building a sense of creeping dread that explodes into hair-raising action. He's also deft at bringing complex characters to life and at pointed humor. . . . [A] riveting ride." —*Tampa Bay Times*

"The latest novel by a new American crime-writing master . . . I'm envious of anyone who's just discovering S. A. Cosby—he's one of crime fiction's biggest talents, skilled at merging the darkest human behavior with robust and indelible characters."

—Sarah Weinman, *The New York Times*
(Best Crime Books of 2023)

"Cosby's thriller is Southern Gothic at its most visceral and profound." —*Star Tribune*

"A dark, wildly entertaining crime novel . . . *All the Sinners Bleed* is rough, smart, gritty, intricate, and Southern to the core."

—Gabino Iglesias, NPR

"On the basis of four novels, each better than the last (and *All the Sinners Bleed* the best of them all), it's fairly easy to say that American crime fiction has found its future, and his name is S. A. Cosby."

—Dennis Lehane, *New York Times* bestselling
author of *Small Mercies*

"Superb . . . A thoughtfully plotted, unflinching look at Cosby's familiar themes, with precise character studies, crackling dialogue, and the backdrop of a small town in Virginia. Cosby's characters are flawed and fragile but with spines made of steel and an unwillingness to bend in the face of adversity."

—*South Florida Sun Sentinel*

"A vintage serial killer cat-and-mouse about systemic indifference."

—*Chicago Tribune*

"A bold new voice in the thriller landscape. *All the Sinners Bleed* has a dark, raw, Southern Gothic / noir feeling combined with a hard-edged look at the dark places in our past."

—Kristin Hannah, #1 bestselling author of
The Nightingale and *The Four Winds*

ALL THE SINNERS BLEED

S. A. COSBY

FLATIRON
BOOKS
NEW YORK

ALL THE SINNERS BLEED. Copyright © 2023 by S. A. Cosby. All rights reserved. Printed in the United States of America. For information, address Flatiron Books, 120 Broadway, New York, NY 10271.

www.flatironbooks.com

Designed by Donna Sinisgalli Noetzel

The Library of Congress has cataloged the hardcover edition as follows:

Names: Cosby, S. A., author.
Title: All the sinners bleed / S. A. Cosby.
Description: First Edition. First International Edition. | New York : Flatiron Books, 2023
Identifiers: LCCN 2023001596 | ISBN 9781250831910 (hardcover) | ISBN 9781250906540 (international, sold outside the U.S., subject to rights availability) | ISBN 9781250845641 (ebook)
Subjects: LCGFT: Thrillers (Fiction) | Novels.
Classification: LCC PS3603.O7988 A55 2023 | DDC 813/.6—dc23/eng/20230123
LC record available at https://lccn.loc.gov/2023001596

ISBN 978-1-250-83192-7 (trade paperback)

Our books may be purchased in bulk for promotional, educational, or business use. Please contact your local bookseller or the Macmillan Corporate and Premium Sales Department at 1-800-221-7945, extension 5442, or by email at MacmillanSpecialMarkets@macmillan.com.

First Flatiron Books Paperback Edition: 2024

10 9 8 7 6 5 4 3 2 1

To my brother, Darrell Cosby.
What we know only we could ever know.

The belief in a supernatural source of evil is not necessary; men alone are quite capable of every wickedness.

—JOSEPH CONRAD

Behold, I make all things new.

—REVELATION 21:5

Charon County

Charon County was founded in bloodshed and darkness.

Literally and figuratively.

Even the name is enveloped in shadows and morbidity. Legend has it the name of the county was supposed to be Charlotte or Charles County, but the town elders waited too late and those names were already taken by the time they decided to incorporate their fledgling encampment. As the story goes, they just moved their finger down the list of names until they settled on Charon. Those men, weathered as whitleather with hands like splitting mauls, bestowed the name on their new town with no regard to its macabre nature. Or perhaps they just liked the name because a river flowed through the county and emptied into the Chesapeake like the River Styx.

Who knows? Who could know the thoughts of those long-dead men?

What is known is that in 1805 in the dead of night a group of white land-owners, chafing at the limits of their own manifest destiny, set fire to the last remaining indigenous village on the teardrop-shaped peninsula that would become Charon County.

Those who escaped the flames were brought down by muskets with no regard to age, gender, or infirmity. That was the first of many tragedies in the history of Charon. The cannibalism of the winter of 1853. The malaria outbreak of 1901. The United Daughters of the Confederacy picnic poisoning of 1935. The Danforth family murder-suicide of 1957. The tent revival baptismal drownings of 1968, and on and on. The soil of Charon County, like most towns and counties in the South, was sown with generations of tears. They were places where violence and mayhem were celebrated as the pillars of a pioneering spirit every Founders' Day in the county square.

Blood and tears. Violence and mayhem. Love and hate. These were the rocks upon which the South was built. They were the foundation upon which Charon County stood.

If you had an occasion to ask some of the citizens of Charon, most of them would tell you those things were in the past. That they had been washed away by the river of time that flows ever forward. They might even say those things should be forgotten and left to the ages.

But if you had asked Sheriff Titus Crown, he would have said that anyone who believed that was a fool or a liar. Or both. And if you had an occasion to speak with him after that long October, he would have told you that maybe the foundation of Charon was rotten and fetid and full of corruption, not only corruption of the flesh but of the soul. That maybe the rocks the South was built upon were shifting and splitting like the stone Moses struck with his staff. But instead of water, only blood and ichor would come pouring forth.

He might touch the scars on his face or his chest absentmindedly and lock eyes with you and say in that harsh whisper that was now his speaking voice:

"The South doesn't change. You can try to hide the past, but it comes back in ways worse than the way it was before. Terrible ways."

He might sigh and look away and say:

"The South doesn't change . . . just the names and the dates and the faces. And sometimes even those don't change, not really. Sometimes it's the same day and the same faces waiting for you when you close your eyes.

"Waiting for you in the dark . . ."

ONE

Titus woke up five minutes before his alarm went off at 7:00 A.M. and made himself a cup of coffee in the Keurig Darlene had gotten him last Christmas. At the time she'd given it to him he'd thought it was an expensive gift for a relationship that was barely four months old. These days, Titus had to admit it was a damn good gift that he was grateful to have.

He'd gotten her a bottle of perfume.

He almost winced thinking back on it. If knowing your lover was a competition, Darlene was a gold medalist. Titus didn't even qualify for the bronze. Over the last ten months he'd forced himself to get exponentially better in the gift-giving department.

Titus sipped his coffee.

His last girlfriend before Darlene had said he was a great boyfriend but was awful at relationships. He didn't dispute that assessment.

Titus took another sip.

He heard the stairs creak as his father made his way down to the kitchen. That mournful cry of ancient wood had gotten him and Marquis in trouble on more than one late Friday night until Titus stopped staying out late and Marquis stopped coming home.

"Hey, while you standing there in your boxers, make me one of them there fancy cups out that machine," Albert Crown said. Titus watched his father limp over to the kitchen table and ease himself down into one of their vinyl-covered metal chairs that would drive a hipster interior designer mad with nouveau retro euphoria.

It had been a year since his father's hip replacement and Albert still walked with a studied caution. He stubbornly refused to use a cane, but Titus saw the way his smooth brown face twisted into tight Gordian knots when a rainstorm blew in off the bay or when the temperature started to drop like a lead sinker.

Albert Crown had made his living on that bay for forty years, hauling in crab pots six days a week, fourteen hours a day off the shore of Piney Island on boats owned by folks who barely saw him as a man. No insurance, no 401(k), but all those backbreaking days and the frugality of Titus's mother had allowed them to build a three-bedroom house on Preach Neck Road. They were the only family, Black or white, that had a house on an actual foundation. Envy had crossed the color lines and united their neighbors as the house rose from the forest of mobile homes that surrounded it like a rose among weeds.

"When we retire, we can sit on the front step in matching rocking chairs and wave to Patsy Jones as she drives by rolling her eyes," Titus's mother Helen had told his father at the kitchen table one night during one of those rare weekends his father wasn't out gallivanting down at the Watering Hole or Grace's Place.

Titus put a cup in the Keurig, slid a pod in the filter, and set the timer.

But, like so many things in life, his mother's gently petty retirement plan was not meant to be. She died long before she could ever retire from the Cunningham Flag Factory. Patsy Jones was still driving by and rolling her eyes, though.

"Which one you put in there?" Albert asked. He opened the newspaper and started running his finger over the pages. Titus could see his lips move ever so slightly. His mother had been the more adventurous reader, but his father never let the sun set on the day without going through the newspaper.

"Hazelnut. The only one you like," Titus said.

Albert chuckled. "Don't you tell that girl that. She got us that value pack. That was nice of her." He licked his finger and turned the page. As soon as he did, he sucked his teeth and grunted.

"Them rebbish boys don't never let up, do they? Now they gonna have a goddamn parade for that statue. Them boys just mad somebody finally had the nerve to tell them they murdering traitor of a granddaddy won't shit," Albert spat.

"Ricky Sours and them Sons of the Confederacy boys been knocking down the door of my office for the past two weeks," Titus said. He took another sip.

"What for?" Albert asked.

"They wanna make sure the sheriff's office will 'fulfill its duties and maintain crowd control' in case any protesters show up. You know, since Ricky is Caucasian, I'm biased against them because of my 'cultural background,'" Titus said. He kept his voice flat and even, the way he'd learned in the Bureau, but he caught his father's eyes over the top of the newspaper.

Albert shook his head. "That Sours boy wouldn't have said that to Ward Bennings. Hell, Ward would've probably marched with 'em with his star on his chest. 'Cultural background.' Shit. He means cuz you a Black man and he a racist. Lord, son, I don't know how you do it sometimes," Albert said.

"Easy. I just imagine Sherman kicking their murderous traitorous great-granddaddies in the teeth. That's my Zen," Titus said. His voice stayed flat, but Albert burst out laughing.

"Down at the store last Friday, Linwood Lassiter asked one of the boys with the sticker on his truck why don't they put a statue to . . . what's that boy name? The one with them eggs?" Albert said.

"Benedict Arnold?" Titus offered.

"Yeah, build a statue to that boy, since they like traitors so goddamn much. That boy said something about heritage and history and Linwood said all right, how about a statue to Nat Turner? That boy got in his truck and spun tires and rolled coal on us. But he didn't have an answer," Albert said.

Titus narrowed his eyes. "You get a license plate number? What the truck look like?"

"Nah, we was too busy laughing. It looks like every truck them kind of boys drive. Jacked up to the sky and not a lick of dirt in the bed. They do them trucks just like some of them fellas that come up on the bay in them big fancy boats but don't never catch no fish. Use a workingman's tools for toys," Albert said.

Titus finished his coffee. He rinsed out the cup and set it in the sink.

"They don't care about Benedict Arnold, Pop. He didn't hate the same people they do. I'm gonna go get dressed. I'm on till nine. There's still some beef stew left from Sunday in the refrigerator. You can have that for supper," Titus said.

"Boy, I ain't so old I can't make my own supper. Who taught you how to cook anyway?" Albert asked.

Titus felt a tight smile work its way across his face. "You did," he said. But, Titus thought, not until Mama had been in the ground and you'd finally found Jesus.

"Damn right. I mean, I'll probably eat the stew, but I can still turn up something in the kitchen," Albert said with a wink. Titus shook his head and headed for the stairs.

"Maybe I'll get some oysters and we can put some fire to that old grill this weekend. Get your trifling brother to come over," Albert said as Titus put his foot on the first step. Titus stiffened for a moment before continuing up the stairs. Marquis wasn't coming over this or any other weekend. The fact that his father still clung to the idea was at various times depressing and infuriating. Marquis worked for himself as a self-taught carpenter. He stayed on the other side of the county in the Windy River Trailer Park, but he might as well have been in Nepal. Even though he made his own hours, they could go months without seeing him. In a place as small as Charon County, that was a dubious achievement.

Titus went into his bedroom and opened his closet. His everyday clothes were on wire hangers on the left. His uniforms were on wooden hangers on the right. He didn't refer to his everyday clothes as his "civilian" wardrobe. That gave his uniforms a level of militarization he didn't like. His everyday clothes were color-coordinated and hung in alphabetical order. Blacks first, then blues, then reds, then so on. Darlene had once commented that he was the most organized man she'd ever met. His shoes were ordered in the exact same manner. Kellie, his former girlfriend from his time in Indiana, used to rearrange his clothes whenever she spent the night. She said she did it for his own good.

"Gotta loosen you up, Virginia. You're wound too tight, one day you're gonna snap. I'm trying to help you with your mental health," she'd say.

Titus thought she did it because she knew he hated it. She knew they would argue about it and she also knew they'd make up, furiously.

He let out a sigh.

Kellie was the past. Darlene was his present. And despite what Faulkner said, that part of his life was done. Best to leave it where he'd left it.

He pushed his regular clothes to the left. His uniforms were all on the right side of the closet. They were all the same color. Deep brown shirt, lighter tan brown pants with a dark brown stripe down the leg. He had two bulletproof vests that hung at the far right of the closet. Two pairs of black leather shoes sat on the floor. A brown tricorne hat sat on a shelf. Darlene called it his "Smokey the Bear" hat.

"Because you're my big ol' bear," she'd said one night as she lay across his chest. Her fingers playing across the scar on his chest like a pianist playing the scales. The scar was a gift, of sorts, from Red DeCrain, white supremacist, Christian nationalist, militia leader, and for seven minutes a wannabe martyr.

Those seven minutes had changed all their lives. Titus's, Red's, and those of Red's wife and his three sons, who all had been outfitted with grenade vests. The youngest boy had only been seven years old. His vest had hung loose on his shoulders like a hoodie he'd borrowed from one of his brothers. When he'd pulled that pin his face had been as blank as a sheet of notebook paper.

Then it had—

"Stop it," he said out loud to no one. He rubbed his face with both hands. The shrapnel from the explosions had left that question-mark-shaped burn scar on his belly. The scars on his soul were not visible but were no less horrific.

Titus put on his uniform in an oft-practiced ritual that calmed him. First he put on the vest and strapped it in place. Then he grabbed his shirt. Then a brown necktie that hung next to its two brothers on a hook on the inside of the closet door. Next were his pants, then his shoes. He went to his nightstand, opened the drawer, and grabbed his service belt. He cinched it tight before grabbing the key from the nightstand and carefully dropping to his haunches. A sheriff couldn't be seen in his county with wrinkled pants. A Black sheriff had to have an extra pair of pants in his office just in case.

He pulled a metal box from under the bed, unlocked the box, and retrieved his service pistol. The county would only pay for a Smith & Wesson nine-millimeter. Titus wanted something with more stopping power. He'd purchased the SIG Sauer P320 out of his own pocket. It was the same sidearm the Virginia State Police used. He checked the clip and the chamber before sliding it in the holster. There were two pairs of mirrored sunglasses on top of the nightstand. Titus grabbed one pair and slipped them in his shirt pocket. His radio was on top of the nightstand next to the sunglasses. He picked it up and clipped the transponder to his belt and the mic to his collar.

Lastly, he reached in the drawer and grabbed his badge. He pinned it to his shirt above his left pocket and headed down the stairs.

Albert was still sitting at the table, but now the newspaper was gone. In its place was an envelope bearing Titus's name.

"What's that?" Titus asked, even though he was pretty sure he already knew.

"It's been one year. Reverend Jackson said last Sunday it was still a miracle worth praising. Who knew Ward Bennings getting hit by a logging truck would mean the first Black sheriff of Charon County would win the special election?" Albert said.

Titus picked up the envelope. He tore it open with his thumbnail. A greeting card with a comical penguin holding a devilish pitchfork was on the front. On the inside, an inscription read:

GUESS HELL REALLY FROZE OVER, YOU TWO ARE STILL TOGETHER! HAPPY ANNIVERSARY!

Titus raised his eyebrows.

"Walmart didn't have a card for being proud of your son for being the first Black sheriff this county ever had. But I am proud. My boy back home and changing things. You don't know how much seeing you in that uniform means to people, Titus. If you mama was here, she'd be proud too," Albert said, his voice breaking around the edges. Titus's mother had been gone for twenty-three years and yet the mere mention of her still wrung heartache from his father like water from a washcloth.

Would she be so proud if she knew what had happened in Northern Indiana at the DeCrain compound? I don't think so, Titus thought. No, I don't think she'd be proud at all.

"Not all our people are proud. But thanks for the card, Pop," Titus said.

"You talking about that Addison boy over at the New Wave church? *Pssh,* ain't nobody thinking about that boy. He thinks Jesus wears blue jeans," Albert said. It was the worst insult his Pentecostal Baptist father who wore his best suit every Sunday could utter in reference to the dreadlocked New Age minister.

"He's doing good work over at that church, Pop," Titus said.

"You call that place a church? It sounds like a juke joint when you drive past," Albert said.

"You don't? Anyway, Jamal Addison ain't the only person who thinks I'm an Uncle Tom," Titus said with a rueful smile.

"Well, Reverend Jackson always preaching about being aware of false prophets," Albert said.

Titus thought that was ironic but didn't say anything.

"You know, it would be nice if you came to a service once in a while. Don't nobody at church think you no damn Uncle Tom," Albert said. "They worked hard for you, Titus. I'm just saying." The amount and depth of his gratitude to Emmanuel Baptist Church for their support of his surprise campaign was a conversation his father kept trying to have and Titus kept trying to avoid. Not because he wasn't grateful. He was well aware it was the support of congregations like Emmanuel that propelled him to the sheriff's office. Along with an influx of liberal-minded latter-day hippies and good ol' boys and girls who hated Ward Bennings's son Cooter more than they distrusted the former football hero and FBI agent. A rare coalition that wouldn't come together again for a generation. But now everyone had their hands out. His father's church was no different. He knew that the support of his father's congregation came with conditions that he wasn't inclined to meet. Never mind the fact that he hadn't attended an actual church service since he was fifteen. He'd stopped going about the same time his father had started. Two years after his mother had died.

"I'll let you know, Pop. It's the week before Fall Fest. You know that's gonna be busy for me," Titus lied. Fall Fest was mainly an excuse for the citizens of Charon County to get drunk and dance in the street before slipping off to some dark corner of the courthouse green for a whiskey-soaked kiss from a lover. Either theirs or someone else's.

Albert was about to press his case further when Titus's radio crackled to life.

"Titus, come in!"

The voice on the radio was his dispatcher, Cam Trowder. Cam worked the morning shift and the other dispatcher, Kathy Miller, worked at night. Cam was one of the few holdovers from the previous administration.

He was an Iraq War vet who was calm under pressure, who also possessed an encyclopedic knowledge of every road and dirt lane in the county. Despite those impressive credentials, Cam's most important attribute was proximity. He lived less than a mile from the sheriff's office. He never missed a day, come rain or shine. His all-terrain electric wheelchair could get up to twenty miles per hour. Cam had souped it up himself with help from a YouTube video and some PDFs he'd downloaded off the internet. The man was nothing if not determined.

That was why the sheer hopelessness that seeped from his voice and came spilling out of the radio set Titus's nerves on edge.

"Go ahead for Titus," he said after he depressed the talk button.

"Titus . . . there's an active shooter at the high school. Titus, I'm getting a hundred calls a minute here. I think . . . I . . . think . . . Titus, my nephew's there," Cam said. He sounded strange. Titus realized he was crying.

"Cam, call all units. Have them converge on the high school!" Titus shouted into his mic.

"My nephew is there," Cam said.

"Call all units! Do it now!"

Cam groaned, but when his voice came through the speaker this time it was smooth and resolute.

"Got it, Chief. Calling all units. Active shooter at Jefferson Davis High School. Repeat, active shooter at Jefferson Davis High School."

Titus dropped the greeting card and sprinted for the door.

"What's going on?" Albert called after him as he barreled out the back door.

But the only answer he got was the sound of the screen door slamming against the jamb as the autumn wind caught it in its chilly grip.

Titus was already gone.

TWO

There is a sense of chaos that can seem to move with its own order. When a chaotic situation becomes rote, there are certain patterns that emerge from the repetition.

As Titus came screaming into the parking lot of Jefferson Davis High on two wheels, he observed these distinct behaviors as they unfolded like an origami sculpture moving in reverse.

Students and teachers were pouring out from every point of egress of the huge brick building. They were running out the front door. They were slipping out the side doors. They were jumping from the windows. Some had slipped out the back through a metal roll-up door that was the exit and entrance for Mr. Herndon's auto mechanics class. The tide of students and teachers poured past and around his car like a river passing over and around a stone. Their faces were etchings from a Francis Bacon painting, shadowed by a memory that ten years from now would make them burst into tears at a baby shower, in the middle of the grocery store, after watching a commercial for an exercise bike.

This was the first part of the chaos of this particular type of event. The unrelenting atavistic panic that sprang forth from the deep recesses of the animal part of our brains. Fight or flight went from an abstract concept in health class to a necessary component of survival.

Titus hopped out of his SUV with his gun drawn. The screams of the children were like a storm cloud moving east to west. Their cries were thunderclaps that shook him down to his heels. He looked to his left and saw two of his deputies drive over a shallow ditch that ran parallel to the front lawn of the school. Davy Hildebrandt was driving one patrol car and Roger Simmons was in the other. Carla Ortiz was just seconds behind them in the D.A.R.E. van she drove to the middle and elementary schools. Roger hopped out carrying a riot gun. Davy had his sidearm drawn. Carla had hers as well. Roger was running toward the crowd of teenagers. He was holding the gun by the stock with the barrel pointing toward the sea of bodies coming toward him like a rogue wave.

"Roger, gun up! Gun up!" Titus yelled. Roger stopped and stared at him. He blinked hard, then looked down at his hands. Titus saw him tremble like he'd taken a shot of whiskey, then he raised the gun so the shortened barrel was pointing up in the air.

"Davy! Get everyone across the road! Across the road!" Titus screamed. Davy holstered his gun and started waving to the kids and the teachers and began herding them across the road into a pasture that belonged to Oakfield Farms. A few Angus cows grazed haphazardly in the field. They seemed nonplussed despite the screams of terror echoing through the crisp early morning air.

"What do we do, boss?" Carla asked. She'd sliced her way through the crowd and was standing at Titus's side. Titus saw a red pickup truck with an emergency light attached to the roof come flying into the parking lot. Tom Sadler was in the truck. He was off today but must have heard the call on his scanner. There were only a few more members of the Charon County Sheriff's Office that weren't here today.

Titus prayed they wouldn't need them. He prayed the shooter didn't have an AR-15 or an AK-47 or some other machine designed to deal out death in bunches like a spreader tossing seeds.

"We move in and clear the building," Titus said. He grabbed his mic. "Davy, get Tom to watch the crowd. You come on back and help us clear the scene. You got your vest on?"

The radio crackled when Davy responded. "Sure do. I'll get Tom."

"Come on with it, Davy," Titus said. He motioned for Carla to follow him as he began to move through the stragglers and headed for the school.

"He shot Mr. Spearman!" a slight blond girl said. Titus registered she was Daisy Matthews's daughter. He'd graduated with Daisy. Her name was . . .

"Lisa, get across the road!" Carla yelled.

"Who shot Mr. Spearman? What does he look like, Lisa?" Titus asked.

Lisa turned her head and gazed at him like she'd just noticed his six-foot-two frame had appeared. "I . . . I . . . don't know. He was wearing a mask. He shot him in the face. Oh my God, he shot Mr. Spearman!" Lisa's eyes were as wide as tractor wheels. She wasn't crying, but her face was pulsatingly red. Titus knew the tears would come later. Either tears or screams in the night.

"Was he tall? Taller than me? What about his clothes? What was he wearing?" Titus said.

Lisa closed her eyes and fell against Carla. "I don't know!" she screamed into Carla's shoulder.

Titus took a breath. He realized he had been yelling. A deep-voiced police officer yelling in your face never produced pertinent information. He knew this, preached about this to his deputies, and yet he'd done it anyway.

Titus touched his mic.

"Suspect is wearing a mask. That's all we got. Let's move in," Titus said.

"Honey, I'm gonna need you to go across the road, okay?" Carla said as gently as she could. Lisa didn't respond but took off for the pasture like a startled gazelle.

"Okay. Let's go," Titus said.

This was the other half of the tradition born from chaos that resembles order. Guns drawn, men and women walking toward a man, it's almost always a man, with his own gun drawn, the barrel still hot from spraying a classroom or a theater or an office full of cubicles with chunks of lead in steel jackets moving at twenty-six hundred feet per second.

Titus felt his stomach tighten so hard and so fast it was like a cramp. His breath was slow and steady, but his head was pounding. The wind picked up and cooled the sweat wicking into his collar. Rays of sunlight reflecting off the windows were muted by his sunglasses as he moved forward. His feet crunched across the asphalt. The sound was polyphonic in his ears. To his right Carla was taking deep sharp breaths. To his left Davy was emitting a sort of keening noise like a bleating lamb. Roger was taking point. Titus could see the muscles in his thick shoulders knotted up like coils of deck rope.

In the past fifteen years Charon County had notched exactly two murders. One was solved in fifteen minutes when Alice Lowney confessed to stabbing her husband, Walter, with a pitchfork after she'd caught him sleeping with their next-door neighbor Ezra Collins, Pip's cousin. The other one was unsolved, and if Ward Bennings's file notes were to be believed it would remain that way for time immemorial. The victim had been a white male, age twenty-one to forty-five, found sliced in neat sections inside a suitcase that had washed up on Fiddler's Beach. Conventional wisdom said the remains had come in from the Chesapeake Bay on a strange tide that wouldn't come again. Folks liked to say Charon wasn't a place where terrible things like that happened with any regularity.

Titus thought folks had short memories.

Charon's recent history was indeed relatively quiet, but the past held horrors and terrors that had moved into the realm of legend. His father would sometimes share a quote from one of Reverend Jackson's fire-and-brimstone sermons and say that Charon was long overdue for a season of pain. Titus didn't think Gideon had the gift of prescience, but he did believe in the rise and fall of time. That what had happened before would happen again. The wheel spins and spins and eventually it lands on the same number it landed on twenty, thirty, forty years ago. No matter what they found inside the school, the season of peace had passed. Now the season of pain had returned, on his watch.

They were about fifty feet from the front steps of the school when the doors opened and a man carrying a leather mask with a wolf's snout in his left hand and cradling a .30-30 like a newborn in the crook of his right arm walked out onto the top step. The man wore a weathered black peacoat buttoned in the middle and dirty blue jeans. His hair was twisted into fuzzy cornrows that needed to be redone. His mouth was frozen in a grimace that seemed to take over his whole face.

For a moment the world was calm again. The sounds of the crowd were snatched out of the air by the breeze. It was just the morning sun, the blue sky, and this man that Titus recognized peering down at them.

"Latrell, put down the gun!" Titus roared. The time for the inside voice had passed. Latrell turned his head toward Titus. The fact that five police officers had five guns pointed at him didn't seem to disturb him at all. His smooth brown face was eerily calm despite a golf-ball-sized bruise on his right cheek. Pupils the size of pinpricks assessed Titus with a profound impassiveness. Titus figured it was the effect of either Oxy or heroin. Both were plentiful in Charon despite his best efforts. Latrell was here and not here. He looked like a toddler who had escaped the watchful eyes of his parents and who did not yet know he was in fact lost.

Titus knew Latrell's parents. Calvin and Dorothy Macdonald. He'd gone to school with Calvin. He and Calvin and Patrick Tines and Big Bobby Packer had brought Charon their one and only state football championship. Calvin was a wide receiver to Titus's quarterback. The night of the championship, Titus had lost his virginity in the back of Calvin's Ford Mustang with Nancy Tolliver. She liked being choked, but Titus couldn't bring himself to do it. Not back then. He used to wonder how a seventeen-year-old even realized she liked erotic asphyxiation, until he realized he didn't really like any of the answers to that question.

Nowadays Calvin worked at the shipyard in Newport News. He was coming up on twenty-five years there. Dorothy was a nurses' aide at Pruitt Nursing Home. They had another son, a twelve-year-old named Lavon. Latrell was their oldest and their most troubled. In the year since Titus had taken office, he'd arrested Latrell once for possession of drug paraphernalia after he was kicked out of a 7-Eleven for starting an altercation about not being allowed to purchase beer after midnight. That night he'd appeared much as he did now. Disheveled but mostly harmless. Except that night he hadn't been carrying a long rifle and a leather mask. When Calvin had bailed his son out, all he'd said to Titus was that Latrell was "messed up."

Titus had sensed his old friend had wanted to say more. Yearned to say more. But instead, he'd collected his son and kept his own counsel. Titus had watched them leave, fully aware Calvin was struggling with Latrell's demons. Titus was also aware that he was no longer a shoulder for his former teammate to cry on or a listening ear for him to share his problems. The badge on his chest had slammed that door shut.

It seemed whatever demons Latrell were battling had multiplied tenfold.

"Latrell! Drop. The. Gun," Titus said. He enunciated each word with as much clarity as his tongue could muster. He wanted to break through whatever fog had enshrouded Latrell's mind. He needed him to hear him. He needed him to see the guns trained on him. He needed him to realize that, whatever he'd done, he could still leave this place upright. This was Calvin's son. And even if he had been the son of a man Titus didn't know, he still deserved that opportunity. A man Titus hadn't drunk moonshine with or run two-a-days with for four years. A man Titus hadn't grown up with under the shadow of that giant Confederate flag out by the county line.

"He's one of the archangels," Latrell said. His timbre was tremulous but loud and clear.

"Latrell, I'm going to need you to put that gun down and get down on the ground," Titus said.

"He said he was the Black Angel. Angel of Death. Mr. Spearman used to say he just liked to hear himself talk," Latrell said. Titus watched as tears trickled down Latrell's face.

"Latrell, you need to put that gun down now," Titus said. He said it loud and clear, but the threat had ebbed. This didn't need to end with bullets.

"He made them call out for God. Then he'd tell them he was the Malak al-Mawt, the Destroyer. But that wasn't true either. He was just a sick motherfucker, just like Mr. Spearman," Latrell said. He dropped the mask and put the barrel of the rifle under his chin.

Titus stopped. He lowered his gun a fraction of an inch. He didn't want Latrell to pull the trigger, but he knew how quick someone could go from suicide to murder. The words coming out of the young man's mouth could be dismissed as the ravings of a broken mind.

Yet . . .

Titus saw the agony that wound its way through Latrell. It twisted his body. It contorted his limbs. It was as if his arms and legs were being pulled and drawn by the weight of a guilt and shame Latrell couldn't properly articulate. His hands gripped the rifle with manic desperation, fingers undulating in and out like the tentacles of a deep-sea creature who had no knowledge of the sun.

"Latrell, listen to me. Whatever's happened, we can talk about it. Whatever you've done, this isn't the way to fix it. Put the gun down. Please. Put the gun down and let's talk. It doesn't have to be this way," Titus said. He took one hand off his gun and held it palm up toward Latrell. Through his splayed fingers he watched as Latrell gingerly removed the barrel from beneath his chin.

"That's it. Now put it down on the ground and walk toward me," Titus said. He changed the orders he had given Latrell because he didn't want him to be within an arm's reach of that rifle if he changed his mind. Madness was coming off him in waves like heat rising from asphalt in the middle of July.

"Put the gun down, bitch!" Roger screamed.

"Deputy, stand down!" Titus yelled back.

Latrell closed his eyes.

"No . . . ," Titus murmured.

"You don't know the things I've done. I tried to stop, and they said they'd kill my little brother. The Angel, he never took off his mask. But Mr. Spearman, he liked for them to see his face. He liked that a lot," Latrell said. The words came out in one long sentence like a chant.

"Latrell, wait," Titus said.

Latrell opened his eyes. "Check his phone," he said. Titus lowered his gun one more fraction of an inch.

Latrell held the rifle above his head.

"I HAVE BECOME DEATH!" he howled as he tore down the steps toward Titus and his deputies.

Later, as Titus replayed the scene over and over again like a film on loop inside the theater of his mind, he'd come to this part in the movie and pause. The moment would become a turgid series of movements that seemed hidden by an opaque sheen. Had Latrell pointed the rifle at them? Had he begun to point the rifle at them? He'd close his eyes and strain for the memory, but it dissolved even as he grasped it, like a cobweb.

Titus heard the first shot before Latrell had taken his third step. Buckshot from Roger's riot gun turned half of Latrell's head into a red mist. Tom Sadler popped off five shots from his .357 Smith & Wesson six-shot. Tom was an excellent marksman. All five bullets found their target in a tight grouping in Latrell's chest.

"HOLD YOUR GODDAMN FIRE!" Titus screamed at the top of his lungs. Davy hadn't fired a shot yet, but he holstered his gun so quick it might have been a magic trick. Carla pointed her sidearm down but held on to it with a tactical grip. Davy was muttering, but Titus couldn't make out the words. The gunshots were still echoing in his ears.

Latrell's body rolled down the last nine granite steps of Jefferson Davis High like a rag doll discarded by a child. The .30-30 clattered to the ground far out of his reach, as if that mattered anymore. As Latrell came to rest at his feet, Titus saw the trail of blood his journey had left behind. It stained the steps with streaks and slashes like rose-colored calligraphy.

THREE

They found Mr. Spearman at his desk.

He was leaning back in his chair with his mouth agape and his tie askew and the tail of his gray mullet spilling over his collar. Anyone who'd taken ninth-grade geography in Charon County in the past thirty years was familiar with that frazzled blue tie with the Rorschach-inspired coffee stains. If a poll were taken at Jefferson Davis High asking who was your favorite teacher, Jeff Spearman would most likely have come in at number one for twenty-five out of his thirty years as a member of the Jefferson Davis faculty.

If it weren't for the dime-sized wound in his cheek and the cavernous hole in the back of his head, you could be forgiven for thinking he was taking a nap.

The section of the blackboard that was directly behind Mr. Spearman was painted in bits of bone and clumps of brain matter and gray hair. The pieces were held in place by a patina of blood.

Titus thought that part of the blackboard resembled an arts-and-crafts project inside an abattoir created by a lunatic.

Titus went over to the body and put two fingers on his neck. There was little doubt Jeff Spearman had shuffled off his mortal coil, but Titus believed in being thorough. In college in an anatomy class, he'd read about a man who had taken a two-foot iron rod through his brain during an industrial accident and driven himself to the hospital.

"Clear the rest of the school. Room-by-room. Go," Titus said.

No one moved.

"The fuck he shoot Mr. Spearman for?" Davy asked. The hurt in his voice made Titus wince. He wondered about that himself, but the time for questions would come later. Right now they had to secure the scene.

"Fucking terrorist. Hear what he hollered when he came at us? Some Islam shit," Roger said. He was breathing hard, like a bull. Titus spun on his heel and stepped inside Roger's personal space.

"We don't know anything about anything yet. We don't know why he did it or if he even did it. Maybe he has an accomplice. Maybe Mr. Spearman shot himself and Latrell just picked up that rifle. Maybe we are dealing with terrorists. Maybe we are dealing with someone with a mental health issue who should never have had access to a rifle that can take down an elk. We don't know shit. So, what we're gonna do is secure the goddamn scene. Now go. I'm not gonna tell y'all again," Titus said. He used a plural noun but he was talking to Roger. He stared into his eyes until Roger dropped his head and turned away.

Roger moved toward the door to the classroom. The rest of Titus's deputies followed him. He and Davy shared a brief moment of eye contact before Davy too headed toward the door.

"And what he was yelling wasn't Arabic. It was Aramaic. Don't make any assumptions about what's happened here," Titus said to the empty room.

An hour later they were in the parking lot joined by ambulances and fire trucks and throngs of terrified parents searching for their traumatized children. Dozens of husbands and wives holding their spouses, many of whom had probably logged their last day as an employee of the Charon County school system. Coming face-to-face with the possibility of your imminent demise forces you to reckon with the career path you've chosen.

"They both need to go to the ME?" a large, light-skinned man asked Titus. He was from the funeral home. Virginia was still a largely rural state, interspersed with medium-sized cities surrounded by great swaths of forest and nestled in the bosoms of hills that were just a few feet shy of being mountains, and mountains that were old when the pyramids were new. Even large counties like Red Hill or Queen didn't have a local coroner's office. The state appointed a local doctor as a medical examiner. This medical professional pronounced unattended deaths. Aunt Emma dead in her bed after swallowing a peanut the wrong way or Mama Jane finally succumbing to a stroke as she canned peaches for the fall. Anything that could be called natural and expected was handled by the local medical examiner.

People with bullet holes went to Richmond to be dissected by the state medical examiner's office.

"Yeah, both of 'em gotta go, but Maynard's is gonna take Spearman," Titus said. The light-skinned man nodded and bent down to grab the stretcher with Latrell's body on it. He squeezed a lever and stood at the same time. The foot of the stretcher came up with him. He went to the head and repeated the action. Once he made sure everything was locked and loaded, he started pushing the stretcher into his van.

"Hey, hold on a minute," Titus said. The funeral home attendant paused. Titus unzipped the body bag.

"Can you give me some gloves?" Titus asked. The attendant leaned into his van and then tossed him a pair of black latex gloves. Titus put them on and opened Latrell's coat. He ignored the sickly pungent scent of voided bowels and the metallic aroma of spilled blood. A memory so powerful it felt like a hallucination tried to force its way into his mind, but he held it at bay by focusing on Latrell's body. He unbuttoned the man's coat. There was a bleeding honeycomb in the center of his sternum. He went through Latrell's pockets with a practiced thoroughness. After a few moments he found Latrell's phone. Latrell had mentioned Spearman's phone in his ramblings. Had they been communicating before the shooting?

One way to find out was to let the body go to Richmond and let the evidence sit in a drawer for four weeks. Another was to take Latrell's and Spearman's phones back to the office and go through them.

"Carla, get me an evidence bag out of my truck," Titus said. Carla nodded and jogged over to his SUV. When she came back, Titus dropped the phone in the evidence bag.

"You can take him now. Carla, tell Maynard that Spearman can go too, but check and see if he has his phone on him first," he said. He dropped the "Mister." Latrell was a broken soul with troubles he couldn't begin to imagine. He was also a thief, a drug addict, and could be an irritating nuisance anywhere in the county he happened to appear. Common sense said Titus shouldn't trust a thing Latrell had to say. Common sense said if Latrell Macdonald told you it was raining you should probably stick your head out the window and see if it got wet.

But Titus couldn't reconcile common sense with the look in Latrell's eyes when he'd started talking about archangels and Jeff Spearman. The darkness in those eyes that expanded like a black hole as he ran at them screaming about the Angel of Death contained no lies. Titus knew that for a fact. Knew it in his bones. His instructors at the FBI Academy would have chided him for that kind of thinking.

"Gut feelings are full of shit," Bob McNally, his behavioral science instructor, was fond of saying. That idea, that only empirical evidence had any investigative value, was a philosophy that Titus had espoused with enthusiasm at the Academy. That same idea was shown to be as fragile as new ice on a pond, when you were in the field.

"Evidence makes convictions, your gut gets you to the heart of the case," Ezekiel Wiggins, the only other Black agent in the Indiana Field Office, was fond of saying. Titus thought the truth was somewhere in the middle. Evidence could be tainted. Your gut could lead you astray. You had to find a balance between technique, intuition, and the truth.

The truth here was that Latrell had walked into Jeff Spearman's classroom, shot him, then walked back out and died on the same steps he'd been running up four years ago as a senior. The evidence was in the rifle, in Jeff Spearman's cranium, and maybe on Jeff Spearman's phone.

"Titus, what the hell is going on here?"

The sound of Scott Cunningham saying his name made Titus want to grind his teeth like a grist mill. He took a breath and turned to face Scott.

"There was a shooting, Scott. I'm gonna need you to get back behind the tape," Titus said.

Scott put his hands on his hips and jutted out his chin. Titus had seen him do this at Board of Supervisors meetings when things weren't going his way, which in all honesty wasn't that often.

"Who was shot? See, this is why I been saying we should let the teachers arm themselves," Scott said.

"Scott, I'm gonna tell the whole county everything I can once we get the scene cleared and get the shooter and the victim moved and their families notified. But right at this moment you're in the middle of my crime scene stepping on evidence, and I'm gonna need you to step back. Now," Titus said.

Scott looked down at his feet. He was standing in the middle of a puddle of Latrell Macdonald's blood.

"Goddamn it. Shit to hell," Scott groaned with disgust. He took two large steps backward before scraping the soles of his shoes on the grass to the side of the front steps.

"Behind the tape," Titus said.

"I'll expect a full report," Scott said. He waited a beat before he started walking back to his truck. Titus knew he wanted to make it seem like it was his decision to leave.

"Scott, you're the chairman of the board. You're not my boss. You'll get the same report the rest of the county gets," Titus said.

Scott blanched, then just shook his head. "I'm not your enemy, Titus."

Liar, Titus thought.

When Titus had announced his candidacy, Scott Cunningham had thrown all his considerable influence behind Cooter. Titus knew Scott's reasons for supporting Cooter had nothing to do with Cooter's law enforcement philosophy, which in its purest form could be articulated as "harass Black and Brown people and anyone who voted Democrat."

It had everything to do with Scott's desire to have his own personal puppet in the sheriff's office. A sheriff who wouldn't look the other way, per se. but perhaps could be counted on to squint when the need arose. And what better marionette than the son of the former sheriff? A man best known for three things: roughing up teenagers caught necking down at the river, shaking down folks for cash or weed during traffic stops, and once getting into a fight with a goat. If you got Cooter the slightest bit tipsy, he'd regale you with stories about how the goat suckered him with a head butt out of nowhere. The goat, as was the tendency of victors, didn't comment on the altercation.

When the election results had come in Titus was nearly as shocked as Scott. In the past year they had butted heads more than Titus thought was necessary for a county the size of Charon. Things really reached a turning point when Titus arrested Alan Cunningham, Scott's cousin and the county building inspector. Jamal Addison had made a complaint that Alan was denying well permits for Black families without cause. Titus had investigated and found an almost comically inept conspiracy between Alan Cunningham and Reece Kanter, a local real estate developer. The two had conspired to keep Black families from building homes on land that Reece coveted near the Conyers's Beach for a new subdivision. Alan had received a kickback for each refusal.

Scott had been the titular figurehead for the collective rage of the Cunningham family. But there was nothing he could do for his cousin. Whether through arrogance or stupidity, Alan had left a paper trail Wrong Way Corrigan could have followed.

Titus didn't usually enjoy arresting people, but slapping a pair of bracelets on Alan Cunningham had been the highlight of his week and the nadir of his relationship with Scott.

"Uh-huh. And I'm not yours. I'm also not one of your cutters at the flag factory or one of your crab pickers at the fish house. My department will handle this. You wanna help, get the board to approve some funds for counseling for everybody that was here today. You do your job and I'll do mine," Titus said. He turned his back on Scott and took the evidence bag from Carla. On any other day the constant dick-swinging contest that Scott Cunningham was convinced they were both participating in wouldn't garner a second thought from him, but people had died this morning. Their bodies were still warm even as their blood cooled on the steps and the walls of Jefferson Davis High. Men like Scott, men consumed by their egos and their desire to assert dominance at the top of hierarchies only they could see, didn't have the capacity to set aside their petty aspirations even in the face of death.

They craved power and control in any quantity or amount they could find. Titus thought you could offer Scott the job of head shit shoveler at a manure farm and he'd take it if it meant he got to tell someone else what to do. Scott's small-town megalomania was fed by equal parts hubris and tradition. The Cunninghams were one of the biggest families in a county where they owned the two largest companies that were the county's two largest employers. By most metrics they ran Charon County.

Except one.

Titus was the sheriff and they weren't, and today, of all the days since he'd pinned that badge on his chest, was not the day he was going to indulge their feudal fantasies.

"If Spearman has his phone on him, bag it up too and take them both back to the office," Titus said to Carla as he handed her the evidence bag. Carla had been his second hire behind Davy. She was a short slim woman who had a blue belt in jiujitsu and dreams of joining the FBI herself. Davy was friendly and loyal, but Carla was smart and tenacious. One day in the future Davy might be sheriff himself. One day in the future Carla might be halfway across the country leading cartel members on a perp walk.

"Got it, boss. I'll take care of it," Carla said.

She paused.

"This is gonna get bad, isn't it? The shoot, I mean. Most of those kids back there were recording it. I . . . I thought he was surrendering, then he just . . . it looked like he was running at us. I mean, that's what it looked like, right?" Carla said.

"Right now I just need you to get that phone. We'll deal with everything else later," Titus said. Carla nodded and went off to rifle through Spearman's pockets. Behind his mirrored sunglasses he closed his eyes and ran his tongue over his teeth without opening his mouth. How long would it take for one of the kids' or staff members' videos to go viral? A day? An hour?

At the final debate before the election, he and Cooter were given a chance to make their case one last time to the citizens of Charon County with a closing statement.

Titus had gone up to the lectern in the cavernous East Charon Ruritan Club and shared a fraction of his guilt disguised as a personal mission statement.

"George Orwell wrote that we sleep safe in our beds because rough men stand ready in the night to visit violence on those who do us harm. I just want a sheriff's department that makes sure those rough men don't visit violence on the people they are supposed to keep safe. I was born here, graduated from high school here. Grew up swimming in Fiddler's Bay, learned to drive on Route 15. Had my first taste of liquor over behind the Watering Hole. Charon is my heart and my home, but I know that those rough men have not always been judicious with their violence. I think the least a sheriff can do is make sure those rough men are bound by the same rules they are sworn to enforce. Because we all know it hasn't always been that way," Titus had said. As far as closing arguments went, he'd thought it was rather eloquent, especially since Cooter's final statement had consisted of ursine grunts that sounded like a bear trying to say the words *law and order* and *border control*. Even though Charon was two thousand miles from the southern borders. When Titus had returned to his seat a few people clapped, but everyone had listened.

Now his rough men had visited violence upon Latrell Macdonald. Latrell had visited violence upon Jeff Spearman. But could there have ever been any other outcome?

In Titus's penance-driven mind he'd thought so, but now he realized that was the height of naivete. You pick up an axe, you're going to chop down a tree. You pick up a gun, whether you are wearing a star or not, eventually you're going to chop down a man.

Titus knew that was always a possibility. The algorithm of law enforcement made it a near-inevitability. That didn't make it any easier to reconcile the fact that he held the power of life and death.

When Jamal Addison had first approached him about running for sheriff after Emmet Thompson had gotten pulled over by Cooter Bennings and ended up being beaten to within an inch of his life, he'd gone to the cemetery to talk it over with his mother. Under the mournful pine trees that stood sentry over his mother's grave he'd sworn that he'd change things. Change himself. He'd seen what the width of the thin blue line could hide, and it sickened him. Almost as much as what he'd done, no matter the provocation, sickened him. He'd run for sheriff with the weight of a promise to a spirit on his shoulders.

And in the end his deputies had killed a man whose mind was held together by a delicate amalgamation of heroin-induced fever dreams and moonshine. A man who was suffering. A man who had needed his help.

Titus walked over to his SUV and slid behind the wheel. He started the car and immediately put it in gear. There was paperwork to fill out, there were phone calls to make. He had to notify Latrell's parents. He was going to do that personally. He couldn't hand that off to anyone else. He hoped to God he could get to Calvin and Dorothy before they saw the news online or, even worse, someone called them.

He'd have to find out who to notify about Spearman. The school would obviously be closed for the day, and probably the rest of the week. The walls and steps would have to be scrubbed clean of gore.

The exorcism by bleach and water would wash away the carnage but would have a minuscule effect on the consciousness of every person who'd walked the halls this morning. He was going to have to pull Roger and Tom into the office. That was a given. Hundreds of moving parts were now set to begin locking into place like rusted gears in an old engine. Any or all of those parts could bite him in his softest places. But that knowledge wasn't the only thing paramount in his mind.

He also wanted to see what was on Jeff Spearman's phone.

FOUR

B y the time he got back to the sheriff's office, news of the shooting was burning through the county like a fire in a tinderbox. Titus could hear Cam answering call after call from his desk. As soon as he ended one call another would sound, and he'd answer with the generic response Titus had told him to use in case of a mass casualty event.

"Yes, there has been an incident at the high school. At this time, we cannot release any more information. The sheriff will provide an update as soon as possible," Cam said again and again in his weathered rawhide rasp.

Titus pointed to his own ear, then pointed at Cam. Cam removed his headset. He pushed an errant strand of dirty blond hair out of his eyes.

"My nephew?" was all he said. The words came out clipped and harsh, as if he were already preparing himself to speak about the boy in the past tense.

"He's fine. There was only one casualty besides the shooter," Titus said. Cam sat back in his wheelchair and closed his eyes. Relief, that voraciously selfish emotion, washed over his entire face.

"The board is blowing up. I can keep up but just barely. Maybe we should record a message on the 911 line about the shooting? Might cut down on the calls," Cam said.

"That's a good idea. I'll do it now," Titus said.

"What . . . what, uh, happened over there?" Cam said. He'd put the headset back on and opened a bottle of water.

"You know Calvin Macdonald? His son, Latrell, shot Jeff Spearman with a .30-30. Then Roger and Tom shot Latrell," Titus said. He didn't try to explain how he'd attempted to disarm Latrell or how he felt Roger and Tom had been a half second too quick on the trigger.

"Jesus H. Christ. Mr. Spearman's the nicest teacher I ever had. He used to give me a ride home after basketball practice. My folks only had one car, and my dad used that for the night shift at R&J. Goddamn, man. We got any idea why?" Cam asked. Before Titus could answer, the board went off again.

"I'm gonna go record that message," Titus said. He went into his office and shut the door. He hung his hat on a peg on the wall that was level with the top of the frosted glass in his office door. Easing down in his chair, he considered how quickly what's important can shift and transform. A week ago, the biggest thing on his immediate radar was Ricky Sours and the Sons of the Confederacy planning a parade to protect a statue that no one was seriously talking about removing. Granted, he would shed no tears if someone reduced Ol' Rebel Joe to a pile of crushed pea gravel, but the Sons' parade was a grievance in search of a reason. Now he was going to have to record an incoming message letting folks know they had killed the man who shot a schoolteacher in front of his students. Ricky Sours and his band of neo-Confederate apologists were sandcastles washed away by the incoming tide of Charon County's new reality.

That reality was as simple as it was traumatic. They were now the latest locality that had to add "site of a school shooting" to their town's history.

Titus started to open his laptop when a scowl crossed his face.

"Cam, you been in here?" Titus yelled.

"I needed a pen!" Cam yelled back.

"Next time don't move the laptop!" Titus yelled in response.

"Sorry, boss," Cam said before answering another call.

Titus adjusted the laptop so that it was back to its usual ninety-degree angle perpendicular to his pen holder and the telephone. There was also an ink stamp embossed with his signature to his left and a yellow legal pad to his right below the laptop. Much like his closet and his personal truck and, despite his father's best efforts, the kitchen cabinets, Titus's desk was rigidly organized to a degree that bordered on obsessive. He wasn't always so consumed by order. After his mother died when he was thirteen, he became possessed by a desire to give his life structure. Partly because his daddy had crawled into a bottle of JTS Brown and wouldn't emerge for the next two years, and partly because he craved a new type of religion. The one based on blood and wine magic had failed them, in Titus's opinion. Structure became his religion. Discipline was his crucifix against chaos.

But there were moments like today when the true nature of existence was revealed to him. Moments when the ephemeral curtain of divine composition was pulled away and entropy strode across the stage. For all his attempts at control, days like today, when he'd seen a boy he'd known since infancy get his chest cratered, reminded him that chaos *was* the true nature of things.

The DeCrain family could attest to that.

Chaos was king.

Titus sighed. He would keep setting the pieces of his life in straight lines. It was all he had. It was all that brought him a modicum of peace.

Titus opened his laptop and scrolled to the voice recorder app. He cleared his throat, clicked, and spoke in his calmest, most succinct manner, recording a straightforward message and assuring the town that there were no active threats.

He pulled up the emergency system administrative page and added the file to the incoming message. Then he went to the Charon County Sheriff's social media page and typed the same message and pinned it to the top of the page. Performing these tasks, steeped in mundanity, always felt strange after he'd had to pull his gun. Writing reports seemed hopelessly inconsequential in the aftermath of holding someone's life at the end of the barrel of his gun. Yet he knew from firsthand experience that writing the reports was the most important part. It was the record of how you upheld or dishonored your oath. In a perfect world that record was sacrosanct.

But Titus knew the world was much less than perfect.

The phone on his desk rang.

"Hello?"

"Calvin Macdonald is on line one," Cam said.

"Shit," Titus said. "Okay, put him through." He rubbed his forehead with his thumb and forefinger. "Sheriff Crown," Titus said.

"Is my boy dead, Titus?" Calvin asked. He breathed in deep gasping swallows of air.

"Calvin, where are you?"

"I'm in my truck. Dorothy called me. Said they was saying Latrell had shot up the school."

"Calvin, can someone drive you home? I want to come over and talk to you," Titus said, knowing as soon as the words left his mouth, they confirmed Calvin's worst fears. But Titus said them anyway, even if they felt hollow as bird bones. He was not going to tell Calvin about Latrell on the telephone. The man deserved to see his face.

"Is my son dead, Titus?" Calvin sobbed. It was a frank and uncomplicated sound. The sound of all hope being lost.

"Calvin, go home. I'll meet you and Dorothy over there in an hour," Titus said.

Calvin moaned. "Aw, fuck. Fuck you, Titus."

The line went dead.

Titus put the handset back in the cradle. There was going to be more of that. A lot more. He was prepared to take it, but that didn't mean he liked it.

He opened up the reports tab and started detailing the shooting from his perspective. Roger and Tom would have to write their own reports. In an effort to encourage more accountability he'd instituted a rule that deputies couldn't discuss the details of any ongoing investigations, including deputy-involved shootings. He didn't want to give the appearance of impropriety or give anyone a chance to get their stories straight.

When he finished, he went back into the dispatch area. Cam was still juggling calls. Titus pointed to his ear again.

"Yes, ma'am, the message is correct. That's all the information we have at this time. 'Bye, now," Cam said. He removed the headset and let out a sigh.

"The message might have saved us from maybe two less calls," Cam said.

"I'm going over to Calvin and Dorothy's place. Do you still have Tom's number? I got it in my phone if you don't," Titus said.

"Yeah. He gave it to me when we had that cookout at his place in June."

"Give him a call. Tell him I need to see him by four today. Tell him to bring the gun he used at the school," Titus said.

Cam looked down at his desk, then raised his eyes. "It was a good shoot, right? I mean, you said he killed Mr. Spearman," Cam said. The statement hung in the air between them, ensconced within Cam's unspoken assumptions. There had been a bad man who had shot a good man, then other good men had killed the bad man. What more was there to talk about?

Titus wished it were that simple. He really did.

"I need to talk to him, Cam. Pass the message along," Titus said. It was no longer a favor.

Titus got in his SUV and slipped out of the parking lot of the sheriff's office and onto the road that wound its way through downtown Charon County, past the Safeway and the Dollar General, past what used to be Herndon's Furniture and Appliances. The road took him by the county library and Gilby's Southern Dining, then past the courthouse building and the Confederate War Memorial that stood not ten feet from the front door. Past the high school, the parking lot a ghost town after this morning.

Past Soapy Suds Car Wash, the third most profitable business in Charon County. Lots of boys liked to take their jacked-up trucks mudding on Friday night and drove through Soapy Suds Saturday morning to cruise the back roads and tear up and down Route 15 Saturday night. Finally, Titus drove past what was once Sommers Pharmacy. Titus had arrested Billy Sommers for prescription fraud six months ago. When he'd gone to the house with Davy and Carla, they'd found Billy sitting in his den with his wrists slit down to the bone. A pearl-handled straight razor was in his lap and a picture of his wife and two boys was in his hands. His café au lait carpet looked like someone had spilled a carafe of merlot. They'd tied him up with tourniquets and ferried him to the hospital in Newport News, then arrested him proper two weeks later.

A new pharmacist had tried to take over the Sommers building but Billy's cousins, still stinging from his arrest and subsequent conviction, started a rumor she didn't really have a degree, and within a month the rumor was an immutable fact, and by the fall the young woman who'd tried to help the good people of Charon with their medicinal needs soon lit out for greener pastures. Titus thought the fact that she'd been a Black woman hadn't helped to endear her to the white citizens in the county. Normally the Black folks in Charon would have tried to rally around a sister taking on a new venture, but the young lady wasn't a *native* of Charon. She was a come-here, and people in Charon were loath to cotton to new faces. In this the citizens, both Black and white, were united.

Titus escaped the bonds of the thirty-five-mile-per-hour speed limit in town and stepped on the gas as he turned onto Route 15. The road sliced through most of the teardrop-shaped county like an incision, with side roads that broke off from the main highway like asphalt stitches.

Titus passed First Corinthian Methodist Church. A sprawling edifice encased in bright red bricks, First Corinthian was where a lot of the white folks on this side of the county went for Sunday service. A few miles down the road he passed Second Corinthian Methodist Church. The result of a schism in the First Corinthian congregation, Second Corinthian was not as large as her mother, but what she lacked in square footage she made up for in garishness. Stained-glass windows stretched from the foundation to the steeple. A fountain large enough to swim laps in dominated the green space in the front of the building. The church sign, a billboard framed in stonework that advertised salvation with clever quips and pithy proverbs, was a good ten feet tall and festooned with golden cherubs.

Titus thought the members of Second Corinthian missed the part about the meek inheriting the earth.

First and Second Corinthian and the New Wave Temple were three of the twenty-one churches in Charon County. When he was growing up there had been nineteen churches in the county. His mother had been a member of Emmanuel Baptist Church. She'd taught Sunday school until her illness forced her to step down, then it forced her to lie down, then it made her go still. Before it took her speech, she would say that a place like Charon didn't need such an overabundance of salvation.

"God can be everywhere at the same time if he wants, but he ain't in every building that calls itself a church. You can stand in a pulpit and call yourself a minister. I can roll around in mud and call myself a pig too. Don't mean you was called to preach, and it don't mean I was meant to be pork chops," he'd heard her say on more than one occasion.

Then she'd laugh and laugh.

When he was a boy, he'd thought his mother's laugh was full of the prettiest notes he'd ever heard. It had been a high and sparkling sound, like something Mozart might riff on a harpsichord. All these years later, nothing had come along to change his opinion.

After fifteen more minutes of driving, Titus turned onto Salt Lick Lane and headed down to Calvin and Dorothy's double-wide. When he'd first come back, before he announced he was running for sheriff, he'd come down here in his father's truck and sat on the back deck with Calvin and passed a mason jar back and forth and spoken of people they'd known and memories they'd shared. Of good times they'd had that seemed in Titus's mind to be bathed in a sepia tone as they faded bit by agonizing bit. Once he'd put on the star, the invites had faded away as well. Titus couldn't say he hadn't expected it, but he was hoping this was one time he was wrong.

Titus saw Calvin's truck parked at a haphazard angle as he pulled into their yard. Dorothy's little two-door sedan was parked in much the same way. Titus could see them pulling in hard, slamming on the brakes, and rushing toward the house. The grapevine being what it was, they'd heard fifteen different versions of how their son had died. None of them correct and all of them sickening.

Titus walked up to the door and knocked hard three times. Calvin had bricked in the double-wide a few years ago, turning the mobile home into an actual house with four pallets of baked red clay. Footsteps came to the door in frantic rhythms. Calvin tore open the door and locked eyes with Titus.

"Say it. Say it to my face, motherfucker," Calvin croaked.

"Calvin, can I come in?" Titus asked. Calvin was a few inches shorter than Titus but twice as wide, with a wide head on a bull's neck. He still held the Jefferson Davis High dead-lift record. His dark brown face had a few more wrinkles around the eyes, but for the most part he still looked like the foulmouthed, irreverent kid Titus had known since first grade.

"You can stand on that step and tell me you killed my boy. I already know, Titus. I just want to hear you say it. I want you to look me in the eyes and say . . ." Calvin trailed off. For a half second he just went quiet. The light in his eyes dimmed and Titus could tell he was somewhere else. Some place where one of his best friends hadn't killed his child. Then he came back with a vengeance. Tears streamed down his face. He grabbed his head with both his hands. Sobbing, he stepped backward away from Titus and bumped against the wall. His legs gave way and he slid to the floor.

Dorothy appeared like an apparition and went to his side while keeping her gaze on Titus.

"What happened, Titus?" she asked. Her jaw was set in a rigid line. Dorothy was a slim woman, but she put her arm around Calvin and helped him to his feet. A sentiment passed between her and Titus, as invisible as electricity but just as powerful. She wore the expression of a person who has prepared themselves for the most awful thing they could imagine every day of their life.

Titus took off his sunglasses.

"We got a call that someone was shooting at the high school. When we got there, Latrell came walking out with a .30-30 in his hands. He . . . he didn't put it down. He said some things about Jeff Spearman, then charged at us," Titus said. A sour taste crawled up from the back of his throat and settled in his mouth. Calvin and Dorothy exchanged a pained look. Titus picked up on it like a hound dog catching a scent.

"Was that .30-30 yours, Calvin?" Titus asked.

Calvin looked toward Dorothy again, but his wife had closed her eyes. Calvin whipped his head back in Titus's direction.

"You gonna arrest me now?" Calvin barked. His grief had emerged from its cocoon and become anger.

"No. I was just asking. Just trying to get things straight, that's all," Titus said. He put his sunglasses back on and stepped back onto the second riser. He fought the urge to explain. To tell them how he'd tried to talk Latrell down. Tell them how he hadn't wanted this to end with half of Latrell's head splattered across the parking lot.

"When he was in school Mr. Spearman had been his favorite teacher. He'd even given Latrell extra help with his geography classes. Used to keep him after school and tutor him. Why would he wanna shoot him, Titus?" Dorothy asked.

Titus swallowed the lump trying to form in his throat.

"He didn't shoot him. They setting my boy up. That's what they do!" Calvin said. Spittle flew from his lips. Titus felt a few drops land on his cheek. Another silent conversation took place between him and Dorothy. Her eyes told him things about Latrell Calvin didn't want to accept.

No one knows the hidden rivers of a man's spirit like his mama.

"Cal, we didn't set him up. Nobody in my office gave him that .30-30," Titus said. He did his best not to saddle the statement with an accusatory tone. He was just speaking facts. People who said facts don't care about your feelings had never had to tell a father his son was dead and before he died he'd become a killer.

All the fight seemed to seep out of Calvin abruptly. Without warning, he turned and walked away. Titus watched as he ducked into the living room and disappeared from sight. That left him and Dorothy standing in the doorway with the cold stealing the warmth from their bodies.

"A few weeks ago, he came here with a machete. Was swinging it all around, hollering about how he was the devil. Scared the hell out of us. Had Lavon crying. Then he dropped the machete and fell in my arms. He was hurting so bad, and I didn't know how to help him. He was my son, and I didn't know how to help him. We had thought he was doing better, ya know? He'd gotten a job at the fish house. We thought he was getting himself together." Dorothy hugged herself against the cold. "When can we get him?"

"He's at the medical examiner's right now. It'll be a couple of days. We'll be in touch with the funeral home. I'm assuming y'all gonna use Spence and Sons?" Titus asked.

"I hadn't even thought about it. Yeah, I guess we'll use Spence. Did he . . . hurt anybody besides Mr. Spearman?" Dorothy asked.

Titus shook his head. "No. No one else. Not the kids and not any other teachers."

"That's good. I'm gonna go check on Cal. Then I guess we'll figure out how to tell Lavon his brother is dead," Dorothy said. She closed the door. Titus stood there for a few seconds before heading back to his SUV. There was so much more to say, and at the same time there was nothing he could say that would stanch the wounds Calvin and Dorothy and Lavon would carry from this day until their last.

As Titus was starting his truck his mic squawked.

"Sheriff, what's your twenty?" Carla said.

"Making the notification for Latrell. What you got?"

Carla didn't respond.

Titus felt his phone vibrating in his pocket. He pulled it out and looked at it.

It was Carla. He hit the answer button.

"Something you want to talk about you can't discuss on an open channel?" Titus said. He heard heavy breathing on the line like some obscene phone call from the eighties.

"Sheriff, we have the phone but we can't get into it. It's locked. It's got one of those thumbprint security apps. I called Harold at the funeral home. He still has Spearman's body. He was going to run him up to the ME, but he got caught up with some folks who wanted to order a headstone for their mama. I was calling to ask if you wanted me to run over there and see if I can use Mr. Spearman's fingerprint to open the phone. But . . ."

"But what, Carla?"

"Sheriff, Jamal Addison is in the parking lot with about twenty people from his church. They asking for you. They asking why we couldn't take Latrell alive. They asking if he was really the shooter. Davy went out there to try and talk to them, and . . ."

"It didn't go well," Titus said.

"Not at all," Carla said.

"Tell them I'll be there in ten minutes. Don't go to the funeral home just yet. I might need you and Davy," Titus said.

He hated the fact that he even had to acknowledge the possibility that things might get out of hand. Jamal was a dynamic pastor who was as passionate about social justice as he was about saving souls. He inspired intense devotion among his congregants. That intensity coupled with the righteous (and sadly justified) skepticism of the veracity of anything the Charon County Sheriff's Office said under Titus's predecessors mixed with the raw emotions that were still being processed by everyone across the county after today's event set the table for a volatile situation where words could quickly become actions and those actions would invariably be violent.

Titus didn't think Jamal and his folks wanted that to happen, but that was the thing about violence. It didn't always wait for an invitation. Sometimes it saw a crack in the dam and then it flooded the whole valley. For his part, Titus didn't want to see anyone else get hurt today. He'd had his fill of both the sound and the fury.

Nine minutes later, Titus was driving past a small crowd waiting for him as he pulled into his parking space at the sheriff's office. Jamal Addison and twenty or so of his congregants were standing near the entrance to the drab brick building that housed the sheriff's office and one holding cell.

Titus rolled his head from left to right like he was loosening up before a fight. He knew this conversation was going to be a different kind of battle, but he was sure he wouldn't escape unscathed. An African American man had been shot by two white deputies. Didn't matter who was sheriff, there were going to be serious questions asked. Titus knew this, and even though some people wouldn't believe it, he agreed with them. The history of policing in America, especially south of the Mason-Dixon, made those questions necessary.

He also knew Jamal wasn't going to like the answers to those questions. He would see them as the language of conspiracy. Didn't matter that Titus was a Black man who had run on a platform of reform. To a lot of Black folks, including Jamal, he was now blue instead of Black. That Jamal thought this way was both ironic and disheartening.

When they had discussed the possibility of Titus running, he'd gone to great pains to ensure that Jamal realized he was going to be a sheriff who was Black, not the Black community's sheriff. He'd told Jamal he'd do everything he could to enact real change, but at the end of the day he couldn't and wouldn't ignore the law. Unfortunately, he'd failed in his attempt to make him understand that idea. Or maybe Jamal felt Titus had used him to get in office and had now betrayed him. It certainly felt like that was Jamal's position. Either way, it weighed on Titus every time circumstances brought them together that ultimately only served to drive them further apart.

As for the rest of Charon's Black community, he understood that for some of them he would always be the enemy. It was the price of wearing the badge. The moment he announced his candidacy he had made a choice to live in a no-man's-land between people who believed in him, people who hated him because of his skin color, and people who believed he was a traitor to his race. He tried his best to stand on the border of that undiscovered country, bloodied but unbowed. For most of the past year he thought he'd succeeded. Then a day like today slapped that notion into the dirt and all he could do was watch it shatter at his feet. He couldn't blame that on Jamal. That was the nature of the beast. And that beast liked to bite.

Titus got out of his SUV. He nodded to Carla and Davy. They were standing on the other side of the concrete island that separated one row of parking spaces from another. The crowd was on the side closest to Titus. When Carla and Davy didn't move, he nodded again, this time more forcefully. Carla got the hint and nudged Davy. He could see Davy's face was beet-red.

They both disappeared through the front door.

Titus wanted them nearby but he didn't want them standing guard outside. If things went sideways, they were only a few steps away, but he didn't want Jamal and his people to feel like they were in a standoff.

"Sheriff Crown, can we have a moment of your time?" Jamal said. He was a handsome young brother with a booming voice. He had the tone and mannerisms of an old-school pastor but the vison and passion of a millennial activist. A lot of the older Black folks in the county didn't cotton to his long braids or his casual attire. Jeans, brown Timberland boots, and throwback football jerseys weren't how they expected a minister to dress. Titus thought Jamal's wardrobe was a welcome change. He actually preferred that to the pimp/prophet outfits some pastors wore these days.

"Reverend Addison. What can I do for you?"

Titus had noticed that Jamal stopped referring to him by his first name around six months after he'd been elected. Titus decided he should probably do the same. If a man decides you aren't his friend, then you look like a fool trying to hang on to that title.

Jamal put his hands together as if he were going to pray. He took a moment to gather his thoughts.

"Sheriff, we've been told there was a shooting today at the high school. Calvin Macdonald called me crying and said your department had killed his son. Now I'm hearing that he is suspected of shooting Mr. Spearman, and I'm also hearing that he was about to surrender when he was shot down like a dog," Jamal said. He spoke slowly and with such deliberate pronunciation Titus knew he was enraged.

"Reverend, the shooting is still under investigation. The two deputies involved will be placed on administrative leave pending an internal review. I'll be making an official statement tomorrow. But I can assure you that every effort to resolve the situation peacefully was made," Titus said. He hated the way that sounded. It was like he was code-switching with another Black person.

Jamal put his fingertips to his lips.

"Sheriff, I'm sorry, but frankly that's not good enough. Can you assure us right here and right now that the state police will be called in to investigate this shooting? I mean no offense, but if you catch a fox in a henhouse, you don't get other foxes to investigate his intentions," Jamal said. A gentle murmur of agreement rolled through the crowd.

"As of this time I don't feel it's necessary to have the state police carry out the review. I give you my word we will employ complete transparency in regards to—"

"Your word ain't shit, Oreo." Titus recognized the young man standing next to Jamal who said it. The name on his driver's license was Ervin Jameson but everyone called him Top Cat. Until six months ago he was one of the main recreational pharmaceutical reps in Charon County. Then he'd overdosed on his own product. When he came back to this side of the veil after a week in a coma, he pronounced himself saved. He'd seen the other side and he'd glimpsed where he was going. He joined up with Addison's church not long after that proclamation. Titus didn't doubt the veracity of his conversion. He knew from firsthand experience how coming within kissing distance of the Grim Reaper can change you. What annoyed him about Top Cat was the overabundance of self-righteousness he now possessed. It was a trait common to the recently saved. Especially if one suffered from some form of dependency in their previous unsaved life. It was like they traded a secular addiction for a sanctified one.

"I don't think I heard you right. Say that again," Titus said. He was tired and stressed and his mind was reeling from all he'd seen this morning. One of his best friends' sons was killed in front of him. A teacher who had written a letter of recommendation for him to attend UVA had his brains blown out the back of his head. And now his Blackness, a thing that was as intrinsic a part of him as his arms and legs, was being challenged by a man who six months ago was selling more Oxy and molly to his own people than he sold to the Tylers and Madisons of the county.

The audacity was palatable. The hypocrisy was infuriating.

"Say it again," Titus said. He didn't use his cop intonation this time. It was all back-road Charon County in his voice now. Moonshine and cornbread. Fistfights and honeysuckle.

"You heard me," Top Cat said, but this time with the volume turned way down.

"Ervin, it's okay. Sheriff Crown, I hear you, but do I have to really explain to you why we might be a little doubtful?" Jamal said. Titus cocked his head to the side just a bit. In many ways what Jamal was saying was worse than Top Cat's insult. Of course he understood why Jamal was doubtful. Of course he was aware of the long history of bias and bigotry that persisted, not only in the Charon County Sheriff's Office but in many police departments across the country. Of course he'd grown up seeing Ward Bennings wielding his badge like a mace that he pressed on the neck of every Black man, woman, and child in the county. Titus wanted to grab Jamal by the collar of his old-school Houston Oilers jersey and yell at him, "Why the fuck do you think I ran for sheriff?"

But that wasn't the only reason, was it? Red DeCrain's voice whispered in his mind.

"Reverend, I understand your concerns. But that's all I can say right now," Titus said.

Jamal shrugged his shoulders. "All right. But I want you to know this. We are going to be watching how you handle this review. And if it looks like you're trying to sweep the murder of another Black man under the rug, then we are going to make our voices heard, no matter how long it takes. The truth is never out of season, Sheriff."

Titus remembered when Jamal was leading a rally to get out the vote for him last year. He wondered when exactly he'd lost the pastor's trust. He understood why he wouldn't trust the police in general, but it bothered him that Jamal and his church didn't trust him specifically.

"I give you my word we are going to do a thorough review," Titus said.

"I guess that's going to have to be good enough for Calvin and Dorothy and their living son right now," Jamal said.

"Lavon," Titus said.

"What?" Jamal said.

"Their other son. His name is Lavon. I was home visiting when he was born. I was the fifth person to hold him after his mama and his daddy and his two grandparents. They were afraid for him because he was born with a slight heart defect. Doctors went in and fixed it. Now he's a twelve-year-old ball of fire. Likes to draw. Before I was sheriff, I was over at Calvin's for a cookout. Lavon drew me a picture of me and his daddy. I know it won't be good enough for

Calvin right now. His oldest boy is dead. Nothing is going to change that. Not my promises and not your preaching. Now, if you'll excuse me," Titus said. He brushed past Jamal and his congregants and went into the sheriff's office.

Carla and Davy were standing near the entrance to the holding cell. Roger was positioned near the evidence room with his back to him. He had one hand against the wall with his head down. The only sound in the office was Cam's deep voice as he answered the phone.

His other deputies were as solemn as mourners at a funeral.

One would think this was because they had killed a native son of Charon. And while that may have impacted their demeanor, Titus could tell that wasn't the primary reason for their sorrowful expressions. That native son had killed Jeff Spearman. Geography teacher, coach of the debate team, and sponsor of the Drama Club. Jeff Spearman, who always seemed to side with the students whenever there was a confrontation between the administration of the high school and the student body. Titus remembered during his tenure at Jefferson Davis High School when the principal had tried to cancel the Ring Dance. Ostensibly it was because of a mono outbreak, but everyone knew it was because too many interracial couples had made it known they'd be attending the dance together. Jeff Spearman had stood with the students. He'd even threatened to organize a backup dance at the Ruritan Club if the principal canceled the one at the high school.

When Titus had shared that anecdote with his college roommate, the kid, who was from Trenton, New Jersey, had asked whether or not Charon was stuck in a time loop from 1958.

"I mean, it's the year 2000, man, and principals are still trying to protect the virtue of little white girls from the big bad scary Black penis monster?" Malik, his roommate, had said.

"Yeah, but Mr. Spearman had our back," Titus had said.

"Him having your back shouldn't have been necessary," Malik

had said. Titus remembered feeling foolish for praising Mr. Spearman. Not because Mr. Spearman didn't deserve it but because the whole situation had been a sad, pitiful anachronism.

"Y'all come on in the office," Titus said. The three of them followed him, silent as stones. He put his hat on the peg and sat behind his desk. Carla, Davy, and Roger stood in a semicircle in front of him.

They were all staring at the cell phone sitting on his desk just to the right of his laptop. The phone was facedown inside of a tie-dyed cover. Roger's face was pale as the belly of a trout. His lips were slick with spit. Titus thought he might have thrown up recently. Davy had his fist pressed tightly against his mouth. His jug ears were still bright red like he'd been slapped. Carla had her hands behind her back in a military stance.

Titus took a deep breath. He could smell the acrid scent of sweat and beneath that, another fragrance. A bitter aroma, both familiar and disturbing in equal measures.

Fear. He could smell their fear in the air like ozone before a lightning strike.

All of them, with the exception of Cam, had heard what Latrell had said about Spearman. His plaintive accusations hadn't sounded like the ravings of a madman, not entirely. There were no half measures here. Titus had a feeling that once they opened Jeff Spearman's phone, he would either be a beloved teacher murdered by a mentally ill former student or he would be a monster. Titus knew it was going to be one or the other. There was no middle ground. Taking one look at his deputies' faces, he could see they knew it too.

"Where we at on witness statements from this morning?" Titus asked.

Carla cleared her throat. "We took as many as we could. Got about thirty. A lot of people didn't want to talk," she said.

"I tried to get all the adults to make statements," Davy said.

Titus took off his shades. "Let's see if we can track down a few more. I want to make sure we've got this covered," Titus said.

"What's there to cover? That fucker shot Mr. Spearman and we took him down," Roger said. His eyes were wild and his words were full of bravado, but his thin lips quivered when he spoke.

"Y'all go on and get on that. I'll take the phone over to the funeral home," Titus said. Davy and Carla moved toward the door. Roger trailed behind them.

"Roger, not you. Have a seat," Titus said. The big man stopped and moved toward the wood-framed leather-bound chair on the opposite side of Titus's desk. Carla took a quick look over her shoulder before heading out the door.

Titus interlaced his fingers, leaned forward, and rested his forearms on the desk. He looked Roger in the eye.

"Roger, you were involved in a shooting today."

"Yeah, and it looks like we killed a crazy bastard," Roger said. He crossed his arms over his wide chest like a child about to refuse to partake of the brussels sprouts on his plate. Titus went on.

"As you know, as I explained after I was sworn in, any officer involved in a fatal shooting is placed on administrative leave for at least two weeks," Titus said.

"What? You can't be serious! Latrell shot Mr. Spearman in front of a whole classroom of kids. Kids we know. Kids you know, Titus. We did what we had to do, and now you putting me on desk duty? Really? You . . ." Instead of finishing his statement he suddenly popped straight up out of his chair.

Titus studied his deputy with cool, dispassionate eyes. Roger was a big man and he often used that to intimidate suspects, prisoners, and folks racing him for a table at the Watering Hole. He had never tried it with Titus, in much the same way a coyote won't try to intimidate a grizzly if it's alone. But now he came over to the desk and put his hands palms down as he leaned forward. His huge squarish head blocked out the fluorescent light in the ceiling.

"You gonna need all hands on deck, Titus. The shoot was good, but it ain't gonna be good enough for Addison and those folks over at that cult of his," Roger said.

Titus unlaced his fingers and leaned forward even more. "We

will need all hands on deck. That's why I need Trey to come back and give this a good look and make sure the shoot was above reproach. If I just ignore the fact that we killed a man on the steps of the high school, regardless of what he may or may not have done, then that will taint this office and our investigation of the murder of Jeff Spearman. Never mind the fact that everybody and their mama was videotaping the shooting from more angles than in a geometry book. I figure those videos are all over Twitter, Facebook, Instagram, hell, there might even be some folks posting to MySpace. It's gonna get rough around here. I don't need nobody thinking we sweeping something under the rug."

"You mean people like Addison gonna be upset a white cop shot a Black kid. You put me on leave, then people are gonna think the shoot was bad anyway," Roger said.

"Roger, there are some folks that are always gonna think it was a bad shoot because of that reason. We can't worry about them. We gotta worry about keeping our own house in order. That means desk duty for two weeks while Trey investigates the shoot and the rest of us see what's going on with Spearman, this phone right here, and Latrell. When Trey is done, you'll be back," Titus said.

Roger straightened. He crossed his arms again. "You don't believe any of that shit Latrell was rambling about was true, do you? You can't. You ain't gonna find nothing on that phone except pictures of Jeff Spearman at Phish concerts," Roger said.

"Whatever is or isn't on this phone, I don't need you on the road right now. Things are going to be heated. We need to do our due diligence. You can keep your sidearm, but put the riot gun in the evidence room," Titus said.

Roger glowered at him.

Here it comes, Titus thought. I'm either going to be a Black bastard or he is going to go there and drop the N-bomb. He didn't want to fire Roger, but that would be his ticket out the door. A good leader doesn't tolerate disrespect. He'd read *The Art of War* in college unironically, which set him apart from a lot of the trust fund babies he walked with through the halls of UVA. They read it for style points at corporate meetings. He was reading it for the actual battles he'd face in the Bureau. Both in the field and in the office. He'd read one phrase over and over from Sun Tzu's seminal tome:

"*Even the finest sword plunged into saltwater will eventually rust.*"

He couldn't have people around him who didn't respect him. Disrespect was a pestilence. If you let it go unchecked it would infect the entire department. That was doubly true if you were a Black man. No matter how much folks protested to the contrary, their preconceived notions carried weight when they dealt with you. He didn't need Sun Tzu to tell him that.

Roger uncrossed his arms. "You making a mistake. A big one," he said.

"You think you're going to see him tonight in your dreams?" Titus asked.

Roger's face softened. "What?"

"Latrell. You think he'll be waiting for you tonight? I think he will. He'll be there with half his head gone. Roger, even if I wasn't going to have Trey do an investigation, I'd take you off the road. You can pull your gun a thousand times, but pulling that trigger is a whole 'nother thing. And before you tell me it's not, I know you threw up before I came in here. It's because of what you're seeing in your head, isn't it?" Titus asked.

Roger opened his mouth a crack. His thick tongue appeared, then disappeared.

He didn't answer Titus's question.

"It's just two weeks, Roger. You help Cam on the phones and type up warrants and summonses. It was gonna be Davy's turn this week with summonses but you're gonna take it for him."

"I got some sick leave," Roger said.

"Suit yourself," Titus said.

Roger turned on his heel and left the office.

Ten-to-one he runs for sheriff in three years, Titus thought.

His cell phone buzzed in his pocket. He grabbed it and checked the screen. It was Darlene. He touched the decline button. He sent her a text.

Cant talk. Im OK. Will call later.

He knew she was probably worried sick. She'd told him more than once that she wished he was in another line of work. Being a cop's girlfriend hadn't been her childhood dream.

His phone buzzed again. She'd sent him a text back.

Okay.luv u.

Titus typed a two-character response.

U 2

He did love her. He did. He simply had a hard time expressing it. He realized that made him a walking cliché. The tough lawman who had a hard time sharing his emotions. He was lucky that Darlene didn't blindly accept that cliché. She'd pushed past his defenses and deciphered the vagaries of his love language.

To an extent.

He hadn't told her everything that had happened in Indiana at the DeCrain compound and, to her credit, she had only asked him once. She accepted that he wasn't ready to talk about it, but he knew she was also quietly confident he would one day confide in her all of his secrets.

Titus picked up the evidence bag and headed out the door, bound for the funeral home where Jeff Spearman was currently lying in repose. Latrell's cell was an old flip phone. It didn't have any fancy security apps on it. They'd be able to pry open Latrell's secrets with ease.

But what kind of secrets were you keeping, Jeff? Titus thought as he started the SUV.

Titus didn't have the heart to tell Darlene that no one told anyone all their secrets. Even the people we loved kept pieces of themselves hidden away from the light.

arold Bigelow met him at the door when he got to the Maynard Funeral Home. Maynard's was the funeral home most white people in the county used. Spencer and Sons was the one most Black folks patronized. Titus thought the only place where segregation was practiced without reproach besides the church on Sunday morning was a funeral home. Both were the last bastions of Ole Southern social conventions.

"Hello, Sheriff. I wish we didn't always have to meet under these circumstances. God, I can't believe we've had a school shooting here in Charon. You always think those things happen in other places," Harold said.

"People in other places think the same thing, Harold. Can you take me to Spearman?" Titus asked. Harold nodded and led him through the sparse yet elegant lobby and down the hall to the prep room. Harold unlocked the metal double doors marked PRIVATE and stepped aside as Titus entered the room.

The prep room was as sparse as the lobby but not quite as elegant. There was a stainless-steel embalming table in the center of the room. To the right against the wall was a dressing table, also stainless steel. To the left was a rolling metal tray with numerous scalpels, clamps, and tools of the mortuary trade. Next to the dressing table was a stretcher with a black body bag strapped to it.

"Has anyone got in touch with his brother yet? Last I heard he was in North Carolina," Harold said.

Titus shook his head. "That's part of the reason I'm here. I need to see if I can unlock his phone and get a number for a next of kin." That wasn't an outright lie. He did need to notify Spearman's next of kin. Titus knew Spearman had dated a few women in the county over the years, but he was still a bachelor. His brother would have to take charge of the remains and the funeral arrangements. But that wasn't the main reason Titus was here. Not by a long shot. For what felt like the umpteenth time that day, Titus put on a pair of latex gloves and unzipped the body bag.

Spearman's face was fixed in a wide-eyed rictus of surprise. It was as if at the moment Latrell's bullet had entered his skull, he'd finally realized he was indeed mortal. Titus pulled the evidence bag out of his pocket and retrieved the phone.

"I don't mean to tell you your business, but you probably won't be able to open it with his thumbprint now. Body temperature affect—" Harold said, but Titus cut him off.

"It affects the shape of the swirls on a fingerprint. I know. But Jeff had his phone set with a cold-weather app. So I'm betting it will still work," Titus said. He grasped Spearman's right hand. Rigor mortis was slowly settling into his limbs, so Titus had to wrench on the arm to turn Spearman's hand around to get to the thumb.

Harold looked on as Titus pressed Spearman's thumb against the lock screen of his phone.

The phone remained locked.

"I don't want to say I told you so, but . . ." Harold trailed off. Titus didn't respond. He grabbed Spearman's left hand, pried the fingers apart, and pressed the thumb to the screen.

This time the screen went from red to green.

Titus said, "I don't like saying I told you so either."

Titus went back to his truck. Sitting in Maynard's gravel parking lot, he started scrolling through Jeff Spearman's phone.

His daddy would have told him to pray for strength before he started scrolling, but Titus hadn't prayed since the day his mama had died.

Jeff Spearman must have been an avid fan of the Grateful Dead. His screen saver was the band's whimsical dancing bear mascot. Titus dragged a gloved finger over the screen and went to photos. There were photos in two different apps. One was a Google app that could be accessed on the phone or the computer.

The other app was specific to the phone and could only be accessed on this device. Titus went there first. He didn't think Spearman would put anything that could get him arrested on an app that could be hacked.

The first few pictures were relatively benign. Spearman on a hike. Spearman under the marquee of a concert venue. Titus kept scrolling. There were more innocuous pics. Then he saw a tab within the photo app titled "Favorites."

Titus touched the file icon.

"Oh God," Titus said.

He never realized he had called on the deity.

Titus's SUV came flying down Jeff Spearman's crush-and-run-gravel-covered driveway. Titus pulled up next to Davy's cruiser. He got out and immediately made a beeline for Spearman's small white and gray rancher. He ignored the few neighbors who were milling around in their front yards trying to pretend they weren't interested in what the sheriff was doing at Spearman's home. He'd called Davy and Carla after he'd finished scrolling through Spearman's phone and told them to forget about witness statements and meet him at Spearman's place. He'd given them the basics of what he'd found on the phone. The basics were enough to make both of them go silent.

He'd put the phone back in the evidence bag after fighting the urge to put it under his front tire and roll over it five or six times, then set it on fire. Titus had seen his share of horrific things in his twelve years as an FBI agent. The ability of one human to visit depravity upon another was as boundless as the sea and as varied as there were grains of sand on a beach.

The images on Jeff Spearman's phone were the worst he'd ever seen.

He kept thinking about purification by immolation. It seemed like that was the only thing that could remove the stain of those images from his mind, his heart, his soul. Burn the phone. Scald his eyes with hot oil. Put Spearman and Latrell on a pyre and reduce them both to ashes, then scatter those ashes to the four winds. Erase all proof of their existence and the things they had done. But the children in those pictures deserved to have their story told. They deserved justice. Whatever that was these days.

Looking at the pictures Jeff Spearman kept within easy reach, Titus had done what they had trained him to do at the Academy. Focus on the details. Force the pain and the perversion to the periphery and zero in on what could be used to make the case. He'd noted that there were usually two people in the pictures. At times it was two individuals wearing leather wolf masks like Latrell had been carrying on the steps. Titus knew one of the individuals was Spearman. He saw his gray ponytail trailing down his back in a few of the pics. Other times it was Spearman with no mask and Latrell. And at other times it was Spearman and a third person. This person never removed their mask. This person wore all black. This person always wore gloves and affixed the gloves to the ends of their sleeves with duct tape.

In the pictures Latrell was present but didn't seem to be participating in what Spearman and the last wolf were doing to the children. And they were children. Titus guessed they were teenagers, the youngest looked about thirteen or fourteen, the oldest no more than seventeen. All of them Black or Brown. Every one of them helpless.

Titus felt any sympathy he'd had for Latrell dry up like ditchwater in August. Latrell might not have been participating, but he hadn't tried to stop what had happened to those kids either. What would they find on *his* phone?

Titus swallowed hard.

What had been done to those children in those pictures was nothing less than an abomination. An atrocity before a God that didn't seem interested in forestalling the actions of his most accursed creations as they attacked his most innocent ones.

If Titus had harbored even a flicker of belief, those pictures had extinguished it. He'd called Mack Bowen and gotten him to agree to write up a search warrant for Spearman's house.

"Is it bad, Titus?" Mack had asked. Titus knew, in addition to being the commonwealth's attorney, Mack was the president of the local Rotary Club. They'd given Jeff Spearman an award last spring. He'd been their Teacher of the Year.

"If it wasn't, I wouldn't be calling," Titus had said.

"What you got so far?" Titus asked Davy.

"We got his computer, but it's password-protected," Davy said.

Carla stepped out of the house carrying a plastic milk crate full of correspondence.

"This was in the back room. It looks like he used it for an office. I figured we should go through it," she said. Titus had never been to Spearman's home. He'd called Cam for the address. He could have gotten it through the DMV database, but Cam was faster and didn't put him on hold.

"Is there a shed or something in the backyard?" Titus asked.

"No. It's just woods," Davy said.

Titus put his hands on his hips. "Where's Steve?"

"He said he was coming. Had to make sure his boy was okay," Carla said.

"Shit, that's right. He takes an afternoon class at the high school," Titus said.

"That boy is scary smart," Davy said.

"Did you . . . I mean, is it really . . ." Carla stammered.

"I can't believe it. The stuff you said was on his phone. I can't believe Mr. Spearman was into . . ." Davy's face trembled.

"Kiddie porn," Carla said softly.

Titus kept his gaze straight ahead.

"It wasn't just porn," Titus said. He took off his shades and rubbed his eyes. "It's real bad. He was . . . he was in the pictures."

He heard Davy choke out a swear. Carla shook her head from side to side.

"And based on some of those photos, they didn't just hurt them. They killed them. They murdered those kids," Titus said. He put his sunglasses in his breast pocket.

Carla made a noise that was halfway between a retch and a whimper. "You're sure? Positive?"

Titus didn't answer.

Carla set her shoulders and nodded. "You're sure."

"Spearman and Latrell and a third person. They weren't doing it here, though. Not enough room. Wherever they were at, they'd fixed it up just the way they liked. You find any books about that kind of stuff?" Titus asked.

Carla and Davy shared a glance.

"I mean, he got a lot of books," Davy said finally.

"We've just started going through his things. I mean . . . I don't think he'd have those kinds of books out for just anybody to see," Carla said. Her voice sounded hollow, like she was speaking inside a tin can.

"How are we supposed to know if . . . like, what do those kinds of books look like?" Davy asked.

Titus sighed.

"The books will have titles that refer to the deflowering or destruction of a young boy or girl. The covers will be mundane, but inside it'll go into great detail. Excruciating detail. The magazines will be more . . . explicit. Both the books and magazines will be weathered, dog-eared from constant handling. He'll have them hidden but within easy reach. There may also be . . . souvenirs," Titus said.

"I'm gonna throw up," Davy said conversationally. He wandered over to the far side of Spearman's house and vomited.

"Did you learn how to do that when you were with the Bureau? That profiling?" Carla asked. Her face had gone green, but she hadn't joined Davy yet.

"Yes," Titus said.

"How do you deal with having that in your head?" Carla asked.

Titus put on his sunglasses.

"I try not to dream," he said as he walked into the house.

"I know Steve is worried about his boy, but we need another set of hands. Give him another call," Titus said as he moved a pile of magazines on a coffee table.

"What about Roger? He can help too," Carla said with just a hint of frustration.

"Roger is on desk duty for the time being. So is Tom, I just haven't talked to him yet. Standard procedure for a fatal shooting."

"But if what you're saying is true, if what's on that phone is what you say it is, then Latrell got what he deserved. Spearman too. What we gonna punish Roger and Tom for?" Davy asked.

Titus turned his head toward his deputy.

"Latrell being involved in this . . . whatever this turns out to be . . . doesn't change the fact that we follow procedure. And following procedure is we are going to have an internal investigation. Do I need to explain that? Is there something about that idea that is confusing you?" Titus asked. Davy shook his head. Titus walked up to him. He bent slightly and spoke directly into Davy's face.

"We follow the rules. Not just enforce them. Now get Steve. We have a lot of work to do here," Titus said.

By the time Steve got there they had taken apart Spearman's bed and cleaned out all his closets. As they continued to work, they found random scraps that chipped away Jeff Spearman's John Keating image. Carla found a book called *The End of Alice* under Spearman's mattress. There was another book about Tiberius, with several sections highlighted about Tiberius's "minnows." They found a few porno DVDs that were marketed as "jailbait," featuring both male and female performers in the jailbait role. The performers were obviously over eighteen, since they'd had stickers on them from the old Video Hut that had long since closed, indicating they had been purchased legally. Steve found a few magazines in a lockbox in the laundry room that pushed the envelope even more but had a clarification in bold letters on the back that all performers were of legal age and had fully consented to the acts depicted in the magazines. These items on their own were evidence only of Jeff Spearman's venial sins. Perhaps perverse but not illegal.

Titus thought it was all disgusting, but it was nothing compared to what had been in those pictures on the phone. These magazines and DVDs and books were twisted and borderline unhealthy, but no one had died to create them. Everyone walked away with their lives, if not their dignity, intact. That didn't seem to be the case for the kids in the pictures on Spearman's phone. The speech he'd given Roger about nightmares danced tauntingly around in his head.

Steve was the one who found the wolf mask.

He'd been poking around the baseboards of Spearman's bedroom, peering in the floor vents, when he found a section of cove molding that sounded hollow. A push and tug later, and the piece of molding pulled away from the wall on a slim hinge. There was a small hidden compartment behind the molding.

"Titus, look at this," Steve called. Titus put down the sofa pillow he was about to cut open with his pocketknife. He walked in the bedroom and saw Steve holding a leather mask similar to the one he'd seen Latrell holding. The mask had a rigid snout that extended about six inches from the face. The ears ended in sharp points. The eyeholes were narrow slits in the leather that gave the mask an alien appearance. Less like a wolf and more like an insect. Steve wasn't wearing a glove on the hand that held the mask.

"Where's your glove?" Titus said. He made no effort to hide his disappointment.

"I took it off to wipe my eyes. I'm only holding it on the corner," Steve pleaded. Carla had entered the room and dropped to her haunches without saying a word, reaching into the compartment. She pulled out a plastic pencil box and opened it. There were two external drives in the box.

"Guess we don't have to worry about breaking the password on his computer now," Titus said.

"If there's evidence on these, and I think we're all pretty sure there is, why did he have that shit on his phone?" Carla asked.

"He wanted to look at it whenever the mood struck him. It gave him a thrill to have it with him all the time. It made him feel powerful. It also excited him. Not the acts in the pictures but having them with him while he was around people. People who thought they knew him. I bet he got off on that," Titus said.

"He was looking at that shit while he was in the same building with my son?" Steve said. Titus couldn't tell if he was incredulous or incensed. Steve's timbre rarely changed, no matter the circumstances.

Titus didn't respond to the question because the answer was obvious and nothing he could say could offer Steve any comfort.

"Carla, you got your computer in the van?"

"Yeah."

"Go get it. We need to look at these thumb drives. Anybody who doesn't want to see this shit can stay outside," Titus said.

"You seem to know a lot about these freaks," Davy said.

Titus gave him the smallest of shrugs. "It used to be my job to catch them."

"There's something else down here," Carla said. Carefully, she pulled out a rolled-up length of canvas. She stood and untied the black ribbon tied around the roll. When she unfurled it, Titus felt he wasn't the only one relieved it didn't have another set of gruesome images. It was a painting of a forest scene. A bosk of young maple and birch trees encircled a small clearing. In the center of the clearing was a tall, majestically gothic weeping willow tree. There were three words scrawled across the bottom of the canvas:

The Secret Garden.

Davy rubbed his face with his gloved hand. After licking his lips and tasting the residue from the latex, he gagged, then cleared his throat. "Well, thank God it's just a painting. I don't think I could take anything else."

"That's Spearman's handwriting. I recognize it from his calendar in the kitchen. And geography class," Carla said.

"I guess we should bag it along with this," Steve said, holding up the mask.

"Who are those kids in those pictures?" Carla said, seemingly asking herself the question.

Titus didn't say anything. He gently plucked the painting from Carla's fingers.

"What did he and Latrell and the Last Wolf do with them? With the bodies?" Titus said. He spoke in a murmur. He too was talking to himself.

"Dumped them in the river, maybe?" Davy offered.

"We would have found them. The Wercomico is brackish. Has a little salinity to it. Bodies float. Ain't you ever heard Pip's story about the baptismal drownings back in . . . what was it, '68? No. They had to put them somewhere else. A place that was special to them. A secret place," Titus said.

"Okay, but where is this?" Carla said, pointing at the painting.

"I don't know. But I know I've seen that tree before. That tree is their secret place. We find it, we find the bodies. I'd put money on it," Titus said. He rolled the canvas up and replaced the ribbon.

"Go get your laptop," Titus said.

"Titus, I gotta be honest with ya. If he's hurting kids, I don't think I can watch that," Davy said.

"It's okay, Davy. Nobody wants to see that shit in their head," Titus said.

"But you're going to look at it?" Steve asked. He seemed relieved that Davy had said what he was thinking.

"Someone has to bear witness," Titus said. Twenty years removed from the last time since he willingly attended a church service, and he still found himself using the jargon of the devout. It never left you, not completely. The cadence, the syncopation, the King James syntax. It was all there waiting to reemerge like seventeen-year cicadas.

If the pictures had been obscene, the videos were abhorrent. Titus felt like pieces of him were being sullied that could never be cleaned. He was being infected with a rot that would never heal. Carla had tried to stay and view the contents of the thumb drives with him, but after the first video she went running out of the house. She stood in the yard with Steve and Davy as the sun began to slide behind the horizon. There were a total of fifty-one videos on the one thumb drive. Seven of those videos depicted the torture and murder of young Black teenagers. The other videos featured younger white children. These victims appeared drugged and unconscious. There was also a coded mailing list. The other thumb drive held thousands of still images.

Titus shut off the computer. He went in Jeff Spearman's kitchen and ran cold water from the sink faucet. He took off his hat and his shades, then splashed cold water on his face. He'd heard a few people at the Bureau say you got numb to the cruelty that lives at the core of some creatures that passed for human. Titus thought if he ever got numb to the things he'd seen today he'd eat his gun.

He went back in the living room and closed the laptop. He gathered the thumb drives and put them in an evidence bag. He picked up the computer and his notepad and went outside to join his deputies.

"Take these external drives and the phone and his computer back to the office. Put it in the evidence room. Don't talk about anything we've found today. Not yet. We are going to have to get the state police involved, the Bureau may want a piece of this too. Child pornography is a federal offense," Titus said. It felt good to talk, to speak about taking action. That was the least he could do for the children Spearman, Latrell, and the Last Wolf had murdered.

"Spearman and Latrell are dead. What the state boys gonna do with our case?" Carla asked. Titus sensed a shift in her demeanor. She had gone from horrified to righteously enraged.

"The third man in the videos is still alive. He is still walking around like he isn't a monster. We're not giving up control of this case. But we need the resources to track down these victims. Find their bodies, find their families. Then we find him," Titus said. He handed Carla her computer, then pulled out his notebook.

"He's at least six feet tall. Spearman was five-nine, and he's taller than him. He's muscular, probably around two hundred pounds. He was using a fake voice. He tried to make himself sound . . . demonic. He was white or really light-skinned. You can see it through the eyeholes. Left-hand-dominant, but he used both to . . . he used both hands. The location was either a shed or a large outbuilding. Walls were sheet metal, painted black, but covered with dozens of paintings depicting angels. LED rope lights were strung up on the perimeter of the ceiling. Didn't see a door in or out. Could be a gutted-out trailer. They made Latrell hold the phone to video them, except when they made him get in the shot. Seven videos end with the demise of the victim." Titus closed his notebook with a sharp snap.

Seven, Titus thought. They killed seven kids. Seven families are out there somewhere wondering where their children are. Seven innocent little kids strapped to a table and suffering for these fuckers to get their kicks. And Latrell knew, and he didn't say anything.

He didn't say a word. If there was a hell, he and Spearman would be on the same spit.

Hell got plenty of room, Red DeCrain whispered to him in his head.

"Let's get all this back to the office. We got a lot of work to do," Titus said.

"I guess you never really know what people are really like, do you?" Davy said.

"I don't think anyone really wants to know," Titus said.

When he got back to the office, he typed up an email to the state police, but he saved it in his drafts. He'd send it when Trey got back and broke into Spearman's computer. Titus guessed that everything incriminating was on the thumb drives, but it didn't hurt to be thorough. Then he went over the monthly expense reports, checked his inbox for any BOLO requests, summonses that needed to be served, warrants that needed to be processed. Roger had sent him a sick leave request for two weeks but he'd miscalculated his PTO. He only had three days of sick leave left. He signed the evidence tags and initialed the time and date on all the items they took from Spearman's house. He sent Steve home to finish what was left of his day off. He sent Davy back on patrol. Carla volunteered to take up Roger's shift, so he approved her overtime and sent her out as well.

That he went about these tasks so adroitly after staring into the depths of the abyss that was what passed for the souls of those three sociopaths made him feel unclean. He knew better than most that the wheel of life would keep spinning, with little regard to the families who had lost their children or the children who had lost their lives. Waiting for the world to shed tears for your pain was like waiting for a statue to speak. So you filed the reports, you answered the emails. You carried on as best you could. And if you were like Titus, if you wore a badge on your chest, you promised you'd do all you could to find the Last Wolf and peel off his mask. Show the world the face of the monster.

There were times when he thought that badge gave him too much power. When he was with the Bureau, he'd seen what that power could do. How, to a certain degree, the badge was a shield that protected you from consequences and repercussions in the name of justice. Titus had been allowed to leave the Bureau under that mantle of protection. When he ran for sheriff, he promised himself he would use that power to help, not to hurt. Not ever again.

He took a deep breath and grabbed the evidence bag holding Latrell's phone. He slipped on his gloves and retrieved the phone from the bag. Titus opened the phone and started scrolling through the different screens. Latrell's phone was so old Titus felt like he was an archaeologist. No apps, plain HTML script. No pictures, no videos. Just lots of text messages and phone numbers with no names. Most of the texts were from Latrell's mother, begging him to call her. Pleading with him to get help. Quite a few were from people Latrell had queried about where he could score. A few texts were from a woman with whom Latrell seemed to be involved. He pushed a small button on the phone and advanced the scroll of messages. A text popped up that stopped him in his tracks. It was a simple declarative sentence, but it dripped with menace:

I saw your brother walking all alone today.

It was the last text Latrell had received. Titus checked the date. It was three days ago.

Titus dialed the number attached to the text. A robotic voice told him the number was out of service. He'd put in a request for Latrell's phone records, but his gut, that old unreliable narrator, told him the number was probably to a burner phone. It only showed up once in Latrell's phone. There was another number that called Latrell frequently, most recently last night. Titus touched the screen and hit the call button above that number. He was not surprised at all when he heard Jeff Spearman's phone begin to vibrate on his desk.

SIX

By the time Titus was done with the daily minutiae that wasn't connected to the quickly expanding murder case against Jeff Spearman and company, it was nearly 8:00 P.M. He hadn't eaten anything all day. The only thing he'd tasted was that cup of coffee at around six in the morning. Titus got up and grabbed his hat. He was going to head home. True, he was leaving an hour early, but he figured he'd earned it.

As he was heading for the door, the desk phone rang.

"Of course," he said. He answered it.

"Scott on line three," Cam said. He was due to go home in a few. Kathy was coming on to do the night shift. Titus pushed line three.

"Titus, what's the status of the investigation? I haven't heard from you all day," Scott said.

"I posted a report on the sheriff's office home page. That's all you need to know for now," Titus said.

"What that's supposed to mean? All I need to know for now?" Scott said.

"It means that's all you need to know, Scott. That means we are still investigating. It means you need to handle county business. Pass a budget. Approve some new stop signs. I don't report to you. And I'm getting tired of having to remind you of that fact," Titus said.

"You know, it's ironic a school shooting happened on the anniversary of the day you were elected. Seems to me that's the kind of thing people remember. Seems to me if I was an elected official, I'd want to keep people who could help me in my good graces," Scott said. Titus knew that was supposed to be a threat, but Scott hadn't helped him get elected and he damn sure wasn't going to stop him from getting reelected if Titus chose to run again.

"That's not ironic. Irony is a state of affairs that seems deliberately contrary to what one expects. If I had said that there would never be a school shooting on the anniversary of my election and then there was a school shooting, that would be ironic. What happened today is tragic, not a political football," Titus said.

Scott chuckled ruefully. "Showing off that fancy college degree, huh, Titus? You know I couldn't get into UVA. Too many quotas had to be filled."

"If that's what lets you sleep at night, Scott, you go right on believing that," Titus said.

"I guess I'm a racist now, right? Seems like anybody who speaks the facts gets called that nowadays," Scott said. Titus could hear the aggrieved sneer through the phone. Scott was the type of man who complained about the world being too sensitive these days without ever acknowledging the irony of his own fragility or privilege. Where some saw equality, he saw conspiracies against his manhood, his identity. He would tell anyone who would listen that he had the biggest house in the county and a Jaguar and a Hummer because of his own hard work, not because he was white or the son of the richest family in the county. Scott seemed to think he was a brave new soldier in the current culture wars.

Titus thought Scott was a spoiled brat. A spoiled brat who had never had to work for anything, who truly appreciated nothing but thought he was owed everything. Even a spot at the premier university in the state.

"Two things. First, I didn't get into UVA on a quota. I got a football scholarship *and* an academic one. Second, if I ever thought you were thinking about saying something to me that could be construed as racist, we would have a conversation about that. In person." Titus paused between "that" and "in person" just long enough so Scott could pick up the threat *he* was implying.

"There is going to be a candlelight vigil on the courthouse green for Mr. Spearman tonight at nine. Just thought you should know," Scott said.

Titus switched the handset to his other ear.

"We're still in the midst of an investigation, Scott," Titus said. "Might be better to hold off." That was as much of a warning as he felt comfortable giving Scott. He could have told him that Jeff Spearman was most likely a pedophile and possibly a serial killer. He could have told him Latrell had indeed done them all a favor. He could have told him that there was a third, as-yet-unidentified, coconspirator walking around free as a bird. But all that information was part of a currently active investigation. Titus wanted to get the tapes to the state police or even the Bureau to verify their authenticity. Same with the photos. They needed to crack open his computer and see what sickening evidence might be on that as well. There were *t*'s that needed to be crossed and *i*'s that needed to be dotted. Let the county have their communal moment of silence. They could grieve for who they thought Jeff Spearman had been before he told them what Jeff Spearman really was. Tonight was the end of innocence for a whole generation of Charon County citizens.

After he made an official announcement, every person who had ever walked through one of Jeff Spearman's geography classes, who had laughed at his silly suit of many countries he wore every year on Earth Day (a hodgepodge garment made of flags from almost every country on the planet), who had high-fived him after a debate or one-act play competition, would question every single interaction they had ever had with the man. Every hug, every shoulder pat, every conversation would become a clouded crystal ball that had failed them.

Let them hold on to their idea of Jeff Spearman for one more day. The awful truth would be with them all forever soon enough.

"Well, now, I don't answer to you either, and the community wants to gather. Tonight at nine. I assume you'll have some of your people there. The people of Charon County are watching you. They are watching you very closely," Scott said.

"Good night, Scott," Titus said. He hung up before Scott could say something else to make his blood pressure rise. Titus put on his hat and walked through the front lobby. Cam was watching the front door. Kathy was a few minutes late.

"She'll be here in a few," Titus said.

"I know. It's . . . today is one of them days I kinda wanna go home and hug my nephew and my sister real tight," Cam said. Titus nodded.

Cam rubbed his chin. "When I first came back, Mr. Spearman saw me in the Safeway. He spoke to me. He didn't look away. He didn't . . . it didn't seem like he felt sorry for me. A lot of people couldn't even look me in the eye."

"There's people who thought Danny Rolling was a hell of a singer," Titus said.

"Who's Danny Rolling?" Cam asked.

"The Gainesville Ripper. Killed five college students over four days back in 1990. Cut one of their heads off and put it on a shelf near the body. He was one of our case studies at the Bureau."

"Jesus Christ," Cam said.

"Terrible people can do good things sometimes. But they like doing the terrible things more. I'll see you tomorrow," Titus said.

Titus pulled out of the parking lot and slipped onto the road. The night had come and covered the sky above Charon County like a black blanket full of pinpricks. He turned right and drove past the courthouse building. Ricky Sours and his neo-Confederates had installed solar lights around the statue of Ol' Rebel Joe. Titus thought the lights looked cheap and disposable, much like the statue itself. It had been erected in 1923 by the United Daughters of the Confederacy, part of a coordinated and extensive propaganda campaign to reframe traitors as patriots.

After World War I, thousands of Black veterans returned home after saving democracy from the Kaiser with a renewed sense of dignity. They were heroes, after all. Why should they have to bow and scrape to anybody? Then the Red Summer happened and white men, like Everett Cunningham, Scott's great-grandfather, made it their mission to remind these heroes of their place. One didn't have to dig too far into the back issues of *The Charon Register* to see an article about Everett leading a group of "patriots" up to D.C. to show these Black men they were still just boys to them. That Everett came back minus an eye but with gallons of blood on his hands was a bit harder to find in the public record.

To cement their perceived dominance, the Daughters had erected hundreds of Civil War monuments across the South as the Red Summer waned. Most of them were made of low-grade bronze or limestone, mass-produced and erected as fast and inexpensively as possible. These effigies served two purposes.

To create a false narrative of honor and sacrifice that Confederate sympathizers could embrace in place of the shameful pall of treason that was their actual birthright.

And to remind Black Southerners that to some of their white neighbors they were just escaped cattle meant to be sacrificed on the altar of the Lost Cause.

When they were kids, around the time they got their driver's licenses, Titus and Cal and Big Bobby had talked about looping a rope around that statue that sat in front of the courthouse and dragging it down off its pedestal and down the road to the dump. If Titus closed his eyes, he could see the cloud of sparks that would have followed Big Bobby's '84 red and black Dodge Ram as they dragged that hunk of tin and copper slag down Route 18.

But talk was all it had been. The jejune declarations of young boys trying to find their way as men. Black boys who may not have been able to truly articulate how seeing that statue every day on their way to school made them feel but knew without a shadow of a doubt what that statue meant.

As Titus turned in to Gilby's he remembered his grandfather telling him how the Charon chapter of the Daughters of the Confederacy met its untimely end. The short and sweet version was that Sarah Anne Denning, the vice president of the local chapter, distressed that her husband, Norris Denning, had been charging his picket into many of her fellow revisionists, had made a sweet potato pie for the 1935 May Day UDC picnic. She'd used all the normal ingredients. Pureed sweet potato. Milk. Nutmeg. Butter. Cinnamon. She'd also added one extra ingredient. Five heaping tablespoons of laudanum.

"My daddy told me by the time the sheriff back then found 'em they'd been dead for half the day. Laid out like rabbits after the hunt. He say you could see the buzzards circling from a mile away," Grandpa Crown had told him and Marquis as they sat in the floor in front of his recliner. His mother had admonished his grandfather for telling her boys such a gruesome story, but she'd done so with a smile. Titus recalled there hadn't been much sympathy in his house for dead antebellum enthusiasts.

He took his hat off as he walked into Gilby's. The original Gilby didn't cook anymore, but she still came to the restaurant and held court in the corner. Gillian "Gilby" Hayes was at least eighty years old, but she might be one hundred. The colloquial axiom that "Black did not crack" could have been coined in her honor. She sat at her table with a pack of Virginia Slims in one hand and a coffee cup full of whiskey in the other. Tall and lean, with a crown of snow-white hair that was layered like a dollop of whipped cream that contrasted sharply with her dark black skin. Once, while he was in New York City for a regional meeting for the Bureau, he had gone to an art museum in Brooklyn. He'd come around a corner and seen a sculpture carved from obsidian called *Martinique Woman*. It was like Gilby was staring at him from atop a pedestal enclosed in glass.

Gilby's served down-home, unadulterated, nutritionally dubious

Southern cuisine. Fried chicken, mashed potatoes and gravy, hominy grits, black-eyed peas, turnip greens, buttermilk biscuits the size of your hand, baked and boiled ham, fried fish of every ichthyological designation, shoofly, pecan, chess, and chocolate pie, and iced tea so sweet it made your A1C rise two points just by looking at it.

Titus loved it.

He wasn't alone in his infatuation. Gilby's was one of the few places in Charon where everyone seemed to feel at home. A lot of that had to do with Gilby herself. She was your big mama and your auntie. Your nana and your grammy, and in later years she'd become something of an abuela for the migrant workers who found their way into town during the summer to help supplant the thinning ranks at the fish house. Her smile was a welcome invitation to anyone who came through the door to sit a spell and get yourself a good plate. As long as you treated her with respect you got respect in return.

And if you didn't, Titus knew there was a .44-caliber hand cannon under the counter ready to teach you your manners.

"Hey, now, Titus, you not gonna come over and speak to me?" Gilby asked.

Titus smiled. The sensation felt alien after all that had happened today. Then Gilby flashed one at him in return and for a moment he felt the weight on his shoulders and the shade hovering over his heart dissipate a bit.

Gilby took Titus's hand when he reached the table that was also her de facto throne. Her grip was stronger than he had anticipated. Years of chopping vegetables, rolling dough, and rendering chickens had given her hands deep strength, the kind that didn't wither with age. He wondered why her hands had retained their power and his father's had become distorted. They both had worked with their hands. But only Gilby owned her time. She could rest whenever she wanted. Albert's hands had been tethered to another man's whims.

"I heard about Calvin's boy. You know, Latrell won't never right. Then he got on that stuff and that didn't help," Gilby said in a low, hushed tone. Titus moved his head up and down in a quick motion of assent as he strained to hear her whispery voice. He couldn't comment on Latrell or the shooting even if he agreed with Gilby's assessment. Titus didn't have to survey the dining room to see that he was being simultaneously observed and ignored. Scott had only been half right. People were watching him, but they also liked to pretend he wasn't there. No one liked cops interrupting their dinner except the folks who liked cops too much.

"It's a rough situation for sure," Titus said.

"I know you hurting. You and Cal was like brothers. Bobby too," Gilby said. She let go of his hand and lit up a thin cigarette, completely ignoring the commonwealth's health guidelines. She exhaled slowly. Twin tendrils of white smoke streamed from her nostrils like plumes of steam from a train engine.

"Yes, ma'am, we were," Titus said.

"That Bobby Packer had the right name. He'd come in here with his people, and Lord if he wouldn't eat a whole goddamn chicken by himself."

"Bobby sure could eat. Speaking of eating, I better go and order my food," Titus said.

"You look like your daddy, but you talk like your mama. Helen was as sharp as a tack. She knew how to get away from an aggravating old woman too," Gilby said. She plopped her cigarette in the corner of her mouth and smirked.

"You ain't aggravating me, Miss Gilby. I'm just hungry."

"You tell Patrice I said don't charge you for nothing. You get the special platter."

"You ain't gotta do that, Miss Gilby," Titus said.

"I know. I ain't gotta do nothing but stay Black and die, but I want you to have a good meal. Darlene's a good woman, but she could burn water," Gilby said.

Titus hoped he lived long enough to say whatever was the first thing that came to his mind without fear of reproach.

"Well, uh, thank you. I appreciate it," Titus said.

"Don't you never no mind about it. Tell your Daddy and them I said hey," Gilby said.

"Yes, ma'am," Titus said. He threaded his way back through the crowd on his way to the counter. Few folks acknowledged him. A couple of white teenage girls sitting by the ancient jukebox that still had CDs glanced at him over the top of their phones and snickered. He recognized them from the scene at the high school this morning. A few hours ago they had been running for their lives, and now they were hiding their faces behind their phones and giggling. He wondered if this was how they were processing their ordeal. If the impermanent nature of social media was a refuge from the finality of death.

Or was he overthinking things again?

"Sheriff, I . . . I just wanted to say thank you. Y'all saved some lives today. Jesus Christ in a juniper tree, that boy was crazy as hell," a voice said.

Titus stopped and saw it was Cole Marshall. Cole drove a delivery truck for Cunningham Seafood and ran his own land-clearing and bush-hogging business on the side. Like a lot of people in Charon, he needed multiple revenue streams. He was sitting with a young woman Titus thought had to be his girlfriend. She was sitting on the same side of the booth as him. Her hands were resting on his forearm. She was idly playing with the fine blond hair that lay there. Their body language whispered of new intimacy. On the other side of the booth were Dallas and Megan Processer. Their married mannerisms moved in long-practiced concentric paths.

"No need to thank me," Titus said.

"Glad you had the nerve to put that boy down. Mr. Spearman was a good fella, he didn't deserve that," a man at the table opposite Cole and his group said. Titus narrowed his eyes behind his shades. The man's name danced on the edge of his memory. It came to him after a second. Royce Lazare. He was wearing an old-school TEXACO trucker cap over a thick head of brown hair.

"He wasn't a dog. We didn't put him down," Titus said. He removed his glasses and stared at Royce.

Royce frowned, readjusting his TEXACO hat. "I was just saying . . ." He let the end of the sentence die on his lips.

"We didn't mean . . ." Cole stammered.

Titus bore down on them, letting his eyes say the things a Black sheriff couldn't, until the awkwardness made each man drop his eyes and their dates turn their heads.

Titus put his sunglasses back on.

He recognized the rancorous taste filling his mouth. It was abasement, pure and uncut and as bitter as vinegar. What Latrell had done was horrendous. Not what he had done to Spearman, but what he had done with Spearman and the Last Wolf. The images of their inhuman actions would live unbidden and unbound in Titus's mind until the last day of his life.

That didn't mean he had to stand there like an extra in *Gone with the Wind* and take it while this jackass in the faux-retro hipster hat got his rocks off talking to one Black man about another Black man being killed. He could despise Latrell's actions without reveling in his death.

Those two things were not mutually exclusive.

"Y'all have a good evening," Titus said.

When he pulled into his yard, Darlene's two-door hatchback was sitting next to his father's truck and Titus's off-duty vehicle, a Jeep Wagoneer. Titus parked the SUV and walked over to Darlene's car and touched the hood. It was still warm.

He walked into the house.

Albert and Darlene were in the kitchen. Albert was sitting at the table like he'd been that morning. Darlene was sitting across from him in the chair that Titus usually occupied. They both had a container of Chinese food in front of them.

"Boy, you don't know how to use a phone?" Albert growled. He got up from his chair, limped over to Titus, and grabbed him in a vise-like embrace. Why had he ever thought his father had given in to infirmity? Albert was squeezing the air from his lungs like he was trying to pop a balloon.

"I heard about the shooting on the news. I was scared something had happened to you, big head," Albert mumbled into his neck. The bristles of his father's beard rubbed against his bare cheek. The sensation took him back to his childhood. Another hug, another prickly sensation, but this hug came with the scent of whiskey. Sharp and pungent as green isopropyl rubbing alcohol. His father taking him into his arms as they lowered his mother into the cold ground.

Titus hugged him back with his free arm. He was carrying the bag with the food in it in the other.

"I ain't going nowhere, old man," Titus said. His father gave him one more squeeze before releasing him. When he stepped back Titus saw him pass his hands over his eyes. He made his tears disappear like a magic trick.

"You okay?" Albert asked.

"I'm all right," Titus said. His mind played him images of what Jeff Spearman had on his phone and made his statement a lie.

Darlene stood up from the table and moved past Albert to encircle him in her arms. She was shorter than his daddy and her head came to rest on his chest.

"I hate this. Every day I'm so scared something is going to happen to you," Darlene said. She hugged him, and Titus hugged her back. Titus respected her honesty. Darlene didn't pretend that his job was normal. She never denied that it made her anxious. She spoke about her concerns often and yet she never asked him to choose between her and the badge. She was able to separate her fears from his needs. He knew that was a quality as rare as hen's teeth and it was one of the reasons he found himself still falling in love with her.

"I know. But I'm here and I'm okay," Titus said.

"I got you food. I didn't know you were going by Gilby's," Darlene said. Titus frowned. He should have called her back.

Albert coughed. "I think I'm gonna take my food upstairs. Let you young'uns have time to yourselves."

"Pop, you ain't gotta go nowhere," Titus said.

"Eh, I'm tired anyway. I went out to the garden and fooled around with those collard greens and snow peas. There's a rabbit eating them damn carrots like Bugs Bunny, so me and Gene put up some chicken wire. Took more out of me than I thought. Don't ever get old, boy," Albert said. He and Gene Dixon ran the church's community garden. The garden itself was carved out of a plot of land across the road from Emmanuel. The church gave away most of the vegetables to the county Social Services Department. His dad had taken up gardening in place of his carousing and drinking after his mother had passed. After he and Marquis moved out, he'd volunteered his skills to the church. He used to give some of his bounty to Gilby until one day he stopped.

Titus was fairly certain his father and Gilby had once been involved. If pressed, he would have guessed it started around his junior year in high school and had ended around his sophomore year in college. She'd never been over to the house, but his father had spent a lot of time at the diner.

Gilby had started coming to Emmanuel around Thanksgiving of his junior year, even though she was a member of Calvary Baptist Church. That Christmas his father took them to Gilby's for dinner. Titus didn't begrudge his father's need for companionship. He hadn't liked it, but he didn't begrudge it. He never thought his father was trying to replace his mother.

Marquis never stepped foot in Gilby's again after that Christmas dinner.

"You sure, Pop? You don't have to go," Titus said over Darlene's shoulder. His father smiled at him.

"Yeah, I'm sure. You take care of him, now. He think he ten feet tall and bulletproof," Albert said to Darlene.

"I always take good care of him, Mr. Crown," Darlene said. Both she and Titus were over thirty, but these moments with his father always made him feel like they were teenagers again. It wasn't an entirely unpleasant sensation. There was comfort in nostalgia, however fleeting it was.

"I know that, darling. Just keeping you on your toes. Good night, y'all," Albert said. They watched him shuffle upstairs with his beef and fried rice. Darlene stood on her tiptoes and planted a kiss on Titus's lips.

"He was so worried about you I thought he was going to pass out," Darlene said.

"And you weren't?" Titus said. He hugged her again.

"Of course I was, but I had to stay strong for him. Now give me that bag and sit down. I'll make your plate," Darlene said.

"You don't have to do that."

"I know I don't have to. I want to. Go change. I'll meet you back in the living room in five minutes," Darlene said. Titus handed over the bag without any further protest. He went upstairs and changed out of his uniform and into a pair of gray sweatpants and a black T-shirt. He came back downstairs in his bare feet, savoring the coolness of the laminate flooring that extended from the kitchen to the living room.

He sat on the couch, laid his head back, and closed his eyes.

"Don't fall asleep before you eat, Smokey," Darlene said. He snapped his eyes open and took the plate from her hands. She also handed him a beer from the fridge. His father didn't really drink anymore, but he didn't mind Titus having beer in the house. He twisted the cap and took a long swig while balancing his plate on his lap.

She sat down next to him and watched him eat. He glanced at her as she stared at him. Her wide eyes took him in, studied him, saw him through the prism of adulation. He teased her that she had anime character eyes. Her skin was a deep dark brown as smooth as fresh ice on a mountain lake. Her hair was cut short in the back and piled in curls on the top of her head. In the past few months, she had started going natural, eschewing chemical relaxers for more organic hair products. Titus thought his mother would be skeptical of

Darlene's new hair care regimen. Helen Crown had been devoted to her Dark & Lovely relaxers.

He took another long sip of his beer and finished it off. She took the bottle from him with her left hand and carried it to the trash can in the kitchen. She told him she was born right-handed, but after an accident at her mother's flower shop that took the tip of her little finger, she used both hands equally. Titus had his suspicions about the flower shop accident story. The last time he'd talked to Marquis, his brother had told him word around the county was Darlene's ex had slammed her hand in a car door.

Titus didn't press the issue. Part of him wanted to believe Darlene's story. That way he wouldn't be tempted to find the ex. She only talked about him in vague anecdotes, but he knew it wouldn't be hard to get a name from her. It wouldn't be difficult to pull his record. It would be barely an inconvenience to find his address and pay him a visit.

It would probably be immensely satisfying to pay him a visit.

But Darlene had never given him any indication that was what she wanted. She stuck to her story about a mishap with a sharp pair of shears and he allowed himself to believe it even though she never looked him in the eye when she talked about it.

A tapping erupted against the living room window and they both jumped. A large horned owl was sitting on the windowsill. Titus felt a chill run through him. His granddaddy—who used to regale him and Marquis with murderous historical lessons about Charon County—was a repository of folkloric legends and used to tell him owls were harbingers of doom. Titus didn't believe in superstition any more than he believed in the wizard in the sky, but seeing the owl staring at them through the window with its silver-dollar-sized eyes made him think of dark portents and ill winds. Titus stomped his foot. The owl extended its wings, then took off in a silent explosion of power.

"Well, that was creepy," Darlene said.

"Yeah. I think he's after the squirrels in the backyard," Titus said. He ate a forkful of succotash.

Darlene put her hand on his thigh. "I can't believe Latrell shot Mr. Spearman. He was a nice teacher," she said.

Titus chewed his food. He swallowed it, then took a deep breath. "I tried to talk him down. I thought I had him, then he charged at us, swinging that rifle. I've never seen a man look sadder than Latrell did this morning. Until I saw Cal and had to tell him his son was dead," Titus said. A silence settled between them that lasted for longer than Titus thought was normal. Darlene turned her body so she was staring at his profile. She fidgeted, pulling at an invisible thread on her pants. Titus knew she wanted to ask him a question. He waited for her to finally get her nerve up.

"Did y'all find some bad things at Mr. Spearman's house today?" Darlene said.

There it is, Titus thought.

Titus sat his plate on the TV tray next to the couch. He turned and faced her.

"Why'd you ask me that?"

"When we was closing up the shop today, Bucket Miller came in and said that Joyce down at the Safeway told him that Davy said he wasn't going to the vigil tonight. Said that y'all had found some stuff at Mr. Spearman's house and that people was gonna be mad they'd wasted their candles on him. Then I saw Gladys at the gas station and she said somebody said they saw you taking stuff out his house today. I mean . . . I was just . . . He was one of the few nice white teachers when we was in school. It felt like he really cared about us," Darlene said.

Titus made a mental note to have a talk with Davy tomorrow about his loose mouth. The grapevine in Charon County was as invasive as kudzu. By morning everyone would have a different version of what they had found at Spearman's house.

"Yeah, me too," Titus said.

"Is it true?" Darlene asked.

Titus didn't answer. He took her hand in his. Felt the rough end of the nub on her pinkie. He felt like the words trapped in his throat were like hornets in a nest. They were ready to burst forth and sting.

What he wanted to say but couldn't bring himself to was:

"Think of the worst thing you've ever seen. Now imagine seeing it dozens of times. See it and hear the screams that come with it and the cries for mercy or for God or for mama and knowing that there will be no mercy, no rescue, no divine hand of God coming down to smite the devils. Think of seeing that and knowing that it will stain you forever like the fucking mark of Cain."

Instead, he said:

"Let's go to bed."

SEVEN

Titus was up by seven making coffee. Darlene had slipped out of his bed around 6:00 A.M., giving him a kiss on the cheek before she eased down the stairs. She had to take her mom to an early morning appointment with the physical therapist, then go and open the flower shop by ten. Mrs. Gilchrist was recuperating from her own major surgery, a complete knee replacement. That was how they had met, in the lobby of the physical therapist's office. Adult children who had switched roles with their parents and were now the ones who soothed the patient when the doctor approached with the foot-long needle.

"You was trying to make me walk funny last night, huh? Call me later, Smokey," Darlene had whispered in his ear with a laugh before she left.

Titus sipped his coffee.

She'd thought he was being extra-passionate last night. Over the past year he'd learned their definitions of *passionate* differed greatly. He didn't mind, not really. She never left him totally unsatisfied. Darlene wanted to make love even when they'd just been friends with benefits. Not have sex. Not fuck. She wanted to make love.

That was fine, and if he'd had any problem with it he should have spoken up when they had first started dealing with each other. It wasn't like he wanted her to re-create *Story of O*, but when so much of his life was dedicated to his religion of order and control, there were times he felt the need to be a sinner and give in to the forces of tumult and discord. To dive into the center of the maelstrom and come back to the surface with wounds that told a story of real passion.

"Dig your nails in my back," he'd whispered last night. In the cold light of morning, he didn't know why he had asked. He supposed the lizard part of his brain had taken over and it had conveniently forgotten that Darlene didn't like to be the aggressor. But he had needed that aggression last night. He had needed it to chase away the pictures on Jeff Spearman's phone that were now pictures in his head. He had wanted to feel . . . anything besides disgust. Say what you will about her, but Kellie never had a problem with aggression. In fact, she craved it. If she had been in his bed last night, he'd—

Stop it. You got a good woman. Appreciate that, he thought.

He finished his coffee and headed out the door. His father was still in bed. He'd checked on him before he'd come downstairs. Going into his father's bedroom was like stepping through a time machine. His father hadn't changed anything in the room since his mother had died. The curtains were the same. The carpet was threadbare. Her nightstand with her reading glasses and her copy of *The Autobiography of Miss Jane Pittman* was exactly as it had been the night he'd heard his mother's death rattle rumble up from her mouth like someone shaking dice in a cup.

His father had been on his side of the bed. Always on that side, never on his mother's side. Titus saw the steady rise and fall of his chest. Heard him snoring and watched him shift his position a bit. His father never spoke about his dreams, but Titus hoped he saw his mother there. He hoped his father's dreams were not like his own.

As he was opening the door to the SUV, his phone vibrated. He pulled it out of his pocket and checked the screen.

"Huh, that's a surprise," he said under his breath.

It was a text message from his brother. It was only two words long.

you alright

Titus sent back his response in kind.

Yeah, I'm good.

Okay.

Titus's finger hovered above the screen. He felt like there was more to say, but then he reconsidered. Why should he be the one to say it? Marquis liked to act like he was the only one who missed their mother. Then he used that as an excuse for the life he was living. After Titus had been elected, he'd taken the opportunity to go through the archive reports. His predecessor hadn't been the most devoted record keeper, but the arrest reports were mostly intact. He'd seen Marquis's name again and again. Seen how his father had put up the house for bail. He'd also seen how his father had almost lost it because Marquis was late to his court date. Titus loved his brother, but he hated that he seemed to think he had a monopoly on grief.

After a long minute he typed a response.

Hey you gonna be around this wknd? Pop
wants u 2 come ovr he wants to get some
oysters

Marquis's response was so quick Titus wondered if he had rehearsed it.

Working this wknd. Building a shed for
Vanessa Ferguson over by Tank Billups place

A gear locked in place in Titus's mind. Tank Billups owned Norton's Marina. Had a big brick house over on Stamper Hill Road near the Cunningham homeplace. That was where Marquis was working this weekend, supposedly. Tank's name had shaken a memory loose. A memory that he shared with dozens of people in the county.

He jumped in the SUV and tore out for the office.

Titus saw Trey leaning against his car talking to Pip when he pulled into the parking lot. Trey was wearing a dark brown suit that was a few sizes too large for his wiry frame. His hair was cut into a short flattop that was going prematurely gray at the sides. Trey was the first Black investigator for Charon County. He'd been Titus's third hire. He had an associate degree in criminal justice and, like Carla, planned to leave Charon after a few years under Titus's learning tree. Titus had little doubt that Trey would succeed wherever he decided to go. He was smart, ambitious, and tenacious. Those were the qualities that could make for a very good cop or a very bad one. Titus was betting Trey would be the former.

Pip was in his uniform. The bottom three buttons on his shirt were performing a labor of Hercules as they kept his belly from spilling out. Pip was Titus's oldest deputy and looked like every stereotypical characterization of a Southern deputy. Wide head, jowly face, and a balding buzz cut that screamed "cop" even when he was in street clothes. The only thing he was missing was the virulent racism.

Pip had been raised Mennonite. He'd left his family's farm on the northern end of the county for the Peace Corps for a decade, then had come home and joined the sheriff's office. When he was growing up, Titus learned to see Pip as the nuanced ying to the rest of the sheriff's office's belligerent, frothing-at-the-mouth yang.

When Pip asked Titus if he could stay on, Titus was surprised.

"You're sure you wanna do that? I don't mind having you, but I think there are folks who might see you as a traitor," Titus had said.

"I suppose so, but I think it might be nice to finish up my career working for a sheriff who ain't meaner than a rabid weasel. One who keeps his white sheets on his bed," Pip had said.

"If he was so bad, why'd you stay on for all these years?" Titus had asked.

A pall had come over the old man's face. "Ward was a nasty piece of work. Person like that, well, if they think there's a pair of eyes on them that might be taking note of the things they doing, it might give them pause," Pip had said. Titus had just nodded. He didn't ask Pip if it had worked. He knew the answer to that question. He did wonder if Pip thought about that answer when he faced the man in the mirror.

"Gentlemen," Titus said as he walked over to Trey's car.

"Sheriff Crown, my granddaughter told me to tell you that you ruined her graduation," Pip said.

"No, she didn't," Titus said.

Pip grinned. "Nah, but she was thinking it."

"My fiancé said it. She said it more than once on our way back," Trey said.

Pip stopped grinning. "It's . . . bad, ain't it?"

"It's not bad. It's about twenty-five miles past bad. Let's get inside," Titus said.

Davy, Steve, Carla, and Douglas, who'd been handling a domestic assault call when the shooting at the school went down, were waiting in his office when he got there. He hadn't talked to Tommy yet, but Tommy was off, so he could catch up with him later today.

Titus sat at his desk. The deputies made a semicircle around him.

"First thing, we need to make sure we aren't sharing the details of the investigation into the shooting yesterday with anyone. Not our loved ones or our neighbors or our friends or folks at the market. The details of the case are changing rapidly. We don't need rumors floating around town. Understood?" Titus said. He locked eyes with Davy. Davy's face turned maroon.

"Second, Trey, I forwarded you all the reports on the fatal shooting of Latrell Macdonald. I want you to take a look at everything. Make sure it was a good shoot. I want to think it was, but what I think don't matter right now. We need fresh eyes on it."

"Yes, sir. Gotcha," Trey said.

"Carla, can you get the painting we took from Spearman's house?" Titus said. He slipped on a pair of latex gloves. "I knew that tree looked familiar."

When Carla returned, he took the painting from her and unfurled it. He held it in front of him by the corners.

"Davy, you ever do any hunting out on Tank Billups's seventy-five acres? Over on King Field Road?" Titus asked.

"Yeah. Me and my daddy went deer hunting over there a few times," Davy said.

"Me too," Steve said. "Me and my daddy and my uncle used to go over there. Tank charges fifty for the day for each person in your party."

"Me and my brother and my daddy went a few times too. I got a twelve-pointer over there. He charged us a hundred a person."

"He charged you that much?" Steve asked as if he hadn't heard what Titus had said thirty seconds before.

"Privilege is a hell of a drug. Now look at this tree. Where have you seen a weeping willow this tall before?" Titus said.

Davy and Steve exchanged confused expressions.

"It's on Tank's property. About four or five hundred yards in. I've seen it when we was tracking the blood trail on a buck my brother had shot. I remember it because it's rare to see one this big in the middle of the forest. On the videos, Spearman mentioned a secret garden. I think this is it," Titus said.

"Goddamn, you're right. I remember it now," Davy said.

"So, why is that tree important?" Steve asked. Titus turned to answer him, when Trey spoke.

"You think that's where they buried them, don't you?" Trey asked.

Titus nodded. "I do. There are at least seven different victims on the . . . videos. They aren't under Spearman's house. They aren't in the walls. There is always the possibility they could have been disposed of in other ways, but this painting was important to Spearman. It was so important he hid it with his external drives. Killers like Spearman and his partner are driven by fantasy. They think about their fantasies all day. If possible, they like to relive them until the fantasy isn't enough and they need a new victim. I think they buried them near this tree and then went back to visit the site. More than once," Titus said. Talking about it this way, in cop jargon, helped him, albeit slightly. It gave him a measure of distance from the memories of those children and their screams.

"What you wanna do?" Douglas asked. Unlike Trey and Carla, Douglas didn't have any higher aspirations. He was a former bouncer who'd gotten a job with the sheriff's office for the health insurance. He didn't feel like it was his calling like Roger, but he didn't see it as a career like Trey. It was just a job to Douglas. Titus could respect that. There were times when Douglas's dispassionate demeanor came in handy.

"I want to call Warren Ayres and have him bring both the volunteer fire department and the volunteer rescue squad out to Tank Billups's property. We are going to excavate the area around that tree and we are going to need help. Pip, I'm gonna need you to handle the patrol in the northern part of the county. Steve, you and Douglas ask around with the teachers at the high school, Spearman's friends. Find out if any of them saw Latrell and Spearman together. Rest of us are going to go over to Tank's. Right now, this stays quiet as kept until we find something," Titus said.

"You really think Jeff Spearman buried those kids out under a tree in the woods?" Steve asked.

"Spearman and the Last Wolf. I think they did it and I think they got off on it. They liked knowing those bodies were out there. They liked having that secret. But secrets can be corrosive. You hold it in, and it starts eating your insides. Pretty soon you find yourself willing to do anything to stop the pain. For Latrell that meant blowing a hole in Jeff Spearman's head wide enough to put your fist through," Titus said. It occurred to him he could have been talking about himself as well as Latrell. His secret was patiently waiting to be revealed. Hanging over his head like a dull sword of Damocles.

"There's nothing we can do to Latrell or Spearman. But that third man? The one who never took off his mask? We can find him. We can make him answer for what he did. Take off that mask and show him to the world. The things they did on those videos . . ."

He paused, took a breath, then continued.

"No one should get away with that. No one. That kind of sickness won't stop because his partners are dead. I'll be damned if I let him take somebody else's child on our watch. The scales gotta be balanced. First step in that is finding the bodies. Bodies hold secrets of their own," Titus said.

"They called it their secret garden. What the hell is wrong with people like that, Titus?" Davy asked. Titus rolled up the painting and laid it on his desk.

"Everything, Davy. Everything."

Like most back roads in Charon County, the way to Tank Billups's wooded seventy-five acres was beset by shadows even during the brightest part of the day. Deciduous and coniferous trees lined the ditch banks like the first regiments of an army trying to reclaim a captured kingdom. Titus thought the trees seemed to be encroaching on the narrow ribbon of asphalt like the Great Birnam Wood from Macbeth.

Titus did some math in his head as he drove. The date codes on the video files from the thumb drives went back five years, to 2012. The photos were older. Way older. In the earliest ones Spearman had black hair and was alone with a child who was obviously a young Latrell. Later there were other children. Titus recognized some of the faces. He'd seen them around town, lined and weathered, with beards or tattooed eyeliner. Adults who had once been scared little children in the hands of a man who was the second-most-trusted grown-up they knew after their parents.

Titus fought the urge to drive to Richmond and pump some bullets of his own into Spearman's body.

After the meeting Titus had sent his team home to change out of their patrol uniforms and get into clothes they didn't mind getting dirty. Titus kept on his uniform. If the good citizens of Charon County saw him in a filthy, soiled uniform they would fixate on that image like a posthypnotic suggestion. It would become fodder for gossip at the post office or the grocery store. They would subconsciously file it away as another reason he wasn't fit for his office. The color of his skin was reason enough for some folks. He didn't intend to give them any more kindling for that hateful fire.

Titus led a caravan down East Wood Road for nearly ten miles. He'd finally spoken with Tom on the phone and informed him of his two-week suspension. A phone call wasn't the ideal way to communicate that decision, but things were moving fast and the secret garden was taking precedence.

"Sure. I get it. Titus, I had to shoot him. He was coming at us. He could have drawn down on us, on you. I had to do it. You know that, right?" Tom asked. Titus could tell his *h*'s and *t*'s sounded bent. He figured Tom was three sheets to the wind.

"Get you some rest, Tom. Is there somebody you can talk to?" Titus asked.

"Can I talk to you?" Tom asked.

"Well . . . yeah, but later. We're heading out to Tank Billups's field."

"What's happening out there?" Tom asked.

"We're following up on some things we found on Spearman's phone," Titus said.

Tom went quiet for a beat. "What kind of things was on his phone?" he slurred.

Titus ignored the question. Tom was drunk. That didn't bode well for his ability to maintain confidentiality.

"I'll be in touch. Drop by the office and give Trey your gun," Titus had said before ending the call.

Titus turned off East Wood Road onto a dirt lane with a horse gate across it, mounted to two ancient four-by-four posts. Titus stopped, hopped out, and opened the gate. Tank wasn't sure if the gate was locked when they had called and asked for permission to go onto his land. He was in his sixties and he admitted to Titus he hadn't personally been out to the property in years.

"I can't see so good no more. And my boy Jerry got the DMV to take my goddamn license. I know why. He wants to put me in a goddamn home. And he don't go check on the property. He just wants to sell it. That land been in our family since my grandaddy came back from World War I. Yeah, we moved to town later, but don't mean we need to give it up. Land is the only real thing that has value in this world," Tank had intoned.

Is that why you charged Black people double to hunt on it? Titus thought.

"We just need permission to look around, Mr. Billups."

"What y'all looking for out there?"

Dead kids, Titus thought. "We have reason to believe that certain parties may have left evidence of a crime out there," Titus had said.

"What kind of crime? I think I have a right to know, if y'all be out there tearing up my property. Am I gonna be compensated for this? Y'all go out there tearing up hell while I'm stuck here at the house without someone there to look out for my interests, I think I need some assurances," Tank had said. Titus thought Tank probably didn't talk to a lot of people anymore. He was enjoying this negotiation, as it were. The art of the deal and all that nonsense.

Titus didn't have time for that. "Murder, Mr. Billups. Now can we go on the property?"

That ended the negotiation abruptly.

Titus led the caravan down the lane until they came to a place where the road ended and the forest began. Behind him was not only his deputies but four pickup trucks and one emergency vehicle from the Charon Volunteer Fire Department. The pickups held two people each. The emergency vehicle held three. Each pickup

had shovels and work lights in the back. The emergency vehicle had
body bags.

Titus got out of his SUV. He waited as the men and women piled
out of the vehicles. Once everyone was accounted for, he started to
speak.

"I don't know how many of you have hunted or run your hounds
through here, but we're heading for that willow tree. If you've
been here before, you've seen it. It ain't really got no reason to
be here in that clearing. That's what makes it stand out. I'll give
more details about the radius we're working with when we get out
to the tree."

"You really think Jeff Spearman and Latrell killed some kids and
buried them out here?" a voice said, basted in incredulity.

Not just Spearman and Latrell, Titus thought.

"You didn't see what we saw on that phone. Let's head out," Titus
said. He led the group down among the pines, oaks, elms, and the
odd cypress. As they marched, slivers of sunlight pierced the dense
forest canopy and bathed them in incandescent chains of gold.

Every now and then as they walked Titus would glance up toward the crown of one of the trees they passed. He thought trees
were the closest living things to immortal on earth. How many of
these arboreal giants had been saplings when the first indigenous
people hunted whitetails here? When the Jamestown settlers ate
their shoes as the first Virginia winter tested their resolve? How
many men who looked like him were lynched from their branches
in the years following the failed rebellion of Southern landowners
and poor hired men? What would these eternal elementals say if
you asked them about the children Jeff Spearman, Latrell Macdonald, and the Last Wolf tortured? Would they say anything at all? Or
would the affairs of men be like the affairs of ants to them?

"You think too much," his pops used to tell him when he'd ask
questions like that as a kid.

"That's his superpower, Albert," his mother would say before kissing him on the forehead. Before her flesh started turning to bone.

They crunched over dead leaves and pine needles until they reached the clearing.

"Here," Titus said.

The willow tree towered over them as it stood in the center of a clearing that was at least a hundred feet in circumference. Multifarious branches stretched up toward the sky from a girthy trunk. These branches winnowed down to slim, jade-colored vine-like leaves. These leaves fell toward the ground like strands of hair that were the crown of glory for some eldritch elder god. The wind moved the leaves like the god was shaking its head.

"We need to excavate this whole area. We start from the outer edge and work our way in. Warren, if you and Derry could sweep the ground with your metal detectors first, then we'll dig some exploratory samples. If they're out here, they didn't bury them deep."

"We'll sweep it, Titus, but I gotta be honest. I can't believe Jeff Spearman could hurt a fly," Warren said.

"He had videos showing him and Latrell and another man hurting boys and girls. Do you want to see them?" Carla asked. Warren's face bloomed red.

Titus went on. "If you find anything, holler and we'll mark it. Try your best not to disturb the remains. We need to preserve as much of the evidence as we can." He searched their faces. The yearning there was plain and desperate. They didn't want to believe it. They wanted to pretend that Jeff Spearman was what he had presented himself to them and nothing more. We all choose to be skeptics when the truth is inconvenient.

"Let's get to it," Titus said.

Three hours later the sun was hanging low in the sky and the shadows that stood watch over them had grown exponentially.

Warren came up to Titus with his shovel over his shoulder. "Titus, ain't nothing here. Whatever happened to those poor children, it didn't end here." His face was slick with sweat despite the cool temperature.

"Let's move closer to the tree. Did anybody bring an ax? We need to break through those roots," Titus said.

Wayne frowned. "Titus, I know you used to be some fancy hot-shot FBI guy, but I'm telling you, we done dug twenty holes and we ain't seen shit."

"Men like this, like Spearman, they don't like to let them go. We need to chop through those roots and get closer to the tree," Titus said. He ignored Warren's dig about his past. He was used to the people who voted for him deifying his time with the Bureau and those who didn't vote for him dismissing it. Titus thought if they knew why he'd stepped down, the roles would be reversed. He took no solace in that knowledge.

"This is a waste of goddamn time. You do what you want with your deputies, I'm taking my people home. We're a volunteer squad. We can't be playing around in the woods when we need to be fresh," Warren said.

"Give me forty-five more minutes," Titus said. He could just say he'd deputize the members of the fire department. Take advantage of an arcane proviso in the county's charter. He'd read the charter from beginning to end. The likelihood that Warren had also read it was probably between zero and nil. No, he didn't feel like arguing the merits of a two-hundred-year-old codicil. If Warren wanted to leave, he could go. They would carry on, with or without him or his volunteers.

"I'm sorry, I can't do—"

"OVER HERE!"

The words echoed through the woods, ricocheting backward and forward until they came back around like the moaning of a banshee.

"I guess I won't need those forty-five minutes," Titus said.

They walked over to Anita Denton, the one who'd sent up the alarm. She was holding her shovel with both hands, one near the spade, the other near the tip of the handle. She took two steps away from the fresh hole she'd been digging. Her face was ashen. A flock of crows flew overhead, raining down a chorus of caws.

Titus peered down into that hole.

The skull was painfully small, as most are when the skin and muscle has fallen away. A few scraps of hair were still attached to the top of it. The skull was attached to a spine that looked fragile as a twig. The torso was wearing a shirt, brown and tattered with age. The roots of the willow tree were notoriously invasive. Most homeowners are warned not to plant one near their well or their septic tank. These roots were no less aggressive. They had wrapped around the body like an anaconda. One of the roots had found its way into the skull and was coming out the eye socket to reconnect with its brethren.

Titus dropped to his haunches. There was a small plastic rectangle near the top of the skull. He reached out his hand and a pair of latex gloves were placed in his palm. He put them on and picked up the piece of plastic.

It had darkened with age, but Titus recognized it. His high school girlfriend had worn one in her hair. A tortoiseshell claw clip.

"There are more here. Let's take care of them. Let's get them out of this ground and get them home," Titus said. He raised his voice just enough that everyone heard him. They had formed a semicircle around him but were standing as far away from the hole as they could.

He stood. "They been out here long enough."

They were still at it two hours later. Work lights were employed to give them light as the darkness chased the sun back to her den. The creatures of the night, the whip-poor-wills and owls, the crickets and mockingbirds, the random coyote, vocally affirmed their presence. A nearly full orange-hued moon shone down upon them, its light lost among the illumination from the work lights. Titus watched as red survey flags on thin, flexible wire posts sprouted from the ground like wildflowers.

"How many?" Titus asked.

Davy wiped his forehead with the back of his hand. "Seven so far. Boys and girls, just like you said was on the videos."

Titus took a deep breath. "Call the funeral homes."

"Which ones?"

Titus exhaled. "All of them. Bigelow's, Blackmon's, Spencer and Sons. All these bodies going to have to go to Richmond. I'll put in a call to the state police. We're gonna need help with analyzing the remains. They're all going to need full autopsies," Titus said, silently wishing Virginia had an actual coroner's office instead of just four district offices for the medical examiner.

Davy let his chin hit his chest. Words tumbled from his mouth, but under his breath.

"What?" Titus asked.

"I said, why wasn't nobody looking for them? Some of these bodies been here for years, it looks like. . . . Why wasn't somebody trying to find them? They was just kids!"

Titus took off his hat and ran a hand over his close-cropped hair. "They were Black children, Davy. People are probably looking for them, but blond hair and blue eyes make the news."

"Don't make it about that," Davy said. Indignation spilled from him like water from a sluice.

Titus readjusted his hat on his head. "You look over there and tell me it ain't about that," he said. Davy didn't respond.

"I'm going back to the office. Gotta get things going with the state boys. I want to run this jointly. I'm not letting them take this over. This is our case. This is our home. Set up a perimeter, then you and Carla go get some sleep. I'm going to get Douglas to post up at the entrance to the property overnight."

"That's a long shift," Davy said.

"We're all going to be working long shifts from here on out, until this is finished."

"And when is that gonna be?"

Titus looked past Davy to the graveyard that had rapidly grown around them. The killing field hidden in plain sight for so long. The willow tree swayed gently in time with the cold wind.

"When we catch him," Titus said.

Titus got back to the office thirty minutes later. He saw Kathy's car in the parking lot.

"You're here early. Cam was supposed to be on till eight," Titus said when he entered the office.

"Yeah, but he called me and asked if I could come in early, seeing as I was late yesterday. He's still pretty shook up about what happened yesterday. He told me to tell you Ricky Sours been blowing up the phone," Kathy said.

"I'll call him later."

"Is it true? About Latrell?" Kathy asked. She'd dated Calvin for a hot minute when Dorothy had broken up with Cal. Three months later they had made up and Kathy was with Bobby Packer, Titus's other old high school teammate. They'd gotten married a year after Calvin and Dorothy. They'd stayed together until Bobby died in an accident in his dump truck in 2012.

After the election Kathy had applied for the dispatcher job, since both dispatchers, two older white women, had quit out of loyalty to Cooter. Titus had hired her almost on the spot. When she was filling out the paperwork, he noticed she had gone back to using her maiden name. He hadn't asked her about it, but she noticed him noticing it.

"It's hard to hear it. Packer. Every time I hear it I think of Bobby. It's . . . it's tough," she'd said. Titus understood that kind of grief. He used to love reading Greek mythology as a kid. He especially loved the *Iliad*. After his mother died, he couldn't read it anymore. He couldn't stand to see the word *Helen* over and over again on the weathered pages of his book. Eventually he'd burned it in their woodstove. When Kathy had told Titus the story behind reclaiming her maiden name, he'd felt a wave of grief so powerful he'd felt his chest tighten. Sometimes grief is love unexpressed. Other times it's regret made flesh.

"Yeah. It's true," Titus responded.

"Jesus be a fence around us," Kathy said.

"I don't think Jesus is getting involved in this one."

"Titus!"

"There's more going on than just Latrell shooting Jeff Spearman."

"Like what?"

"We found a lot of disturbing things on Jeff's phone. Things are going to get crazy 'round here in the next few days."

"Oh Lord. Well, you the man for the job," Kathy said. She smiled at him.

"I'm gonna make some calls, then I'm gonna head home. Pip is working a double. If you need me, you can get me," Titus said, side-stepping Kathy's compliment.

"Okay. Oh, Darlene called too. She said she was trying to get your cell phone."

"I must have been out of signal range. All right, thanks."

Titus could handle the proprietary tendencies of the state boys if it meant they'd bring the full arsenal of the Virginia State Police's forensic capabilities to his county.

His county. When he was in Indiana, he'd often sidestep talking about Charon the way he'd sidestepped Kathy's embarrassing compliment. If he was honest with himself, he had been ashamed of his hometown. Of the backward people and the small-town pettiness that flourished there. Only after Red DeCrain's family had exploded in front of him did he find comfort in the familiar highways and byways of Charon County. Being home, being with Pops, after losing everything, made him look at Charon County in a different light. It was his home and it was his heart. And he'd be damned if he let men like Ricky Sours think they could claim it as their sole property or men like the Last Wolf get away with making it a killing field.

Titus had no illusions about who or what he was. For many

people he was the devil. He accepted that. Only he was a devil that chased down demons.

When he got home his father wasn't there. He found a note on the refrigerator that said Albert had gone to give Bernice Gresham's granddaughter a jump. Bernice was a member of his father's church, and since his father was chairman of the deacon board his number was on the emergency contact list for church members. Titus thought his father was still trying to make up for his misspent youth. If his father's early morning gas station buddies were to be believed, Albert Crown was once a hellion. Quick with his fist and fearless as only young men can be. Only when his father's temper flared up did he get a glimpse of the man whose fists were so strong from years of pulling crab pots they called him the Maul. Because when he hit someone, it was like they'd been attacked with a hammer. Titus thought that both the scrapper and the gardener existing in the same man was a testament to the multifaceted tapestry that lives in us all.

"Like Jeff Spearman being a teacher and a child killer," Titus said under his breath.

Titus changed out of his uniform and into a pair of jeans, boots, and a sweatshirt. He went outside and let the air pinch his cheeks for a moment before he went over to the woodpile. His father had a furnace installed a few years back, but they still used the woodstove now and again. Albert liked to say the heat felt more real than what came from the furnace. A few of the floor vents didn't seem to work correctly, either. So they kept the woodstove.

As a child Titus would sit and listen with a touch of fear when the old cast-iron cube would start to roar like a lion after his father got a good fire going. The heat that came off it was biblical. Marquis would complain that the woodstove made the house too hot. His mother would bop the back of his head playfully and tell him it was hotter than this in hell.

She used to make them laugh a lot. Before.

Titus grabbed an ax and started on the cord of wood that had been dropped off last week. Most of the wood was stove-length, but was a hair too wide. Titus grabbed one of the pieces of firewood and placed it on the tree stump he used as a block. Above him an arc of sodium light hummed like an old blues man about to start singing an old tune.

Titus raised the ax and brought it down in a vicious whistling arc. The wood split in two. Both halves hopped off the block and danced across the grass. Titus started a stack against the back of the house. He grabbed another piece and repeated the vicious ax strike. As he worked, he caught a whiff of the last blooms of the magnolia tree that dominated the backyard. He paused and looked at the tree. Even though the air was cold, they hadn't had a true frost yet.

His mother had loved magnolia flowers. She'd enlisted his aid in making perfume out of the blooms. The scent would hang in the house for weeks. A cloying, sweet scent that was half old-women-sachet, half a sickeningly sugary odor like a rotting body right before it sprouted maggots. There were days after she'd boiled the petals in a big pot that he thought he could see the scent in the air.

Titus grabbed another piece of wood and split it in two. He bared his teeth as he brought the ax down.

He and Marquis had plucked a bouquet's worth of magnolia flowers for his mother the day before her funeral. The petals on the flowers had turned brown and brittle overnight. Marquis had thrown his in the trash. Titus had taken his and tossed them into the grave after the service. He'd watched the dead brown petals fall over his mother's casket like scraps of burned paper. In the years since, Titus thought there was a truth in the rapid desiccation of those beautiful white flowers that all the preaching and hollering ministers did from the pulpit couldn't deny.

Titus grabbed another piece. When he struck it with the ax he grunted deep in his chest. It wasn't a sob, but it was damn close.

No one had picked flowers for those children buried under the weeping willow tree. There had been no fall or spring arrangements to mark their final resting place. Only the cold embrace of the earth and the ever-tightening roots of the willow closing around their frail bodies in the dark.

Titus grabbed another piece. When he swung the ax, this time he yelled. There were no words to his exclamation, only unarticulated pain.

Titus thought when this was over, when he'd caught the bastard who kept his wolf mask on, he was going to go back out to that willow tree. He was going to take a chain saw with him. He was going to chop that motherfucker down; Tank Billups be damned.

Headlights blazed behind him, and for a moment he saw the outline of his shadow projected on the side of the house. It was a slouching giant with an ax in its bulbous hands. His father got out of the truck and pulled his coat tight.

"You all right, boy?" Albert said.

Titus placed another piece of firewood on the block and split it in two. "I'm fine."

"You sure? Because it's nine thirty and you're chopping wood in the dark."

"Got the pole light," Titus huffed.

"Titus."

Titus grabbed another piece of wood and split it with a sharp crack.

"Titus!" his father yelled. Titus faced him. He gripped the ax handle so hard his hands ached.

"They killed kids, Pop. Latrell, Spearman, and a third person. They tied them to a table and cut on them and . . . and . . . then they killed them and buried them under a willow on Tank Billups's land. They killed them. Black boys and girls. Did things to them. Things I can't even say because I don't want you to have that shit in your head," Titus said. He knew he was breaking his own rule about confidentiality, but he couldn't hold this in anymore. His deputies hadn't seen what he'd seen. They hadn't watched those children die. That duty had been his and his alone.

"Lord, son. Are you sure?"

"It was on video, Pop."

"Oh Lord. Those poor children. They in God's hands now. Let him keep and sanctify their souls," Albert said. The statement went from an exclamation to a prayer in the blink of an eye.

"God didn't save them. He let them die screaming in the dark," Titus said. He knew this would spark an argument but, like his knowledge of their deaths, his disdain for the appeals to a pernicious supreme being couldn't be contained.

"Titus, you know I don't like that kind of talk. We can't know God's plan but the Father is still in control," Albert said.

Titus turned and slammed the ax into the chopping block. "I used to believe in God's plan. I believed he would heal Mama. Even though he'd never spoken to me. He'd never answered any of my prayers, but I still believed he'd heal her. Stop her muscles from turning to bone. Touch her with his heavenly hand and take away her pain. Stop her from howling all night. But he didn't," Titus said. "She died at forty years old and the world just moved on. So, when you tell me it was God's plan for them boys and girls to end up under that weeping willow tree, I have to ask myself, which one of us is the bigger fool? You for saying it or me for listening to it?"

His father took his hands out of his coat pockets. He held them out in a gesture reminiscent of supplication. He closed his eyes. Titus watched as his lips moved silently for a few moments.

"I prayed for you. Because I know you're hurting. She was my wife. She was the best woman I've ever known. So I know how much you're hurting, because I'm feeling it too. But, son, faith is never foolish," Albert said.

"Pop," Titus said as he brushed past his father and went into the house, "faith broke my fucking heart."

EIGHT

Two state police investigators were waiting for Titus when he got to the sheriff's office the next morning. Sergeant Adam Geary and Sergeant Ian Wright. They were accompanied by two state medical examiner vans with three assistant medical examiners each.

"Good morning, Sheriff Crown," Geary said.

"Sorry we're meeting under these circumstances," Wright said. Titus nodded. Geary and Wright reminded him of the lead actors from *Starsky & Hutch*. Geary was blond and blue-eyed, while Wright had dark hair and deep brown eyes. They all shook hands as firmly as etiquette would allow.

"You secured the crime scene?" Geary asked.

"Secured, and posted a deputy there overnight," Titus said. The condescension was implicit, but Titus ignored it. Interdepartmental jockeying was par for the course in cases like this. He'd been on the other side of the divide when he was with the Bureau. He would put up with it, to a point, if it meant he was able to take advantage of the state police's forensic lab. He wanted to catch the Last Wolf. That was all that mattered. He didn't care if the state boys wanted to take the credit. He wanted the Last Wolf's head on a spike.

Metaphorically speaking.

"Well, I'm sure your team did their best," Geary said.

Titus let that one slide too. "Let's head out."

Titus leaned against the hood of his SUV while the medical examiners and field techs took measurements and soil samples of the graves. He watched as they examined each yawning maw with meticulous precision.

Geary walked over to him.

"How'd you find this place?"

"Spearman had a painting of the willow tree in his belongings. Me and my father and brother used to hunt on this property. I recognized the tree."

"Really?" Geary asked.

"Really. I killed my first buck about two hundred yards to the west. Eight-pointer," Titus said.

"How long ago was that?" Geary asked.

"I was eleven, so twenty-five years ago."

"When was the last time you been out here?" Geary asked. Titus faced him. Geary was interrogating him. Like he was a suspect. That was the thing about being a cop. Gradually you became suspicious of everyone. Eventually you'd cut the deck twice on your own wife.

"I stopped hunting when I was thirteen."

"And you remember that tree? Remember where you shot a deer twenty-five years ago?" Geary asked.

"I've got a really good memory," Titus said.

"Well, that's a blessing, I guess," Geary said with a smile.

Titus didn't respond.

After a few moments Geary cleared his throat. "You said you found some thumb drives?"

"We have Spearman's computer too. I'm guessing you would want to take that with you."

"Yeah, was gonna ask about that. Hey, just so we're clear, we're here to assist. This is a joint thing, but this is your county. You know this place better than we do. I mean, you found the tree," Geary said.

"Does that mean you have no objections to me going up to Richmond and talking to the coroner?" Titus said.

"I mean, no objections, but we can just email you the reports," Geary said.

"I know, but I've found talking to the actual person who did the examination can sometimes be more useful," Titus said.

"You get many murder cases out this way?" Geary asked.

"I . . . I used to be with the Bureau. Started in Behavioral Science before moving to Domestic Terrorism," Titus said. Sharing his past with other cops usually led to one of two different responses. Adulation or dismissiveness. Adulation from the ones who wanted to shed their small-town stripes and tin stars for the hallowed halls of the FBI, and dismissiveness from the ones who enjoyed treating their county or city or state like a fiefdom.

"No shit? How'd you end up out here in the boonies?" Geary asked.

Adulation it was.

"My father had a serious surgery, so I came home to help him. Ended up running for sheriff," Titus said. Geary frowned. Titus figured him for a hard charger. Probably graduated at the top of his class. Smart and hungry like Trey and Carla. The kind of person for whom the idea of leaving the Bureau to write speeding tickets and break up fights in the parking lot of the Safeway was inconceivable.

"Well, that's . . . I mean, family is important," Geary said. He looked over his shoulder at the techs.

"What's your feeling on this? Mr. FBI."

Titus adjusted his shades.

"The third person is somebody local. They knew this place. Not just the burial spot but the county. I'm guessing a white male between thirty and fifty. Physically strong. Organized. He's not flipping from job to job. Probably doesn't have a steady girlfriend or wife. If he does, they have a dysfunctional sex life. He's got land. Enough land to build a shed or outbuilding that he soundproofed. Some place semi-remote. Where nobody noticed him bringing in live teenagers and taking out dead bodies. The . . . injuries he inflicted on the victims were horrific. He has a lot of anger. Lots of rage. There was a lot of religious iconography on the walls of the building where the crimes took place. He may have theomania. He's obsessed with God or thinks he's God or is angry with God. Maybe that's the source of his rage," Titus said.

"Your email mentioned that they wore wolf masks. You think that was to hide their identities, or was it mostly ceremonial?" Geary asked.

Titus crossed his arms. "I think for Spearman it was just a costume. Latrell too. Not for the Last Wolf. I don't know, I don't think he was trying to hide his identity. The wolf plays an antagonistic role in Christian theology. Especially the New Testament. I think . . . I think that's how he sees himself. He thinks he's the Wolf. The Angel of Death. And his rage is both in service to and directed at God." His voice had dropped to barely a whisper.

The cry from a loon cracked through the air. Geary shivered.

"That's that FBI training, all right," Geary said.

Titus blinked his eyes behind his sunglasses and uncrossed his arms.

"That's just some inferences based on past experience. It's not magic," Titus said.

"No, but if we catch this guy, it helps. I put in a request for Spearman's phone records. See if we can track his movements based on cell tower triangulation," Geary said.

"That's good, but I bet he didn't carry the phone with him when he went to see his partner," Titus said.

"But the pictures . . ."

"Are on a SIM card. And the videos were on thumb drives. Probably used a burner phone to take the pictures, then swapped the card. I'd put in a request for Latrell's phone records too. Hopefully either he or the third man carried their phones with them. It's not much, but it's a start," Titus said.

Geary shook his head.

"What?"

"You're not bored out here? Gotta be a change of pace from chasing Al-Qaeda," Geary said.

"We targeted domestic terrorists. White supremacists. Environmental extremists. Radical religious fanatics of all the Abrahamic faiths," Titus said.

Geary cleared his throat. "Ah, gotcha."

Before an uncomfortable silence could descend upon them, Titus's radio crackled to life.

"Sheriff, we got a 415 down at the courthouse. Two groups arguing in the road. Deputy Ortiz requesting backup," Cam said on the mic.

"Ten-four. Relay to Deputy Ortiz I'm on my way," Titus said into the receiver.

"We'll let you know what we find. You're gonna have to tell me some of your FBI stories sometime," Geary said.

"They aren't that interesting," Titus said.

Red DeCrain's face came to him like a message from Morpheus sent to him in a waking nightmare.

Ricky Sours and his cabal of revisionists were surrounding the statue like a phalanx minus the pikes. Jamal Addison and a large group of young people were halfway in the road, halfway out. Between the two groups was Carla, doing her best to keep them separated. Titus parked in one of the diagonal spaces directly in front of the courthouse building. There was a long black streak on the statue that had the indistinct edges of spray paint. A Confederate flag lay on the grass, ripped in half.

"Heritage not hate! Heritage not hate!" Ricky screamed at the top of his lungs. His doughy face was speckled with red splotches. A black baseball cap with the characters 2A emblazoned in white was pulled down tight over his stringy dirty blond hair streaked with gray. He wore a shirt emblazoned with both Old Glory and the Confederate battle flag. He held a pole in his hands that had a few tattered pieces of the Stars and Bars attached to it.

Titus knew if you asked Ricky he'd say he was incensed because wokeness was trying to erase his history. He'd say he was only trying to protect the story of his ancestors. Titus wondered if folks like Ricky really believed that tale when they told it to themselves. Titus knew what men like Ricky were really disturbed by was the fact that people, mostly people of color, had the temerity to challenge the lie of antebellum honor and chivalry that had been shoved down the throats of every child in the South for generations.

A lie that people like Ricky embraced with the darkest part of their hearts.

"Jamal, get across the road!" Titus roared. He used every ounce of bass he could muster so he could be heard over the growling din of the opposing forces.

"Sheriff, they tried to assault this young man!" Jamal yelled back.

"He vandalized the statue! We was just trying to hold him until the police came!" Ricky hollered.

"Jamal, get these people across the road. Ricky, you ain't got no right to put your hands on nobody," Titus said.

"You taking their side, why am I not surprised?" Ricky said. A few of his fellow neo-Confederates voiced their agreement.

"I'm not taking sides. I'm trying to ascertain exactly what happened. Jamal is taking his people across the road. Now you calm your folks down and let's talk about this. Or do you want me to start arresting everybody?" Titus asked. Ricky tried to find Titus's eyes behind his shades so he could register his disgust, but the mirrored aviators stymied his attempt at a standoff. Even without seeing his eyes, Ricky must have sensed a steel in Titus that wasn't prone to bending to the whims of others. He turned and herded his group across the lawn until they were standing on the steps of the courthouse.

Titus walked up to Carla.

"What happened?"

Carla was breathing hard. A few strands of her coal-black hair had freed themselves from the tight bun she wore for work. They snaked their way down around her neck.

"Got a call that a kid had vandalized the statue. When I got here,

Ricky and a few of his crew were holding the kid down. Then Jamal was driving by and he pulled over and hopped out. Next thing I know, Ricky's got twenty people here and Jamal's got fifty and everybody's screaming bloody murder," Carla said.

"Was it the white kid with the dreads?" Titus asked.

Carla nodded. "They were holding him down when I got here. How'd you know?"

"Grass stains on his jeans. Black spots on his hands. Also he keeps looking over at me. Who ripped up Ricky's flag?" Titus asked.

"I . . . I don't know. Things were out of hand by that point," Carla said.

"Things always get out of hand when Ricky is involved. I wish he'd just stick to running his trash trucks. Go to that kid and ask him does he want to press charges. I'm gonna talk to the rebs," Titus said. Carla walked across the road to the sidewalk in front of the library.

Titus approached Ricky and his group.

"You gonna arrest that boy?" Ricky said.

"You should be asking am I going to arrest you," Titus said.

Ricky blanched. "What for?"

Titus took off his shades. He pointed at the statue with the temple of his sunglasses. "That statue sits on a square of land that was donated by the Daughters of the Confederacy. The statue technically belongs to them. It's not public property. That means you have no legal standing to detain anyone for any reason in respect to anything done to that statue. Holding that boy down could be considered unlawful detainment, assault, and/or battery," Titus said.

"Bullshit," one of Ricky's compatriots spat.

"Hey, Denver, have you read the statutes? Because I have. So you might want to watch your mouth. And is that Canadian Mist I smell? I hope you didn't drive up here," Titus said.

There it was again. Charon County, raw as the throats of freshly butchered calves, came pouring out of him. Not a litany of threats but a promise of consequences.

The fact that Titus knew Denver Carlyle was a drunk with a

CDL license that he was barely holding on to, who nonetheless still decided to drive to and from the Watering Hole in various levels of inebriation, only added to their fear. It was the fear they respected. For Ricky and Denver and their ilk their fear was twofold. They feared him as a man and they feared the invincibility they thought the badge gave him. The idea that the invulnerability their grandfathers had used to brutalize people who looked like Titus could be turned against them was what had chastened them.

"Now, if you want to have that young man, I think that's William and Renee Dolson's son, prosecuted for vandalism, go find the nearest Daughters of the Confederacy chapter and have them file a complaint. Other than that, I think y'all should go on home. Now." Titus heard a few grumbles. He didn't put his hand on his gun, but he did let it drop to his side.

The grumbling ceased.

He saw how all their faces were contorted into knots of self-righteousness and contempt. He'd gone to school with many of these men. Or with their children. Reggie Wilson had been on that state championship team. Kevin Cross's daughter, Stephanie, had sat in front of Titus from kindergarten to twelfth grade.

None of that mattered to them now. They wiped all that away until he was just a nigger with a badge. To a few of them even the badge disappeared as they reduced him to a form they felt comfortable disparaging. He felt it in the air between them, like the charge before a lightning strike. It wasn't surprising, and that in and of itself was tragic.

"Go on, now," Titus said. He spoke the words to the crowd, but he zeroed in on Ricky Sours.

"Our permit is still good for Fall Fest," Ricky said as he turned away. He hurled the words at Titus, flecks of spittle flying from his thin lips. Titus didn't acknowledge him. Ricky was trying to save face in front of his fellow reenactors. It wasn't Titus's job to assist him. He noticed Royce, with the TEXACO trucker hat, walking with Ricky back across the courthouse green. He knew Royce drove one of Charon's school buses. He was also apparently a Confederate apologist.

Once he saw them get in their trucks and cars (noting that Denver Carlyle got in Ricky Sours's truck instead of his own late-model Buick), he walked across the road to the library.

"I was just telling Mr. Trevor Dolson if he wanted to press charges he could come by the sheriff's office," Carla said.

"Is that something you want to do, Trevor?" Titus asked. Trevor shrugged.

"I think you should. Evil wins when good men do nothing," Jamal said. The crowd surrounding him rumbled with agreement.

"Am I in trouble?" Trevor asked. Titus looked over his shoulder at the statue of a Charon County Confederate soldier with the black line of paint across the base.

"I don't know. If you did it, then the people who own the statue would have to file a complaint. That would be the Daughters of the Confederacy. Seeing as there hasn't been a chapter here since the thirties, I'd guess you'll be okay. That's if you did it," Titus said.

"I . . . I just wanna go home," Trevor said.

"How old are you, Trevor?" Titus asked.

"I'm eighteen . . . sir."

"Okay. Well, seeing as you're eighteen, I'm not legally bound to tell your parents. But I'd let them know, if I was you," Titus said. He turned to the rest of the crowd. It was a mixture of New Wave members and young white men and women who adopted an aesthetic similar to Trevor's. Titus recognized them as members of Charon's small but vibrant art scene. He recognized some of them from the flea market in the parking lot of the high school every third Saturday of the month. A few more were members of a band that played the Tuesday night open mic at the Watering Hole.

"The rest of y'all head on home, now. Nothing else to be done here," Titus said. A few people started to amble down the sidewalk. The majority didn't move. Their adrenaline was still surging like electricity in their veins. His father would say their blood was up. He recognized it and he knew he needed to dissipate it.

Titus crossed his arms. "Unless y'all want to get arrested for disturbing the peace." More promises, more threats. The words PRO-TECT AND SERVE were inscribed on his badge, but in moments like this, it felt like INTIMIDATE AND FRIGHTEN should replace them.

Part of the job, he thought. On the heels of that thought was another one, from a place in the cellar of his mind: If this is a part of the job, is this the job you were meant to do?

Titus pushed it away and spoke to the crowd again. "Y'all get on, now." The crowd dispersed with whispered insults and vague mumblings. Jamal was the last one to leave.

"'This is what the Lord says: Do what is just and right. Rescue from the hand of the oppressor the one who has been robbed,'" Jamal said.

"Jeremiah, twenty-second chapter, third verse," Titus said.

"You did what was right for Trevor. Wish you could have done that for Latrell," Jamal said.

Titus checked his watch. It was a little after 10:00 A.M. "There is going to be a press conference today around four. You should listen to it."

Jamal continued to speak as if he hadn't heard him. "I can't believe you gonna let them wannabe Nazis have a white power parade during Fall Fest. Ain't you the sheriff? What good was it us getting you elected if you can't stop Ricky Sours and the Confeda-idiots from marching through town?" Jamal said. Titus bit down on the inside of his cheek. He didn't want to see Ricky Sours and his cosplaying rebels walking down the street any more than the good reverend did.

"The Parks and Rec Committee approved the permit. I don't like it, but I can't stop it. But they've whined and cried about being protected, so I'll be there. Trust and believe if they get out of pocket we will handle it."

Jamal shook his head. "You the last person I thought would turn coon. Your mama used to teach us in Sunday school that the righteous are never forsaken, and here is her son letting these damn demons walk all over God's people," Jamal said.

"Carla, why don't you go write up this report?" Titus said.

"Yes, sir," she said. She walked back across the road to her cruiser.

Titus took off his shades. He took off his badge and put it in his pocket. The sharp edges of the star dug into his thigh. He stepped closer to Jamal.

"You stand there and you quote Bible verses to me about the oppressed, and then have the nerve to accuse me of tap-dancing for these motherfuckers. Like I stopped being Black when I put on that star. Watching them boys march down Main Street waving Confederate flags and wearing T-shirts extolling the honor of Jefferson Davis and Robert E. Lee makes me sick to my stomach. But unless they break the law there's nothing I can do." Titus leaned closer to Jamal until his mouth was inches from his ear. "This is Titus talking now, not the sheriff. You ever say anything about Helen Crown again, you gonna wake up with your teeth down your throat. You feel me?" Titus said. He stepped back and replaced his sunglasses and his badge.

"Come to the press conference, Reverend. You need to hear what I have to say." He turned and headed back to his own SUV cruiser. He got in and started the engine. He watched as Jamal shook his head and walked back to his own vehicle. Titus caught his own image in the rearview mirror. The man staring back at him kept finding himself tossing hard words out to the folks he was sworn to defend.

Titus put the SUV in gear.

It made him ask himself, who was at fault here? The man or the folks?

NINE

Titus turned right onto Jackson Street and pulled into the parking lot of the state medical examiner's office. A tall, nondescript concrete building across from the crumbling Richmond Coliseum, the medical examiner's office held generational horrors and gut-churning terrors that were all detailed and collated with a cool, practiced detachment that Titus could not seem to master.

Titus parked the SUV and entered the building through the front entrance instead of the large metal roll-up door that accepted bodies of all shapes, sizes, ages, and ethnicities. In the former capital of the Confederacy, equality's surest foothold was found on the autopsy table.

Titus was waved through the lobby and took the elevator up to the morgue. The pungent scent of antiseptic slapped him in the face the moment he stepped out of the elevator. It forced its way into his nostrils and stung the back of his throat. It was like a portent that warned you that you were crossing over into the land of the dead.

"'Abandon all hope ye who enter here,'" Titus whispered.

Titus pushed the speak button on the intercom to the right of a massive set of stainless-steel doors that were eerily similar to the doors of the elevator. A voice crackled up from the intercom.

"Yes, may I help you?"

"Sheriff Titus Crown from Charon County. We sent some bodies up here yesterday. Was wondering if I could talk to someone about the preliminary findings," Titus said. The intercom was silent. He knew they were probably not even halfway through their examinations, but he needed—no, he wanted—to jump on this as soon as possible. He needed something, anything, any type of clue, to jumpstart his investigation. Those seven dead children and their families demanded it of him. It was a new millstone he willingly wore. Sadly, the best clues would probably be found on their poor broken and twisted bodies.

Titus didn't want to look at them again, but he would. It was the job. It was his penance.

"Come on in," the voice crackled.

The doors whooshed open and Titus stepped into the land of the dead.

He stood in the small anteroom that separated the morgue proper from the ME's actual office. A young Asian woman came to the door wearing a blue surgical gown and cap. She took both off and disposed of them in a plastic biohazard container before swiping her badge in front of the door and stepping into the anteroom.

"Sheriff, I'm Dr. Julie Kim."

"Nice to meet you," Titus said. Dr. Kim nodded. She had long black hair that was tied into a tight bun that resembled the one Carla wore. She gestured toward the office. Titus followed her as she sat behind a huge oak desk. He took off his hat and shades and sat in one of two leather office chairs on the other side of the desk.

"Sheriff, I have to be honest, we've only examined two of the seven bodies you brought to us. We are a little short-staffed these days."

"Not a huge interest in pathology nowadays?" Titus asked.

Kim smiled. "No, more like there's a big interest in the American Aquarium concert tonight at the National. Some members of our staff seem to have come down with playing hookyitis," Dr. Kim said.

"Yeah, I see cases of that around the first day of hunting season. But I'm not here to press you, Dr. Kim. I just want to hear some of your preliminary findings, whatever they may be," Titus said.

"I was going to say I could have emailed them to you, but I get the feeling you are a hands-on individual," Dr. Kim said. She smiled and Titus found himself smiling back. Then he thought of the seven Black boys and girls currently stretched out on metal tables with Y incisions in their chests, and the smile died on the vine.

"I'm having a press conference later today. Charon County is a small town, Doctor. There're already wild rumors making their way across the county and on social media. We had a school shooting day before yesterday and then we found these bodies. My county is reeling. If you can give me something to hang my hat on, then I can at least tell my folks we are doing our best," Titus said.

Dr. Kim flexed her fingers. She pressed a button on the telephone sitting on her desk.

"Peter, can you bring me the Charon file?" Dr. Kim said.

"Yes, Doctor."

A few seconds later, a young white man came in and handed Dr. Kim a thick manila folder. He left so quickly he might have been a figment of Titus's imagination.

"Here you go, but I'll give you the highlights. Or the lowlights, as it were," Dr. Kim said as she handed Titus the file. He opened it, and the first thing he saw was a body flayed open on the autopsy table. The leathery skin was pulled back and the rib cage had been bisected with a bone saw. Titus flipped that picture over. The next picture was a close-up of the arm of that body.

"Are . . . are those words?" Titus asked.

"Yes. The bodies that still have a viable epidermis have words cut into the skin of their arms, their chests, their buttocks. I suspect the rest of them will have similar incisions."

"Cursed . . . be . . . Canaan," Titus whispered as he read the words.

He flipped the photo.

The next one depicted the desiccated face of one of the victims. The photo had been taken with some kind of black-light or infrared device that gave the face a spectral countenance. Titus couldn't tell if it was a boy or a girl. The lips had run away from the opening of the mouth, leaving it in a rictus of agony.

Titus squinted and read the words carved into the forehead of the face in the picture.

"Those words are just the tip of the iceberg of what these children went through. These children suffered. A lot," Dr. Kim said.

Titus felt something wash over him as she spoke. A feeling both familiar and fearful. He'd felt it at the DeCrain compound when bits of the DeCrain boys were embedded in his face.

Righteousness. The kind of righteousness that made you feel above petty things like laws and amendments. The kind of righteousness that came from the barrel of a gun. He knew now it was a false piousness. A lying piety that seduced you into believing the end justified the means.

Titus closed the file. He promised himself he would never heed that siren's call again. His soul, whatever was left of it, couldn't bear it.

"Any DNA? Any fiber evidence? Insect or larval markers?" Titus asked.

"We tested them for DNA. Found a few viable samples, but we don't know how degraded they are. We're also running their DNA against the national and state databases. Going to run the dental records too. None of them had any form of ID. Funny you mentioned fibers. We found synthetic hairs on the two we've examined. Most likely from an expensive wig. We're running textile typing on them now. We've also identified most of the metallic objects we excised from the bodies. There were nails, straight pins, lengths of baling wire, razor blades." Dr. Kim paused and took a deep breath. "We identified all the metal objects except one. Go to the last page of the file."

Titus did as he was asked.

Sitting on a small table next to a metal ruler for scale was a rusted T-shaped object. The arms of the T were as thin as pipe cleaners.

The bottom of the T was cylindrical and rounded at the bottom. It reminded Titus of a toy he'd had as a kid. It was called a cap bomb. It resembled an old World War II bomb. You put pop caps in it, then tossed it on the ground. They would explode like gunshots.

"We've done image searches, reached out to the state police. I've emailed the pic to the FBI. So far no one can tell us what it is," Dr. Kim said.

"The Bureau will probably have a database with five different examples of whatever it turns out to be," Titus said.

"You're familiar with their thoroughness," Dr. Kim said.

Titus smiled ruefully. "Intimately."

Dr. Kim nodded. "And that's all we have so far. I'll have toxicology and the DNA back in a few weeks."

"I know the state has a backlog, but is there any way to bump this up to the front of the line?" Titus asked.

"Sheriff, these aren't the only kids we have on the table. But I'll see what I can do."

Now it was Titus's turn to nod. He closed the file again and put it back on the desk.

"Well, thank you for your time, Dr. Kim," he said. He stood and put his hat back on.

"Do you ever wonder how they do it? Or why? Why would someone . . . do what they did to those children?" Dr. Kim said. For a brief moment the cool, detached mask fell away and Titus could see the face of Julie Kim. A human being with empathy and kindness in her heart. If the pictures on her desk were to be believed, she was also a wife and mother in addition to being the chief medical examiner.

Titus straightened his hat. "I usually try not to think about it. I try to focus on who they are, not why they do it. But if you want an answer"—Titus pulled his shades from the pocket of his shirt—"they do it because they like it. They do it because they can," he said. He put on the aviators. "It's not really deeper than that."

"You really think it's that simple?" Dr. Kim asked.

"Evil is rarely complicated. It's just fucking bold." Titus touched the brim of his hat and left.

Once he was back in the car, he pulled out his notebook and wrote down the information Dr. Kim had given him. While it was true he had an excellent memory, he always backed it up with detailed notes.

"Poor rabbit that only got one hole," his mother used to say. Her homilies and colloquialisms were usually intended to be responses to some particularly juicy bits of gossip, but that didn't change the veracity of their wisdom.

Titus wrote down all the details that Dr. Kim had shared. At the top of the page he wrote the phrase "Curse of Canaan." He was sure that was a reference to the Curse of Ham in Genesis. A bit of Old Testament vitriol that multiple empires had used to justify subjugating various peoples and keeping them in chains. Titus could remember one social studies teacher who had said without a hint of compunction that Black people were cursed to be slaves by the word of God. When he'd gotten home from school that day and told his mother, he watched as a tornado brewed behind her eyes.

"We going up there to talk to that wench tomorrow. Listen to me, Titus, and don't ever forget this. The Word is perfect, but the way men interpret it is corrupt. And your teacher is full of shit."

Titus could still remember the shock of hearing his mother curse. It was like seeing Jesus drinking Henny. Later, after his mother was in the ground, he realized the Word was just as corrupt as the men who read it. Old Testament, New Testament, it was just words with a little *w*, written by zealots as PR for their new cult founded in the memory of a dead carpenter.

Titus wrote another phrase at the top of the page: "Our salvation is his suffering."

That had been carved into the forehead of the body in the third photograph. That wasn't a biblical phrase, but Titus was still familiar with it. Of the twenty-three houses of worship in Charon County, six had used that phrase at one time or another over the past three years as an attention-grabber for their church signs.

He'd noticed it on a sign in front of St. Ignatius. Then he'd seen it on a sign in front of his father's church. Later he'd seen it at Trinity Baptist Church and Nazareth United. First Corinthian had taken it up as well, but the first church to actually put it on a sign had been the Holy Rock of the Redeemer, a nondenominational family-run church on Piney Island, a little spit of boulders and sand that was attached to Charon by the world's most rickety bridge. The Holy Rock of the Redeemer was known as a fire-and-brimstone, holy-roller, snake-handling, and strychnine-drinking church of true believers. Or, as his father said, "A bunch of racist loony tunes sons of bitches."

Titus put his notebook away and started the SUV. It wasn't much, but it was something to grab on to even if he was just using his fingertips. Was the Last Wolf a member of one of the six churches that had used that phrase? Or was he a sick bastard who lived in the county and thought it was cute to cut that phrase into some poor child's forehead with a razor? Either way, he was local. Titus was sure of that. Only a local would know where the willow tree was located. Only a local would work with Spearman and Latrell. Only someone who had Charon tattooed on their bones could hate the county enough to sow its soil with the blood of innocents.

Titus got back to the office by noon. Cam was at the switchboard fielding dozens of calls. Titus noticed how his face was set in a series of hard lines.

"The sheriff is going to answer those questions at the press conference, Toby. I can't tell you nothing because I don't know nothing, all right?" Cam said. He hung up on Toby and answered another call.

"Charon County Sheriff's Office. Ma'am, the sheriff is holding a press conference today at four to talk about all that. Thank you,"

Cam said. His voice cracked with exasperation. The phones were quiet for a moment, a brief lull that plunged the office into silence.

"Been busy, I guess," Titus said.

Cam grunted. "Everybody talking about what we found out in that field. People flipping out. Ricky Sours called up here talking about deputizing his crew. Folks talking about should they leave town. Scott calling up here talking a bunch of trash. I swear to God, that man got a face made for punching," Cam said.

Titus clapped him on the shoulder. "Scott's the least of our worries. Do me a favor. Call Freddie Nickels at Channel Seven and get him to put the word out about the press conference. I sent him an email, but I wanna follow up. I sent one to Dan Dawson at Channel Twelve and Stacy Weddle at Channel Twenty-three. Call them too."

"Want Charlie from *The Charon Register* too?" Cam asked.

"The more, the merrier," Titus said.

Cam nodded. "Roger called."

Titus sighed. "What he talking about?"

"Just wanted to know where you were. Said he had talked to Scott about his suspension," Cam said. He said the last part hesitantly, like a child reluctantly tattling on a sibling.

"He can talk to Scott all he wants. Long as this badge says SHER-IFF he can talk to anybody he wants. Gonna do him about as much good as a wagon with square wheels," Titus said.

He went into his office thinking that if his former colleagues at the Fort Wayne Field Office had heard him roll that particular bon mot off his tongue, they would have left a pair of bib overalls and a packet of hayseeds on his desk.

As a joke, of course. They were always full of jokes.

Titus turned on the laptop and started writing his speech for the press conference. He knew he had to strike the right tone. Concerned but not afraid. Stern but not demanding. There was a balance one had to strike when you told your constituents three of their fellow citizens had turned their county into a killing field.

Titus paused and peered at Ward Bennings's photo on the wall in the lobby. He was there with all the other previous sheriffs of Charon. Some of those bodies had been under that willow tree for more than five years. Spearman and Latrell and the Last Wolf had carried them out there, passing under branches and tearing through brambles, without so much as a wink from Ward or anyone else. How had they done it? They must have been careful, but they weren't magicians. They should have been seen, even if only once. Charon was too small for a trio of men carrying bodies into the woods to go unnoticed. At least that was what he hoped.

He looked at the row of past sheriffs. A lineage of stewards who had protected some citizens of Charon while ignoring others. A tradition of watchmen who had turned a blind eye to the suffering of anyone who didn't look like them. Each one had passed through the world, generation after generation leaving the pieces of their broken county for the next man to try to repair. Now Titus found himself standing in the shadow of a specter with a wolf's head while he did his best to hold those shards, even as they sliced his hands to ribbons.

"Damn, everybody and their mama is here," Davy said.

Titus peeped through the window. The parking lot was jam-packed. Not only were the vans for the three main TV stations that served Southeastern Virginia here, but three of the stations that served the greater Richmond area were here, along with a couple from Northern Virginia. Titus saw Frank from *The Register* and a couple of other folks with tablets and notepads and that sly gaze that only reporters on the hunt for a good story have. Filling out the rest of the parking lot was about sixty percent of Charon County. Cars and trucks were parked down the street to the Safeway.

"All right, well, let's get to it. Davy, you, Carla, Pip, and Steve are crowd control. I'll go to the mic, say my piece, and end it. We're not taking any questions right now. We all on the same page?" Titus asked. The deputies nodded in unison.

Titus checked his uniform in the reflection in the window. The crease in his pants was sharp enough to slice a cake. His hands and face were moisturized with lotion. His badge was gleaming like a diamond. For some folks it wouldn't matter, but for the majority of Charon's citizens he had to be a larger-than-life character for them to even pretend to respect him. And he needed that respect today more than he ever had before. He was about to shatter their fantasies of safety and security. He was set to smash one of their idols. He was going to have to drag them into a new reality where people they knew, people they'd known all their lives, were monsters with human faces.

Folks hated receiving that kind of news.

They often ended up hating the messenger too.

"Let's get to it," Titus said.

A hush came over the crowd when Titus tapped the microphone. It was Davy's. He used to be a DJ before he joined the sheriff's office. Titus watched as a sense of expectation flowed over the crowd and made its way into every crack and crevice like shellac. Folks had heard things, been told things, made things up, and now they were about to get it from the horse's mouth, so to speak. Titus could feel the weight of those expectations on his broad shoulders. The pressure of those hundreds and hundreds of eyes bearing down on him nearly made him drop his head, but he took a deep breath and looked straight ahead. Submission was not an option. He could not afford to look defeated for even a fraction of a millisecond. Staring down a crowd was like dealing with a feral dog. You showed fear, and you'd find yourself without a throat.

"I'd like to thank everyone for coming today."

The hunt was on.

TEN

Titus took off his hat and put it on his desk. He sat down and removed his sunglasses and rubbed his hands across his face. The crowd outside was starting to disperse, but he could still hear their voices through the walls like a quiet rumble of thunder.

Carla came into the office. "Do you think we're going to catch him?" Carla asked.

Titus smoothed down his tie. "We have to," he said.

The landline rang. "Someone asking for you on line one," Cam yelled.

"Do me a favor. Run back out to the dig site and see how the state boys are getting on. Let them know you're there as my rep. They say they gonna keep us in the loop, but sometimes they tighten their circle and leave us out," Titus said.

"Got it." Carla turned and headed out the door.

Titus picked up the landline. "Sheriff Crown. How can I help you?"

"Damn, you sound all official like you a real officer of the law. They give you your own set of handcuffs?" A throaty laugh came across the line. Titus felt the bottom drop out of his belly for a moment.

"Kellie. Why are you calling here?" Titus asked.

"Wow, nice to hear from you too," Kellie said.

Titus cleared his throat. His face felt hot as a griddle. "I mean, how you doing? I can't say I expected to hear from you," Titus stammered.

"Relax, Virginia. I'm not stalking you. This is strictly a professional call," Kellie said.

"Professional? So, you're calling in your capacity as a reporter for the Fort Wayne *Journal Gazette*?" Titus said.

"Not exactly. And I'm over in Indianapolis now. Working at *The Times*. But a little birdie told me there's something going on in your hometown that might help with my new side project," Kellie said.

Titus didn't respond.

Kellie chuckled. "You haven't heard about my podcast, have you?" she asked.

"I don't . . . I don't have a lot of free time," Titus said.

Another throaty laugh.

"I know you have Spotify on your phone. I'll send you a link. You can listen to it while you ride to and from the cross burnings," Kellie said. Another laugh.

Once again Titus didn't respond.

"I guess that was in bad taste," Kellie said.

"Not really, more like a pot-and-kettle scenario. Indiana isn't exactly progressive central," Titus said.

"Point taken. But, seriously, give me your cell and I'll text you a link."

"What exactly do you think is going on down here?" Titus asked.

"My podcast is about true crime. I started it when I got laid off from *The Journal Gazette*. Originally we were just chronicling crimes against sex workers in the tri-city area but we've been expanding our content. A friend of mine at a news station in Richmond texted me that you just found some murdered kids in a field. I was wondering if the man I shared a bed with for two years might be inclined to give me an interview when we get to town?" Kellie asked.

Titus exhaled like he'd been punched in the chest. "Why are you coming to town?"

"You know, for an FBI agent you're not great at listening. I have a true crime podcast. You seem to have discovered a serial killer. I've got some vacation to burn at *The Times,* so I thought I'd come to town to do an episode about said serial killer. And I was hoping you'd talk to me about it," Kellie said. "Look, I was kidding about the whole man-I-was-sleeping-with-for-two-years thing. Was just trying to make you laugh. You never laughed enough."

"The investigation just started. I'm already going to have reporters and concerned citizens lining up to get in our way. No offense, but we don't need anyone else getting in our way right now," Titus said.

"Would you say that if I wasn't your ex?"

"I'd say that if you were Anderson Cooper," Titus said.

Kellie chuckled. "Well, if he was your ex, it would have made our time together interesting. Look, Titus, we're coming to town. I just wanted to see if you wanted a chance to get your message out. Shake some folks up. Maybe get a few leads. You don't have to talk to me, but you can't stop me from doing my job."

"Nobody can stop you from doing something you've set your mind to. I'm just telling you you're wasting your time. We literally are just starting to sort this thing out. There's nothing anyone can tell you because we don't know anything. All you going to do is burn up some gas driving down here."

"You really don't want to see me, do you?" Kellie said. The laughter in her throat was gone. It had been replaced with a quietness that softened her voice. The phone hummed as neither of them spoke. Memories, charged like electrons, ran along the phone line like nerve impulses.

He'd met Kellie Stoner during an investigation into the deaths of several sex workers in the Fort Wayne area. Kellie was one of two crime reporters for the Fort Wayne *Journal Gazette.* She also volunteered at a community center that focused on sex workers and the homeless. She was a five-foot-three ball of energy and sarcasm that had kept him on his toes during their entire interview. Long dark hair and matching eyelashes. Smooth, darkly tanned skin that he'd find out later was the product of her Filipino and Italian heritage. Light brown eyes like drops of honey that changed to amber when she was angry. Like she'd been that day.

"I'm sorry, Agent Crown, but it doesn't seem like the FBI cares about murdered sex workers. This is the sixth body found this year. What progress have you made? And why did it take you so long to get involved? I mean, no offense, but folks around here have been begging the police to do something for these missing women," she'd said as they'd sat in the office he'd borrowed from the local chief of police.

"Ms. Stoner, I assure you the Bureau is doing all we can. I can promise you I'm doing all I can. I don't believe in leaving anyone behind. My word is my bond," Titus had said.

"Wow, next thing you're gonna tell me Santa Claus is real," she'd said under her breath.

"Excuse me?" Titus had said.

"I'm sorry. But you can't blame me for being skeptical. Folks in this part of town don't usually see the cops until it's a rich white girl that's late for a bridal shower," Kellie had said.

"I don't work my cases based on the social standing of the victims, Ms. Stoner. Either we all matter or no one matters. Everyone deserves to have someone speak for them," Titus had said.

"You mean that, don't you?" Kellie had asked.

"I do. My mama raised me right. And I can tell how much you care. Not just about the victims but the people here. That kind of passion is all too rare," Titus had said. "And I think Santa Claus usually uses his Kris Kringle alias this time of year," he had added.

And she had laughed. That full, throaty laugh that would soon become music to his ears.

Titus and his team eventually found the man who killed the

eight sex workers. Titus felt the team had avenged them as best they could. They had spoken for them.

Then he and Kellie had begun to dance to a song that had lived in that strange undiscovered country that existed between love and lust.

Until the DeCrain raid, and the song had ended abruptly.

"It's not like that, and you know it. I had to come home. You had to stay in Indiana. A long-distance thing wasn't going to work. I thought we ended things as well as you can end things," Titus said.

"Is that what you thought?" Kellie said.

Titus gripped the phone. "I guess I was wrong."

"No, you're right. But that doesn't make it any better. But we've both moved on. I'm seeing someone and I'm sure you are too. But I'd still like to send you a link to my show. If that's okay," Kellie said.

Titus thought about Darlene. He had moved on. He had come home and found someone who was good and honest and devoted to him. That wasn't to say Kellie hadn't been all those things too. She was, but she was also a smart-ass with a singular intensity that had constantly challenged him in ways he had both craved and feared. If Darlene was sunny days and lemonade, Kellie Stoner was moonshine and a sky gone full dark with no stars . . . but he was happy living in the light.

That didn't mean he couldn't listen to her podcast, did it? He probably should, just to know what to expect once she hit town.

"Sure, send it on," Titus said.

"Same number?" Kellie asked.

"It hasn't changed. You still got it?"

"Duh. If I had deleted it I wouldn't have said same number," Kellie said.

Titus suddenly felt exceedingly foolish.

"We'll talk when I get to town. Later, Virginia."

The line went dead.

Titus hung up the phone.

Titus had asked his neighbors to report anyone who was acting strange or suspicious, especially someone who owned a large shed or outbuilding or had been behaving erratically. The tips would come flooding in soon enough, most of them worthless but all needing attention, so Titus spent the rest of the afternoon going over the minutiae of small-town administrative bureaucracy. He'd put in a request for body cams and more beanbag guns to the Board of Supervisors three months ago that had been denied so forcefully it immediately made him think someone was embezzling from the county treasury.

He filled out a new request and sent it on over for the next board meeting. Titus hoped they would be more receptive to the idea of body cams after their kids had almost had their heads blown off. It wasn't his proudest moment, but if it was possible to pull something constructive out of this tragedy, then he had to try. It would probably be the only good thing that came out of all this.

He went over the expense reports and the gas receipts. He posted on the county social media page about the press conference. He went over the arrest reports from the last twenty-four hours. As inconceivable as it seemed, the seven holes in the ground that held the bodies of those murdered children that surrounded Tank Billups's weeping willow tree like a honeycomb were not his only responsibility. Ben Thomas and Wayne Hodges had been found passed out in Ben's truck, ODed on what appeared to be heroin laced with fentanyl. Louise Tallifero had thrown a bowl of hot chicken soup on her daughter because the little girl wouldn't stop crying. The little girl was two years old. Darryl West had called in to report that his neighbor Lenny Barkers and his wife, Stephanie, were beating the shit out of Lenny's father, an eighty-nine-year-old World War II veteran who had moved in with them last year. Darryl had reported that he saw Lenny and Stephanie kick the old man after he had fallen in the front yard. Darryl said he thought the old guy had Alzheimer's. He had a tendency to wander. By the time Steve had gotten there they had cleaned him up and gotten him back in the house, but they couldn't hide the fracture in his forearm.

As he clicked on report after report, Titus couldn't help but feel like he was a character in an old *Twilight Zone* episode. A man cursed to forever miss a departing train by just a few minutes. That was what policing a small town felt like some days. You were always a day late and a dollar short. You stood there over a broken body covered in bruises or a wrecked car that reeked of whiskey, with your broom and your dustpan and a mouthful of regret. Just a janitor tasked with picking up the pieces of someone's broken life.

By the time Titus finished reviewing all the reports, he felt like he needed a bath. Ugliness seemed to fill the world like a dark elixir.

Titus rubbed his hands across his face.

That wasn't the whole truth. There was ugliness, sure, but there was beauty in the world, there was grace, if you knew where to look. It was there if you were brave enough or foolish enough to seek it. The star on his chest dictated that he wade through the muck and the mire, but it wasn't an anchor. It didn't have to drown him in the slurry unless he let it.

Titus checked his watch.

It was 9:00 P.M. He got up, stretched, heard his back pop like a campfire, grabbed his hat, and headed for the door. He'd had enough poison for the day.

Titus pulled into his driveway and parked next to his father's truck. When he got inside the house he found his father dozing in the recliner he had tried to dissuade Titus from buying for him. Titus got a blanket out of the closet near the front door and spread it across his father's lap. Albert snorted once, then pulled the blanket around himself. Titus went upstairs, stripped out of his uniform, and put on his sweats. He came back downstairs and got the leftovers out of the fridge and made himself a plate.

After he ate, he washed his dishes and the plate his father had left in the sink. He dried them and put them away. He went back to his father.

"Hey, old man. Wake up and go to bed," Titus said as he gently touched Albert's shoulder. His father's eyes opened languidly as he yawned.

"Was working in the garden today. I guess it took more out of me than I thought," Albert said. He stood up slowly, wincing as he rose.

"Don't push yourself too hard. You might have titanium hips, but you ain't Iron Man," Titus said.

Albert shook his head. "The Lord done seen fit to keep me around this long, I don't guess I'm going anywhere no time soon. Except to bed. See you in the morning, boy."

"Hey, Pop," Titus said.

Albert paused at the bottom step. "I know that look."

Titus gave his father a tiny bit of a smile. "What look is that?"

"Same look you had when you and Marquis knocked your mama's sweet potato pie off the counter that Thanksgiving y'all was wrestling in the kitchen," Albert said.

"Remember I told you about that girl I was seeing when I was in Indiana, the reporter?" Titus said.

"The one you told me got in that fight at the pool hall?" Albert asked.

Titus nodded. "Yeah, well, she coming to town to do a story about the kids we found under the weeping willow tree."

"Mm-hmm. Coming to see you too, I reckon," Albert said.

"Well, she wants to interview me," Titus said.

"Titus, you still got feelings for this girl?"

"What? No, I guess . . . I'm just thinking how I should tell Darlene about this. You know she can be a little . . . I don't know, insecure sometimes. I just don't want her to get upset. Like, I can't stop Kellie from coming, and I didn't ask for her to come," Titus said.

"But you ain't mad about it, though, are you?" Albert asked him.

Titus cleared his throat. "I just don't want this to upset Darlene," he said.

Albert shuffled back over to him and put a hand on his shoulder. "Son, the only way this gonna upset Darlene is if she see the same look on your face that I'm seeing right now. You got you a good woman, boy. But if that ain't what you want, you owe it to her to tell her. Don't wait till that girl comes to town," Albert said as he squeezed Titus's shoulder.

"I hear ya, Pop. Good night."

"Good night, son."

Once Albert had gone upstairs, Titus texted Darlene.

Hey im home

Almost immediately Darlene responded.

U want me to come over?

Titus stared at his phone for a long minute before responding.

Nah that's ok. I'm beat. Maybe we can go to Newport News tomorrow night for dinner

Darlene's response was slower this time.

K

Titus didn't need to have a master's in criminology to deduce Darlene was upset he didn't want her to come over. He could have said yes, but the last few days were finally catching up with him. He felt a wave of exhaustion coming on that felt like it was enveloping him like a cocoon. He knew he'd be poor company for Darlene if she did come over. He could be surly when he was tired. He would take this skirmish to avoid a full-blown argument. That was the nature of long-term relationships. Dozens upon dozens of tactical decisions and one-sided negotiations to keep the peace, or some facsimile thereof.

Titus climbed the steps to his room with legs that felt encased in lead. By the time he reached the bed he was nearly asleep on his feet. He had just stretched out when his cell phone rang.

"Fuck," Titus said into his pillow.

He rolled over and grabbed his phone and looked at the screen. It was Davy.

Titus touched the screen.

"What's up, Davy?"

"Hey, Titus. Uh, I'm down here at the Watering Hole and, uh, well, I just wanted to call you, um, because . . ." Davy stammered.

"Davy, spit it out," Titus said.

"Right, well, Titus, Marquis is here, and he just done about tore up hell around here. And Jasper's hollering about pressing charges and I don't know what to do," Davy sputtered.

Titus closed his eyes. He was too tired to sigh.

"I'll be right there."

ELEVEN

Twenty minutes later Titus was pulling into the parking lot of the Watering Hole. The rotating rack of blue and red lights on top of Davy's cruiser cast ghostly images on the side of the brick building. Unlike many local bars in this part of Virginia, the Watering Hole was a freestanding structure, not a suite in a strip mall. A rugged rectangle with a squared-off roof that resembled the cardboard boxes Titus had used to file active case reports at the Bureau, the Watering Hole wasn't the only bar in Charon County, but it was the one most people patronized. The Celtic Tavern usually picked up the scraps that the Watering Hole left behind. Folks who had been banned by Jasper for various slights or offenses, or people who balked at the seven-dollar cover charge.

Jasper felt no compunction charging his customers to cross his threshold. He had a live band four nights out of seven. Comedy shows and open mic nights were sprinkled across the calendar to add some variety. Jasper had recently updated his sound system and added a fancy LED light system for the stage. He was constantly adding the newest or most expensive hospitality accessory to the Watering Hole's skill set.

Titus put his SUV in park.

One of the first things Titus had noticed when he took office was how much money seemed to be moving through the Watering Hole, for a local bar in a small rural county of less than twenty thousand people. It seemed like Jasper was a creative financial genius. He was squeezing this desolate turnip out on the far edge of the county and blood was pouring forth in copious amounts.

That was one scenario.

Titus was of the mind that Jasper Sanderson was moving heroin, meth, and whatever other illicit substances he could get his hands on through his bar in quantities that could choke a horse. In the year since Titus had been elected, there had been twenty-two overdoses within a five-mile radius of the bar. Ben and Wayne had left the Watering Hole an hour before they were found percolating in the middle of Severn Road. Several informants had sworn in affidavits that Jasper had a connection to a chapter of the Rare Breed motorcycle club, who got him as much China White and high-quality meth as he could handle. Titus had broken up a fight in the parking lot and found two ounces of crank on one of the combatants. Chucky Crowder had said he'd testify that Jasper and his cousin Cotton had supplied him with eight ounces of methamphetamine. Titus had gone to the Regional Drug Task Force and made his case for a multi-county raid, but no one in Hampton seemed much interested in putting Jasper in an orange jumpsuit. The lack of interest made Titus think Jasper must have some good friends. Then Chucky Crowder skipped town, minus most of his teeth. Carla said her cousin, who had an on-again, off-again thing with Cotton, told her Cotton had the teeth in a jar in the back office of the bar.

Titus got out of the truck and walked over to Davy and Pip. They were standing in front of the bar. A small crowd had gathered nearby, full of swaying patrons who felt safe in their inebriation by virtue of the police's preoccupation with the handcuffed men sitting on the front step of the bar.

"Davy, Pip. What's the deal?" Titus said. Davy bit his bottom lip. Pip pushed his hat back on his head, revealing a small wine-colored birthmark that resembled Florida above his right eye.

"Well, it seems like your brother here took offense to something Austin McCormick said and decided to make him eat a barstool. Austin's buddy Brent Johnson didn't think Austin had an appetite for barstools and tried to intervene. He's headed to Riverside General with what's left of his face. Austin here fared a little better."

Titus sucked at his teeth. Austin was Cotton and Jasper's cousin. He approached Marquis.

His brother was roughly the same height as Titus, but Marquis was a bit wider across the chest. He was wearing a white T-shirt and an unbuttoned red flannel shirt. There were huge blotches of red on his white T-shirt shaped like uncharted islands. A small mouse was growing under his left eye. Other than that there wasn't a mark on him. Titus was fairly sure the blotches were blood and he was positive the blood didn't belong to Marquis. His brother's hands were cuffed behind his back, but Titus remembered what they had looked like the last time he'd shaken Marquis's hand. Wide as ax heads, with nicks and scars from teaching himself carpentry.

"Davy, take Austin over to your car. Give me a minute here," Titus said.

"Sure, Titus," Davy said. He and Pip helped Austin to his feet. Titus noticed Austin's nose was broken in several places. As he rose he took great heaping gulps of air. Pip and Davy shuffle-walked him to Davy's cruiser.

Titus looked down at his brother. Marquis shook his head and moved his dreads out of his face. He smiled at Titus, the blood on his teeth changing from blue to red as the light from Davy's rack was caught in his mouth.

"How's Pop?" Marquis asked.

"You should come by and see him sometime. You high?"

"Nah, might be drunk, though."

"You know I have to take you in. Brother or not. At least until we sort this out," Titus said.

"You gotta do your job, lawman," Marquis said. He laughed.

"What?"

Marquis craned his head up and smiled again. "I guess I'm just meant to look up to you."

Titus swallowed hard.

"That motherfucker tried to kill Austin!" a voice yelled from the right. Titus turned his head and saw Cotton Sanderson come striding out of the crowd. He stumbled to his left, righted himself, and kept coming, a bull seeing red.

"Cotton, stay over there," Titus said. He raised his voice but he didn't yell.

"Fuck you, you think I don't know you? You think I don't know how you work? Gonna let your brother walk after he sucker-punches Austin in the face?" Cotton slurred. He was less than ten feet away now. Titus saw he had the business end of a pool cue in his hand.

"Cotton, stay over there. You aren't going to find nothing over here but regrets. I'm taking Austin and Marquis to the holding cell. We gonna sort this thing out. Now, if Jasper wants to make something of it, or Austin, Marquis, and Brent wanna press charges against each other, well, we'll cross that bridge when we come to it," Titus said.

A few people from the crowd came over and got between Titus and Cotton. They gently tried to corral Cotton and lead him back across the parking lot. It seemed like it was working until he executed a deft spin move and spun away from his friends and came charging at Titus and Marquis. For a big man, Cotton was surprisingly agile. He made a beeline for Marquis.

Titus took a step to his right. He opened his left hand and made a sort of V with his thumb and the rest of his fingers. He planted his feet and thrust that V into Cotton's thick neck. He felt a shiver run up his arm as his hand connected with Cotton's Adam's apple. The big man dropped the pool cue and fell to his knees, clutching at his throat as his face bloomed in full crimson.

Titus grabbed Marquis by the arm and helped him to his feet.

"He gonna feel that in the morning," Marquis said.

"Y'all help Cotton, here," Titus said to the crowd. He saw Sawyer Hudgins, Arnold Atwell, and Royce Lazare come over and try to help Cotton to his feet.

As Titus walked his brother to his SUV, Marquis laughed again.

"You a real detective. I thought that ol' boy ain't had no neck, but you found it," he said.

Ezekiel had told him once, "You can demand respect. You can treat them with it too. You can save their children. You can find their wandering grandparents. You can judge the goddamn pie contest. But sometimes you still have to remind them you're not to be fucked with. It's the only thing some people understand."

Titus thought about that as he put Marquis in the back of his truck.

That thought made him incredibly sad.

Titus brought a folding chair over to the holding cell and sat down in front of his brother. He crossed his legs at the ankles, took off his hat and put it on the floor, then leaned back. He checked his watch. It was a little after midnight.

Titus stared at Marquis, willing him to wake up. It was a technique he had employed when they were children. He usually only brought it out on special occasions like Christmas morning or the first day of summer vacation. The memories of those days threatened to drown him in a river of time.

Marquis sat up and laid his head against the cool cinder-block wall of the holding cell.

"You thinking twenty-four hours in the drunk tank will get me right?" Marquis asked.

"No. I'm just trying to keep you from getting in any more trouble," Titus said.

Marquis laughed. "Liar. You ain't never stopped trying to fix me. You always trying to fix everything. Been that way since . . ." Marquis trailed off, but Titus knew the end of that sentence.

"Since Mama died," Titus said.

Marquis leaned forward. Titus crossed his arms, then immediately uncrossed them when he realized how aggressive that appeared.

"You shouldn't have had to do that," Marquis said.

"Somebody had to," Titus said.

Marquis yawned. "It shouldn't have been you, even if you was the oldest. Hell, it should have been Pop, but we both know how that went. He traded the bottle for the Bible and thought that would fix it all. But we both know that's bullshit."

"It's not all bullshit. You can try to fix things. Pop just used the wrong tools."

"You can't fix everything, no matter what tools you use, Ty. Shit, you can barely fix anything. Most days you gotta just hold on and keep your head down," Marquis said.

"I don't believe that," Titus said.

Marquis smiled at him, but it never reached his eyes. "That's why you're miserable, big brother." A quiet bloomed between them. The kind of quiet that was neither awkward nor filled with any specific potentiality. The kind of quiet that can only exist between brothers of a certain disposition.

Finally, Titus broke the spell. "You wanna tell me what all that was about? Jasper says you broke two of his tables and a barstool," Titus said.

"Them tables rickety as fuck. You gonna call the magistrate so I can bond out?" Marquis asked.

"Let's hold on a minute. I wanna know what that was all about. What set you off like that?" Titus asked.

Marquis rolled his massive head and stretched his arms above his head and yawned. "I got tired of hearing them talk shit about my brother," he said finally.

Titus leaned his head back and stared at the ceiling. "Marquis, if you gonna fight everybody who says something bad about the sheriff, you better get a good lawyer on retainer."

"You ain't just the sheriff," Marquis said.

Titus stared at him.

"Just for curiosity's sake, what were they saying?" Titus asked.

Marquis stretched again, and this time his back popped. "They was saying you was lying about Mr. Spearman. That you didn't know your ass from a hole in the ground. Then one of them called you an uppity nigger. So I sat down my rum and Coke and picked up that barstool and made them think about their life choices."

Titus didn't want to laugh. He knew he shouldn't, but it came out unbidden and unbound. Soon Marquis was joining him. They hadn't shared a laugh in a long time. It echoed through the holding cell like a church bell. As it ebbed, Titus felt his eyes begin to sting. How many times had they had a moment like this since their mother had died? Three, maybe four?

"Look, I'm not gonna hold you all night. Austin has declined to press charges. Brent was telling anyone that would listen he was going to handle it in the street as they took him away in the ambulance, so I'm assuming he isn't pressing charges either. Unless you want to press charges against them, I'm gonna let Austin go, then let you go an hour later. You need a ride back up the road to get your car?" Titus asked.

"Nah, I'll call Tisha," Marquis said.

"You don't need to do that. I'll take you," Titus said.

"I know you're tired as hell. I'll get Tisha. She ain't doing nothing."

"How long y'all been messing around now? Ten years? You need to go ahead and marry that girl," Titus said, instantly realizing he sounded just like his father.

"Like you gonna marry Darlene?" Marquis said. He winked at Titus.

"That's different."

"That's one way of saying it," Marquis said.

"What's that supposed to mean?" Titus said.

"Nothing. Just . . . you really think you gonna spend the rest of your life here? Like, you winning was luck. You know these white folks ain't gonna let you get a second term. Then what? Pop don't really need you to hang around. You used to be in the F-B-fucking-I. Why in the hell would you stay in Charon? Besides Pop, I can't believe you came back. Darlene is a good woman, but she a Charon girl. The only way she would leave here is feet first. I know you, Ty. This place ain't enough for you. It never was," Marquis said.

"We've seen each other five or six times in the last seven years. You really think you know me, know what I want?" Titus said. His voice was tight as a drum.

Marquis got up off his cot and walked over to the bars of the cell. He gripped them with his wide ax-head hands and leaned forward. His tightly coiled dreads fell into his face.

"Better than anybody who's still breathing, big brother," Marquis said. More quiet descended upon them like a fog. After a few minutes Titus got up and folded his chair.

"You'll get your stuff from Pip. He'll cut you loose. Everything except your belt. I'm pretty sure that buckle knife is illegal in the state of Virginia. Why do you even have something like that?" Titus asked.

"To stab people," Marquis said. He laughed.

Titus didn't join him this time. "Watch yourself, little brother. Jasper and Cotton can hold a grudge."

"I'm not the one that throat-chopped Cotton and probably made him shit his pants," Marquis said.

"I'm the police. They know better."

"No offense, big brother, but that star don't mean a lot to them boys. They've seen how little they cost," Marquis said.

Titus walked over to the cell. "What you saying?"

Marquis moved his dreads out of his face. "I ain't saying nothing. But people talk. I hear things."

Titus stared at his brother. Stared into his dark brown eyes. He'd heard rumors about Cooter Bennings having his hand out to local businesses, but he'd assumed most of his graft took the form of free gas and a good loan from the bank.

"You know something I don't?" Titus asked.

Marquis shook his head. "I don't know nothing. But don't you think it's mighty funny you can't never run up on them white boys? I'm just saying."

Titus walked up to the cell and put his hands on the bars. "If you knew something you would tell me, wouldn't you?"

"If I knew something for sure, you damn right I'd tell you. You my brother, ain't you?" Marquis said.

Titus let go of the bars. "Pip will let you out in an hour. I'm heading home. You should . . . you should think about coming over this weekend."

"I might. See you later, Ty," Marquis said.

"See you, Key," Titus said. He walked back down the hall.

Just as he reached the door, Marquis hollered to him, "You can keep that belt. You probably need it more than I do!"

Titus stopped by the switchboard desk. He expected to see Kathy, but Carla was there, out of uniform with her hair down and in a Dartmouth hoodie.

"You aren't Kathy. And you don't really look like Carla," Titus said.

"I know, but Kathy called and asked could I cover her for the rest of the night. Apparently she's been messing around with Brent and she had to go get him from the hospital," Carla said. "Side note, we really need more than two switchboard operators."

"Small-town living. You know, even though I grew up here I'm still shocked about who's seen who naked," Titus said.

Carla chuckled. "FFD."

Titus arched an eyebrow.

"My brother Luis used to say, 'Ain't nothing to do in small towns except fighting, fucking, and drinking.' We've seen the results of all three tonight," Carla said.

"Your brother spoke the truth. Pip is gonna let Austin go in a minute. Then he gonna cut Marquis loose about an hour later. Hopefully that will keep them from running into each other. Make sure you mark these hours you working down as overtime. I'm heading home, going to try and catch a few hours with my eyes closed," Titus said.

"Gotcha, boss. Oh, by the way, those state boys said they would probably be done with the crime scene by tomorrow. They took some soil samples, pictures, stuff like that. What's the plan for tomorrow?" Carla asked.

"We'll talk about that tomorrow. I'm beat," Titus said.

"Right. See ya, boss."

"Later, Carla," Titus said.

He was almost to his car when he heard Carla calling his name. She was standing in the doorway with her finger on the earpiece of the headset.

"Titus! Someone on the phone says he got a tip on the case. Says he has to talk to the sheriff," Carla said. Titus trotted back to the station. He took the headset from Carla and put it on his head.

"Sheriff Crown, how can I help?" he said. He pointed at Carla and pantomimed writing, then pointed at the screen of the switchboard. Carla wrote down the number on a scrap of an envelope.

"Huh . . . it's me that thought I was helping you," a voice said. The speaker was talking through a piece of fabric or paper over his or her phone. They were also slurring their words and breathing like they had just run a panther-assisted mile.

"Well, we do appreciate any help you might be able to give. You told my operator you had some information for me?"

"Shit, man, it might not be nothing. I don't know. Heard that press conference. Got me thinking. Jesus Christ in a *juniper* tree, I feel bad. I been drinking all day."

"Look, what you might think is nothing might end up being important. Even a tiny detail might help. Just tell me what was on your mind," Titus said. He dropped his voice an octave.

"I don't know, man. If it's nothing, I don't want to put y'all in this man's business," the voice said.

"If it's nothing, he doesn't have anything to worry about. If it is something, those children out in that field deserve their justice," Titus said.

The caller took a deep breath. "I mean, I did some work for a boy. Helped him put in this building. We took some girls out there. Had some fun, ya know. It was . . ." The caller stopped talking.

"Who was it?" Titus said casually. He didn't want to spook the caller, but a name this early in the investigation would be huge.

"It was weird, ya know? Bunch of angels on the walls. Creepy angels with weird faces," the caller said. His voice was soft as crepe paper. Titus gripped the phone. No one knew about the angel paintings from the video.

"Who was it? Who'd you do the work for?" Titus asked. His gut, that old reliable resource, was telling him this was big. This was important. He was possibly on the verge of solving the case. He could feel it in some deep recess beyond his conscious mind.

"Fuck, man. I . . . shouldn't have called. He's a good dude. I'm sorry."

The line went dead.

"Call that number back!" Titus said. Carla redialed the number, but no one answered.

"It's probably a burner, boss. It didn't come up attached to a name. What did they say?" Carla asked as Titus handed her back the headset.

"Said they had done some work for a guy. Sounded like they worked on an outbuilding. An outbuilding with pictures of angels on the walls," Titus said.

"Did they say a name?"

"No. But there were angel pictures on the walls of that dungeon in the video. Now somebody calls and says they know someone with a building covered in religious iconography. Those two things don't feel random," Titus said.

"Could be a coincidence," Carla said.

Titus thought of the autopsy photos. Of those twisted bodies and the corruption and violence visited upon them like some Old Testament smiting.

"Could be. I could also have monkeys fly out of my butt. Don't mean I'm gonna start buying bananas for toilet paper," Titus said. He put his left index finger to his lips.

"What's on your mind?" Carla asked.

"I know that voice. They were trying to disguise it, but I've heard them before. Shit, it's Charon, I've heard everyone's voice before," Titus said as he rubbed his eyes.

"Ain't that the scary part? Whoever did . . . did this is someone you know. Someone I know. Someone we all know," Carla said.

"No," Titus said flatly. "It's someone we thought we knew."

TWELVE

Cam was mixing up a batch of his special coffee when Titus walked through the front door of the station. He wasn't sure what Cam put in it, but one cup was strong enough to make you paint a house by yourself.

"They all here?" Titus asked.

"Yep. Well, everyone except Tom and Roger," Cam said.

Titus nodded. He'd sent a group text out before falling into a fitful sleep last night. Dreams filled his head like spirits trying to possess him. Dreams of his mother, of the DeCrain family, of the not-so-anonymous voice on the phone, of him and Marquis as children. Memories of events that never took place and words that were never said that felt as real as the floor beneath his feet right now. Dreams at first, then nightmares, then he was up and getting ready to have a meeting with his whole squad.

A soft babble of conversation ceased as soon as he stepped through the doorway to his office. They parted silently to allow him to get to his desk. He sat down and took off his hat and laid it on the desk.

"Let's get right to it. Our top priority is the Spearman/Macdonald case, but that doesn't mean we are going to let the county go to hell in a handbasket. To that end, I'm going to make a mini–task force that is going to be helping me investigate these murders exclusively. Of course, if anyone not on the task force finds a piece of important evidence, you share it with the team, but I'm really going to need the rest of you to keep the peace while we work with the state police and their team. Now, my task force will be Carla, Steve, and me. When Trey is done with investigating the shoot, he will be on the task force too. The rest of you will carry on with your regular duties. Any questions before we continue?" Titus asked.

Davy's hand shot up.

"Davy?"

"Uh . . . so, I heard, I mean, I saw it on Facebook, that a few people was already starting to call him, the third guy, the Weeping Willow Man. I mean, are we calling him that? I mean, it's not a bad name," Davy said.

Titus would bet his father's house and every dollar in his savings account that Davy had come up with that name himself. Titus stood up and walked to the front of the desk and sat on the edge.

"No, we are not calling him that. We aren't going to give him any kind of moniker except 'suspect.' If the media wants to call him something that will boost their engagement, that's on them. It's been my experience you give these killers names, you make them into myths. That's what they want. They crave it. They get off on it. They aren't myths. They ain't Hannibal Lecter or Red John or the Mastermind. They are just killers. Nothing more, nothing less," Titus said.

Davy lowered his head, but Titus could still see the red tide rising over his neck on the way to his cheeks.

"Now, we got a phone call last night from someone who thought they might have some information about the murders. Unfortunately, they hung up before we could get a name or track the call."

"Who was the dumbass that let them hang up?" Douglas said. This was followed by a smattering of chuckles.

"I was the dumbass," Titus said. The chuckles ceased immediately.

"But I think I recognized the voice and we do have the number. I'm going to send in a request to the phone company to get the logs attached to that number. Unless it's from a burner phone we should be able to get some info by the end of the day. Okay, everyone on the task force, stay. The rest of you get to work. Those of you that were off, thanks for coming in, don't forget to put your time in," Titus said.

After the other deputies had shuffled out, Titus motioned for Steve to shut his office door. He pulled out copies of the autopsy photos and the report out of a folder on his desk and passed them out to the four of them. He'd called Cam and had him make the copies from his email.

"What you're looking at are photos of the first two autopsies the ME has completed. The abuse you see there is in line with what was on the video clips. Does anything stand out to you?" Titus said.

"Besides this is sick as shit?" Steve said.

"Look closer. The body of a murder victim is our best evidence," Titus said.

"This phrase 'Our salvation is his suffering,' I've seen that before," Carla said.

"It's been on six church signs in the county. We are going to split up and go talk to folks at all six churches," Titus said.

"What are we looking for?" Steve asked.

"Ask them about anyone in the congregation that seems off or odd. Anyone who is secretive but also aggressively helpful. Anyone who is prone to mood swings but also someone who is hyper-religious. Someone who seems like a quiet person but also too good to be true. A lot of times sociopaths will overcompensate with extreme emotions. They don't really understand how real empathy, real emotions work, so they parrot it but they sometimes go overboard," Titus said. He paused.

"We all wear masks. We have a public face and a private face and our real face. A person like this, someone who could do to another human being what you see in those pictures, once you strip away all their masks there's nothing there. They are just a shell. So they fill it with fantasy, with desires that would make a normal person vomit. But that's how we'll catch them. They've let that mask slip in front of someone. They've made a mistake. We just have to track it down," Titus said.

"What if they haven't made any mistakes?" Carla asked.

"They've already made one. They did something that made La-trell crack. There was some precipitating incident that made him kill Spearman. If we hadn't confronted him, I think he would have killed the third member of their little murderous trio too. So they've made that first mistake. I'm willing to bet they've made more. Let's go find out how many," Titus said. He nodded toward the door.

Titus had given himself Second Corinthian and the Holy Rock of the Redeemer to investigate. They were the last two churches that had used that inflammatory phrase on their signs. Second Co-rinthian was led by Reverend Calhoun Wilkes. He stayed in a rec-tory near the church, a simple one-story brick house encircled by ancient pink crepe myrtles, with a brick walkway that bisected the circle as it snaked out to the driveway, where he parked his equally ancient Volvo sedan.

Titus parked next to the sedan and knocked on the door of the rectory. A slim man with a long gray beard and wearing a white button-down shirt and a fluffy brown cardigan answered the door.

"Sheriff Crown, come in, please," Reverend Wilkes said. Titus ducked his head as he stepped through the doorway. Reverend Wil-kes gestured for him to sit in an old but well-cared-for Queen Anne chair while the reverend sat in a recliner. The coffee table between them had a small silver tray with a teacup, a bowl of sugar, and a silver teakettle.

"Would you like a cup of tea, Sheriff?" Reverend Wilkes asked.

"No, thank you. I just want to ask you—"

"How are you, Sheriff? This terrible thing with Mr. Spearman and that young man must be just a horrible thing for you to deal with," Reverend Wilkes said.

"It is, but it's part of the job. Just not the part I like," Titus said.

"You know, usually where there is a tragedy in life, I find solace in the Word. I'm able to compartmentalize the situation as a part of the Master's plan. And His understanding is not my understanding. This situation with Jeff Spearman has tested my obedience and my resolve. I keep thinking, how did Jeff allow the devil to enter his heart to such an extent?"

Titus cleared his throat. "Reverend, do you really think a fallen angel took over Jeff Spearman's body and made him kill those kids?" Titus asked.

Reverend Wilkes poured hot water from the teakettle into his cup. He dumped a teaspoon of sugar into the cup and stirred his tea. He took a sip, closed his eyes, then took another sip. He placed the cup on a coaster and then leaned forward and stared into Titus's face.

"Is it easier to accept that a man who this county trusted with their children for over thirty years was a sociopath and a charlatan who had visited his unnatural desires on those he was supposed to protect? The devil takes many forms, Sheriff. A snake, an angel with flaming wings, madness. You don't believe in the devil, Sheriff?" Reverend Wilkes asked.

Titus placed his hat on his knee and cocked his head to the right.

"Reverend, if you've seen the things I have, you'd realize the devil is just the name we give to the terrible things we do to each other," Titus said.

"That's a rather dim view of humanity, Sheriff."

"From where I sit, that's the only view that makes sense, Reverend," Titus said.

Reverend Wilkes nodded slowly. "I can't imagine what you've seen, Sheriff. But I'll keep you in my prayers," he said.

Titus ignored the minister's supplication on his behalf and asked the question that had brought him there.

"Reverend, the reason I came by was to ask you about a phrase that was on the church sign last year. It was, 'Our salvation is his suffering.' I wanted to ask who was it that came up with that phrase and who suggested putting it on the sign." He zeroed in on Reverend

Wilkes's face. He let his eyes take in the minister's movements, his posture, the way he gently pulled at his beard. Titus was trying to read the cryptic language of his involuntary gesticulations.

"Well, as I recall, it was Miss Maggie Scott who suggested we put that phrase up on the sign."

"Do you have her number?" Titus asked.

"Oh, Miss Maggie died earlier this year," Wilkes said. Titus leaned back in his chair. "Sheriff, why are you investigating a church sign, if you don't mind me asking?"

Titus stood. "Just chasing phantoms, I guess, Reverend. Thank you for your time."

"Of course. Is there anything else I can do for you?" Wilkes said.

"Just one more thing. Has there been anyone in your congregation who seems a bit . . . off? Anyone acting strange since the shooting at the school?"

"Nothing comes to mind, Sheriff. Anything else I can help you with?" Wilkes said.

"No, Reverend. I guess I'll get going," Titus said. He put on his hat and headed for the door.

"Sheriff, I asked you earlier, but you didn't respond. Would you mind if I included you in my prayers tonight?" Reverend Wilkes asked.

Titus paused. "I don't mind, but maybe you should pray for someone that believes, Reverend."

"God loves the believer and the nonbeliever all the same."

Yeah, but I don't love him back. I left that abusive relationship a long time ago, Titus thought. "Have a good evening, Reverend," he said.

Titus drove out to the edge of the county and past the county square toward Piney Island. The pine trees gradually gave way to huge mounds of pampa grass and wild irises and cattails that shot up from the marshland like the quills of a porcupine. Titus cracked his window and let the salt-tinged air slip in and kiss him on the lips. He crossed the Piney Island bridge with the slightest frog in his throat. The rusty metal plating on the old bridge looked like it had been washed in ocher. The aged iron creaked and whined under the weight of the SUV like an old man getting up off the floor.

Titus had joined a small contingent of citizens at a recent supervisor's meeting who literally begged the board to replace the Piney Island bridge. The request was denied four-to-two. Most people in the county hardly considered Piney Island a part of Charon, and those who did didn't seem to understand the severity of the situation with the bridge. Titus hoped it wouldn't happen, but he was beginning to think the only way people would ever understand was if the forty-foot-long structure fell into the Chesapeake.

The Holy Rock of the Redeemer sat at the far western point of the wide exclamation point that was Piney Island. Past a bend in the gravel road sharp enough to slice bread, then down a long stretch bordered by wild unkempt yucca plants that led right up to the narrow parking lot that ran the length of the wooden church. Beyond the church lay the Chesapeake Bay, and in the bay lay the abandoned Old Piney Point lighthouse. When he was a child, he and his friends would try to scare each other with stories of the haunted Old Piney Point Lighthouse and the two lighthouse keepers who went crazy in the 1920s.

Titus parked near the front door of the church next to a tan late-model Chevrolet Celebrity, a car that Titus was sure had ceased being produced more than fifteen years ago. He went up the well-worn wooden steps and knocked on the door. Most churches in the county were only open on Sunday or for special occasions, but Titus knew Pastor Elias Hillington, the pastor of Holy Rock since Titus could remember, lived at the church with his wife, their eight children (most of whom had moved out of the county after reaching adulthood), and a collection of snakes. Most of the parishioners who made up the congregation of Holy Rock were Hillingtons and Crenshaws, from Elias's side of the family tree, and Rollinses and DeButtes, from his wife Mare-Beth's side.

To Titus's knowledge, the entire congregation, like most of the population of Piney Island, was white. They were watermen who toiled on the bay and sold the bounty they pulled kicking and scream-ing from the ocean to the Cunningham Seafood processing plant. Rawboned men and women with faces weathered and toughened by years of cold winds coming off the water at five o'clock in the morn-ing. Titus's father had worked side by side with these men and women for decades and yet was always separate from them. An outsider on this island even though his family went back over one hundred years in Charon proper.

Anyone who didn't take their first steps along the oyster-lined shores of Piney Island or take their first sip of Communion wine in Holy Rock would always be an outsider here.

Titus banged on the door with an enormous brass knocker in the shape of two hands clasped together. He listened as the echoes reverberated through the church and made their way through the sanctuary. After a few minutes he heard steps coming toward the front door.

"What?" Pastor Elias Hillington said when he opened the door. Titus didn't need to go too far out on a limb to assume Pastor Elias hadn't cast a vote for him during the election. Elias Hillington and his congregation made no secret about their political leanings. In between the fire and the brimstone, Pastor Elias railed on in oner-ous tones about gay marriage, the liberal agenda, and how all lives mattered. The congregation of Holy Rock didn't wear hoods and they hadn't burned a cross in anyone's yard, but Titus had no illu-sions about their thoughts about him and people like him. It came off them in waves, like the rot from a gangrenous wound. A putre-faction of the soul.

"Pastor Elias, I was wondering if I could ask you a few ques-tions," Titus said. He used his pleasant voice. He would slip into his cop voice if Elias gave him any undue insolence. If he got nasty, well, then he'd go full-on Charon and see what happened.

"I'm feeding the snakes. You can come on out back and ask your questions there if you want," Elias said. He turned on his heel and walked back down the center aisle of the sanctuary without uttering another word. Titus followed the tall, slim scarecrow of a man through the sanctuary and past the pulpit, past the stairs that led to the second floor of the church, and into a back room lit by a pale indigo grow light that flickered overhead like mini–lightning strikes. Against the back wall of the back room were twelve aquariums on four metal shelves. Three glass boxes per shelf. To the right there was a large utility sink and a short counter made from a rippling sheet of Formica over a piece of plywood supported by stained cinder blocks. The counter was full of plastic containers that tittered and squeaked. Pastor Elias reached into one of the containers with his bare hand and snatched a white mouse from his comrades. He went to one of the aquariums and opened the lid and tossed the mouse inside.

Titus watched as a speckled brown serpent slithered over a fake tree limb and struck the mouse with startling speed. As the mouse writhed on the floor of the aquarium, the snake began to swallow it whole.

"Ask your questions, Sheriff," Elias said as he reached into one of the aquariums and pulled a snake from it, putting it in a separate container with tiny holes punched in the lid. He took the aquarium and placed it in the sink and began to clean it. Elias stood at the sink with his back to Titus.

"A man who don't look you in the eye when you talk to him is a man that don't respect you," his father had told him the week before he'd left for UVA. Albert Crown was full of homilies, but that particular one had proven to be true more than once.

"Pastor Elias, are you going to talk to me out the back of your head?" Titus asked.

Elias's shoulders tensed. When they relaxed, he shut off the water and turned to face Titus. His clean-shaven face was folded into wrinkles that resembled the bellows of an accordion. He tried to lock eyes with Titus, but he saw something there that extinguished his truculence.

"What are your questions, Sheriff? Don't you have your hands full with them there children they found under that there tree? Why you come all the way out to the island to harass us?" Elias asked.

"Pastor, I'm not here to harass you. I just want to ask you who put the phrase 'Our salvation is his suffering' on the church sign out there in your parking lot. Just answer that and I'll let you get back to handling your snake," Titus said. Elias frowned. Titus didn't know if he got the joke and that had elicited the frown, or if it had gone over his head and his frown was the only way he knew to respond.

"I did. It's from one of my first sermons. I put it on the sign once a year to commemorate when we built this here church. When we broke ground all those years ago. God's righteous people spreading his real Word. Not that watered-down version that makes them there folks feel good about their sins. No, sir. We preach the divine Word of God here at Holy Rock. His suffering *is* our salvation. Jesus the Christ died on that there cross for his people. His righteous people protected by his Father's archangels, Michael, Uriel, Gabriel, and Raphael. He purchased that protection for us on that there cross. Through his suffering we are saved. And when it's time for us to join him, Azrael comes to collect our immortal souls," Elias said.

Titus watched as his slack face was slathered in sweat and animated like he'd taken a hit of some pure crystal-clear crank.

"Who are his people, Pastor?" Titus asked. He had other follow-up questions, but he wanted to see how far Elias would go with his definition of who qualified as God's chosen people.

"The righteous. The incorruptible. The pure of heart. The holy anointed."

The white? Titus thought.

"Pastor, the reason I'm asking is because that phrase has come up in our investigation of the murders of those children you mentioned. Is there anyone in your congregation who has been acting . . . strangely since news of the murders broke? Anyone who has stopped coming to church or said anything fatalistic?" Titus asked.

Elias's frown transformed into a snarl. He opened the plastic container with the snake and pulled it out of the plastic box. He let it wrap itself around his left arm.

"Sheriff, I told you my congregation is full of the anointed. We are God's children, full of his grace and his supernatural piety. No one who walks through that there vestibule and gives themselves over to the power of the Son, the Father, and the Holy Ghost could ever do there what you say. 'For they shall take up serpents and not be bitten, and they shall drink poison and it will not harm them,'" Pastor Elias said as he raised his left arm and extended it.

"Pastor, I'm not here to pass judgment on your congregation. I'm looking for a killer. A killer who took the lives of young boys and girls. And just for the record, Mark, chapter sixteen, verse eighteen doesn't say anything about not being bitten or not being harmed by poison. You fixed that to say what you wanted it to. And since that's a king snake, not a coral snake, a bite from him won't mean much," Titus said.

Elias's face bloomed scarlet. He had that befuddled look most self-righteous people got when someone they considered a heathen could quote the Bible more accurately than they could.

Elias took a step toward Titus.

"But only the sinners bleed, Sheriff," Elias said.

"Pastor, like I said, I'm not here to judge you. But you come any closer to me with that snake, I'm going to send him to hell on a bullet," Titus said.

Elias stopped, turned, and put the snake back in the plastic container. He resumed washing the aquarium.

"Like I said. Nobody who comes to this here church could do what you say. If that's your question, I'll thank you to leave me to my work," Elias said.

Titus sighed. He thought back to a movie he'd seen once where a character said if you can't be respected, be feared. Elias may not have respected him, but he could see he feared him. It wasn't a win, but it wasn't exactly a loss either.

"If you think of anything, Pastor, give me a call at the sheriff's office. Anything at all. Those children deserve justice and I'm going to do my best to get it for them," Titus said.

Elias didn't respond.

Titus left him among his serpents.

THIRTEEN

Paul Garnett had a secret.

He liked to grumble and complain about walking the husky his wife had brought home a year ago without asking if he wanted a goddamn husky. The kids loved the dog, his wife fed the dog better than she fed him, and everyone down his road thought the dog was friendlier than he was.

They were right.

But the secret he kept close to his heart, the lie he kept alive, was that despite his protestations to the contrary, he loved the dopey-ass furball. The kids, his two sons and his daughter, had named the dog Rider, and as names went that wasn't a bad one. Paul worked nights at the flag factory, so it had fallen on him to walk the dog first thing in the morning after his wife had left for her shift as an ED nurse and the kids had climbed on the school bus. Once he was sure the coast was clear, he'd get a handful of treats and put Rider through a series of simple tricks before taking him down the road for his daily constitutional.

Paul knew that if he ever admitted how much he loved Rider, neither his wife, Holly, nor his kids Kent, Chad, or Nikki would look at him any differently. They wouldn't think of him as less of a man because he loved a seventy-pound ball of slobber and barks that liked to sleep at the foot of the bed he and Holly shared. He knew this, yet he still kept up the act. By now it was just a part of his daily routine. He was pretty sure his oldest, Kent, knew it was all a performance. Little ass had caught him petting Rider one Saturday morning when Paul had thought everyone was still zonked out from a cookout the night before. But he didn't say anything. It had become a part of his routine to pretend he didn't know his father thought of Rider as his third son. They shared the chicanery. In a strange way it made Paul feel close to the boy. God knows they didn't share many other interests.

Paul didn't walk Rider on a leash. The big dope never strayed too far from Paul's side when they walked down the narrow strip of asphalt that was Ten Devil's Hop Road. Paul had lived in Charon all his life, and he couldn't figure out how in the hell some of the roads in the county got their names. It was like one of the founders had gotten drunk off mead or moonshine or both and just picked names out of a goddamn hat.

He stepped down off the porch with Rider by his side. The sun was only a suggestion behind the heavy gray, almost blue clouds in the east. The wind pawed at his hoodie, seeking an opening as they started down the road. Paul could hear a few birds and another dog barking in the distance, but that was about it. At this time of morning there were no cars on the road and no neighbors in their yards. Ten Devil's Hop belonged to him and Rider alone.

They made their way down the road on the wide shoulder that separated the gravel-covered shoulder of the road from the ditch bank. Rider stayed on Paul's right for most of their walk. Every once in a while he got in the road, but Ten Devil's Hop was nearly a straight line from Route 143 till it joined Chapel Neck Road. A few locals would use it as a cut-through if they were trying to get around a tractor or a truckful of hay bales during the fall, but that rarely happened this time of day.

When they came upon the service road for one of the county's four cell towers, Rider took off down that road. Paul saw a fat gray squirrel running for its life as Rider bore down on it. Paul didn't worry about Rider running off. The big goof would chase a squirrel or a rabbit without any real intention of catching it. All Paul had to do was stop and stand in one place while Rider found his way back.

While he waited for Rider to run down that squirrel (who probably had five escape routes memorized), Paul checked his phone. He scrolled over a few social media apps, checked on the score from the Wizards game the night before and was pleasantly surprised to see they had won. That mean Todd Robbins owed him fifty bucks. After a few minutes he saw Rider come bounding toward him.

"Rider, boy, what's wrong with you? Oh my God, are you bleeding?" Paul said. He was shocked to hear himself yelling. He ran to Rider and dropped to one knee. There was blood on his muzzle and in the fur on his face. Blood so bright red it looked fake. Like Rider had gotten into a can of barn paint. Paul threaded his fingers through Rider's fur, searching frantically for a wound.

"Boy, what did you get into? Thank goodness, you're not cut. You find a dead deer or something?" Paul said. He got up and went to the ditch bank. He wiped his hands on the grass with a promise to himself to soak them in a heavy bleach-and-water solution when they got back to the house.

Rider bounded back into the woods. He stopped and barked at Paul. Then he continued through the brush and undergrowth.

Later, Paul would tell his friends down at the Watering Hole that he had followed the goddamn dog because he didn't want it to get lost so he wouldn't have to hear Holly's mouth. But that was a lie. He'd followed Rider because he didn't want him rooting around some rotten deer carcass and getting an infection. Either from some parasite on the deer or whatever kind of bacteria was on its corpse. So, cussing under his breath, he worked his way through the undergrowth and the brush and the wild blackberry thorns. He followed Rider's barking until he came to a narrow culvert. He hopped over it and pushed his way through some vines he prayed weren't poison ivy until he found himself in a clutch of pine trees.

Rider was standing there barking, his ears drawn back and his tail wagging furiously.

Paul had been working the day Oscar Tillman got caught in the industrial threader. A forty-foot-long Lovecraftian nightmare of a machine that sewed the hem of the American flags with laser-like precision. Unfortunately, when Oscar had tried to work on the machine without locking it out properly, he felt that precision up close and personal. By the time they'd shut off the threader, Oscar's body resembled a piece of cured meat that had been cut into sections and wrapped in waxed cotton in a deli.

Nightmares had plagued Paul for months after seeing Oscar Tillman rendered like a slaughtered lamb.

He thought what Rider had found would give him nightmares for the rest of his life.

Titus studied the dead man.

The body was suspended by the wrists between two pine trees that had grown up less than four feet apart. Yellow nylon rope, the kind you could pick up at Sadler's Hardware or any big-box retailer anywhere in America, was wrapped around the wrists and the forearms and wrapped around a couple of low branches on each tree.

The body had no face.

The skin had been peeled away like the rind of an exotic fruit. What was left behind was a terrible contortion that seemed to be half a scream, half a laugh. Lidless eyes stared out at nothing, like a blind man staring into the sun. It was a cool day in mid-October, so there were no flies buzzing around the corpse, but other insects had found the remains. A few ants trundled across the mouth and over the tongue. Fat black beetles crawled over the body's naked chest. A smooth gash ran across the body's throat and opened it like a secondary mouth.

A crown of blackberry thorns encircled the head like a wreath. Titus could see what he had at first taken to be the cleaned and scoured skin of some large animal, maybe a deer, attached to the victim's arms was actually the victim's lungs. The killer had sliced the man's back open and then pulled the lungs through the slits.

Titus knew this was a form of torture allegedly used by Vikings and other wild tribes from the Scandinavian northlands, but the way the arms were positioned, the crown of thorns, Titus thought this was less like a bloody eagle and more like a bloody angel. If the symbolism wasn't obvious enough, someone had carved URIEL in the victim's chest, right above a death's-head tattoo over a Dixie flag background over the victim's heart. The force of the arterial spray had launched blood away from the body, leaving residual streaks that ran over the wound in the chest and the tattoo.

Blood had pooled in front of the victim's feet like a puddle of syrup, appearing almost black on the ground covering the pine needles and other detritus.

"It's like a monster got hold of him," Carla whispered.

"No, it was just a man. Monsters don't care about all this pageantry," Titus said. Trey was taking photos before they cut him down. Titus had temporarily pulled him off the shooting investigation. He was the best photographer in the department and Titus wanted everything here documented to within an inch of its life.

"That's Cole Marshall," Davy said.

"How can you tell? I mean, without a face and all?" Steve asked.

"We used to play rec league basketball. Time to time we'd play shirts versus skins. I've seen that tattoo going up for a layup more than once," Davy said. He said the words in a near-monotone.

"Jesus Christ in a juniper tree," Titus said under his breath. He knew he had recognized that voice. He pulled on a pair of latex gloves.

He'd just recognized it too late. Far too late.

"You got it, Trey?"

"Yeah, we good."

"Dr. Leonard, we good?" Titus asked.

The diminutive physician lit up a Pall Mall, took a deep drag, and exhaled. "Yeah, he's definitely dead," Dr. Leonard said.

"Cut him down," Titus said.

Steve and Douglas cut the ropes and laid the body down inside a heavy-duty black body bag provided by Blackmon's Funeral Home. The big, light-skinned brother nodded at the body.

"I'm assuming he needs to go to Richmond. That don't look like natural causes," he said.

Titus looked at him for a hard ten seconds.

"I guess that's a yes," he said, and zipped up the bag. Davy and Steve helped him lift the bag onto a stretcher. The attendant, who said his name was Nathan but you could call him Nate, pushed the stretcher through the undergrowth to his van.

"If that was Cole Marshall, he has to run two-forty, two-fifty. How strong would one man have to be to cut his throat, slit his back, then string him up between these two trees?" Titus said to Trey.

"Strong enough I wouldn't want to fight him one-on-one," Trey said.

"Maybe it was two people? One holds him while the other cuts his throat?" Carla said.

Titus stared down at the ground. At the broken twigs and branches and brown pine needles that littered the floor of the forest.

"No, it was just them. When we got here it barely looked like a struggle had taken place. It was one man. A man he trusted. Trusted enough to ask him about the special place he'd helped him build. Trusted him enough to let him get close and cut his throat left to right." Titus moved his right hand from left to right in a slicing motion. Titus walked over to the two trees and grabbed the dangling length of rope. He studied the frayed edges. He cut them down and motioned for an evidence bag. He carefully stepped around the pool of blood and walked around each tree, staring down at the ground.

"He tied him up first. Did you notice how his feet were off the ground? He incapacitated him, then strung him up, still alive. Then he cut his throat. That's where all the blood came from. He cut his throat first, then sliced the face off, then did the bloody eagle. Cole didn't struggle during any of that. No blood splatter on either of these trees or near the ditch. They met on the road; the killer knocked him out, then carried a two-hundred-forty-pound man into these woods and cut him up like he was butchering a calf. Pulled his lungs up so they would look like wings and then put a crown of thorns over his head. Uriel, the angel of wisdom, of knowledge. Is that because Cole knew too much?" Titus said in a low murmur.

"Is he talking to himself?" Davy whispered to Steve.

"Yeah," Steve said.

"Kinda creepy," Davy said.

"Yeah."

By the time Titus got back to the station, Cole Marshall's girlfriend, Jessica Twitchell, had called three times. Each call more frantic than the last. She hadn't heard from him since he'd left at around eight thirty last night. She'd heard they'd found a body on Ten Devil's Hop Road. Cole wasn't answering his phone. Was Cole dead? Wouldn't someone tell her if the man she loved was dead? Titus knew she wouldn't stop calling until a man or woman with a badge eventually broke her heart for her.

"What do I tell her if she calls again?" Cam asked.

"The truth. We haven't identified the body yet and we can't comment any further."

"But it's Cole, ain't it?" Cam asked.

"Just tell her what I said, Cam," Titus said. He went into his office and shut the door. He fell into his chair, took off his hat and his aviators, lay back, and stared at the ceiling. The nooks and crannies of the acoustic tiles resembled the Nazca Lines in Peru. Cole Marshall was the anonymous caller. He was positive of that fact. And now Cole Marshall was dead, filleted like a trout.

Filleted.

They used fillet knives at the seafood plant. Titus made a mental note to ask the ME if they could tell him specifically what kind of knife was used to kill Cole Marshall.

Titus sat up straight.

He called Carla on her cell phone.

"Yes, sir?"

"Carla, do me a favor. Grab Steve and go by the fish house and ask around about Latrell and Cole. Find out if they were friendly or did they have any friends in common."

"You think the connection is the fish house?"

"Well, Latrell worked there and he was involved with two killers. Cole Marshall worked there, and now he's dead. If it ain't a connection, I'd be mighty surprised," Titus said.

"Okay, boss, got it."

She hung up. As soon as Titus set his cell phone down on his desk, his landline rang.

"ME's office, line one," Cam said.

Titus clicked over. "Sheriff Crown."

"Sheriff, its Dr. Kim."

"Doctor, you must be prescient. I'm sending a body to you as we speak."

"Another victim from the Spearman case?" Dr. Kim said.

"In a manner of speaking, I think so," Titus said.

"Well, that's not why I'm calling. I could have sent you an email about this, but I got the feeling you'd want to be notified personally. We identified one of the victims."

Titus gripped the handset so tight he heard the plastic creak. "Were they in the system?"

"Yes, he was. He and his mother were convicted of shoplifting in 2015. His name was Tavaris Michaels. Was reported missing last year. He was seventeen," Dr. Kim said. She said each word slowly and distinctly, as if fearing that just speaking them aloud could curse her own children to a similar fate.

"Do you have any contact info for the mother or father?"

"The mother is Yasmin Michaels. Last address is Baltimore, Maryland. I have a phone number too, but I don't know if it's still good," Dr. Kim said.

"Give it to me," Titus said.

"You're going to call her to make the notification?" Dr. Kim asked.

"If I take 301 I can be in Baltimore in an hour and a half," Titus said.

"You're . . . going in person?"

"She deserves that, don't you think?" Titus said.

Dr. Kim didn't answer for a beat. "Yes, she does," she said at last.

Titus hung up the phone and got up from his desk. He put his hat back on and grabbed his sunglasses. It felt good to be moving, to be acting, to be doing something instead of waiting for another brick to fall. There was a moment in every investigation when things felt like they were spiraling out of control. When a snowflake becomes an avalanche dragging the men and women who were dedicating their lives, however briefly, to the case down into a crevasse as cold and lonely as Dante's final circle. If you were lucky, that moment passed and you found yourself on the other side of it with a suspect in custody.

Titus hoped the murder of Cole Marshall wasn't the avalanche moment in this case. He hoped his small band of local boys and girls could find the strength to grab hold of the shadow that they were chasing and drag this killer of children and men kicking and screaming into the light.

Titus walked into the lobby of the office and found Scott Cunningham standing next to the dispatch desk talking to Cam.

"Titus, can I have a moment?" Scott said. He smiled, showing too many teeth, like a chimpanzee. Titus considered telling him to kindly fuck off, but he knew if he avoided him here, he would just come back later or, better yet, raise the issue in the next board meeting:

"Sheriff Crown keeps avoiding me, for some reason."

Titus could see Scott in his mind, fake sincerity and concern painted on his face like he was a cheap whore as his cronies on the board nodded along in subservient unison.

Titus took his hat off and motioned to his office.

Scott sat down and crossed his legs, letting his wingtip dangle ever so slightly as he shook his foot. He exhaled long and hard before he began to speak. Titus thought maybe that was how he expelled some of his hot air.

"Titus, Titus, Titus. Word has it that you found Cole Marshall pinned to a tree like a butterfly. You care to enlighten me as to what is going on? First Mr. Spearman is murdered in front of our kids, then those poor children are found in Tank's field, and now this? What is going on down here, Titus?"

Titus drummed his fingers on the desk.

"Do you think I work for you?" Titus asked.

"I think as the chairman of the Board of Supervisors—"

"Let me disabuse you of that idea, Scott. Let me be as clear as fucking glass. I work for the people of Charon. Every last citizen of my hometown. My job is to protect them. To make sure they feel like they can go about their lives without getting their throats cut or mourning their children. And even though you are in fact a citizen of Charon, I don't specifically work for you. You're a part of the collective. And every time you break off from the pack and come down here to stomp around and bitch and moan and try to piss in the corners to mark your territory, you keep me from doing the job I was elected to do. You impede my ability to do my duty. Do you understand that? Do you get that?" Titus asked. He fought with all his might the desire to make a fist.

Scott smiled again.

"Titus, do you know how we keep Charon County from becoming a ghost town? I mean, the young people can't wait to leave. You know that firsthand. As dear as they are to my heart, it isn't the fish house or the flag factory. Oh, they keep money in the pockets of the folks that work there, but that's not what keeps Charon from becoming a 'was' on the map. No, sir, what keeps Charon trucking along is those fat and happy Northerners that come down here and wander around Main Street buying knickknacks for three times what they are worth. We get 'em drunk at the Celtic Pub and then we let them wander around Greenway Plantation so they can pretend they give a fuck about some poor ol' dead slaves. Now, if those fat and happy Northerners think there's a serial killer running around nailing people to trees, they're not gonna be inclined to spend their hard-earned hipster dollars. So you can see how important it is to the people of Charon that you get a handle on this. Quickly. Unless you don't think you can. I hate to have to make a motion for a recall or a special election. Maybe Roger can find this psycho," Scott said. He didn't smile this time, but Titus was sure he wanted to.

Titus got up from his chair and walked around to the front of his desk. He crossed his arms and looked down at Scott.

"The population of Charon County is fourteen thousand two hundred and eighty-seven people. Sixty percent of those people are Black. Folks who never thought they'd have a chance to vote for a sheriff who wouldn't pull them over and feel up their wives or daughters or beat their sons or husbands within an inch of their goddamn lives. Add to that a large number of white folks who don't carry water for Robert E. Lee or worship at the shrine of Ronald Reagan, and that gives me a pretty good little coalition of voters. I'm betting they would love to walk past that Confederate statue in the county square and cast their votes for me . . . again. So you start your little recall. Meanwhile, I'm going to be catching this killer. A killer who tortured those Black boys and girls right along with Jeff Spearman and Latrell Macdonald. You remember Jeff Spearman, right? Your old golfing buddy," Titus said.

Titus leaned forward ever so slightly.

"I'm going to find him, and you're going to stay out of my way. We are not having this conversation again. And the next time you see me, you address me as Sheriff Crown. Now get the fuck out of my office," Titus said.

Scott held his hands up in mock surrender. "Titus, I just want—"

"Scott, if you don't leave right now on your two feet, you're going to end up leaving on a stretcher," Titus said. Scott must have sensed the lack of hyperbole, because he got up and walked to the door. He paused, started to say something else, saw Titus's face, and thought better of it. Titus kept standing until he saw Scott walk out the front door, then he walked into the lobby.

"Cam, I'm heading out for a while. Going up to Maryland. It's eleven now; I should be back by four P.M. Check in with Trey if you can't reach me if anything comes up," Titus said.

"What's in Maryland?"

"A mother who doesn't know her child is dead."

The traffic on 301 was sparse until he crossed over into Maryland. Then it became a *Mad Max*–like dystopia of distracted drivers, harried bureaucrats, and D.C. commuters desperate to beat the noonday rush. Titus got off 301 and got on the equally congested 95 to take him into Baltimore. He drove down narrow streets flanked by row houses and corner stores until he reached Yasmin Michaels's house. Titus parked in front of the tiny one-story building. He got out of his SUV and knocked as gently but firmly as he could. He didn't want to give a grieving mother the "cop knock," but his heavy hands made that a near impossibility.

He had called ahead to make sure she still lived here, so he knew she was home. But she didn't immediately respond to his knocking. Titus couldn't say he blamed her. After all this time, she had to know, in some intrinsic way, that he wasn't here to deliver joyous tidings. Who would rush to their door for such devastating news?

Eventually, after two long minutes, the door opened and a slim woman with a mini-'fro answered the door.

"Hi, I'm Sheriff Crown," Titus said.

"I kind of figured that, with the badge and the Smokey the Bear hat. Come in," Yasmin said. She turned, and Titus followed her into a small but neat living room. She sat down in a weathered recliner. Titus could have sat on an equally distressed sofa or a more severe bamboo chair with a threadbare cushion in the seat, but he decided to stay standing.

"You want a drink? Water?" Yasmin asked as she fired up a Newport cigarette.

"No, ma'am, I'm fine, but thank you for asking," Titus said.

"You miss that traffic out near College Park? It gets bad around lunchtime. I don't even leave the building for lunch anymore. Too congested," Yasmin said.

"You said you work at a medical facility?" Titus asked.

Yasmin shook her head. "Nah, I work for a company that makes first-aid kits. For the Army and shit. Been there for a year. When Tavaris . . . didn't come home it was kind of a wake-up call for me. I don't know. I stopped getting high. Just quit. Got this job. I think I thought I had to be in a better place when he came back than when he left. I thought . . . I guess I thought it would make a difference. Seeing you here, I guess it don't," Yasmin said.

Titus steeled himself. He needed to say it. Say it now and not let it linger between them. The longer he did that, the harder it would be for Yasmin.

"Ms. Michaels, I am so sorry to have to tell you this, but we found the remains of your son in Charon County two days ago. It appears he died as the result of a homicide," Titus said. The sentences felt like bullets in a gun as he spoke. Each one aimed right at Yasmin's heart.

Yasmin inhaled deeply, then expelled a cloud of smoke from her nostrils like a dragon awakening from its thousand-year slumber.

"My mama used to say he was in a better place. When we was little she made us go to church every damn Sunday. You go that often, you can't help but believe. For a while anyway. It's like believing in the Easter bunny or some shit. And I believed. I used to believe so damn hard," Yasmin said.

Titus noticed the faded outline of a crucifix on the wallpaper over Yasmin's left shoulder. The indistinct outline reminded him of jailhouse tattoos.

"Faith is a fragile thing, Sheriff. Do you know that? They like to talk about mustard seeds and not walking by sight and all that shit, but the truth is it don't take much to break your faith. Get sick, get broke, or lose your only son. Your faith will run out of town faster than a deadbeat daddy," Yasmin said. Tears rolled down her smooth brown cheeks.

"I used to pray every night for him to come back. Every single night. Then one day I just stopped. I knew it won't doing no fucking good. Guess me and him getting pinched was kinda a good thing, huh? That's how you found out who he was?" Yasmin said. Sobs played on the edges of her voice. Titus thought he had a few seconds before she either started screaming or crying.

"Sheriff, who hurt my baby?" Yasmin said, and now she was crying in earnest. Great howling cries that wracked her thin body. Ash from her cigarette fell to the floor and she trembled in the depths of her sadness.

"I don't know, but I'm going to find out. I promise you that," Titus said. The words felt full of presage and foolishness. He knew he shouldn't make promises. He was setting himself and Yasmin up for disappointment. The poor woman was broken enough already. Yet it was those shards, the pieces of her heart, that cut into his own broken covenant of faith and made those words bleed from his mouth.

FOURTEEN

Titus got back later than he had predicted. The traffic had gotten exponentially worse in the thirty minutes he'd stood in Yasmin Michaels's home. Titus knew he probably wouldn't be able to notify every parent of every victim they identified, but this felt right. It felt like another step in his own path of penance. A path that was as long and twisted as a winding sheet.

Other than her grief, Yasmin Michaels didn't have much to share about her son.

"We was both using when . . . he left," Yasmin had said.

"He left?" Titus had asked.

"Yeah. We got into a bad fight and he went down to the Inner Harbor. He used to hang out there with those college kids. He used to say he liked pretending he was a college kid. He'd hustle them for drinks, playing pool, doing other things," Yasmin had said. She and Titus silently agreed not to investigate what *other things* actually meant.

Titus had made several notes, but the one that stood out the most was that Tavaris was probably last seen at the Inner Harbor, Baltimore's row of bars and restaurants that catered to tourists and those college students Tavaris admired so much.

Might be nothing, might be everything. Titus thought that summed up the startlingly random nature of most police investigations.

174 S. A. Cosby

"Hey, Titus, sorry I had to run out the other night," Kathy said when he walked into the station.

"No worries," Titus said. He didn't want to make things awkward by asking Kathy how Brent was doing, but a part of him did want to know how committed the man was to getting revenge. Or whether the whooping Marquis put on him convinced him to take up a new hobby of minding his own business.

"Was that Cole Marshall y'all found in the woods?" Kathy asked. No beating around the bush about that particular piece of gossip.

"We don't know yet. Gonna probably take a few days," Titus said.

"I heard they . . . they cut his stuff off and put it in his mouth," Kathy said, her face pinched into a pained scowl.

"A lie can be halfway around the world while the truth is still pulling up his britches," Helen Crown was fond of saying. Another piece of wisdom from his mother that time had borne out to be terribly true.

"That's not true, Kathy. So let's not spread that rumor, okay? Rumors can take on a life of their own," Titus said gently. Kathy's face softened, and Titus hoped she picked up both his obvious and subtextual points. He didn't want her spreading rumors about the case just like she probably didn't want people spreading rumors about her and Brent.

Titus went into his office and booted up his computer. He checked his email and saw Carla, Steve, and Trey had filed reports about their visits to the fish house and the churches, respectively. Before he read the reports, he did an online search for Latrell's name. Almost immediately a dozen or so articles popped up on his screen. Many of them had snippets of the cell phone videos depicting the moments before the shooting. The comments were almost evenly split between folks supporting his deputies with rhetoric he found abhorrent and folks labeling him and his department as racists and murderers. Other articles mentioned his press conference. He'd named Latrell and Spearman as perpetrators along with a third unidentified perpetrator in the murders of the children under the weeping willow tree. The fact they had videotapes that confirmed Latrell's status as an accessory to multiple murders didn't seem to dampen the fury some people felt toward his department.

Titus understood that sentiment. Too many Black men and women had been executed by folks with badges for doing demonstrably less than what Latrell had done. The fact that Latrell had been holding a gun and had killed someone did nothing to negate that tragic fact.

Titus always told himself he was changing things by working the system from the inside. Had promised himself as sheriff he would make sure his department was different. But Latrell had shown him the lie that lived in that promise. What if you couldn't change the system because it was working as intended? And if that was true, then why the hell was he wearing this badge?

The system worked just fine for you, though, didn't it? the voice of Red DeCrain whispered.

Titus shook his head and opened his emails.

He read the reports from Carla and Trey and Steve. In addition to talking to people at the seafood plant, Carla and Steve had gone by their respective assigned churches, as had Trey. Titus didn't consider himself an investigatory genius, but even he could see the visits to the churches hadn't turned up much. Carla and Steve's visit to the fish house, however, had borne a few small pieces of fruit. Apparently Latrell had been working at the fish house up until two weeks ago. That in itself wasn't unusual; most citizens of Charon walked through those heavy metal doors of Cunningham Seafood at one time or another. What stood out to Titus was that Latrell was good friends with Darnell Posey, another casual drug user. Carla had also noted that there were several employees Latrell seemed to avoid. These included Eddie Franklin, shift supervisor (understandable, especially if Latrell was coming to work high), and Carolyn Chambers, one of the crab pickers and the mother of Latrell's ex, Candy Chambers. He also apparently went out of his way to avoid Dayane Carter. Dayane was a trailer-park-pretty young woman who had gotten into her share of fights down at the Watering Hole and the Celtic Tavern. Titus had picked her up a few times for being drunk in public. According to Carla's notes, Latrell avoided her like the plague. Apparently he didn't avoid or engage with Cole Marshall.

Titus didn't know if that meant anything, but he made a note of it.

As he scrolled through the rest of the day's reports, his cell phone rang.

It was Darlene.

"Hey, what's up?" Titus said.

"I wanna see you tonight. Can you make that happen?" Darlene asked.

"Yeah, sure, you okay?" Titus said.

"No. Titus, I heard about Cole Marshall. I'm scared. Aren't you scared?" Darlene asked.

"Aw, D, don't worry, okay? Look, I'm leaving here in a few minutes. I'll meet you at the house by seven."

"You didn't answer my question. Kids buried in the woods, now Cole is dead. You aren't afraid? I'm scared to death. I closed up the shop early today. I've been sitting at the house with Mama and Daddy, trying not to think about it," Darlene said, and Titus could tell she was on the verge of tears. She was the second woman today who was about to cry to him at her most vulnerable moment, and there was nothing in his power he could do to comfort either one of them. Plaudits and pledges wouldn't slake Darlene's fear.

Titus closed his eyes tight. What good was the star on his chest, the title in front of his name, if he couldn't keep the people he cared about from losing hope? All the power and supposed glory that came with being a peacekeeper turned to dust when the woman who shared your bed confessed that she was terrified of the place where she'd been born.

"I'm not afraid. I'm concerned, but I'm not afraid. I know we are going to catch him. I trust my folks almost as much as I trust myself," Titus said. That last part had slipped out, but as his father liked to say, tell the truth and shame the devil. He trusted himself more than he trusted anyone. That included God in heaven, the state police, and even the members of his own department. Titus had learned through trial and error and circumstances beyond his control that when the long black veil came down, he could only really depend on himself.

It made for a long, lonely life.

"Do you want me to bring some food over?" Darlene asked.

"That's fine. I'll see you in a few, okay?" Titus said.

"Okay. Love you," Darlene said.

"You too," Titus said.

He put his phone down on the desk. A question crept into his mind, and he didn't have a good answer. When had he started saying, "You too"?

He was sure Darlene would know the answer.

Titus sat on the couch while Darlene cleared the table. He poured some Jameson into two whiskey glasses with one ice cube each and set them on the coffee table. His father was at a Friday night church meeting.

"Your father still leaves you notes? Why didn't he just text you?" Darlene had asked when she had noticed Albert's chicken-scratch handwriting on the mini-chalkboard next to the refrigerator.

"Albert Crown is nothing if not old school. He still darns his socks," Titus had said.

"What's darning your socks?" Darlene had asked.

Titus handed her one of the glasses as she slid next to him on the couch. She laid her left leg over his right one and grabbed the television remote.

"Whew, this is strong," Darlene said after taking a sip from the glass.

"If you can't handle this, I guess I better not break out the 'shine," Titus said.

Darlene poked him playfully as she changed channels.

"One time me and Marquis got into Pop's 'shine. When he found out, he made us drink it with him. A whole quart. I don't think I touched alcohol again until I went to college," Titus said.

"How is Marquis? I heard he got into a fight at the Watering Hole last night," Darlene said.

"He's okay. You know Marquis. Never takes anything too seriously," Titus said. He sipped his own drink. The Jameson burned as it went down until it found a warm spot in his belly. That warmth started to radiate throughout his whole body. He didn't have any intention of becoming the clichéd hard-drinking cop, but after the last few days a cold beer wasn't enough to start the decompression process.

"My daddy got some shells for his shotgun today. He said there were a lot of people at Bobby Joe's place," Darlene said.

"What?"

"I said Daddy got some shells for his shotgun today down at Bobby Joe's place."

Titus took another sip. Bobby Joe Andrews ran the local gun-and-ammo store. Titus put the glass to his forehead. Charon County had more guns than it had residents because most residents had more guns than they needed. The last thing *he* needed was a bunch of trigger-happy wannabe Doc Hollidays stockpiling ammunition and chomping at the bit to play good guy with a gun.

"I guess a lot of people are scared. Not just people that voted against me," Titus said.

"Daddy getting those shells ain't like him saying he don't think you gonna catch this guy, Titus. But this is Charon. Stuff like this doesn't happen a lot. People don't know what to do," Darlene said.

"I'm so sick of people saying 'this is Charon' like everyone around here is a goddamn virgin and no one has ever stepped on a sidewalk crack or stole a grape from the Safeway. Let me tell you something I learned in the Bureau. Doesn't matter where you are from or where you live, people are people. They can be jealous or hateful or twisted and sick. They steal and they lie, and lie about stealing. They fuck each other's husbands and wives or sons and daughters. They go to church every Sunday and hoot and holler about brotherhood and living in Christ, then they come right out and call you or me a porch monkey before they go home to beat their kids. Then have the nerve, the unmitigated audacity, to point at somebody else, at some other town, and say, 'No, those are the sinners, those are freaks, not us, not Charon.'"

"Titus, I didn't—" Darlene tried to say, but Titus ignored her.

"Flannery O'Connor said the South is Christ-haunted. It's haunted, all right. By the hypocrisy of Christianity. All these churches, all these Bibles, but it's places just like Charon where the poor are ostracized. Where girls are called whores if they report a rape. Where I can't go to the Watering Hole without wondering if the bartender done spit in my drink. People say this kind of thing doesn't happen in a place like Charon. Darlene, this kind of thing is what makes places like Charon run. It's the rock upon which this temple is built," Titus said. He tossed back the rest of his drink and stomped into the kitchen.

Titus rinsed the glass and sat it on the edge of the sink. His shoulders rose and fell as he breathed hard.

He felt Darlene's hands first on his back, then on his shoulders, her touch feather-light. Titus turned and took her in his arms. She pressed her head against his chest.

"I'm sorry. I know you're under a lot of stress. I shouldn't have said—"

"No, I'm the one that should say I'm sorry. Didn't mean to blow up at you. You haven't done anything wrong. Look, I love Charon. I know just now it didn't sound like it, but I do. It's my home and heart. And because I love it, I'm hard on it. I'm brutally honest about it. Because I know it can be better than what it is. But it can't get there if we keep pretending that it's some utopia on the Chesapeake Bay. We have to look at Charon and see the whole picture. Even the ugly parts. That's how I catch him."

"I know it's hard looking at all that ugliness," Darlene said.

"It's my job. Let's go upstairs," Titus said. Darlene nodded. He took her hand, so small yet so strong, in his bear paw and led her through the living room. Titus paused to grab the remote to shut off the television. A commercial was on the screen.

"This program was brought to you by the National Scleroderma Foundation. To donate—"

Titus pressed the power button and the television winked out. Neither one of them spoke for a few seconds.

"That's what your mama had, isn't it?" Darlene asked. The question came out in bite-sized pieces. Titus was familiar with that tone. People were painfully curious about what killed his mother, but they took great pains to hide it. Even his girlfriend had a morbid curiosity about it.

"Yeah. Turned her muscles to bone. It was rough," Titus said.

He could see himself at twelve years old standing in the doorway of his parents' bedroom, half-afraid, half-confused, filled with a yearning that is the sole provenance of sons who want a hug from mothers who can't even raise their arms.

"My aunt used to come by and pray over her. Rub her forehead with anointing oil. She couldn't stand to be touched, but my aunt did it anyway. Most people with scleroderma can live long, productive lives but my mama had a rare form. It moved fast. She would scream like a dying rabbit every time somebody touched her. Whether it was my father bathing her or my aunt laying hands on her. One time I ran in there while my aunt was jabbering away talking in tongues and drowning her in that oil. I kicked her. Told her to get away from my mama. She slapped me. My mama raised herself off that bed for the first time in weeks and grabbed my aunt by the wrist. She told her not to ever touch me again. But the disease had messed up her vocal cords. It didn't sound like her, but it was still my mama, you know? Then she told me she loved me. It was the last time she spoke," Titus said.

Darlene squeezed his hand.

She watched as tremors rolled through his body like tides from a full moon. They went upstairs hand in hand. Darlene pretended she didn't see the tears on Titus's face, and Titus pretended he wasn't crying.

Later Titus crept downstairs and went to the kitchen. The old Felix the Cat clock on the wall said it was 2:00 A.M. His father was sitting at the table with a jar of moonshine in front of him. The cap was off, but the jar was still full.

"Pop? You okay?" Titus asked. His father was no longer a binge drinker, but he did have a sip of the good stuff every now and then, despite his devotion to the church. He was fond of saying even Jesus made water into wine.

"Huh? Yeah, I'm all right. Got a call a few minutes ago. Gene Dixon died. Heart attack," Albert said.

"Aw, damn, Pop. I'm sorry to hear that. I know that was your buddy," Titus said.

"Yeah. Did I ever tell you Gene was the one introduced me to your mama? At a dance at the Honey Drop Inn. A little shot house used to be down bottom of the county. Gene was dating Faye Jones. She and your mama were best friends. They needed somebody to dance with Helen when they went out. Your mama didn't cotton much to being a third wheel, and I was the lucky man who got the job."

"I didn't know that," Titus said. He sat down across from his father.

"Yeah. Gene was a good man. Lord have mercy, what times these be," Albert said.

"Season of pain," Titus said in a low voice.

"What?" Albert said.

"Nothing, Pop. You wanna do a shot?"

"I guess we should do one. For Gene," Albert said.

Titus grabbed two shot glasses from the cabinet. His father said a toast before they swallowed the 'shine.

"To Gene Dixon, a good friend and a good man and the best pool player I ever saw. May his spirit abide with the Lord from now until the end of time," Albert said. They took their shots and slammed the glasses on the table.

"What you doing up anyway?" Albert said with a gasp.

"I don't know. I had this dream. A nightmare, really," Titus said.

"About them kids in the woods?"

"Nah, they wasn't in it, but I'm sure it was about them. I'm standing in this field all alone. A wheat field. But the wheat is dead and brown. Brittle as ice. There's these huge black clouds rolling in like a tidal wave in the sky. And the wind is blowing through the dead stalks. And I'm all alone as the storm rolls in. Lightning and thunder and rain, but the rain hurts. It's hot, boiling-hot. It burns. And I'm all alone." Titus poured himself another shot.

"You're not all alone, son. You got me and your brother and Darlene and, most important, you got the Lord," Albert said.

"We're all alone, Pop. We've just trained ourselves not to believe it," Titus said before tossing back the 'shine.

"Titus, that's not true. God walks with us in every moment of our lives. Even the darkest ones," Albert said.

Titus didn't respond. He did not want to get into this with his father, not now and not tonight.

He nodded at his father.

Titus loved his father, he truly did, but it had been a long time since he really thought he knew what he was talking about when it came to the heavenly hosts.

The night his mother had finally, mercifully died was when the blinders had come off for Titus. He still loved the man, but it was in those painful moments that he realized adults didn't really know more than kids. That everyone was making it up as they went along and religion was just another crutch, like liquor or weed.

After his father had called the doctor who had written Helen Crown off weeks ago and made the official pronouncement and the funeral had come and gone, Albert Crown had said something about Titus's mama being in a better place with Jesus. Then he had left thirteen-year-old Titus and eight-year-old Marquis alone to go down to the Watering Hole. Jasper's father had been running it then. By the time Albert came back drunk and crying like La Llorona, Titus had changed the soiled sheets on his parents' bed and made himself and Marquis some chicken soup. He'd washed the bowls and put them away, then put himself and his brother to bed.

Because someone had to grow up after his mother slipped from this world. His father eventually got it together and even became a deacon, but Titus never forgot that the night his mother died his father had left two little boys alone to fend for themselves with just a vague notion of salvation for their mother.

Time had dulled that injury, but there was still a thirteen-year-old inside of him that hated his father just a little bit for that.

Albert got up and put his hand on Titus's shoulder.

"Long as I'm on this side of the dirt you ain't alone, boy," Albert said before shuffling up the stairs. And that simple action, those gentle words, was why he loved his father more than that little boy hated him. It was the blessing of blood.

Titus put the jar back under the sink and cleaned the shot glasses. He turned off the kitchen light and went out to the porch. Even in the South, mid-October can be chilly. The winds coming off the bay carry the cold down from the North Atlantic like a ghost that caresses your cheeks and makes your teeth ache.

Titus spread his arms and let the cold embrace him. The cool air stung, but in a good way. It sharpened his focus. Tomorrow he'd have Trey talk to the ME. He'd go in at 7:00 A.M. and stay until 9:00. People were afraid. The best way to counteract that was for them to see the sheriff on the road, in their neighborhood. See him doing something, anything, that convinced them he wasn't cowering in his office behind a desk. Ninety percent of his job was enforcing the law, but ten percent, the percentage most folks saw, was creating an image. Titus didn't like it, but he knew it was pointless to fight it. He'd told Darlene he wasn't afraid. That wasn't exactly true. He was afraid, just not of the man who killed those kids, who probably killed Cole Marshall. He was afraid of what that man, the Last Wolf, was doing to his county. He knew he had to use that fear, break it and bend it to his will. There was a chasm everyone had to traverse at one time or another called failure. Fear was the bridge that carried you over that crevasse.

"Titus! Your radio, they calling you!" Darlene shouted. Titus turned and saw her through the doorway standing at the top of the steps. She was wearing one of his old UVA T-shirts. Titus hurried through the door and up the steps.

He grabbed his radio off the charging station.

"Sheriff Crown, go ahead."

"Titus, we got a situation down here at the station," Pip said.

"What kind of situation?" Titus asked.

"Darnell Posey came by here, dropped off a box, then tried to run through the woods. We got him in the holding cell," Pip said.

Titus held the speaker close to his mouth. "What was in the box?"

Titus got down to the station in five minutes. Five minutes less than the usual ten it took for him to get there. Pip and Douglas were waiting for him in his office. There was a cardboard box on the desk with a familiar swoosh design on the outside.

"The parchment has some words on it," Pip said. He handed Titus a pair of latex gloves. Titus slipped on the gloves, then took the parchment.

I Am the Beast Slouching Towards Bethlehem, it said in what appeared to be black ink.

"Is that from the Bible?" Pip asked.

"No, it's from a poem by Yeats," Titus said as he handed the parchment back to Pip, who put it in an evidence bag.

"And it's not parchment. It's skin," Titus said.

"What the fuck?" Douglas said. Pip reached into the box and pulled out a ziplock bag.

"Well, that tracks because this was in the box too," Pip said. He handed the bag to Titus. The older man's hands trembled as he did.

Titus flattened the bag out on his desk.

The eyeless face of Cole Marshall stared up at him, the mouth stretched into an eternal O of pain.

Charon County

Small towns are like the people who populate them. They are both full of secrets. Secrets of the flesh, secrets of blood. Hidden oaths and whispered promises that turn to lies just as quick as milk spoils under a hot summer sun.

The myth of Main Street in the South has always been a chaste puritanical fantasy. The reality is found on back roads and dirt lanes under a sky gone black. In the back seat of rust-mottled Buicks and the beds of ramshackle trucks. The heart of Charon County beats in time with the spirituals sung in church on Sunday morning. But its soul is a truth that can be scried from the sweat of illicit lovers, the blood that drops from the lips of the PTA president after her husband has had one too many, too many times. It can be augured from the serial numbers on the tens and twenties passed from the hands of Charon's favorite sons and daughters to the men and women who sell them a taste of the quiet that sends them to dreamland drooling.

It's there dancing among the fumes of a kerosene heater in a freezing trailer that snatches the breath from a mother, a father, a baby boy.

It persists when all the niceties of civility fall away under the weight of their own impermanence.

It can be divined in the eyes of the Wolf who buried seven young men and women under Tank Billups's weeping willow tree. The Wolf who dreams of angels with their wings unfurled, their four faces rippling with a madness that comes from being too near the throne of God.

The Wolf who revels in its secret. Who delights in hiding its true face.

Yes, small towns are like the people who populate them.

Eventually they will give up their secrets, but the price for those revelations is always paid in blood.

FIFTEEN

Titus walked into the room they used for interviews and sat down across from Darnell Posey. Darnell had his head down on the table.

Titus slapped the table with the palm of his hand.

Darnell popped up, tried to stand, realized he was handcuffed to the table, then sat back down in the steel chair. Titus put a folder on the table.

"How you doing, Darnell?" Titus asked.

"Man, I ain't do shit," Darnell said.

"Well, that's not exactly true, is it? You left that shoebox on our front step, then took off for the woods. What do you call that?" Titus asked.

Darnell licked his lips. "I don't know, man. A joke? Was, like, shit in it or something?" Darnell said. His brown skin had a pasty, ashy patina that gave him a dehydrated appearance, like he'd crossed a vast desert.

"No, not a joke, Darnell. This," Titus said. He took out a photo of the contents of the ziplock bag that he'd blown up to an eight-by-eleven size.

Darnell took one look at the photo and tried to get up again. "What the fuck, man? What is that? Is that a fucking face?"

"Yeah, it's a fucking face. Still got some blood on it. So you better start talking real fast, and Darnell? I better fall in love with every word that comes out your mouth," Titus said.

"Man, I don't know nothing about that shit!"

"Darnell, I'm not feeling like I'm falling in love here. Where'd you get the box?" Titus said.

"Look, man, I woke up around eleven and that box was on my step with five hundred dollars in cash in an envelope. Had a letter said, 'Drop this off at the police station,' so that's what I did. I ain't know it had no goddamn face in the box. What the fuck, man?" Darnell said.

"Darnell, I have to ask, why didn't you just take the money and toss the box?" Titus said.

"Cuz I figured whoever left it was watching to see if I did it. Duh," Darnell said.

Titus put the photos back in the file. He steepled his fingers and pushed himself back from the table. "Darnell, how well did you know Latrell Macdonald, and before you say you don't know him or you don't know anything, you should know I already know y'all were friends."

"What Latrell got to do with this?" Darnell asked.

"Do you want to get charged with the murder? Because that face belongs to a murder victim. Now tell me what you know about Latrell, unless you don't want to ever touch grass again," Titus said.

He studied Darnell, watched him bite his lip and roll his eyes like marbles in a tin can. Did Darnell realize Titus was bluffing? That despite delivering a box to the sheriff's station with Cole Marshall's face in it he really didn't have anything incriminating on Darnell? They'd dusted the box for prints and even though Darnell's were on the outside of the box there were no prints on the inside. There were none on the bag or the piece of tanned skin. Darnell didn't strike Titus as a criminal mastermind so the absence of prints inside the box spoke to a more organized person.

Organized killer. The killer left that box on Darnell's step, Titus thought, correcting himself. The Last Wolf was taunting them. He wanted them to know he was the one who killed Cole. This didn't really shock Titus. A killer like the Last Wolf, who was the dominant personality in their triumvirate, was a narcissist. He would see the police in general, and Titus specifically, because he was the sheriff, as his nemesis. His need to prove his superiority would be his downfall. Titus had seen it time and time again. It's how they finally caught the BTK killer.

"Look, man, me and Latrell used to kick it sometimes."

"Y'all get high together?" Titus asked.

Darnell hesitated. "Yeah . . . we did. Latrell used to be able to get good shit. He did some work for Jasper Sanderson from time to time." His shoulders slumped as he poked out his bottom lip. He wore defeat like a comfortable old coat.

"What kind of work?"

"What kind you think? You know what Jasper do. Shit. Motherfucker runs half the county."

"Did Latrell ever say anything to you about Jeff Spearman or anyone associated with Jeff Spearman?"

"He ain't say shit about Mr. Spearman, but I ain't surprised he was killing them kids. Latrell was crazy, man. He could be the chilliest motherfucker you know one minute, then the next minute he got a broken piece of glass to his throat saying he gonna end it all," Darnell said.

"Did he ever say why he wanted to kill himself?" Titus asked. He thought he might know the answer, but Darnell was like a faucet that had been broken. Everything was pouring out now.

"I don't know. I mean, last time I saw him he was acting weird. Like he was scared. Somebody had popped him upside the head. . . . Look, he said something, but if I tell you, you gotta cut me loose on this box thing. I swear on a stack of Bibles on my mama's back I didn't know what was in that motherfucker," Darnell said.

Titus leaned forward. "That depends on what you have to say."

Darnell bounced his leg up and down, fidgeting violently in his chair. "Look, last time I talked to Latrell was about a week ago. He said he was at the Watering Hole picking up a package for Jasper to take it to somebody in Gloucester. He said he went to the bathroom and heard Jasper talking. Said he could hear the echo or some shit from his office. Said he heard Jasper say he had a deputy in his pocket. That every time y'all try and bust him that deputy gives him a call and he gives that deputy an envelope. He said Jasper was laughing cuz he knew the deputy was putting that cash in the bank like a dumbass. Then when he come out the bathroom he say something to Jasper and Cotton about the deputy they got and he says Cotton smacked him upside the head. Then he says he wasn't worried about Cotton and Jasper. He says he had bigger problems than them two. I don't know what the fuck could be a problem worse than Jasper and Cotton. That's all I know, I swear."

Titus didn't let any emotion show on his face, but he felt his insides roil like a hurricane was swirling in his chest. If he hadn't had that conversation with Marquis, he would have probably dismissed Darnell's statement as the ramblings of a drug addict desperate to get out of a hole of his own making. But he'd had that conversation. And now he was getting a second source saying one of his deputies was dirty. He didn't believe in coincidence, but he did believe in a preponderance of evidence.

He thought back to the bruise he'd seen on Latrell's face on the steps of the high school.

"You making this up, Darnell? You lying to me?" Titus asked.

"Shit, man, you asked and I'm telling you. What I got to lie for? Latrell ain't the first person I heard say it. Lot of people think Jasper got one of your boys in his pocket."

Titus ignored that comment but filed it away for later. "Did Latrell ever say anything about Mr. Spearman in connection with Jasper? Did he ever say anything about them hanging out together?" Titus asked.

Darnell shook his head. "Nah, he never mentioned Mr. Spearman at all. But Mr. Spearman was a freak."

Titus sat forward. "Why you say that?"

Darnell gazed up at the ceiling as he spoke. "When I was in school, I was trying to stay on the basketball team, but all we had was a piece-of-shit car. I was missing practices and shit. One day I smacked the shit out of Chris Mason in geography class cuz he was teasing me about it, right? So, Spearman has me stay after class instead of sending me to the office. He asked me what was going on, so I told him. He was like, 'I'll give you a ride home from practice.' I was like, for real? Bet." Darnell lowered his head and locked eyes with Titus.

"First time he gives me a ride, we shook hands. Second time, he wanted a hug. Third time, it was a long-ass hug. Fourth time . . . well, there wasn't no fifth time. I got kicked off the team, and since I was only going to school to ball, I dropped out. All because that freak wanted me to jerk him off," Darnell said.

Titus felt his gorge rise, but he forced it back down into his guts. "You never told anyone?" Titus asked.

Darnell barked. "Who would you believe? Teacher of the year or a Black dropout?"

"If I'd been here, I would have believed you," Titus said.

"Yeah, well, you wasn't," Darnell said.

Titus stood. "Stay here. I'll be back in a few."

"Where'm I going?" Darnell asked.

"What's he saying?" Pip asked.

They were sitting in the office. Titus had put the box in the evidence locker. He'd put the ziplock bag in a red biohazard bag. He'd have to get it up to the ME tomorrow.

"He said Latrell did some work for Jasper. He told me Spearman tried to molest him once. He didn't seem to know anything about him and Latrell, though. But I'm pretty sure whoever was working with those two is who sent him up here," Titus said.

"Now, what makes you think that? No offense, but I've personally arrested Darnell five times for possession. How he stays on at the fish house is gotta be a miracle. Hell, he probably high right now," Pip said.

"It ain't about him. It's about who sent him. Think about it. We go by the fish house and interview folks about Latrell. One of the people we talk to is Darnell Posey. And then he just happens to show up here with a box with Cole Marshall's face in it? Nah, somebody saw us talking to Darnell and they decided to use him to make a point," Titus said.

"What kind of point?" Pip said.

"They know we're after them. And they are daring us to catch them," Titus said. He yawned for a good while and stretched his arms skyward until his back cracked. "Tomorrow I'm going to have to talk to Elias again. And Jasper."

"Hey, why don't you let Douglas take Jasper? I mean, with Marquis fucking up Austin and you making Cotton sound like Candyman, he might get a better reaction," Pip said.

Titus considered it. "Yeah, that's a good idea. I want to know where Jasper was last night," Titus said.

"You think he's the third man, do you?" Pip asked.

"Darnell said he was using Latrell as a mule. He had Cotton smack him around. Sounds like a person of interest to me," Titus said. He didn't tell Pip about Darnell's bribery accusation.

"So, tell me, why didn't you ever run for sheriff, Pip?" Titus asked.

Pip chuckled. "Every time the thought crossed my mind I would come in here and look at Ward and see the way his shoulders were slumped from carrying that weight. No, sir; no, thank you, I don't need those kinds of problems."

"Smart man," Titus said.

Darlene was asleep when he got back to the house. She was spread out across his bed like an invitation. Her body was positioned perfectly for him to slip up behind and wrap his arms around her midsection. When he did, she put her hands on top of his and pushed herself against him.

"You, okay?" she whispered.

"Yeah," he lied.

SIXTEEN

Later that next morning Titus hit the ground running. He got to the office by seven. By seven thirty he was rooting through the evidence locker for Marquis's belt. His had snapped on him when he bent over to tie his shoe. He hoped that wasn't an omen for the rest of the day.

When Carla came in, he sent her to Richmond with the box that had been delivered to the sheriff's station and all the contents therein. He gathered the rest of the crew to give them their marching orders.

"Steve, go back to the fish house. Push 'em hard. Latrell and Darnell and Cole worked there, and now Darnell brings us Cole Marshall's face. I want to know if Spearman had any connection to anyone at the fish house. Don't leave until you get some answers," Titus said.

"Sure thing," Steve said.

"We haven't gotten the official word, but I'm ninety-nine percent sure that's Cole Marshall at the ME's office. Steve, bring his girlfriend up here. I want to talk to her by the end of the day. I told Carla to check his cell phone while she's up there. See who he last talked to or communicated with. Someone got him to go out to Ten Devil's Hop Road," Titus said.

"I wonder if he got set up. That service road is a well-known hookup spot," Davy said.

"How do you know that?" Douglas asked.

"I . . . I mean, I've run some kids off from there before," Davy stuttered.

"I'm just messing with you, Davy," Douglas said.

"Douglas, you go talk to Jasper and Cotton. I want to know where they were last night and when was the last time they talked to Latrell," Titus said.

"Um . . . I have a question," Davy said.

"Go ahead," Titus said.

"So, you said Spearman did . . . things to them kids and the third man did things too. But you said on the videos Latrell was kinda just there," Davy said.

"Yeah, what's your question, Davy?"

"I'm just trying to wrap my head around why was he there? Like, if he wasn't, ya know, getting off to this stuff, why was he even involved?" Davy asked.

Titus put his finger to his lips for a moment before he answered.

"I think Latrell was an extremely damaged young man. I think Spearman and the third man took advantage of that. I think they used him as bait," Titus said.

"Bait? How do you mean?" Steve asked.

"They were two white men. How you think they got close to those kids under the weeping willow tree?" Trey said.

The room went quiet until Titus ended the meeting.

"All right, get on it. We'll meet back up at three P.M.," Titus said. Everyone got up and filed out of the office.

"Hey, Trey," Titus said. Trey stopped and stood by the door.

"Close it," Titus said. Trey did as he was asked and stood in the middle of the floor.

"I know I've put a lot on your plate, with the investigation of the shoot and everything, but I need a—"

"You need a favor," Trey said with a smirk.

"Yeah. I need you to go over to the Citizen Mercantile Bank and go see Fraser Woodall first thing in the morning."

"The bank manager?"

"Yes. This morning I got Mack Bowen to write up a subpoena for the bank records of everyone in the department that participated in raids on the Watering Hole. That's Roger, Steve, Pip, Carla. I need you to look into deposits they made in the week of or before a raid. Look for any larger-than-normal deposits," Titus said.

Trey frowned. "Titus, are you sure you want to handle this in-house? I mean, I'll do it, but I'm still going through the reports for the shooting. You sure you don't want to turn this over to the state police?" Trey asked.

"Not yet. Look, I got you to investigate the shoot because you're smart, thorough, and I trust you. Right now you're the only person I can trust with this."

"You really think one of them is dirty?" Trey asked.

Titus drummed his fingers on his desk. "I hope I'm wrong. But I rarely am," he said.

Titus banged on the church door again. Locked tight. "Elias!" he called, taking the frustration of the morning out on the door one more time.

"Saw you over here the other day. I was hoping you'd come to shut them down," a three-pack-a-day female voice said. "But I haven't seen Elias today."

Titus turned and saw an older white woman sitting on a small porch attached to a single-wide trailer across the slender ribbon of road. Titus pulled off his shades and walked to the edge of the road. "Have you seen something illegal going on over there?"

The woman chuckled ruefully. She ran a hand through her wild mane of white hair that was peppered with brown streaks. Titus walked across the road and put his foot on the bottom step of her porch and leaned on the handrail. He put her around mid-sixties, but her bright green eyes sparkled with a younger woman's audaciousness.

"Those goddamn freaks have been hollering and screaming and

acting like the second coming of the Peoples Temple since I moved here in '89," the woman said.

"Most people on the island aren't come-heres, Ms. . . . ?"

"Griselda. Griselda Barry. I came out here in '89 when I married my husband, Otis Barry. He died in '95. I decided to stay on. If for no other reason, I know it annoys Pastor Cult Leader and his band of merry lunatics. Otis's people were original island folk. They didn't much care for the wild hippie girl he married from West Virginia and the feeling was pretty mutual, but when Otis drowned I kinda got stuck with them. Took care of them both till they went into the Lake Castor Nursing Home over in Red Hill."

"You were a good daughter-in-law," Titus said.

"Shit, I didn't have anywhere to go either. So it was thumb it back to Wheeling or make them soup and help them not to break their hips."

"My father broke his hip last year," Titus said.

"Jesus, it's the worst. You never really get right after that."

"What have you seen over there that makes you think they should be shut down?" Titus asked. His gut was whispering to him that what this former wild child had to say was important. The former FBI agent in him noticed that Griselda had an obvious ax to grind. That was often how crimes were solved. Animus was a great motivator for vigilance.

"Well, they're crazy, everyone knows that. But there's always been terrible shit going on over there. You don't know about the boy who used to live there, do you?" Griselda asked.

"What boy?" Titus asked.

"Hold on, this is gonna take a minute," Griselda said. She pulled a pack of Pall Malls out of the pocket of her tie-dyed hoodie. She pulled a cigarette from the pack and produced a wooden match from her pocket as well. She struck the match against the heel of her brown Hush Puppies and lit her cigarette in a smooth, practiced motion. She inhaled deeply and exhaled two gray plumes of smoke through her nostrils like a dragon.

The breeze stirred the leaves of the blue hydrangeas that surrounded the porch. Griselda crossed her legs.

"Must have been in '88 or '89. Otis was still alive. His parents had a little bungalow just down the road a piece. Every Sunday they would try and get us to go to church with them, and finally Otis convinced me to give in. That was a mistake. You ever been to one of those hooting-and-hollering services over there, Sheriff? It's like watching *End Times, the Musical*. Then they bring out them damn snakes. I told Otis that was my first and last time attending a service at Holy fucking Rock. That Sunday just happened to be the same day Elias and Mare-Beth tried to pass off that boy as their own," Griselda said.

"A boy? He wasn't their child?" Titus asked.

"Fuck, no. Mare-Beth was fertile as a rabbit, but she carried her children heavy. Always gained a lot of weight, then burned it off chasing all those kids or Holy-Ghost-dancing down the aisles on Sundays. But she hadn't gained an ounce before that baby showed up that Sunday."

"Where did they get a newborn from? Did one of their daughters have it?" Titus asked.

Griselda shook her head. "I used to think that, but all them girls take after Elias. Skinny as a rail, and they stayed that way while they was still at home. No, I don't know where that boy came from, but I wish he could of gone back," Griselda said.

Titus sucked at his teeth. "They were hard on him?"

"Huh, that's one way to put it. Or you could say they kicked that boy around like he was a stray dog. I watched them treat him like a redheaded bastard for twelve years. They worked him like he was a goddamned peasant. Made him cut the grass with a reel mower when he was nine years old. Had him painting the steps during the hottest part of the day during the hottest month when he was ten. I made Otis go say something to Elias when I saw him slap that boy across the face for dropping some wire for his crab pots. I even called the old sheriff a few times. But nobody gave a damn about what was happening with island folk. Especially a mixed-race child that was being homeschooled by the goddamn Heaven's Gate." Griselda took another drag off her Pall Mall.

"The boy was mixed? You sure about that?" Titus asked.

"Yeah. They started cutting his hair in a crew cut when it started coming in kinky. In summertime he got what I'd call a deep tan, but that hair gave it away. Drove Elias crazy," Griselda said.

"Yeah, I can see that. Elias doesn't strike me as the most racially tolerant fella around. But that begs the question, where did the boy come from?" Titus asked.

Griselda grunted. "I figure some poor fool girl gave that boy up thinking she was giving him a better life. Boy, was she wrong. Elias is to the right of David Duke. When he isn't hooting and hollering over here at his church, he goes to Charon proper to cry with the rest of the good ol' boys still mourning Lee's ass-whooping. I think if that child had belonged to one of his girls, he would have killed him."

Titus raised an eyebrow. "Really?"

"He talks an awful lot about God and the Bible, but my mama always said the devil can quote the Good Book as well as any angel. And Elias is as close to the devil as I wanna get." She took a long drag off her cigarette.

"Then there was Elias's brother Henry," she said. Her tone was similar to one his father used when he spoke about rats getting into his bird seed.

"What about Elias's brother?" Titus asked. He didn't push too hard. He could tell this was a story Griselda had been wanting to tell for quite some time.

"Henry Hillington was as mean and nasty as one of those snakes they dance with on Sunday mornings. A man like that hates himself and don't know why, so he blames everybody else for the way he feels. He treated that boy worse than Elias did. He smacked him around, called him names, made fun of the way that boy walked and talked so much I hollered at him more than once to just leave him the fuck alone," Griselda said. She stubbed out her cigarette and lit another one.

"But I didn't do or say enough. Nobody did. Nobody looked out for that boy the way they should have. Then Henry started taking him out on the boat to gather the crab pots alone. Just the two of them," Griselda said. Her eyes bore into Titus, saying things she couldn't bring herself to speak aloud. Titus heard the words she refused to say and felt his skin begin to crawl.

"Then one day Henry Hillington got locked in the outhouse out back of the church and got bit by about seven or eight copperheads and water moccasins. Somebody locked him in there and dumped one of Elias's aquariums on top of him. That was in 2000, I think," Griselda said.

"I never heard about any of this. I graduated in 2000, but my Pop never said anything about a murder on the island," Titus said.

Griselda chuckled. "Shit, even the old sheriff didn't give a damn about Henry. Most people in Charon proper probably don't even remember him. And Elias worked hard to make sure nobody actually called it murder. Didn't want Sheriff Bennings over here taking too close a look at his operation, I reckon."

"Was it the boy? Was he the one who did it? Whatever happened to him?" Titus asked.

Griselda expelled another cloud of smoke. "I don't know. After Henry died, he just seemed to . . . slip away. I think he either ran away or they sent him away. If he did run away, wherever he ended up I hope the people there lock their doors at night and keep an eye on their pets."

"But you think he killed Henry? Poured those snakes down on his head?" Titus asked.

"If I'm being honest, Henry was the kind of man that was going to find someone to kill him sooner or later. And the way he treated that child, I ain't waste no tears on him. But that poor boy. The kind of pain they put him through, the hatred they poured into him all in the name of what they called church, well, I don't think one killing would be enough for him, do you? That kind of hurt stays hungry."

Griselda stubbed out her second cigarette. She said softly, "That kind of hurt has to eat."

SEVENTEEN

Titus pulled into his parking spot at the sheriff's office. He pulled out his notepad and wrote down Elias Hillington's name, then wrote, "Missing boy? Murdered?" next to it. If even half of what Griselda had told him was true, then Holy Rock deserved his full attention.

The phrase carved into the skin of those children originated with Holy Rock. The mystery boy who killed Elias's brother happened to be half-Black, according to Griselda. The fact that Elias, a racist, raised and abused a mixed-raced child. The fact that the victims were Black boys and girls no younger than fifteen but no older than seventeen. It felt like all this was connected in ways that he couldn't yet see. But it also felt like everything he'd learned today was significant.

His instructors at the Academy had their own version of string theory. The way they explained it, there were invisible strings that vibrated unseen in the liminal spaces between sunrise and secrets, between rumor, shadows, and lies. Strings that pulled all this together. All you had to do was find the seam and unravel it. Or rip it apart.

As he got out of the SUV, he noticed a van with Indiana plates parked near the entrance. Titus paused midstep. He should have known she was coming no matter what he said.

Titus sighed. That was Kellie's SOP. Ask for forgiveness rather than ask for permission. Of course, this was America; she didn't need his permission to come to the Old Dominion. He just wished she had listened this one time.

"And if wishes were horses, beggars would ride," he mumbled to himself as he entered the station.

She was standing near the switchboard talking to Carla while Davy, Steve, and another man looked on. Davy had more stars in his eyes than the Andromeda galaxy.

Kellie had that effect on some people.

"Oh, hey, boss. We were just talking to your friend here," Carla said. Davy started to inexplicably turn red around his ears.

"Boss? Do you make them call you that, Virginia?" Kellie asked. She looked at him over her shoulder, long dark auburn hair spilling down her back like the colors of autumn personified. He knew under that mane, under that leather jacket she wore, under the shirt was a tattoo that took up most of her back. It was a medieval castle with the words DOUBT THOU THE STARS ARE FIRE across her shoulder blades and NEVER DOUBT I LOVE across the small of her back. Kellie loved Shakespeare. He remembered kissing those words in the dark. Her voice husky with something deeper than desire as she whispered one word over and over.

"Harder."

Titus blinked his eyes furiously behind his shades. He told himself it was the shock of seeing her in the flesh again after two years that ignited that reverie in his mind. He took off his hat and forced himself to not pause as he walked over to Kellie and her audience.

"I don't make anyone say anything. That's not how this office works," Titus said.

Kellie smiled at him. "Titus Crown is never one to overstep his authority," Kellie said with a wink.

He took a deep breath.

She still smoked, but not recently. She knew he hated it, so if his nose was correct, she'd forgone her morning cig. But the pack she had smoked yesterday still claimed its place on her skin and in her hair. His ego told him she skipped that cigarette specifically for him, but the cop in him said she did it to get close to him to convince him to come on her podcast. He found he didn't really mind either way. He had to admit it was nice to see her. To hear her musical laugh. He didn't want her back and he was more than happy with Darlene, but it was still nice seeing Kellie Stoner and her honey-brown eyes all the same.

"That's right, Ms. Stoner," Titus said. Kellie raised an eyebrow a second before bursting out with that laugh. He remembered when they would take turns raising an eyebrow at each other.

Except that one time you did overstep, with Red DeCrain. You sure overstepped with that motherfucker, a voice said in hushed tones inside his mind.

"It's Ms. Stoner now?" Kellie asked. At first, she seemed slightly irritated, then she noticed the slightest curl at the corners of his mouth. "Ohhh, that's a Titus joke. It's such a rare occurrence I forgot what it looked like. Like seeing Bigfoot riding the Loch Ness monster."

"Did y'all really used to go out?" Davy said. It came out in a burst of syllables, like he'd been holding it in for months.

"Let's go in my office. After I talk to Kellie we'll meet, okay?" Titus said. Carla and Davy nodded.

"I mean, it's none of my business, I was just curious, I mean, really—" Davy babbled.

"You're right. It's none of your business," Titus said.

"Year and a half. We dated for nearly two years, then Titus went home. He did do me the honor of breaking up in person. You know you left your Luke Cage T-shirt at my place? I used it for a pillowcase for a long time." Kellie said. She smiled, but it never got past her cheeks. It never got close to her honey-dipped eyes.

Titus felt his heart flutter in his chest. He cleared his throat. "Um, we can talk in my office," he said. He started to put his hand on the small of her back to guide her toward the door, then stopped himself. He pulled his hand back like he was about to touch a hot stove.

"Yes, sir, boss. By the way, are those your party cuffs or your work ones?" she said. She saluted him, then laughed again.

Titus didn't say another word, but headed for the office. When she and the man following her with puppy-dog eyes were seated, Titus tossed his hat on its hook and took his seat on the opposite side of the desk.

"You can't say stuff like that in front of my team."

"Stuff like what? You mean the handcuffs thing? Jesus, Virginia, it was just a joke. We are all adults here," Kellie said. She chuckled a bit, and Titus knew she wanted to say something else sarcastic. Then he would chastise her, then she'd say another sarcastic statement, then, if this were the old days, they would find themselves pressed against each other as she pinned him against the wall.

But this wasn't the old days.

"Speaking of adults, you haven't introduced me to your friend," Titus said.

"Oh, this is Hector. Hector, this is Sheriff Titus Crown, former special agent for the FBI Fort Wayne Office," Kellie said. Hector held out his hand and Titus took it firmly but not with any type of aggression. Hector tried to match his grip, failed, then pulled his hand away.

"Good to meet you, Sheriff. I do all the sound for the podcast."

"Where's your equipment?" Titus asked.

"Oh yeah, it's in the van. Kellie said—"

"I said let's just stop by, because if I called you and asked for a time for an interview, you'd put me off till Judgment Day," Kellie said.

Titus took off his shades. "You would have been right. We have a lot going on, not just the Spearman case."

"But you haven't told us to leave yet," Kellie said.

Titus shook his head. "I can't stop you from talking to people in town. I can't stop you from asking questions. But I can't give you details about a case that I've just started to investigate."

"Then don't. That's fine. Tell me about you. How do you feel finding out a killer has been in your midst all this time? Three killers, to be precise. Tell me how you feel," Kellie said. She had leaned forward and was punctuating her statements by tapping her index finger on Titus's desk.

How I feel? Titus thought. I feel like the Woodsman when he confronted the Big Bad Wolf. I'm going to have to split someone's belly to return us to any sense of normalcy. That's how I feel.

"I know you well enough to give up any effort to avoid an interview completely," Titus said.

Kellie cut him off. "Hector, go get the equipment! You won't regret this, Virginia."

Hector rose from his seat.

"Sit down, Hector," Titus said.

Hector plopped back down in his chair.

"Let's set the parameters first. I'll give you a statement. I'll say a few things about the investigation. And that's it. Do we have an understanding, Indiana?" Titus said.

Kellie smiled. "Of course."

"All right. Now you can go get the equipment, Hector," Titus said. Hector got up and hustled out the door.

"Is he your . . . ?" Titus let the question hang between them.

"Hector? Nah, he's just my sound guy and helps me produce the show. I'm actually seeing a guy who works at my tattoo shop. Were you jealous, Virginia? Anyway, aren't you and Darlene an item?" Kellie said.

"Which one told you? Let me guess, it was Davy," Titus said.

Kellie nodded. "He's so goofy, he's cute."

"Davy's all right, he's just like a mountain climber with no hands. Can't hold shit. And yes, me and Darlene have been together for almost a year."

"Are you happy?" Kellie asked.

"Are you?"

"I asked you first."

Titus leaned back in his chair. "Yes. She's a good woman and I'm lucky to be with her."

"Well, I'm glad for you. Me and Paul are kind of just kicking it right now. We haven't been together long enough to figure out if we're happy or not. But if she is good to you and good for you, I'm happy for you," Kellie said. Their eyes found each other's from across the desk. He was adept at identifying liars. Kellie wasn't exactly lying, but she wasn't telling the God's honest truth either.

That made two of them.

"I—" Titus started to say, when Hector came back into the office.

"We ready to get it on?" he asked with a grin.

Their short interview stretched on into a forty-five-minute conversation. At the end, as Hector was packing up the equipment, Kellie punched him playfully in his arm.

"Damn, you still doing two hundred push-ups every day?"

"Every other day," Titus said as they leaned against his desk.

"Well, before I got distracted by the guns, I was gonna say if you want to hear the edited track, come by our bed-and-breakfast in a few days."

"Y'all staying over at Todd's Inn?"

"Your powers of deduction are truly astounding," Kellie said.

Titus turned his head and saw her smirking. "One of the benefits of small-town living. It's the only bed-and-breakfast in town."

"Well, like I was saying, let me know if you want to hear the audio," Kellie said. Neither one of them said anything for a few minutes. They just watched Hector pack up his cords and microphones.

"It would probably be late," Titus said.

"That's fine. Not like we're going to be running around the Charon downtown district," Kellie said.

Titus walked them to their van. Hector got in the driver's side. Kellie slid in the passenger's side. Titus watched as the window slid down. She leaned halfway out and motioned for him. He took a step closer and crossed his arms.

"It was really nice seeing you, Virginia."

"You too, Kellie."

"I missed you," Kellie said. Titus noticed she used the past tense.

"You deserve better than what I could give you," Titus said.

Kellie kissed her palm and grabbed his hand. "You could never admit how happy we were. You're too committed to punishing yourself for things you can't control." She pressed her palm against his. To any passerby it would look like they were just shaking hands.

"That's . . . that's not what it was," Titus said.

"Sure, Virginia," Kellie said. She squeezed his hand one more time before releasing him. He watched their van move down the road until the taillights were hazy.

EIGHTEEN

Titus sat at his desk with his fingers interlaced in front of him. Steve, Davy, Carla, Douglas, and Trey were all gathered around the other side of his desk.

"Carla, did you find anything on Cole's phone? What did the ME say about the skin in the box and Cole's face?" Titus asked. Carla pulled out her cell. She read from her notes.

"The ME is ready to identify Cole through his dental records. Gonna take a few days to study the section of skin. She did confirm it was Cole's face, but we knew that. Took a look at his phone, and the last call he got was from an extended warranty telemarketer. The last call he made was to a phone number that is disconnected. The last text he got was from Dayane Carter. The message said, *Meet me at our place*, with a question mark and a devil emoji," Carla said.

Titus sat up straight. "Dayane from the fish house?"

Carla nodded.

"Well, that tracks with some stuff I found out today," Steve said. Titus twirled his index finger in a go-on motion.

"So, Lydia Hart told me that Cole and Dayane were pretty tight. She thought he might have been cheating on his girlfriend with Dayane. And get this. She told me sometimes Latrell would go with Cole on his runs. Especially if they had some big deliveries to make. She said she didn't mention it before because she didn't want to get Cole in trouble, but now that everyone pretty much knows he's dead it don't matter much. Also, Jasper and Cotton were up in Dinwiddie at the track last night watching a race with their girlfriends. The girlfriends back them up and Jasper showed me the ticket stubs. He said he hadn't seen Latrell in weeks, but I think he's lying about that, but he wasn't in Charon last night," Steve said.

Titus stood up and came around the front of his desk.

"Okay, he's off the hook for Cole. So, the phrase on the bodies came from Holy Rock. From Elias specifically. I also got a story about a boy who used to live at Holy Rock," Titus said. He recounted Griselda's sad tale about the boy and the outhouse and Henry Hillington's untimely demise.

"Did Cole go to that church?" Carla asked.

"Nah, he went to First Corinthian. We used to be in vacation Bible school together," Davy said.

"Was Cole hooked up with Ricky Sours and his boys? Apparently Elias is tight with that set," Titus said.

"No. He might have agreed with them, but everything I've found out makes it seem like he was too busy with his two jobs to join them in cosplaying as rebels," Carla said.

Davy sucked at his teeth.

"Is there a problem, Deputy Hildebrandt?" Titus asked.

"Uh, no, I . . . I mean, not everyone in that group is a racist. I'm just saying," Davy said quietly.

Titus turned his full attention to Davy. "So, not everyone in the Sons of the Confederacy Cricket Hill Regiment Number 2239 thinks slavery was an acceptable economic system for the South?" Titus asked.

"I . . . uh."

"I'm sorry, let me put it another way. Not everyone in the Sons of the Confederacy Cricket Hill Regiment Number 2239 thinks the rightful place of the negro is to be subservient to the white man, like Alexander Stephens said in the Cornerstone Speech?" Titus said.

"I was just saying, I mean, my cousin is in that group, and he isn't a racist," Davy said.

Titus walked over to his deputy. He stood behind Davy and leaned forward until his mouth was near Davy's ear.

"Davy, if your cousin ain't a racist, he is mighty goddamn comfortable with being around racists. That's a distinction without a difference. Now, can we get back to our meeting, Deputy?"

"Yes, sir," Davy whispered.

Titus went back to his desk.

"Carla, check back with the ME and see if she's made any more identifications. If she has, let's map out where these kids came from. See if it matches up with the deliveries Latrell and Cole went on," Titus said.

"I see where your thinking is going, boss, but if Cole was the Last Wolf, who killed him? A Fourth Wolf?" Steve asked.

Titus sat down again and drummed his fingers on his desk. "No, there were only three people on those videos. I think Cole knew who the Last Wolf was. We need those bodies to be IDed so we can map out their locations. Steve, I want you to keep an eye on Elias. Do it in your off-duty vehicle," Titus said.

"You got it, boss," Steve said.

"How does Elias fit in this?" Carla asked.

Titus spun around and stared at the wall. He had a bulletin board behind his desk. He stood up and grabbed a marker out of his desk and some sheets of paper. He wrote down Elias, Cole, Latrell, and Spearman's names on individual sheets. He pulled down the flyer for the Shad Planking last fall and put the pieces of paper on the board.

"The phrase on the bodies came from Elias. A child he was raising killed his brother. A mixed-race child. So he's person of interest number one. Latrell and Cole made deliveries together, now both of them are dead. Is there a connection between them and Elias? Is Elias the Last Wolf? He doesn't appear strong enough to subdue Cole. Cole was saying he did some work for a guy, that was why he called the hotline. Then he turns up dead. And Dayane Carter is the last text message he got before he ended up dead," Titus said.

"Maybe it's not Elias. Maybe he is covering for someone. Maybe his boys?" Steve offered.

"What?" Titus said. He turned around. Steve repeated his question.

"That's a good point, Steve, change of plan. Pick up Elias first thing in the morning. I want to know who that boy was and what he did with him. Carla, get Dayane Carter up here. I want to ask her why she was asking Cole to meet her on the night he got butchered like a buck deer. All right, we're done here," Titus said.

The deputies filed out of the office. Trey remained in his seat. Titus waited until everyone else was gone, and then he shut the door. He went to his office chair, sat down, and leaned back.

"You were awfully quiet just now, so I'm going to assume you have something you need to tell me about that project I gave you," Titus said.

Trey nodded. "I went by the bank this morning. Talked with the manager and Nadia Manchester, head teller over there. We graduated together," Trey said.

"And?" Titus said.

Trey reached inside his brown blazer and pulled out a sheet of paper. "Per the subpoena I was only given the records of the people on our list. But all of them were clean," Trey said as he handed Titus the piece of paper. "But, to be on the safe side, I had Nadia pull up everyone's records in the department. Including mine, for transparency. Because that wasn't in the scope of the original order, I don't know if it's admissible or if the county attorney is gonna want to pursue it. I mean, it's all circumstantial evidence, but it does match what Darnell told us."

And what Marquis said, Titus thought as he read the figures on the report and the name that was attached to the account.

"How do you want to proceed?" Trey asked.

Titus raised his head. It felt heavy and unwieldy. "Keep this between you and me. Unless we can get Jasper to testify he gave them a bribe, even a shitty lawyer like Vaughn Callis could get this dismissed.

We can't prove the deposits came from Jasper even if the dates line up, but I sure as fuck can fire him," Titus said. His voice quaked on the words "fire him." It did that when his anger was close to its zenith.

"Okay. Well, this makes things trickier with the shoot," Trey said. He got up and headed out.

"Hey, why'd you think to investigate everyone?" Titus asked.

Trey stopped. His hand was on the doorknob. He looked back at Titus. "It's what you would have done if you were in my place," Trey said.

Then he left.

The rest of the day unspooled like wax running down a candle. A tedious series of events that moved like sap down a pine tree in the winter. As the evening came on, Titus gathered his laptop and his notes and put them in a valise he kept under his desk, to take them home. He needed to look at everything in this case again from different angles. He needed to find that seam.

As he was grabbing his hat, his desk phone rang. He hesitated. He could just holler to Cam to tell him to take a message, but that was just wishful thinking. Dodging a call wasn't an option as long as he had that star on his chest.

He put down his hat and picked up the handset.

"Somebody asking for the sheriff, line one," Cam said.

"Got it," Titus said. He pushed line one.

"Sheriff Crown. How can I help you?"

The voice that came through the handset was demonic. Later he would think how it sounded like Mercedes McCambridge's voice in *The Exorcist*. He subconsciously noted that the caller was using a digital voice modulator. An app that could be downloaded for any phone.

"Revelation twenty-one: four," the voice said.

The line hummed between them like a piano wire pulled taut. Titus switched the handset from his right to his left ear. He strained to hear something, anything in the background. Part of him wanted this to be a lonely kid playing a prank. But he knew, without a moment's hesitation, that this was important. The solemnity in that one statement washed away any semblance of doubt in his mind. He didn't know who was on the other end of the line, but the call itself was serious.

"'He will wipe away every tear from their eyes, there will be no more death, no more pain, for the old order of things has passed away.' Is this some biblical trivia game? Is that what you want to tell me? Because we don't have time to tie this line up with foolishness," Titus said in his best cop voice. There was silence on the other end. He didn't hear any other voices or any extraneous sounds like a leaf blower or a car horn. That meant the caller was inside, probably in a room in the center of a dwelling with the door closed and the phone pressed to their face. Titus could see it in his mind like a painting by Caravaggio.

"Tell me, Sheriff, why do you think Jesus didn't extend his hand from the heavens and wipe away the tears of those boys and girls as I carved the words of the Good Book in their skin?"

Titus stretched the cord of the handset to the door of his office and snapped his fingers at Cam. He mouthed the words, *Get this number,* as he pointed at him.

The detail about the phrases being carved on the victims' skin hadn't been made public. Some of his deputies didn't even know about it. He'd been trying to forget it.

This was the Last Wolf speaking.

"Is that what you wanted to happen? Were you testing him?" Titus said. He kept his voice calm as Cam worked the computer that filtered their calls. He had switched from cop to consigliere. This was another thing they taught you in the Academy. No matter how disturbed and perverse your subject, you had to attempt to establish a rapport. Even if it made you want to wash your mouth out with bleach later.

"Genesis nine: twenty through twenty-seven," the voice said.

"The Curse of Ham? Is that your justification for what you and Spearman and Latrell did? Is that why you targeted boys and girls?" Titus said gently. Empathizing with this monster made him physically ill. He could see those poor children and, despite some of them maybe being in their late teens, that's what they were, in his mind, at the mercy of Spearman and this freak while Latrell cried in the background. The images were as sharp as cut glass in his mind.

"Latrell . . . surprised me. I didn't think he had it in him. I think you saved my life, Sheriff," the voice said.

"Sorry, my mistake. That won't happen again," Titus said. There was only so much empathy he could muster.

The voice chuckled. "John ten through twelve."

Titus frowned. There was more silence. Titus knew the verse, but its exact wording danced just outside the reach of his memory.

"Oh, Sheriff, did I finally get you? Let me give you a hint. Will you flee when you see me coming? Will you flee when the wolf comes to devour your flock?" the voice said.

The line went dead.

Titus ran into the lobby.

"Tell me you fucking got it," Titus said.

Cam bit his bottom lip. "It came up restricted. I'm . . . I'm sorry, boss."

Titus rubbed his face. Charon was a small county in Virginia, not a metropolis with a police force that had their own in-house surveillance department. They hadn't ever really needed anything so elaborate, but right now he'd give his left arm for a halfway decent tech squad.

"It's okay, Cam. We're all doing the best we can," Titus said.

Titus went back to his office and called the Bureau of Criminal Investigations, the official name for the state police's special investigatory unit.

"BCI."

"I need to speak with Trooper Geary. This is Sheriff Titus Crown from Charon County," Titus said.

"Trooper Geary isn't available right now; do you want to leave a message?"

"Yeah. Tell him I need to put a trace on my non-emergency number. The killer just called up here," Titus said.

NINETEEN

Titus left the police station and headed out near the county line that buttressed up next to Strayer County by way of the West River. He turned down Griffin Road, then turned down Kingston Lane. There were three houses on Kingston Lane, three modest ranchers that sat in a row with the marsh and the left bank of the West River in their backyards. One house belonged to Cabot Venturis, a chef at the Pax Romana Restaurant, what passed for fine dining in Charon. Another house belonged to Seth and Sueann Sutcliff. Seth was a shift supervisor at the flag factory and Titus thought he remembered someone saying Sueann sold some candles and air fresheners through a multilevel marketing company that was costing her more money than she was making.

The third house belonged to one of his deputies.

He turned down that driveway and passed the white oak trees that lined the exposed aggregate. The trees were bathed in Spanish moss that hung down like the hair of banshees. The afternoon light billowed through the branches and helped to cast dark shadows across his path.

Titus parked next to a red truck and a gray sedan and a jaunty little blue two-door coupe. He got out, straightened his tie, and adjusted his hat before heading for the door. Titus rang the doorbell and waited.

Barbara Sadler opened the door.

"Hello, Titus," she said. Her long blond hair was tied up in a messy bun. She was wearing an old dirty T-shirt and a pair of cut-off jean shorts. She didn't smile at him or ask him to come in. She stood there with her hands on her hips and her mouth set in a tight line. Her demeanor told him she didn't think much of Titus suspending Tom.

"Tom here?" Titus asked.

"He's out back. We been draining the pool," Barbara said. She still didn't invite him inside the house.

"I need to speak with him. Can I come in?" Titus asked. Barbara looked at him like the last thing she wanted was him to walk through the door into her home, but she stepped aside all the same.

"He's on the deck," she said. Titus walked through the living room, through the kitchen, and out the sliding glass doors that led to the deck. Barbara didn't follow him.

Tom was sitting in a wooden Adirondack chair, sipping from a large yellow plastic cup. Titus stood in front of him. Tom took a long swig from the cup. He grimaced, then set the cup down on a table next to his chair.

"How's it going, Titus? Y'all making any headway with the Spearman thing?" Tom asked.

Titus looked down at him. He studied his baggy eyes and his narrow nose full of broken veins. His jaundiced eyes. How long had Tom been an alcoholic? And why hadn't Titus noticed before? Perhaps it was Tom's easygoing manner that had masked his dependency on spirits. Not the holy kind, but the kind that came in a bottle. Tom went along to get along and never made much noise. That helped hide his addiction and his duplicity.

"I'm not here to talk about that, Tom," Titus said.

"You here to take me off suspension?" Tom asked, but even he didn't seem to believe that notion.

"Tom, I know about you and Jasper," Titus said. No use beating around the bush.

Tom grabbed his cup and took it to the head. Light amber liquid dribbled down his scruff-covered chin. He put the empty cup back on the table. "What about me and Jasper? I go by the Watering Hole every now and then. Other than that, I don't know what you're talking about." His voice was barely above a whisper.

Titus took off his shades. He used the temple of his sunglasses to tap the badge on his chest.

"You know this thing here, it's more than a badge. It's a promise. You put this on and you're supposed to be giving your word that you will protect and serve, but more than that, you're promising to do your very best to keep the people you serve safe. Keep their children safe. Their sons, their daughters. Their brothers and their sisters. That's what it's supposed to mean, anyway. That's the dream, ain't it? But when you break that promise, this star becomes a cheap piece of tin and you become a liar," Titus said.

"Titus, what are you talking about?" Tom said. He spoke so low he might as well have been talking to himself.

"You took money from Jasper to tell him when we were gonna raid him. We tried to pop in on him four times in the last year. And all four times in the week before we moved on him you made a huge deposit in the bank. Nine thousand nine hundred and ninety-nine dollars. Just one dollar under the automatic report threshold for the IRS. For a total of forty grand," Titus said. He didn't state it as an accusation but as an immutable fact. Tom studied his empty cup.

"I make twenty-eight thousand dollars a year as a deputy. My daughter wants to go to University of Mary Washington this fall. My wife has had one mastectomy and might need another," Tom said.

"Tom, I'm sorry about Barbara and I hope Allison gets into Mary Washington, but don't sit and tell me your hard-luck story when you pushing a Gladiator truck and Barbara is rocking a Lexus and Allison is in a Mini Cooper as we sit on your twenty-by-twenty deck on the back of your brick house overlooking your in-ground pool. Don't disrespect me like that. At least don't disrespect me any more than you already have," Titus said, thinking of his own off-duty vehicle, an eight-year-old Jeep Wagoneer.

"I'm not saying anything. I'm telling you where I'm at right now. You don't understand. I . . . I got a lot of things on me," Tom said.

"That why you shot Latrell? Because you had a lot of things on you?" Titus asked.

"What . . . Why would say that?" Tom asked.

Titus moved closer to Tom's chair. In the distance a loon sent its love song over the marsh.

"Latrell had seen you at Jasper's. Seen you talking. He knew you were on the take. So, when he came down those steps after blowing Jeff Spearman's head off you saw an opening to get rid of him and make sure he never breathed a word to anyone about seeing you with Jasper. It was just a happy coincidence for you that he was armed and dangerous. You saw an opportunity and you took it. And the fucked up thing is you're probably going to get away with it. The county attorney will never touch you now that you killed that crazy Black boy who endangered the best and brightest of Charon County. You're a hero now, and no one wants to peel back the mask on a hero," Titus said. He leaned forward and put his hands on the arms of the chair. He and Tom were less than an inch apart. Almost close enough to kiss.

"So, I can't put you in jail for first-degree murder, but I can damn sure take that piece of tin and take your gun and make sure you never wear a Charon Sheriff's Office uniform again. It ain't much. In fact, it's just a whore's hair above nothing, but it's how I'm going to fulfill my promise. It's how I keep my people safe. And, Tom? You better not put so much as your pinkie toe across the line from now on. I'm going to be watching you, and if you fuck up just a little bit, I'm going to make it my mission to put you under the jail. You better not even tear the tag off a goddamned mattress," Titus whispered.

He stood up straight.

"You can mail the badge. Drop the gun off tomorrow."

"Titus . . . I didn't—"

"Tom, how many of your neighbors' children ODed because you

was carrying water for Jasper? How many of them are in the fucking ground because you needed a new pool pump? You think about that for a while before you ever try to speak to me again," Titus said.

He went down the steps of the deck and walked back to his SUV through the front yard. He thought he heard Tom sobbing as he walked away.

He caught his father making pork chops when he came through the front door. He could smell the onions and peppers and garlic from the living room. Titus took off his hat and his sunglasses and joined his father in the kitchen.

"What you doing in here, old man? Trying to burn the house down?" Titus said in a deadpan voice.

"Boy, shut your mouth. I'm fixing pork chops for the repast tomorrow," Albert said.

"These ain't for dinner? Pop, you falling down on the job," Titus said.

Albert let out an exasperated sigh. "You think I wouldn't cook for my son first?" There's some in the icebox for you, just gotta heat them up."

Titus went and pulled a plate of pork chops, mashed potatoes, and collard greens out of the fridge. He popped it in the microwave and got a beer while the radiation did its trick. Albert flipped the pork chops in the sizzling grease while Titus sipped. Titus watched as his father's shoulders flexed and then relaxed, then flexed again.

Finally, he turned to look at his son.

"I was wondering, and I know you're busy with all this stuff going on, and I know you ain't much for church, but I was wondering if . . ."

"Pop, spit it out," Titus said, even though he was pretty sure he knew what his father was going to ask. It was written in the slope of his posture, the lines of his face.

"Would you come to Gene's funeral with me tomorrow? He don't have much family, and there probably won't be a lot of folks there, and . . . well, the truth is I could use you there, son. I . . . Gene was one of my best friends." Albert wiped his hands on his apron, then wiped his mouth with the back of his hand, careful to keep the hand he chopped onions with away from his eyes.

Titus sipped his beer. "I don't know, Pop. I'm in the middle of this thing. And I just had to let one of my guys go."

"What? Who?" Albert asked.

"Don't matter. I just don't think I'm gonna be able to go, Pop," Titus said.

Albert turned back to his frying pan and turned down the heat. The sizzling became a light bubbling. He spoke with his back toward Titus.

"I don't ask you for much, son. I know you a man who has responsibilities. Lord have mercy, ever since your mama passed you been responsible as hell. I try not to push, but I'm asking you as your father. I . . . I just was hoping you would come with me. And I thought maybe we could put some flowers on your mama's grave." He sighed. "You know, it's funny. At first you go out there every week. It's all you can think about. Then, little bit by little bit, like a slow leak on a tire, you find yourself going less and less, until one day you look up and it's your anniversary and you realize you're burying your best friend on the happiest day of your life and you haven't been to see your wife since her birthday last year."

Albert paused. "And I don't know if I can do it alone."

Titus sat his beer on the counter. His father was as close to tears as Titus had seen him in a long time.

"Okay, Pop. We'll go. I'll go," Titus said.

Albert took the frying pan off the burner and sat it on the counter. He went to Titus and put his arms around him. "Thank you, boy." He patted him on his back once, twice, three times.

"Now eat your food, I put my foot in them pork chops," Albert said.

———

Later, as he lay in his bed turning the case over in his head like the slow but sure gears of some enormous dieselpunk machine, his phone rang.

"Hello?"

"Hey," Darlene said.

"Hey. What's up?"

"I don't know. Was just wondering what you were doing. Haven't heard from you all day," she said.

Titus closed his eyes. "I know. It's been hectic. I'm sorry. Just a lot going on."

"I wanna come over, but . . . I'm kinda afraid to walk from my house to the car," Darlene said. She laughed, but it was bereft of mirth.

"It's okay. You can come over tomorrow night. I got some stuff to do in the morning, then I'm taking my dad to his friend Gene's funeral in the afternoon. You can come over after that," Titus said.

"I saw Channel Nineteen was in town today. And Wanda Leigh told me some lady is here doing a podcast or something, asking a lot of questions. Was waiting for people coming out the Safeway. I don't know, it's like this ain't Charon no more. Feels like we in a horror movie, except I don't want to be the final girl," Darlene said.

"Hey, so I need to tell you something," Titus said.

The line went quiet.

"Yeah," Darlene said after a few seconds.

"So, that girl at the Safeway? Her name is Kellie Stoner. She came by the office earlier. She's a reporter from Indiana." Titus let the statement sit there between them for a second.

"She was telling people y'all were friends," Darlene said.

More silence.

Titus sighed. "Well, we were more than friends. We dated for a little while. I just wanted you to know that," Titus said.

"Okay."

"You all right?"

"Yeah. I mean, y'all been broke up for a while, right?" Darlene asked.

Yeah, Titus thought. But today when I saw her my mouth went dry and my heart was slamming against my ribs. We used to have borderline-violent sex. To the point I used to feel dirty afterward. But I liked it. And I kinda hate myself for liking it. And there's something wild about her that is alluring and maddening at the same time. And I don't like being wild, feral, out-of-control.

"Yeah. That was all over a long time ago," Titus said.

TWENTY

Titus arrived at his desk by seven the next morning. He was greeted by Cam and a note from the night shift. Mrs. June Baker, an octogenarian with terrible aim, had shot through her window at two kids who lived down the road a piece who'd been knocking on said windows at ten at night. According to Pip, Mrs. Baker thought it was "that boy who killed them children" at her window. The kids were okay, just a little glass in their hair and a little urine in their underwear.

"Medical examiner on line two," Cam said before Titus could set down his coffee. He picked up the phone and cradled it against his neck as he put his valise down on the desk.

"Hello."

"Sheriff, Dr. Kim. Just wanted you to know we confirmed Cole Marshall's identity through dental records and DNA."

"Thank you, Dr. Kim, I appreciate your hard work with all this," Titus said, making a mental note to contact Cole's parents and put a statement on the sheriff's office's social media page.

"Well, as I expect you'd say, it's our job. Also, while I have you, I wanted to let you know we are running tests on the section of skin your office received. Also, we are running DNA on both the samples we found on the bodies and samples taken from the bodies themselves. Using a new technique to make connections through familial DNA. Should have some results by this weekend," Dr. Kim said.

"That would really be some good news. We could use a little bit of that around here."

"Sheriff, I also wanted to tell you we found the same synthetic fibers that are consistent with fibers used in some wigs on Mr. Marshall's body as we found on the remains from the weeping willow tree," Dr. Kim said.

Titus nodded. That confirmed what he had suspected. The Last Wolf had killed Cole Marshall.

"What was Cole's cause of death? I'm assuming it was having his throat slit, but was he alive when that was done? And were you able to identify the kind of knife used?" Titus asked.

"It was a combination of the lacerations to the carotid and femoral arteries. We believe he was alive when the assailant perpetrated the removal of his lungs. We found damage to his hyoid bone. That could have come from either a choke hold or manual strangulation. The knife was probably a wide-blade instrument, like a bowie knife. Extremely sharp," Dr. Kim said. Before Titus could respond, she spoke again.

"The person who did this, Sheriff, they are an incredibly disturbed person. I don't think I'm telling you anything you don't know."

"No, you're not," Titus said.

Titus finished posting the update about Cole on the office's social media page. He'd called on Cole's mother and father at their house an hour ago. As long as he'd been in law enforcement he would never get used to the screams of parents when they realized their child was never going to see the sun again.

Steve knocked on the frame of his open office door.

"Come on in. You pick up Elias?" Titus asked.

"That's what I wanted to talk to you about. I went by there about thirty minutes ago. His wife said he wasn't there. Then one of those creepy daughters blurted out that he hadn't been home for a few days," Steve said.

"Tell Cam to send out a BOLO on him. Pull up his registration and get a description of his vehicle," Titus said.

Steve frowned. "You think he's the guy? You think he ran?"

"I don't know. But I'd rather have him here than not be able to account for him," Titus said.

"I was thinking about something. Elias is, what, sixty-five, sixty-eight? And he weighs a buck-fifty soaking wet. I just can't see him stringing up Cole Marshall between two trees like that," Steve said.

Titus leaned back in his chair. "Yeah, I was thinking the same thing, but I still want to talk to him. The killer using that phrase isn't an accident. Elias said he'd used it for years. He's connected to this; I just don't know how yet."

But I have my suspicions, he thought.

"What about Dayane Carter? She run for the hills too?" Titus asked.

"No, sir, Carla is bringing her in now," Steve said.

"Okay. Get that BOLO out, then go and try to track down Elias's movements. See if anyone saw him last night," Titus said.

"Okay. Hey, boss, we're gonna get this guy, right?" Steve asked.

Titus sat forward. "You think we won't?"

Steve looked down at his feet. "No, I mean, I think we will, it's just, I feel like . . . I mean, do you really think Elias ran, if he isn't the guy? Because Elias doesn't strike me as the type to up and leave town," he said.

"We are gonna get him, but it won't be easy. But the most important things never are. Go put that BOLO out," Titus said.

"Yeah, okay, boss," Steve said.

His old supervisor, Special Agent Tolliver Young, used to say being a good leader was sometimes pretending you were spotless even as the shit was hitting the fan. Things weren't quite that bad yet, but he couldn't afford to let doubt settle into the minds of his deputies. Doubt was gangrenous. Cutting it out was nearly impossible once it started. He wouldn't let that happen here. Finding Elias was now priority number one. The old fire-and-brimstone bastard was tied to all this. His current absence all but confirmed it.

Another knock at the door.

"Boss, got Dayane here. She agreed to come in, but it took some doing," Carla said.

Titus got up from his desk. He grabbed his notepad and a pen.

"Get the case file for Cole. Bring it to the box. I want you to sit in on the questioning. You got her to come in, so maybe she'll feel more at ease with you there," Titus said.

"All right, if you really think it's a good idea," Carla said.

"I do. For her and for you. I know you want my job one day and I wouldn't be doing right by you if I didn't try to give you the experience to get you there," Titus said. He'd never intended to be sheriff forever. He hadn't even expected to win, but now that he'd sat in that chair and worn that badge, he knew he had to do everything to make sure guys like Tom or Roger didn't take over and run the county as their personal fiefdom like Ward and Cooter had.

Carla smiled. "Thank you. I mean that."

"I know you do. Now let's go see what she has to say about Cole getting his face cut off," Titus said.

Dayane was sitting with her arms crossed at the table when they entered the room. She was chewing gum like it was her cud. Titus and Carla sat down, nearly in unison.

Titus thought Dayane had probably been beautiful once. She wasn't hideous now, by any means. But too many late nights, too many long days, had started to take their toll on her. Crow's-feet around the corners of her eyes deep enough to hold a penny, a smile that was yellowed and incomplete. She looked like she had aged five years since he'd busted her and Danny Fields in the parking lot of the Safeway at 3:00 A.M. sharing a hit from some soda-bottle crank. At least she was doing better than Danny. He'd overdosed a few weeks later.

Her thick blond hair was pulled back so tightly in a long ponytail the skin on her forehead looked like it was about to split. She was dressed in a jean jacket and sweatpants. She was also wearing the T-shirt of a band Titus had never heard of called the Dionysus Effect.

"How you doing, Dayane?" Titus said.

"How you think I'm doing? Your girl there comes and drags me out of work and brings me down here. I'm missing time where I could be making money, so I'm not doing so great," Dayane said.

"Well, we are gonna try and get you back to the plant as soon as possible. We just have a few questions for you. Don't worry, you won the shucking contest at last year's Fall Fest, I'm sure you can make up any money you lost," Titus said.

Dayane scowled at him but didn't respond.

Titus pulled an eight-by-ten photo out of the manila folder Carla had brought into the room. He laid it facedown on the metal table.

"All right, I'm not gonna jerk you around. We know you and Cole hooked up from time to time. We don't care about that. What I want to know is, why did you text him to hook up at your regular spot the same night he ends up getting his throat cut?" Titus asked.

Dayane chewed on her bottom lip.

"Y'all got his phone, huh? Ain't no shame in my game. I was trying to get fucked. I texted him, went down to the phone tower, but he never showed up, so I left," Dayane said.

"What time did you go down there and how long was it before you left?" Titus asked.

"I don't know. Like, nine? I waited for fifteen minutes and then I left," Dayane said.

"No," Titus said.

"What you mean, 'no'? That's what happened. The dick was good but it wasn't worth me sitting around all night."

"No, see, Cole didn't leave his house at eight thirty. The service road is ten minutes away. If you got there at nine you would have seen him. You had to have seen him. Try again. Try the truth this time," Titus said.

Dayane stopped chewing. She swallowed the gum while she stared at Titus. "All right, it was probably closer to ten. I get mixed up sometimes."

"Dayane, we found Cole just forty steps off the service road. He was tied to a tree and somebody cut his back to the ribs. They did this to his face," Titus said. He turned the photo over. It was a close-up of Cole's skinned visage.

Titus watched Dayane struggle. She didn't want to look at the photo, but her eyes seemed drawn to it by gravity. Finally, she peered at it, then closed her eyes.

"Why you showing me something like that?" Dayane said.

"Because I know you're lying. Here's what else I know. Cole called up here to tell us about someone he thought might be dangerous. A person he'd done work for with his side job. He told us he partied with this person. That they used to hang out with some girls in a place that had angel art on the walls. I think you're one of the girls. You and Cole and some other folks that we don't know about used to get down at this place. Yeah, you got together at the service road, but that was just for quickies. This place is owned by someone you and Cole trusted. Except after my press conference Cole started thinking about this person. He started thinking about the place with the angel pictures. He called up here but lost his nerve. I think he confronted that person. Then that person asked you for a favor. Get Cole out the house. And you did it and now Cole's dead. Just like those kids under the weeping willow tree. Because the person who killed Cole was the one who killed them too," Titus said. He knew there were holes in his theory, but it held up enough. He'd put it together last night. The fibers from the wig sealed it for him.

"I don't know what the fuck you talking about," Dayane said.

"Dayane, if you know who did this to Cole, your best bet is to tell us now," Carla said.

"I don't know anything, so I can't tell you anything," Dayane said.

"Do you think you're safe?" Titus asked.

"What?"

Titus pulled more pictures out of the file.

"He did this to Cole. Somebody he considered a friend. A friend he shared his secret place with, a friend he shared women with. And he still gutted him like a fish. You think he won't do the same to you? You think he won't take that big-ass bowie knife and slide it across your neck? You know too much. He can't let you live. You tell us his name, and we can help you. You don't, and you might find yourself screaming in the dark," Titus said. He knew his words were harsh, that they were bordering on threatening, but Dayane's resolve was brittle. He could tell by the quick shallow breaths she was taking and the way she was devouring her bottom lip. He had to push her. Because he hadn't been spouting hyperbole. Her life was in danger. If she didn't tell them what they needed to know now, today, the next time they saw her might be on a slab.

"I don't know nothing. If you ain't charging me with nothing, I'd like to go back to work now," Dayane said. She was tapping her left foot so fast Titus suspected it might be a spasm.

"Dayane, are you scared? Because, trust me, no matter how scared you are, it's not nearly enough." Titus spread out the crime scene photos like a deck of cards. "You should be fucking terrified."

Dayane stared up at the ceiling. She wouldn't look at the photos.

"I wanna go back to work."

"Dayane, please think about this," Carla said.

"I said I wanna go!" Dayane screamed. Titus and Carla looked at each other for a moment before Titus nodded. They didn't have anything to hold her on; they couldn't even say she was a material witness.

"Okay, let's go," Carla said. She rose and Dayane rose with her.

Carla opened the door and Dayane followed her out of the room.

"If I was you, Dayane, I'd get something to protect myself," Titus said.

Dayane stopped. "If I was you, I'd worry about catching whoever killed them kids, whoever killed Cole. I'd worry about protecting my own flock."

Titus felt an icicle slide down the back of his neck.

He stood up and followed her out of the room.

"What did you say?" Titus said.

Dayane didn't respond, but Carla stopped walking. Dayane went past her.

Titus caught her by the arm.

"I asked you a question," Titus said. He'd spun her around to face him.

"I just said you should worry about yourself," Dayane said.

"No, you used the word *flock*. What did you mean by that?"

"I don't know. I don't even remember saying it," Dayane said.

"You're lying," Titus said.

Dayane tried to recoil, but he held fast.

"I want you to do me a favor," Titus said. He lowered his voice. "When you talk to him, tell him I'm coming. Tell him I'm going to make him pay for what he did to those kids. And when he slits you open from neck to navel, remember we tried to help you."

He let go of her arm.

"I don't know what you're talking about," Dayane said before heading out the door.

"What's that about?" Carla asked.

"We got a call yesterday from someone who knew details of the case no one besides us and the killer would know. He referenced a flock and how he was the wolf that was going to devour it. Then she says something to me about a flock."

Through the diamond-shaped, reinforced-wire window in the front door of the station, Titus watched Dayane walk out to Carla's cruiser.

"Take her back to work. Then go back by there around the end of her shift. I want to keep an eye on her," Titus said.

"Okay. You really think she knows who killed Cole?" Carla asked.

"Yes, I do. And I think he's the Last Wolf," Titus said.

"If that's true, she—" Carla began, but Titus finished her statement.

"Can lead us to him. Go on, take her back."

Titus left the sheriff's office a little after one to go pick up his father for Gene's funeral. Most days in Charon the roads were chock-full of RVs and lifted trucks pulling cabin cruisers and speed-boats, all set to head down to the river or straight out into the bay. Even this late in the year recreational vehicles and their owners flocked to Charon to squeeze out a few more lazy days of whiskey-fueled shenanigans.

Except today the roads that led to the river were nearly empty. Titus passed a combine with its blades up as he headed to his house. He saw a few locals in pickup trucks and SUVs, but that was about it. Death, that black-clad sentinel, had reaped Charon's tourist season with two swings of its sickle. The first swing was the bodies under the weeping willow. The second swing was Cole Marshall. As much as it pained him, it appeared Scott had a point. Murder had stilled the beating heart of Charon's economy.

All the more reason to find this monster, Titus thought.

He pulled into the driveway, shut off his official truck, and went into the house. His father was standing in the kitchen with a container of pork chops and wearing his old black suit. If it wasn't for the calluses on his hands Titus thought you could be forgiven for thinking his father was a bank president or a lawyer.

"Looking good, old man. I guess it's true about Black not cracking," Titus said.

His father grunted. "Maybe so, but everything else is broke."

"You ready?"

"You gonna wear your uniform?"

"It's got a tie," Titus said. Albert nodded, seemingly content that Titus was actually consenting to going inside a church.

"Let me take that dish," Titus said.

"I got it. You get the string beans and the mashed potatoes. And get the flowers. I put them in the icebox," Albert said.

Titus did as he was bidden. He gathered the plastic containers with the string beans and mashed potatoes, then he retrieved a beautiful bouquet of yellow roses and stargazer lilies out of the fridge. Then he followed his father out the door and to his off-duty vehicle, his Jeep Wagoneer. Titus put the food in the back seat on the floor and the flowers on the back seat proper, then got in the driver's side. His dad grimaced and groaned as he got in the passenger's side.

"You okay?"

"Yeah, just this old hip acting up today. You know that means it's gonna rain later, right?" Albert said.

"All right, Weather Channel," Titus said. His father chuckled.

Titus pulled into the parking lot of Emmanuel Baptist Church and slid in between Bernice Berry's ancient Cadillac El Dorado and Ridley Marks's cherry-red '73 Chevy Chevelle with the black racing stripe. Titus got out of the Jeep and grabbed the food.

"Close the car door, Pop, I'll take these to the kitchen," Titus said.

"All right. I'll go get us a seat," Albert said.

Titus carried the food to the side rear door of the church. One of the deaconesses, Tammy White, saw him at the door and opened it for him.

"Dang, Titus, you didn't want to make two trips, huh?" Tammy asked. Titus remembered Tammy from school. She was five years older than him, but her matronly bearing made her seem much older.

"Pop made this for the repast."

"Here, let me take that from you. It's good to see you. I know you got a lot going on with that Spearman thing. Child, I guess you never know what people doing, do you?"

"People keep their secrets, that's for sure," Titus said. Red DeCrain would have agreed with him if he wasn't already dead.

Titus stopped in the vestibule to take off his hat and his sunglasses. He took a series of slow deep breaths. Kellie had taught him some yoga breathing exercises when they were together. This was the first time he'd used them since they'd parted ways. He felt a flutter in his chest that seemed to envelop his entire body. He recognized he was having what a psychologist might call a mini-panic-attack. This wasn't the first time he'd been in his home church since they'd buried his mother. He'd come here last year, hat in hand, to a Thursday night church meeting to ask for the congregation to mark an X by his name on the ballot for sheriff.

That would make this his second time in his home church since his mother had shuffled off her mortal coil. He went into the sanctuary and found his father sitting in the third pew from the front. Titus squeezed in beside him and took the program with the order of service that Albert offered him. Gene's casket was a deep battleship-gray with black piping. From his seat, he could see Gene in his final repose. He appeared to be in the midst of a not-so-restful slumber. Titus wondered if the body had given the morticians a lot of difficulty, because Gene Dixon was going into eternity with a noticeable scowl on his face.

"Please stand," a deep rumbling voice commanded. Titus followed the rest of the attendees as they stood. The mortician came into the sanctuary leading the minister and Gene's family. Titus recognized Gene's wife. Even if he hadn't grown up running in and out of her kitchen with her sons Gerald and Charlie, he would have recognized the pall that grief cast over her face. The kind of grief only a spouse could carry. He'd seen the same look on his father's face.

Reverend Jackson settled into the pulpit as the morticians closed the casket and the family, Gene's wife, his two sons, his daughter, Rosie, spoke the language of the inconsolable. Howls of anguish that should have made God reach down and touch Gene with the breath of life just to stop their torment.

But he had never seen that miracle, or any miracles, for that matter. And he still carried his own torment deep within the coldest chambers of his heart. In a place where his mother's slack, dead face stared up at him out of the depths like a siren from the void.

As the program progressed, someone turned on all four of the AC window units. Titus knew Emmanuel had one of the larger congregations in the county. On a good Sunday they had to clear at least a thousand, maybe fifteen hundred in the collection plate. Titus thought a church that was bringing in that kind of money should be able to afford a central air unit instead of four rickety ACs that sounded like they all had tuberculosis. They should also be able to afford some better pews. And new vinyl siding.

Titus couldn't help but notice Reverend Jackson's ornately embroidered black robe or his brand-new Lexus parked in the spot reserved for the minister. It seemed like Reverend Jackson got a new car every year. Perhaps that was the miracle that confirmed the true believers' faith.

Or maybe Reverend Jackson took advantage of a congregation bound so tight to the old church at the fork in the road by tradition and tribulations that they closed their eyes and turned their heads from the red in the church ledger. Perhaps they thought the red would change to black like the water turned to wine. Meanwhile, Reverend Jackson lived in one of the biggest houses in the county.

Hallelujah, Titus thought.

As the service came to an end, Albert nudged Titus.

"Hey, when they take the body out, go get them flowers," Albert whispered.

"I'll get them, Pop."

"God, I'm gonna miss Gene, but I'll see him again. Yeah, I'll see him again," Albert said. He wiped at his eyes.

Titus kept his own counsel on the subject of the afterlife.

Titus watched as the pallbearers walked the casket over to the grave. His father winced as they walked down the front steps of the church.

"You sure you don't want me to help you get over to the grave?" Titus asked.

"You can help me when I'm dead. I'll be okay, boy. Get them flowers."

Titus went and retrieved the flowers from his Jeep. He stood back from the crowd gathered around Gene's grave lest someone think his flowers were for Gene. The clouds gathered like young men on a corner getting ready for a fight. The first drops of rain began to fall and splattered on the brim of his hat. Titus could hear the sobbing of Gene's family begin to ebb.

As the crowd dispersed, Titus made his way to his mother's grave. He stood at the foot of Helen Crown's final resting place, waiting for his father to come over and join him. Titus saw Reverend Jackson talking to his father. Even from a distance he could tell his father wasn't happy about the conversation.

Titus made his way over to the two men.

"So, I think that's for the best," Reverend Jackson said. His voice was deep as a coal mine.

"What's for the best?" Titus asked.

"Oh, hi, Titus, good seeing you even if it's under these sad circumstances, brother," Reverend Jackson said.

Titus ignored the pleasantries. "What's for the best?" he asked again.

"Reverend Jackson thinks that since it was just me and Gene

doing the church garden and now Gene's gone, we should raze the garden so the church can sell the land," Albert said.

Titus had never heard his father sound so defeated.

"The land right over there, behind the graveyard, you want to get rid of the garden and sell that, to who? Who's going to buy a quarter acre near a cemetery?" Titus asked.

"Titus, the church just thinks it's for the best. There are many, many things we can do with the money from the sale of that land," Reverend Jackson said.

"Like get you a new car?" Titus asked. Reverend Jackson and Albert both stared at him.

"I beg your pardon?"

"Beg all you want; you won't get it. My father and Gene and Mrs. Jojo Ware built that garden from nothing long before you came in here with your five hundred suits. How many families have they kept from starving? How many people have they kept from robbing the 7-Eleven to get enough money to feed their families? And now you want to sell it? I wish Jesus was real so he could chase you down the aisle with a goddamn whip," Titus said.

"Son, watch your mouth!" Albert said.

"Nah, Dad, this crook needs to watch his. How about this? How about at the next church meeting I come and make a motion to have a forensic accountant go over the books and audit all the church's accounts? See if we really need to sell that land."

"Well, for a member that doesn't attend regularly, you sure seem to have a lot to say about how I run my church," Reverend Jackson said.

Titus stepped forward, brushing past his father until he was towering over all five-foot-six of Reverend Jackson.

"This isn't your church. You just stand in the pulpit," Titus said.

Reverend Jackson stepped backward, stumbled, and almost fell against a headstone. "Deacon, we'll talk about this later," he said. He weaved his way among the stones as the rain began to intensify.

Titus went back to his mother. Albert joined him.

"Titus, I know you . . . ain't a fan of the church, but you didn't have to talk to the pastor like that. I think . . . maybe he's right. You was even worried about me the other day," Albert said.

Titus laid the flowers across his mother's grave.

"That building over there ain't the Church. All that is sticks and stones and vinyl siding. The Church is what you and Gene was doing. I might not believe in it, but I can recognize it. Don't you ever let that con man convince you otherwise, Pop." Titus put his arm around his father.

"You remember Mama's favorite Bible verse?" Titus asked.

"Psalm thirty-seven, verse twenty-five," Albert said quietly.

"'For I have been young and now am old but I have never seen the righteous forsaken nor his seed begging for bread.' You're the righteous, Pop. Because of you, a lot of people have never had to beg for bread," Titus said.

They stood there together side by side for a long time. Any tears they shed were hidden by the rain.

TWENTY-ONE

The rain was coming down in sheets by the time Titus turned down the road to their house. He had his lights on and his windshield wipers on high as he pulled into the driveway.

Titus put the Jeep into park. As the wipers moved back and forth in a robotic staccato rhythm, Titus saw a flash of color on their front door between the blades.

A flash of red that was streaming over the panels of the fiberglass door. Titus shut off the wipers. For an instant, before the rain splashed across the windshield, he thought he saw the source of the red streaks.

"Pop, stay in the car and call 911," Titus said.

"What . . . what is that on the door?" Albert asked as he squinted.

"Pop, lock the doors when I get out."

"Titus, what is that?"

"Lock the doors, Pop," Titus said. He climbed out of the Jeep and drew his gun. The rain was coming down sideways, but as he got closer the door became clearer. Titus used a tactical grip, right hand over his left wrist, as he aimed at the door. He moved to the corner of the house and secured the backyard. There was nowhere for anyone to hide there unless they buried themselves in the woodpile. He went back to the front door. He holstered his gun and put both hands on his hips.

A white lamb, its throat cut with one smooth slice, had been nailed to their front door. The nail was really a tent spike. It went through the poor creature's eye and out the back of its head and into the door. The blood had stopped flowing from the wound, but the wind had driven the rain up into the porch and mixed with the lamb's vital fluids and spread them across the door.

Titus swallowed hard.

The Last Wolf had been to his house. He'd left him a message. But not the one he thought he'd communicated. He thought he was frightening Titus. He was mistaken. Hanging that lamb from his door told Titus the Last Wolf was anxious. He might even be spiraling. When organized killers became volatile, they made mistakes. Like this lamb. Titus was willing to bet it came from River Oak's petting zoo. He knew they had security cameras. This poor creature had lost its life, but, much like sacrifices in the years of antiquity, a blessing might soon manifest from its spilled blood.

The fact that his home had been attacked, that a man who had killed children, boys and girls, had killed Cole Marshall, had killed a baby sheep just to make a point, had literally brought the fight to his front door, well, that fact had to be shoved aside for the moment. He had to use this. He could be angry and afraid another time.

Twenty minutes later the yard was full of vehicles, both police and personal. Red and blue lights blazed through the rapidly encroaching darkness. The lamb had been placed in a biohazard bag. Douglas, Carla, and Davy were canvassing the neighborhood, asking folks what they had seen or heard. Pip and Trey were helping Titus clean the door. Steve was off, but he'd called. They had all come by or checked in with him. He definitely appreciated that.

"You don't have a Ring camera, do you?" Trey asked.

Titus shook his head. "My pop doesn't like tech stuff and, frankly, I didn't think we needed it."

"Well, Cory over at River Oak confirms someone broke in and grabbed one of their lambs. He noticed the fence had been cut this morning, so he did a head count," Pip said as he put his cell back in his pocket. The rain had subsided, but the air was still saturated with moisture. Titus felt like he was walking through a mist.

"Get the lamb to Richmond. Go ahead and dust the door for prints, but I doubt they left any. Somebody take my pops over to my brother's house," Titus said.

"Um, about that. He says he ain't going nowhere," Trey said.

"Yeah, he's pretty adamant," Pip said.

Titus sighed. "I'll talk to him. And who's watching Dayane?" Titus asked.

Pip and Trey exchanged a glance.

"Guys, don't tell me no one is on her. And what about Elias?" Titus said.

"Boss, soon as we heard about Mary's Little Lamb, we all came over to check on you and your dad," Trey said.

"I appreciate that, Trey. But Dayane is our way to the killer. Following her and finding Elias are the ways we finish this. Let me go talk to my pops," Titus said. He tried not to be too hard on them. Not every leader got a team that cared for him the way most of his deputies did. For that he should rise up and be grateful. But that didn't mean they could forget the case. He was glad for their concern, but he was still alive. The dead needed their full attention.

"Pop, you need to go over to Marquis's house for a little while," Titus said. His father was sitting on a stump near the woodpile while the deputies went about their work in the front yard.

"Titus, I've slept on my side of the bed for thirty years. This crazy man ain't gonna make me change that," Albert said.

"Pop, I'm trying to look out for you," Titus said.

"And I'm grateful, son, I really am. But I got a 1911 Colt that belonged to my daddy. I'll get him to keep me company tonight. But I ain't leaving my house." For a moment the years were washed away and Titus saw the old Albert, full of piss and vinegar and not about to move for anyone.

Titus put his hand on his father's shoulder.

"Okay, Pop. We'll stay."

"Titus!" a voice yelled from the shadows. Titus turned and saw Kellie and Hector trying to get through his deputies, who had formed a phalanx to cut them off. He hurried over to the commotion.

"Kellie, what are you doing here?" Titus said.

"We have a scanner. Are you okay? Can you tell us anything? Do you think this was the killer?" Kellie said. She was holding a thin wireless microphone. Her tone was professional, but her eyes were wide and red around the edges. She was scared for him. He didn't need to hear her say it.

"Kellie, go back to Todd's Inn. I'll talk to you later, but right now y'all just getting in the way."

"You heard him, miss," Carla said. She gave Kellie a gentle push on her shoulder.

"Don't touch me!" Kellie said. Rage, as hot as the slag from melted metal, filled her face.

Titus stepped up and got between them. "Kellie, please go. We'll talk later. I promise."

"You might want to teach J. Lo about the first amendment, Titus," Kellie said as she and Hector made their exit.

"What did you call me?" Carla said, but Titus cut her off as she started to walk toward Kellie.

"You ever want to sit where I sit, you have to get a thicker skin, Deputy," Titus said.

"I don't know what you saw in her," Carla said.

Titus sighed.

"That's a long story, Deputy," he said.

Douglas, Carla, and Davy talked to everyone on Titus's road. No one saw anything. Most people were out running errands or at work. Trey went over to River Oak and reviewed the tape, but he called Titus to tell him that the video quality was extremely poor. All it showed was an individual, in a hoodie and a ski mask, wearing gloves cutting a hole in the fence with tin snips and then taking the poor lamb. Without enhancements there was no way to tell if it was a man or woman, tall or short, white or Black. Titus told Trey to get the tape and they would send it to the BCI in the morning. After that there wasn't really anything else for the deputies to do, so most of them went back on patrol or went home. Carla went to check on Dayane. Davy went out to the island to see if Elias had returned.

"You want one of us to sit in the driveway?" Pip had asked.

"No. If he comes back, I'll meet him on my own terms," Titus said. He knew that sounded menacing, but the reality was he didn't want to endanger his deputies if it could be helped. This person, the Last Wolf, the Angel of Death, was falling apart. Titus figured he would do something chaotic soon. Something in his mind was apocalyptic. Pip deserved to retire, not get caught up in some madman's death wish.

So Titus sent everyone to their homes or their duties.

Now he was sitting on his porch with his Jameson and his riot gun across his lap. The clouds had vacated the premises and long-dead stars littered the night sky with phantom light. Frogs, crickets, and night jays competed for his attention. He didn't sleep much on a good night, so he fully expected to be awake until the sun rose. Here in the dark with his father asleep cradling his own pistol, the horror of what had happened finally settled into his bones.

Titus had no one to blame but himself. He'd challenged the killer, sent a message through Dayane, and he had responded. He always told his deputies to never let the job get personal, but it was beginning to feel downright intimate between him and this abomination.

Titus pulled out his phone and called Darlene.

"Are you okay?" she said when she answered.

"We're fine. I was calling because I didn't want you to worry."

"I'm not worried. I'm scared to death."

"It's fine. Everything going to be fine," Titus said.

"Titus, someone nailed a goat to your door," Darlene said.

A lamb, but I guess that belongs to the ages now, Titus thought.

"I know. It's going to be fine, but I think we need to be cautious. I don't think you should come over tonight or for a while."

"How long is a while?" Darlene asked.

"Just for right now. We're going to catch him, but for right now, well, I'd never forgive myself if something happened to you," Titus said.

"And I don't know what I would do without you," Darlene said.

"You're not going to have to find out. I just want you to be safe, okay?" Titus said.

"I love you, Titus," Darlene said.

"Me . . . I love you too."

"Call me in the morning. I'm so stressed I took a sleeping pill and I'm about to pass out," Darlene said.

"Okay. Sweet dreams."

"You too, Smokey."

He hung up the phone.

Titus took a sip from his bottle. He closed his eyes and visualized the case as a jigsaw puzzle. He visualized himself putting the pieces together. Elias had gone missing after Titus had talked to him. Cole Marshall had died. Dayane knew the name of the person they had partied with, the person who had killed Cole and those kids. Now Elias was missing. What if Elias wasn't the killer? What if he was the motive? Or, more accurate, the genesis? Was he a part of the killer's origin story? Griselda had said that wherever that boy had ended up she hoped the people were locking their doors at night.

What if that place was Charon?

What if the boy had come home and had become the Last Wolf?

Titus took another sip. His mind didn't feel dulled by the alcohol. If anything, it was like it sharpened his thoughts.

Say the boy that Elias and his church had abused had come back to Charon to live. But he's got this pain in him. A ravenous pain. He meets Spearman somehow and they realize they have the same prurient interests. Or similar interests. Somehow Latrell becomes a part of it and that's their mistake. Now the boy is settling old debts and tying up loose ends as he spirals down into his own personal black hole. His two acolytes were dead. His mission, his war with God, had been thwarted. Titus was convinced that was what this was all about.

"They cracked something inside you, didn't they? And now it's shattered," Titus whispered.

Titus took another sip.

That meant Elias was probably dead. He was waiting on Carla to call him, but if Dayane was missing that meant she had skipped town or was dead too.

Titus opened his eyes.

He called Trey.

"Yes, sir," Trey said.

"In the morning, go to the judge and get a warrant for Cole Marshall's business files. I know he had a contractor license, so that means he was paying taxes. If he took cash for building that place he talked about for his friend, we're shit out of luck. But if the friend paid with a check, he had to make a record of it. We cross-reference his customers with people who could fit the profile. A physically strong white male, twenty-five to thirty-five, with enough land to build a fancy man cave or something close to it," Titus said.

"That's a good idea, boss. Will do first thing in the morning. Hey, I know this might be a bad time, but how'd that other thing go?" Trey said. Titus could hear a woman's voice in the background. Trey was trying to keep their conversation confidential.

Titus thought he'd make a good agent if that was what he wanted.

"I took care of it."

"Well, good enough, I guess. I'll take care of that thing first thing in the morning," Trey said.

"Good night," Titus said.

He took another sip.

Even with all that he'd seen, all the things he'd done, the image of that lamb hanging from his door haunted him. Children and animals were easy targets. Neither had learned to be wary of good intentions and sweet words.

TWENTY-TWO

Preston Jefferies often wished he could control the weather. The Farm Bureau said they were technically no longer in a drought, but his electric bill for his irrigation system begged to differ. His corn had taken forever to mature and ripen for the fall harvest this year despite the twelve thousand dollars he had sunk into said irrigation system. Here he was in the third week of October finally getting ready to fire up his combine and try to equal last year's yield. He wasn't going to beat it. That bus had left town a long time ago. But if he kept his yields close, he would still qualify for that grant from the state. His was one of the few Black family farms in Southeastern Virginia, and those grants helped stanch the bleeding when they lost out on big ethanol contracts or when feed producers tried to lowball them.

Preston thought capitalism was great if people who looked like you were the ones sitting in the Capitol. For everyone else, well, sometimes it was like trying to climb a greased pole in mittens.

Preston started his combine. The 268-horsepower engine roared to life. He pressed the accelerator and drove it out of the three-wall shed where he stored it. The sun was slowly peering over the edge of the horizon. Despite the long days, the aches and pains, the uncertainty, a morning like this reminded him why he kept making his living in the dirt. Running a farm was a distinct act of will. He pulled his livelihood out of the soil through sheer determination. Yet that act connected him to the earth, to his father and his father's father.

This farm was his legacy. Hopefully it would be his two sons' legacy as well.

Preston drove to the far end of the cornfield and started the harvest. He hummed to himself as the combine stripped the corncobs from the stalks and dropped the stalks back to the ground to help contribute to the next planting season. His humming became an old R&B song he had sung to his wife at their wedding reception. "Always" by Atlantic Starr.

Preston made it to the end of his field. His farm was small when compared with farms in the Midwest, but he worked the land with a practiced eye and a determination to maximize his production. He turned and headed back the other way. Preston was about to hit the high note that had made his wife tear up when he saw a strange object in the middle of his cornfield.

He pulled the hand brake.

Preston climbed down out of the combine.

"Jesus Christ," Preston said when he got close enough to see what was in the middle of his field.

Titus stood in front of his bulletin board staring at the sheets of paper pinned to it with thumbtacks. Carla had given him the bad news when he had arrived at the office.

"I went back to Dayane's place. Her car was gone and her roommate said she packed a bag and didn't say where she was going or when she'd be back. I parked across the street for a couple of hours to see if she came back, but she never did," Carla had said. Titus didn't reprimand her. They had made a mistake and now they had to adjust.

He had added a sheet of paper with Dayane's name on it to the board.

Steve sent word that Elias still hadn't come home.

"Ask his wife about the boy they raised. Ask her about Elias's brother and see if she has any pictures of the boy, if she knows where he is. It seems like he was the product of an illegal adoption and he was homeschooled. So we don't know what he looked like then or what he might look like now," Titus had said.

"You think that boy grew up to be the Last Wolf?" Steve had asked.

"It fits. There are some holes, but it fits. Ask about those pictures," Titus had said.

Trey knocked on the door of his office.

"Come on in," Titus said.

"I checked out Cole's records, if that's what you want to call them. He did most of his side work in cash. And the work he didn't do for cash was for old folks. Like clearing a field or bushhogging. I asked his girlfriend did he ever talk about building a man cave or a big shed for someone, but she said he didn't talk to her about work. I think we struck out," Trey said.

"Well, it was worth a shot," Titus said.

Titus turned to look at the board again. "Let's go over what we think we know. The killer is a friend of Cole Marshall's. He's a friend of Dayane Carter's. He's a local. He might possibly be a boy who was abused out at Holy Rock who killed his play uncle. He got to know Spearman well enough that they shared their dirty little secrets. He was able to get these kids, some of them fairly street smart, to get in a vehicle with him. That was where Latrell came in. Cole and Latrell and Dayane all worked at the fish house."

"Maybe we should go back to his girlfriend and ask her who he was tight with. She should know who his drinking buddies are," Trey said.

"Yeah. Do it. You know, I saw Cole having dinner with his girlfriend and a boy named Dallas Processer and his wife. Ask her how close Cole and Dallas were," Titus said.

"Dallas? I don't know," Trey said. "He was behind me in school. All he ever wanted to do was drive his daddy's dump truck. He was just as quiet as a mouse. I can't see him doing this."

"The mask, Trey. We all wear a mask. Ask how close they were."

"Okay. Can we talk about the shoot?" Trey asked.

Titus turned around and faced him.

"Go ahead."

Trey cleared his throat.

"Well, I looked at the reports, and I looked at a bunch of the videos that are online. I talked to some of the kids and saw their videos. Titus, I've looked at this thing six ways to Sunday, and I can't say this was a bad shoot even with what we know about Tom. He came at y'all with a gun in his hand. I'm not a fan of Roger's, and Tom is suspect as hell, but I think they are in the clear. I'll send you a copy of my report," Trey said.

"You're sure? I don't want you just saying that because it's our department," Titus said.

"You taught us better than that," Trey said.

Titus nodded. He would always have his own doubts, but the truth was the badge would protect them. Latrell had been carrying a gun. He'd killed someone. He'd participated in the killing of children. The Jamal Addisons of the world might lament his death, but for most he was just a problem that had been solved. That was the narrative that would take hold. The details be damned.

Whoever controlled the narrative controlled the truth.

That was another lesson he had learned from Red DeCrain.

The desk phone rang. He didn't wait for Kathy to tell him what line it was. He just grabbed it and answered.

"Sheriff Crown."

"Sheriff, Dr. Kim."

Titus switched the handset to his left ear.

"Yes, Doctor."

"We were able to identify four more of the victims through dental records and DNA. The other victims are still unknown. Would you like their information to make the notifications?" Dr. Kim said.

"Email me that. Doctor, where were the rest of the victims missing from?" Titus asked.

"Let's see here, well, of course you know about Baltimore, then we have Columbia, South Carolina; Hillsborough, North Carolina; Wilmington, Delaware; and Philadelphia, Pennsylvania." Dr. Kim rattled these locations off with detached efficiency.

"Do you have the approximate dates they were reported missing?" Titus asked. He pulled out his notepad.

"Yes. The Columbia victim was reported as missing June twenty-first, 2013; Hillsborough victim was July thirtieth, 2014; Wilmington August first, 2015; and Philadelphia was June tenth last year. The Baltimore victim was in 2016. Now, the unidentified victim is the most recent. We are going to try and do a facial reconstruction."

"Thank you, Doctor," Titus said.

"Sheriff, there's something else," Dr. Kim said.

Davy burst into Titus's office. He didn't bother knocking on the door. He stood in the center of the floor breathing like a pony.

"Titus, you gotta come. They found another body, in Preston Jefferies's cornfield. You gotta come, it's bad, it's fucking bad!" Davy said. The words came out in rapid succession like a string of firecrackers.

"Doctor, I have to go. Send me the rest of the info in an email," Titus said.

"Sheriff, I really think—"

"I'm sorry, Doctor, I have to go. We got another body," Titus said. He hung up the phone and jumped from his chair. He grabbed his hat and followed Davy out the door.

He's playing with us now, Titus thought. The wind blew through the cornstalks, making them chatter like teeth. There was a strange scent in the air that was an amalgamation of the stench of the wet earth, the acrid chemicals Preston used to fertilize his crop, and the body itself.

"Who put the sheet on him?" Titus asked.

"Preston. He called 911, then said he didn't want to leave the body alone but he couldn't stand looking at it either," Pip said.

Blood had soaked through the white sheet, creating abstract expressionist drawings. Titus looked down at the soil. It was a mess of footprints from Preston and Pip and Steve and whoever else came up here to gaze at the body. Most likely the killer's footprints had been trampled under their slow stampede. The road was about four rows over. Titus could hear cars zipping by, but he also heard the sound of gravel being crushed under the wheels of vehicles that had pulled over to get a better view of the proceedings.

Titus pulled on his latex gloves and pulled off the sheet.

"Goddamn," he whispered.

Elias Hillington had suffered.

His body was naked as the day he was born. A wooden stake, about as big around as a baton, had one end shoved in the dirt. The other end was shoved in Elias's anus. It was what was keeping the body upright. Flies buzzed around the body, playing electric blues on their translucent wings. The past few days had been unusually warm. While Cole Marshall had been spared the indignity of flies crawling across what was left of his face, Reverend Elias received no such consideration.

THERE IS NO ESCAPE FROM THIS SAVAGE PLACE.

The words were carved in Elias's chest. From what Titus could see, that was just the beginning of the hell he had suffered. There were dozens of slashes on the body and across the face. Elias's belly had several deep puncture wounds consistent with a bowie knife. There were nails driven through the palms of his hands. His penis had been flayed.

Titus swallowed hard and stepped closer to the body. The smell was horrid. A mix of vomit and shit that enveloped the remains in a noxious cloud. Titus reached out his hands and grabbed the man's chin. There was something in his mouth. Titus gently pulled down on the chin while pulling up on the nose.

A dead rat snake slid out of Elias's mouth.

Titus took two quick steps backward.

"'The Lord is my shepherd, I shall not want,'" Davy said.

"'He maketh me lay down in green pastures,'" Pip said.

"'He leadeth me beside the still waters,'" Steve said.

Soon all three of them were chanting the rest of the Twenty-third Psalm in unison.

Titus didn't join them.

God wasn't here. This was the devil's work. And the devil was a man.

Titus went back to the office while Reverend Elias Hillington's body was taken to Richmond. Pip volunteered to do the notification.

"Once upon a time I went to school with Mare-Beth. She might take it better from me," he'd said before heading out to the island.

Titus locked the door to his office and then sat down in his chair. He was in a race against time. The Last Wolf was spiraling out of control, but in doing so he was taking lives with him. Titus silently chastised himself for calling him the "Last Wolf." He'd given him a name after all. He'd solidified his status as a myth without even realizing it.

Titus rubbed his face with both hands. This all but confirmed the killer was the little boy Elias and his family had abused for all those years. Titus did some quick math. If he was twelve in 2000, then he was around twenty-nine or thirty now. Titus closed his eyes and examined his mental photographs. He tried to think of all the faces he saw every day. He tried to visualize a mixed-race man around thirty years old. Was he passing for white? Was he someone who had positioned himself outside of Titus's standard social circle? Was that why his face was just a blur in his mind?

His door erupted in heavy-handed knocks.

"Titus, open up, we need to talk," Scott Cunningham yelled from the other side of the door.

Titus pinched the bridge of his nose. Hard.

He got up and opened the door. Scott swept into the room with his chest puffed out and his usual air of superiority now a gale-force wind.

"What do you want, Scott?" Titus said.

Scott sat down without being asked and crossed his legs.

"Titus, I think it's time to admit this thing has gone on too long and it's out of your control. Now we've lost a member of the clergy! Not to mention how tourism has fallen off," Scott said.

"I'm glad you have your priorities straight," Titus said.

Scott grinned. It made Titus think that someone somewhere was missing their canary. "Titus, I've told you time and time again I'm not your enemy. I just want what's best for Charon. My family has been here since the county was founded. But I think we both know what's happening now is beyond your skill set. Now, I contacted the state police, and they said—"

"You did *what*?" Titus said. His voice rose like a tidal wave.

"The state police. I asked them to come in and take over this case. Now, they said the only way they could do that is for you to request it because you're the sheriff. And, Titus, you are going to request it. I don't think I'd have a hard time getting that recall now," Scott said.

He hurled the threat with delight, but in that moment Titus suddenly realized he didn't much care about recalls and motions. He just wanted to catch this killer. Maybe . . . maybe it was time to let the state police come in. Not to take over, but to take the lead and bring the full weight of their resources to the party.

"'Humility is not thinking less of yourself. It's thinking of yourself less,'" one of his instructors had said at the Academy. It was years later when Titus realized he was quoting C. S. Lewis, but that didn't make the statement any less true.

He was just loath to humble himself at the feet of Scott fucking Cunningham. But if the state police could stanch the flow of blood flooding Charon, then maybe he should prostrate himself all over his goddamn wing tips.

"Scott, I think—" Titus started to say, when an alert buzzed on his cell phone.

"Titus, this isn't really about what you think anymore. As chairman of the Board of Supervisors it's my duty to do what's best for Charon. And right now, you're not it," Scott said. He tried to appear tortured, but he couldn't quite bring it off properly.

Titus's phone pinged again.

"You want to get that so we can finish this conversation?" Scott said.

Titus felt his temper rising like his voice had a few moments ago, but he tamped it down and checked his phone.

He had an email from Dr. Kim. It was marked IMPORTANT/ CONFIDENTIAL.

Titus began to read it as Scott went on gibbering about the honor of Charon and how it was not to be besmirched.

Sheriff,

I ran the DNA sequence through the CODIS. Unfortunately, we didn't get any hits. I also took the extra step of contacting several online genealogical companies in an effort to run a comparative familial DNA sequence. Sheriff, we got a hit on one of those.

Titus read the rest of the email.

He sat his phone on the desk.

He leaned forward and put his hands flat on his desk.

"I assume we have an understanding, Titus? If you don't mind, I'd like to be here to make sure you do actually call and make that request with the state police," Scott said.

Titus steepled his fingers.

"Scott."

"Please don't make this any harder than it already is, Titus," Scott said.

He then launched into another long harangue that Titus thought sounded like bricks in a washing machine. Sound and fury signifying nothing but one man's insecurities.

"Scott, look at me."

Scott stopped talking long enough to see the fire in Titus's eyes. The ferociousness that erupted in the eyes of a predator when it was closing in on its prey.

"Scott. Tell me about your half brother."

Cunningham's brow folded in on itself with deep furrows.

"What the hell are you talking about, Titus? This some ploy to keep your job? Because I assure you it won't work."

"We're not talking about me anymore. I know your sister, Alanna; I never knew you had a half brother," Titus said.

"I don't have a half brother, goddamn it!" Scott said.

"Yes, you do. On your mama's side. That message was an email from the ME. She ran the DNA we found on the body through some online genealogical services. She found a hit. Last year you sent your DNA to TheFamilyTree.com. The ME found it shares several significant markers with the DNA sample she sent in. Maternal markers. Now, I'm gonna ask you again, tell me about your brother. Because he's the one who helped Spearman kill those kids. He killed Cole Marshall and Elias Hillington. If you really care about Charon, tell me his name," Titus said.

"We did the DNA thing for Mom's birthday. She always said we were related to some Mayflower folks. We aren't," Scott muttered.

"Scott, tell me his name," Titus said. He said each word slowly.

"I don't know! I don't have a half brother!" Scott yelled.

"DNA says otherwise. See for yourself," Titus said. Was there a hint of satisfaction in his voice?

Perhaps.

He slid his phone across the desk toward Scott. He watched the chairman read the email as his lips moved. Scott put his head in his hands. He was hyperventilating.

"Scott, calm down. You're gonna make yourself sick. I'm seeing this is new information for you," Titus said. He tried his best not to sound sarcastic. His momentary pleasure had evaporated. Not for the first time, he found himself sharing a family secret. It was never a good feeling, even if it was directed at an asshole like Scott Cunningham.

"That whore," Scott said. It came out low enough that Titus figured Scott didn't even realize he'd said it aloud.

"Who, Scott?" Titus asked gently, knowing full well who Scott was talking about.

"I have to go," Scott said. He got up and headed for the door.

"I'm going to have to talk to her," Titus said.

Scott froze. "You're not going anywhere near my mother, Titus Crown."

Titus sighed. He was sighing a lot nowadays. "I am going to talk to her, Scott. She had a son, your half brother, who has DNA on the bodies of murdered children. There's no way I'm not going to have a conversation with her. You say you care about Charon? This is how you prove it."

"My mother is a sixty-eight-year-old diabetic who lives alone in our old homeplace. You go near her and I'll sue you for harassment," Scott said. He was back on surer ground now, handing out bombastic threats.

"I'm going to talk to her. Today. And if you try to stop me, I'll arrest you for obstruction. Then I'll make sure the magistrate is occupied so you get to cool your jets for a few days in holding. You're not the only one who can hand out threats, but mine come with a badge and gun," Titus said.

"If my father was alive—"

"He'd call me a racial slur and try to threaten me the same way you did, and I'd ignore him too. I can't believe I have to tell you this, but this isn't 1949. You're the chairman of the Board of Supervisors. You're white and what passes for rich around here. And I don't give a damn about none of that. You're a blood relative to a man who tortured Black boys and girls to death. If I was you, I'd be less concerned about me talking to your mama and more concerned what the fallout from that is going to be."

"Stay away from my mother," Scott said. He stomped out of the office.

"Treat people bad, bad comes back to you," Titus murmured. It was one of his mother's favorite, most prescient sayings.

TWENTY-THREE

Blue Hills Plantation had been in the Cunningham family for more than two hundred years. The sign at the head of the road that hung from a broken chain attached to the arm of a weathered post said it had been established in 1816. It had survived hurricanes, floods, and the end of the Civil War. The Cunninghams had transitioned from producing tobacco, to opening a seafood factory, and later a flag factory, as smoothly as a ball bearing sliding through mercury.

During a pause in vacation Bible school years ago Mrs. Jojo had told Titus's class a dark story about how Hollis Cunningham, wounded from the war and full of hatred and venom, had locked his few remaining slaves in a barn and set it on fire as the U.S. Army approached Charon.

"He would rather see them burn than see them free," Mrs. Jojo had intoned in her razor-sharp articulation.

They haven't changed much, Titus thought as he turned down the pea-gravel-covered driveway. Enormous magnolias with dead brown petals lined the road, wild arboreal entities that reached out toward their brothers across the driveway with thick twisted branches that brushed against the sides of Titus's SUV. The road curved to the right, then slunk back to the left, until it ended in a circular driveway in front of the main house.

Titus parked and shut off the SUV. Time hadn't been kind to Blue Hills. The three-story building was two good storms away from being decrepit. The railing that ran along the outer edge of the wraparound porch that extended three-quarters of the way around the house was missing so many spindles it seemed to have a gap-toothed smile. The shutters were faded and had started to split. Hydrangeas and bougainvillea were on the brink of engulfing the front steps that went up for twelve risers. There was a late-model pickup truck parked off to the side of the house next to an antique Chrysler Fifth Avenue in pristine condition.

Titus got out and walked up the steps to the front door. The wood groaned beneath the weight of his 235-pound frame. He rang the doorbell and heard it reverberate through the structure. How many people who looked like him had seen this building in their nightmares? Seen it in all its glory and known that they would never be allowed the same rights and privileges as the men and women who considered them property?

Titus thought the stain that was slavery was soaked into the bed-rock of the place he called home. A curse of blood that no amount of money nor charity could wash away. A curse that people like Ricky Sours refused to believe in and refused to atone for in any meaningful way.

A young Black woman he didn't recognize opened the door.

"You must be Sheriff Crown," she said. She was wearing nursing scrubs. The name tag on her chest read NATALIE BIVENS RN.

"Yes, I am. I'd like to speak with Mrs. Cunningham if I could, Ms. Bivens."

"Miss. It's Miss, and Scott already called and told me not to let you in . . . but Mrs. Polly said she wanted to talk to you," Natalie said.

"Is Mrs. Cunningham . . . lucid? Her son said she had a lot of medical issues."

Natalie smiled. "She is sixty-eight. She isn't in the best of health and she uses a wheelchair to get around most days, but her mind is sharp as a tack. Like I said, she wants to speak with you." She turned and walked into the house. Titus shut the door behind him and followed her.

The wood-paneled walls of the house seemed to absorb the light from the octagon-shaped dormer windows. Generations of Cunninghams peered down at him from behind the gauze of sepia-toned daguerreotypes. They walked up a two-step rise from the foyer to the parlor. They walked through that room and entered a cavernous living room with cathedral ceilings. The walls were lined with bookshelves that were interspersed with the petrified remains of taxidermied racoons and rabbits and foxes.

Polly Anne Cunningham sat in the center of the room, in a recliner, parallel to a love seat that Titus was sure was at least fifty years old. There was a wheelchair nearby that appeared just as old. Titus took off his hat and his sunglasses.

Polly Anne regarded him coolly. She still had bright, inquisitive blue eyes. Long, lush white hair spilled over her shoulders and over her chest. Her face bore the marks of time, but those marks gave her a gravitas and maturity. In her pale blue and white floral housedress Titus thought she resembled an Old Testament prophet, if women had been allowed to assume that mantle.

"Sheriff. I must say I never thought I'd see the day a Black man wore that badge," Polly Anne said. Her voice was clear and strong, the kind of voice you heard at PTA meetings and fundraisers for the UDC or the Sons of the Confederacy.

"Does that disturb you?" Titus asked.

"Not hardly. I just never thought Charon would let it happen. Goes to show what I know. Please sit."

Titus sat on the love seat. It had a lived-in aroma, not sour or unpleasant, just earthy and raw, the scent of thousands of hours of use, of sweat and tears and the touch of skin.

"Natalie, could you help me into the chair?" Polly Anne said. Natalie came over and slipped her arms under Polly Anne's armpits and transferred her from the recliner to the wheelchair with little trouble. Titus thought Polly Anne must not weigh more than a baby bird.

"Now, let me properly face my guest. Could you tell Crutch to bring us some water?" Polly Anne said.

"Sure," Natalie said. She left them alone.

"Ma'am, I don't know if your son told you why I wanted to talk to you, but it concerns a . . . delicate matter, and I know this might be difficult to talk about, but there are lives at stake, and—"

"You want to talk about my son. The one I gave away," Polly Anne said.

Titus blinked. "Yes . . . yes, ma'am. I know this is a sensitive subject, but I need to hear your story. He may be involved in the murders that have taken place, recently and in the past."

An older Black man in khakis and a white button-down shirt came in carrying a tray with a pitcher of ice water and two glasses. He set the tray on a small circular table next to the wheelchair. He filled both glasses. He handed one to Polly Anne and the other to Titus.

"Thank you, Crutch," Polly Anne said.

"Of course. Don't push yourself too hard," Crutch said. He exited as quietly as he had entered.

"Crutch has worked here since Scott started high school and Alanna was a Girl Scout. He's the only thing keeping me out the nursing home. I hope the water is fine, Sheriff. It's basically all I can have these days. I lost my toes to the dangers of Southern living. Too much sweet tea," Polly Anne said.

Titus glanced down at her feet. They were ensconced in compression socks. Where the toes should have been, the foot just rounded off like a potato.

Titus made a mental note to get his glucose checked.

"Scott wants to put you in a nursing home?" Titus asked.

"He'd rather have me there while he waits for me to die. Then he could sell this place and the twenty-five acres it sits on," Polly Anne said.

"You don't seem like you need a nursing home to me," Titus said.

"It's not a matter of need, Sheriff. It's want. My son, the one I kept, wants me in there. But me and old Crutch, we keep foiling his plans. But you didn't come here to talk about that part of my dysfunctional family."

"No, ma'am, I didn't. I have reason to believe the boy you gave up to Elias Hillington has grown up to become a killer. Elias is dead. So is a man named Cole Marshall and seven young Black boys and girls. And last night someone nailed a lamb to my front door. I need to catch him before he hurts anyone else or himself," Titus said.

Polly Anne sipped her water, then set it on the table. "I love my children, Sheriff, but none of them are what you would call good people. Two of them are spoiled, arrogant brats who only recognize dollar bills as an expression of love. The other one, well, you know what he is. I wonder how much I had to do with that. How much of it was the sins of the mothers and fathers come to nestle in his soul." Her voice quavered, and for a moment Titus thought she might begin to sob. But she just shook her head reproachfully.

"Sheriff, have you ever made what you thought was a good decision only to have it cast shadows over your life for years?" Polly Anne asked.

"Yes, ma'am, I think I have," Titus said. He saw Red DeCrain on his knees begging for the handcuffs.

"When I was nineteen, I met Horace Cunningham at Washington and Lee University. He was the most handsome, intelligent, charming man I'd ever known. A year later I had dropped out and we were married. Horace was a kind and gentle soul. He was wealthy, but he didn't flaunt it like the rest of his family. He graduated and we moved here to Blue Hills. He went to work managing the fish house and I tried my best to be a good partner for him. I learned how to entertain and make polite small talk. And every night I lay down next to my husband and I prayed that he would turn over and kiss me and hold me. But he never did."

"Horace was gay," Titus said.

Polly Anne smiled. "He liked to say he enjoyed a different kind of love. Eventually his father demanded we produce some heirs. Horace cried before and after. And during, he closed his eyes and then I closed mine, and I think we both were far, far away. After I had Scott and Alanna, we came to an . . . understanding. We would be husband and wife in every way but one. He was free to find a different kind of love . . . and so was I."

"The boy, he was of mixed ethnicity," Titus said gently. He wondered when was the last time Polly Anne had talked to someone not named Natalie or Crutch. He wondered how her regrets weighed on her soul. He wondered if this confession was giving her absolution.

"I majored in history in college. I never ascribed to the racist dogma that most of Horace's family embraced. I used to go to the Honey Drop and Club 24 and Gardner's. I would find . . . friends there. Was I protecting myself? Using my privilege as a white woman to find affection in the arms of men I could never have been seen with in public? Yes, but I truly considered the people I met there as my friends. Jojo Ware, Ruth and Jimmy Packer, Gene Dixon, I even knew your father, Albert. I hope you don't judge me too harshly, Sheriff. I was a lonely woman, and those nights in the company of folks who didn't question my presence, who treated me like a woman, not an ornament, were some of the happiest times of my life," Polly Anne said.

"You knew my father?" Titus asked. He cocked his head to the right.

Polly Anne let out a short laugh. "Not that way, Sheriff. Albert liked his whiskey and he liked to cut a rug, but he loved your mama. Don't you ever trouble yourself about that." She took another sip of water.

"In the summer of 1987 Horace started losing weight. He was a big burly man, so losing a few pounds didn't concern either of us. Then he started having these terrible night sweats, where he'd leave the bed just soaked. By January of 1988 he was dead. And three months later I got pregnant."

Polly Anne looked past Titus at a picture hanging on the far wall. Titus had noticed it when he entered the room. It was one of the more recent photos. Horace Cunningham when he was a young man. For a moment the wrinkles in her face smoothed and a smile played at the corners of her lips.

"He was so careful, but I fear someone wasn't careful with him. And so, you see my dilemma? I was a widow who was pregnant long after my husband had been buried."

"And you decided to give the child up to the Hillingtons? Why? Did you know how they were? How they could be?" Titus asked.

Polly Anne shook her head.

"No. After Horace passed, his brothers stepped in and tried to take charge of our lives. Lemuel, his oldest brother, set it all up. I never even got to see my child's face. They forbade me from ever contacting him. I think if I had seen him when he was a baby, I would have tried to keep him. But the Cunninghams would have never allowed me to raise him with Scott and Alanna. They considered him impure." Polly Anne went to take another sip, but her hand started to tremble. Titus got up and put his hand under the bottom of the glass to steady it.

"I went to see him once. I had Crutch drive me over to the island. We parked a little ways away from the church. He must have been nine. It wasn't until Lemuel died that I found myself on that island," Polly said.

She paused.

"He was outside, alone. I was just about to get out the car when I saw him take a blue crab out of a trap and then crush it with a rock. A live crab. He smashed that rock into its shell again and again. I got back in my car and went home. I never saw him again," Polly Anne said, and this time the tears did come slipping down her face like a thief running off into the night.

"I think . . . so many times I think if I had kept him, if I had raised him, that I could've changed him. If I hadn't let the Cunninghams intimidate me I could have helped him. Those poor children, that Marshall boy, even Elias . . . their blood is on my hands," Polly Anne cried.

Natalie came rushing back into the room, but Titus held up his hand. She stopped, then retreated.

Titus took Polly Anne's hand in his own. It felt as insubstantial as smoke. Her sobbing subsided.

"The blood is on the hands of the one who spilled it. You're not to blame for what he's done. But if you help me, I'll try to make sure he gets the kind of help he needs. Do you have any pictures of him? Do you know what the Hillingtons named him?" Titus said.

"I don't have any pictures. I'm ashamed to say I can barely remember what he looks like. But I know they named him Gabriel."

"After an angel," Titus said.

Titus was about to step off the porch when Natalie came to the door.

"This is all gonna get out, isn't it? About the baby and all that," Natalie said.

Titus put on his hat and his glasses. "Yeah, it will. When we catch him."

"She's been wanting to tell this story for years. Scott, he was a teenager when she had that baby. For some reason he blames her for his father's death. He won't like all this becoming public knowledge. Just so you know," Natalie said.

"I don't think there's anything I care about less than what Scott Cunningham likes or doesn't like. I hope she's okay with it, though."

"I think it's a relief for her, honestly."

"Good. She's been through enough."

"I'm not used to cops being kindhearted," Natalie said.

Titus put on his sunglasses. "'We all fall short of grace.' That's what my mama would've said. You have a good day, now."

He went to his SUV and called Trey.

"Hey, boss, I talked to Jessica. She said Dallas and Cole weren't really that close. She and Dallas's wife been good friends since kindergarten. She did say he liked to pal around with Denver Carlyle sometimes and he was cool with Jasper and that crew at the Watering Hole. I talked to Dallas, but he has an airtight alibi for the night of the murder. He was in Harrisonburg picking up a load for his tractor trailer. Denver refused to talk to me. Jasper denied really knowing him all that well," Trey said.

Titus rapped his knuckles against the steering wheel. Just another dead end. Another pathway to nowhere.

"Go back to Denver. Bring him in as a material witness. I'll be back at the station in about thirty minutes," Titus said.

"Can we really do that? I mean, he isn't really a witness to anything," Trey said.

"He doesn't know that," Titus said. He hated how the words tasted in his mouth, but the time for niceties was over. They had to find this killer, and if he had to lean into the darker aspects of his position and his status, then so be it. He could chastise himself later.

Jamal Addison was sitting on the hood of his Prius when Titus pulled in to the sheriff's office. As Titus exited the SUV Jamal slid down and came over to him.

"Reverend," Titus said.

"Sheriff, they told me you'd be back soon. I was wondering if I could have a moment of your time," Jamal said. Titus noticed he seemed subdued, the piss and vinegar seemed to have gone stagnant.

"Reverend, I'm sure you know our time is limited. We have a killer to catch," Titus said. A cool breeze came rolling from the east, snatching away the warmth from earlier in the day.

"That's what I want to talk about. Have you given any consideration to canceling Fall Fest?" Jamal said.

Titus pushed his hat back on his head. "Jamal, I don't have the authority to do that. That'd be up to the Board of Supervisors and the Fall Fest Committee and I don't think they gonna be inclined to do it."

"I know Fall Fest usually brings in a ton of money for the county. But Ricky Sours and his boys are planning on marching down Main Street hollering about blood and soil and the Great Replacement and White Lives Matter. How big of a leap do you think they'd have to make to start blaming people who look like us for the two white men killed in the county?"

"So you heard about Elias?" Titus said. He considered cornering Davy and asking him who he'd told.

"Everyone's heard about it. But my statement stands. I can see Ricky and his boys pulling a Susan Smith and blaming us for Cole and Elias. All those people crushed together at the Fall Fest full of liquor and anger and fear. You gonna have something bad on your hands, Titus," Jamal said.

"Jamal, are y'all planning a counter-march?" Titus asked.

Jamal wouldn't meet his eyes. The young minister studied the asphalt beneath his feet. "You don't know what they saying around the county. They already hate us, now they want to blame us. They don't believe Spearman did anything. They want to put everything on Latrell or some other young Black man who fits their stereotype of the angry Black thug. But this ain't the time of Dr. King, Titus. A lot of people ain't feeling that nonviolent resistance. A lot of people around here, Black and white, are sick of Ricky Sours and his crew."

Jamal got in his car. He rolled the window down and leaned his head out.

"Ask them to cancel it, Titus. Please."

TWENTY-FOUR

itus went to his office and stood in front of his bulletin board. He tacked a piece of paper to the board and wrote the word "Gabriel" on it. Under the name he jotted down notes about what he thought was the man's motivation and his pathologies. He wasn't really working up a profile, more like just organizing his thoughts. He talked to himself in a low murmur as he wrote.

"He's obsessed with religion and angels. He's physically strong as hell. Does he hate the Black side of himself? Is that why he attacks Black kids? He's bold, but most sociopaths are bold. He's probably passing. He was the alpha among him, Spearman, and Latrell. How did he meet them? Latrell didn't seem to be an active participant in the murders. He was purely bait."

Titus stopped writing. One thing he'd learned the hard way was that profiling wasn't magic. It was at best a series of educated guesses based on quantified research and analysis. But some people weren't quantifiable. Some people didn't fit the profile. They didn't even fit within the human race.

Some people were monsters among monsters.

Carla knocked on the frame of his open door.

"What ya got?" Titus asked.

"Talked to the shipping manager at the fish house. The dates that Latrell rode along with Cole don't come anywhere near matching the dates those kids went missing," Carla said.

Titus nodded.

"Okay. It was a long shot anyway. Cole wasn't the killer. He knew who he was, but he didn't know he knew until the press conference. I just can't stop thinking Latrell and the killer were working together to snatch these kids. He used Latrell as bait. I know it, I just don't know the mechanics of it," Titus said.

"Maybe Latrell and the killer just drove up and down the East Coast when the mood struck them," Carla said.

"That's possible. If they did, that makes it that much harder to find the—" Titus stopped himself. He was going to call the killer the Last Wolf. "It makes it harder to find the killer. Randomness is his ally."

"What's ours?" Carla asked.

"Determination."

Titus spent the next few hours returning emails and handling the administrative issues that he'd neglected the last few days. Admittedly, he had good reasons, but the folks he served wouldn't acknowledge those reasons, they'd only hear excuses.

Titus logged on to the various social media pages dedicated to Charon County. Those pages were the new water coolers and fences around which the community gathered. They were also where people had the tendency to expose themselves as racists, misogynists, and amazingly ignorant. Titus thought some people convinced themselves a community page held a sanctity it did not in any way, shape, or form.

There were a lot of posts about the shooting. A few were from concerned citizens who asked for prayer and healing for the county. But the majority were gleefully exuberant about Latrell's death. They used the tragedy as an opportunity to display the vastness of their racist vocabulary. There were quite a few posts about the Fall Fest. Most of them were genial, bursting with anticipation for the pie-eating contest or the crab-pot-pulling contest. Albert Crown had three trophies from that particular competition on his mantel.

A few of the posts hinted at more violent expectations.

Got my flags for the march!
The South will rise again!
Fucking snowflakes can't stand real history!

Titus logged out.

It occurred to him no place was more confused by its past or more terrified of the future than the South. He sent an email to the Board of Supervisors apprising them of the fact that he was going to reach out to neighboring counties for backup during the three days of Fall Fest. He hoped he wouldn't need them, but hoping and praying wouldn't stop some good ol' boy from tossing a Molotov cocktail into a crowd of folks in front of the Safeway.

Titus closed his laptop and checked his watch. It was a little after 6:00 P.M. and he hadn't had anything to eat all day. He considered calling Darlene and having her meet him at Gilby's, but the image of the lamb on his door chased that idea away. He'd go pick up something and bring it back to the office.

As he was walking through the lobby of the office, Trey and Pip came in dragging Denver Carlyle.

"I got rights, motherfuckers!" Denver screamed.

"I'm guessing he didn't agree to being a material witness," Titus said.

"Well, Mr. Big Brain here took off running, got in his car, then ran it in the ditch. That means he got a DUI, resisting arrest, and evading police. And that's if the county attorney wants to be charitable," Pip said.

Titus took a deep breath. Denver smelled like he'd been swimming laps in a whiskey barrel. "Denver, if you're drunk you know that's the end of your CDL, right?" Titus said.

"Fuck you. Fuck all y'all motherfuckers. I got rights. I'm a white man in America. Yeah, I said it, *white* man. I'm not ashamed of my race just cuz some people owned slaves a hundred years ago," Denver said.

"But you want to keep up a statue to those folks. The ones who owned slaves. That's what your march is about, right?" Titus asked.

Denver shook his head. "That's our history you trying to destroy! Trying to erase us."

"So, you don't mind your ancestors being slave owners, you just don't want anyone to complain about it? Take his ass to the holding cell. Call the magistrate," Titus said. Pip carted Denver off to the holding cell.

"Just FYI, I asked him about Cole while he was in the cruiser. He's drunk and it's probably not admissible, but he told me he hadn't talked to Cole in months. He's all about those Sons of the Confederacy bullshit," Trey said.

"When he sobers up, ask him if he will give us a DNA sample," Titus said.

"You think it's Denver?" Carla asked.

"I'm not ruling anyone out," Titus said.

"I mean, I understand that, but I've known that jerk for a long time. He's lived in Charon his whole life. The kid, the one Elias and his family raised, disappeared. Denver's never gone anywhere," Carla said.

"Good point, but I want his DNA anyway. I might be wrong about the boy," Titus said.

"You're not wrong often, boss," Carla said.

"I kinda hope I am this time."

Titus was back at his desk waiting for Denver to sober up when his cell phone rang. He checked it, saw it was from a restricted number. Titus hesitated. It was probably a telemarketer calling about his extended car warranty. Then again, it might be important. He touched the screen and answered it.

"Hello?"

"The flock is not safe," a deep, demonic voice said.

Titus sat straight up in his chair.

"How did you get this number?"

The voice chuckled. It made Titus's skin crawl.

"Anyone can find anyone on the internet. The flock is not safe, Titus," the voice said.

"Is that what you were trying to show me with that lamb . . . Gabriel?" Titus said. He hoped using his real name would throw him off.

"That's not my fucking name."

"That's what your mother said they named you. Your real mother. She regrets giving you up, Gabriel," Titus said. He could hear deep, harsh breaths on the other end of the line.

"How's your mom? Still dead?" the voice said. It had lost its bravado.

"Yes, my mother's dead. But she loved me, Gabriel. She didn't give me up. Is that what this is all about? When you killed those children, did you think you were killing a part of yourself? The part your mother couldn't accept?" Titus said.

"Don't fucking try to profile me. I want you to remember what I told you. Your fucking flock ain't safe."

The line went dead.

Titus tossed his phone on the desk and put his face in his hands. It was like the Last Wolf's insanity was secreting through the cell towers into his brain. Talking to this maniac, thinking like him, was corrosive. It ate away at his soul.

The phone rang again.

Titus picked it up with a pit blooming in his stomach.

It was his father.

"Hey, what's wrong?" Titus said.

"Nothing, calm down, boy. I was just calling to tell you not to pick up nothing for dinner. I'm making baked chicken, greens, cornbread, and tater salad. And I got somebody bringing by some oysters for the grill," Albert said.

"That's a lot of food for just me and you, Pop," Titus said.

Albert chuckled. "Just come on home, boy."

"I got a lot to do here."

"Titus Alexander Crown, you can go back to work after you eat. Now come on home. By the time you get here, the food be done," Albert said.

"What's going on, Pop? I told you I don't want Darlene coming over while all this is going on," Titus said.

"It ain't Darlene, big head. Now come on home."

Titus got out of the SUV and headed for his front door. A pale pink patina still coated the fiberglass. He went in the house and was immediately embraced by the aromas of a long day in the kitchen for Albert Crown.

"You trying to put your foot all the way in it today, huh, old man?" Titus said.

Albert was stirring a pitcher of tea with a wooden spoon. "Sometimes ya gotta."

"Is that your famous lavender sweet tea?" Titus asked.

Albert grinned. "I don't know how famous it is, but yeah."

Titus took in the baking dish full of chicken, the aluminum pan full of macaroni and cheese, the old butter container of potato salad.

"Pop, you got a lady friend coming over?" Titus asked.

Albert laughed. "Boy, sit and shut your mouth. I'm gonna make your plate while we wait."

"I can make my own plate, Dad," Titus said.

"Suit yourself," Albert said, and went back to stirring the tea.

"You really not gonna tell me who coming over?" Titus asked as he spooned the macaroni on his plate.

"You the detective. You figure it out." Albert cackled.

Titus ate a spoonful of macaroni. The old man hadn't lost his touch.

His father had put out three place settings. He was making his lavender tea. Titus glanced at the oven. Behind the tempered glass he saw a pan full of croissants. Only, when he and Marquis were kids, they didn't call them croissants.

"Roly-polys. You made roly-polys. Pop, you think Marquis is coming over?" Titus asked.

Albert grinned. "Finish your plate," was all he said.

Titus sat his plate on the table. "Pop, he ain't been over here in years. What makes you think—" Titus started to say, but a knock at the door stopped him in his tracks.

"Hey, I couldn't get no oysters," Marquis said as he came in the house. He came in the kitchen carrying a six-pack of beer. "Hey, big brother. You look scary, as usual. Pop, you wanna put these in the fridge?" Marquis said.

"Yeah, go ahead. This tea is ready. We can crack open the beers later."

"You sure that tea ain't too much for you, old man? Look like you fighting that stirring spoon," Marquis said as he passed Albert and playfully punched him in the shoulder.

Albert spun around and put up his fist. Titus had taken one step toward them when he saw the grins on their faces.

He grinned too.

After the chicken had been eaten and the sweet tea had been drunk and all the beer was gone, the three of them leaned back in their chairs at the kitchen table with full bellies and cheeks sore from laughing.

"Got damn, I got the itis," Marquis said.

"Everything was good, Pop," Titus said.

"I know. I can still burn up something in the kitchen," Albert said. He yawned and cracked his knuckles. "I'm think I'm gonna hit the hay."

"Pop, it's eight thirty," Marquis said.

"Yeah, past my bedtime," he said.

All three of them guffawed.

"Nah, I took a pain pill for this ol' hip. Mr. Sandman is calling me." Albert rose from the table with a slight grimace. He put his hand on Marquis's shoulder and stared at Titus.

"It's good having both my boys here," Albert said. He squeezed Marquis's shoulder, nodded to Titus, and then headed for the stairs.

"Pop still got some of that good 'shine around here?" Marquis asked.

"Yeah, in the same place," Titus said.

"Remember when we stole one of his jars and he caught us and made us drink the whole thing?" Marquis asked.

"Still can't stand the smell of raspberries. By the time we got to the bottom they was just sludge," Titus said as Marquis retrieved the mason jar.

"Wanna go out on the porch? I feel funny drinking corn liquor in the house," Marquis said.

"Only time I heard him and Mama even kinda argue was when him and Gene and Gary Parrish got drunk at the kitchen table after work that time," Titus said.

Marquis grabbed two glasses and headed out the door. As he passed the mantel he paused and blew a kiss at their parents' wedding picture.

They sat side by side in lawn chairs and passed the jar back and forth until the warmth of a buzz settled over them like a fog.

"I gotta ask. What made you show up tonight?" Titus said.

Marquis took a sip from the jar. "Somebody nails a sheep to your daddy's door, you should probably come check on him."

"Fair enough. I mean, I know it's hard for you to come over here," Titus said.

"If I don't think about hearing that rattle in her throat, I'm okay," Marquis said.

"I think about it all the time," Titus said.

"I don't know why you torture yourself like that," Marquis said.

Titus swallowed his 'shine. "You know, part of me thinks if I don't, if I start to forget that night, I'm disrespecting her. I guess I feel like somebody gotta carry it. Her memory."

"I didn't say I don't wanna remember her. I just don't wanna think about that night, or the six months before. I wanna think about her helping us make them kites," Marquis said.

Titus laughed. "You electrocuted yourself with that thing."

"I'd never seen her so mad and so scared before," Marquis said. He chuckled and sipped some more 'shine. "How you doing? I know you running down behind this boy who cutting people up and leaving 'em in cornfields and shit. I know it's got to be pressing on you."

"It's the job. It's what I signed up for."

"Negro, you did not sign up for no *Silence of the Lambs* shit. This is Charon. The most you should be doing is breaking up fights at the Watering Hole," Marquis said.

"Speaking of the Watering Hole. You was right. Boy on my team was getting paid," Titus said. He held out his hand and Marquis handed him the mason jar.

"That's what I was hearing," Marquis said.

"Was you hearing it cuz you was doing some work for Jasper?" Titus asked.

Marquis turned his massive head to look at him. "You don't wanna know that. But let's say, for the sake of argument, I had done a little something-something for them in the past. If I was any kind of a good brother, I would have stopped the day you got elected cuz I wouldn't want to get my big brother in trouble," Marquis said.

"Well, let's play that hypothesis out a little more. If you was working for them and you stopped and then I fire their inside man, they not gonna come after you, are they? Cuz that's more serious than some broken tables," Titus said.

"They know better than to start some shit with me. Let's leave it at that. Let you have some plausible deniability. I don't want you to lose your golden child status," Marquis said. He winked at Titus.

"I ain't no goddamn golden child," Titus said. He handed Marquis the mason jar.

"Come on, man. I'm the black sheep, no pun intended, and you're the good son. Graduated top of your class from UVA, then Columbia, then worked for the FBI for, what, ten years? Shit, I don't know why you came back here, and don't say Pop's hip." Marquis took a big swig of the 'shine. "And is this my belt you wearing?" Marquis asked. He handed the jar back to Titus.

Titus glanced at his waist. "Mine broke and yours kinda matches the uniform, even if it's got a knife in the buckle," Titus said. He took another sip. "But like I said. I'm no golden child."

Marquis laughed. It echoed through the night and brought a response from a few nightjars and an owl. "Boy, you so straight they can do geometry by your backside," Marquis said as he held out his hand for the mason jar.

Titus first took another long swig of the 'shine. The moonshine burned all the way to his toes. He handed Marquis the jar.

"You asked me why I came home. You was right. It wasn't just about Pop. That was a part of it, but it was more about me," Titus said. "Give me that damn jar back."

Marquis handed it to him without a smart comment. Titus killed the rest of the 'shine in one long gulp.

"I've never told nobody else this. The Bureau swept it under the rug, after I resigned, of course. And there was no family to question the official version we put out," Titus said. He slouched down in his chair. He was rapidly moving from tipsy to drunk, but the story he was going to tell his brother would only come out under the influence of strong liquor.

"In vino veritas," Titus said.

"Huh?" Marquis said.

"Nothing. So, I moved from the Behavioral Science Unit to the Domestic Terrorism Unit. It had more opportunity for advancement, and I wanted to advance. I was seeing this woman who I wanted to take things to the next level with, and I was looking at buying a house and maybe putting down some roots in Indiana. Well, anyway, my first case with that department was a joint operation with the ATF and the DEA to take down a drug-dealing white supremacist who was stockpiling weapons in Northern Indiana named Ronald 'Red' DeCrain. Now, Red was not just a drug-dealing, racist piece of shit, he was also a fucking cult leader. He had about fifty die-hard followers out at his compound. We got a guy on the inside who helped set up a deal where Red and his crew, who were all convicted felons, bought stolen guns across state lines." Titus paused.

"They broke enough laws, everybody could get a piece of the pie. So we loaded up the black SUVs and put on our tactical gear and went to arrest Red and five of his top lieutenants. My colleagues in the BCI gave us an assessment of Red DeCrain. They said he didn't have a martyr complex. That he wouldn't fight to the death. They were partly right. But the part they got wrong . . . well, that was fucking terrible," Titus said. He reached for the jar, realized it was empty, and set it back on the floor of the porch.

"I'll spare you the gory details, but it was a bloodbath. They knew we were coming. Our inside man got compromised and gave up the raid after they cut off three of his toes. We got pinned down for a bit, then we started pushing them back. Me and a friend of mine, Special Agent Tolliver Young, moved into the compound, followed by four ATF agents," Titus said. He stopped talking and blinked his eyes.

"Ty, you don't have to talk about this if you don't want to," Marquis said.

"I need to. And you're the only person I can tell."

"You sure? Because you look like you seen a fucking ghost," Marquis said.

"Let me say it, Key. I have to. I have to tell it all," Titus said.

He paused.

"We cornered Red. We thought he was trying to escape. He was with his wife and his three boys. The oldest was fourteen. The youngest was seven. Little towheaded boy, reminded you of Dennis the Menace." Titus stopped again and swallowed hard.

"I told them to put their hands up and lay down on the ground.

You know what he did? He grinned at me. True madness is like an aura around someone. It glows blue like the flame from a gas fire. That madness can spread. Become like religion for the lost. I saw it in the eyes of his wife and his kids. They were overcome with it like someone catching the Holy Ghost," Titus said. He wiped his face with both hands.

"Then Red yelled, 'Sic semper tyrannis!' And his wife and their three sons pulled the pins on their suicide vests. It was like I'd fallen into the mouth of a dragon. Blinding-white light, incendiary heat that burnt off my eyebrows. If Tolliver hadn't been standing in front of me, I would have died. They had filled their vests with ball bearings. He evaporated like a mist first thing in the morning. The four ATF agents were in a line shoulder to shoulder. They were blown to bits. I got a ball bearing in my abdomen just above my crotch," Titus said as he untucked his shirt and pulled it up over his stomach. He touched the scar with his free hand.

"When I woke up, my ears were ringing so loud I couldn't hardly think. I pulled myself to my feet. I slipped a few times because of all the blood. Bits of Tolliver and Red's family were embedded in my face. They're still there to this day. I lost twenty percent of the hearing in my right ear. Broke most of the teeth on the right side of my mouth. All of this."

He ran his tongue over his teeth.

"It's a plate. I was bleeding, my friend and our team were dead. Red DeCrain's wife and sons were dead. Even the seven-year-old. He'd gotten a seven-year-old to kill himself because his daddy didn't like Black and brown people. Everyone was dead except me . . . and Red DeCrain. Don't get me wrong, he was fucked up. There was a hole in his thigh big enough to step in, but he was alive," Titus said as he pulled his shirt back down.

"I went over to him and looked down at him. That idiot mindless craziness was still glowing around him. He spoke to me. He said he wanted to surrender. He wanted a doctor. He wanted me to handcuff him. He wanted to go be among his brothers inside. He

wanted, he wanted, it was all about his wants. He didn't say anything, not one word, about his wife or his kids or my friend or the
men who walked into that viper's nest with us. Just what *he* wanted,"
Titus said. He flexed his fingers.

"Ever since Mama died, I had promised myself I would do what
it took to keep people safe. That I would live my life with order and
structure, because the world is cruel and capricious and it doesn't
give a damn about you, and the church that she loved and the God
that she prayed to heal her are just placebos that don't fix the poison
we swim in every day. That's why I went into law enforcement. To
try and impose some order on the world, on my life. And here was
Red DeCrain, chaos personified, who was gonna probably make it
and live the next thirty or so years in comfort. Yeah, he'd be in jail,
but he would be a made man inside unless he got the needle. This
sick motherfucker who had made five women widows, who facili-
tated nothing but disorder and tragedy, was going to get to enjoy his
life. I stared down at him and realized, what had following the rules
ever really gotten me? What had trying to make order out of bed-
lam ever really done for me?" Titus paused. He took a deep breath,
a huge inhalation that made him stretch his chest to its maximum
width.

"So I shot him. Two to the head, two in the chest. I shot him as
I stood there covered in what was left of his family and my friend.
Another squad showed up just as I holstered my sidearm." Titus
grunted. "The Bureau quietly asked, well, told me to resign. They
wrote a press release that made it seem like Red was armed when
he was shot four times. I lost all my benefits, but I didn't go to jail.
Six months later, Pop had his operation."

"You never told him? Your name never got in the paper?" Marquis
asked.

Titus shook his head. "By the time my unemployment ran out
and I came home, I had pretty much recovered. And they scrubbed
my name from the official record, little brother. They worked hard
to keep it as quiet as possible. Didn't need another Waco. Only a

few news outlets ran with the story. If you didn't live in Indiana, you probably didn't even hear about it. That was why, when the opportunity came up, I took it and ran for sheriff."

"I don't get it. You took out a racist, and that made you run for sheriff?" Marquis said.

"I killed a man. A terrible man, but a man nonetheless, and I got away with it because I was the law. I ran for sheriff because I didn't want anyone here to get away with the things they did to us when we were growing up because they were the law. I wanted to . . . change things from the inside, I guess. That's a lot easier said than done. But it's my penance."

"For somebody that don't believe in God, you sure talk about religious shit a lot. Look, you don't owe nobody nothing. You took out that racist? Good. You probably saved some lives. And you ain't gotta try to keep stuff straight. Ain't your job."

"It sorta is my job, as sheriff. I keep thinking what would Mama say if she knew," Titus said.

"You chose to be sheriff. And you can choose not to be. It ain't up to you to fix everything cuz you couldn't save Mama. Nobody could save her, Ty. Let me hit you with this one from our old Sunday school days. That idea you gotta save everything? That's pride. And you know what they say about pride and the fall. I'm gonna say it again. You don't owe nobody nothing. Not me, not Pops, not Mama, and not nobody in Charon. And, just for the record, Mama would probably say, 'Shoot that motherfucker four more times,'" Marquis said.

Titus picked up the empty mason jar and studied the way the illumination from the porch light danced across its surface. "What if me trying to hold the world together is what keeps me from falling apart?"

"Fuck, Ty," Marquis said.

He reached out his heavy hand and laid it on Titus's shoulder as the night jays and whip-poor-wills sang a song for them in the dark.

TWENTY-FIVE

Titus woke up with the taste of last night's bad decisions fresh in his mouth. He forced himself to get out of bed and do two hundred push-ups before he took a shower, in an effort to sweat out the liquor.

Marquis was on the couch when he came downstairs. He didn't bother trying to wake him as he headed out the door. He got in the SUV and headed for the office. The windshield had the hint of a frost around the edge. The temperature had dropped twenty degrees overnight. Overcast skies gave the whole county a washed-out countenance. It was like he was watching a faded print of a silent film as he drove through the back roads and headed for the main highway. Titus thought it matched the spirit of Charon, now that a killer had made this place his abattoir.

As Titus pulled into his designated parking space at the sheriff's office, the alert on his cell phone sounded, indicating he had an email.

Dear Sheriff Crown,

    The board has no objection to your plan for added security. However, we hope you will be mindful of the optics of a more robust police presence. We don't want to discourage attendance for Fall Fest.

    Sincerely,

    Julie Narrows

    Vice-Chairman of the Charon Board of Supervisors

"They really don't get it," Titus said to himself.

He went inside and headed for his office.

"Hey, Titus, Denver bonded out about an hour ago. The magistrate had Steve and Davy bring him over to the courthouse and they let him go from there. Steve wanted me to make sure I told you," Cam said.

"Did he ever consent to give us a DNA sample?" Titus asked.

Cam shook his head. "Nope. He lawyered up after you left. You think it's him, Titus?" he asked, pleaded.

Titus didn't let his frustration bubble up to the surface. "I don't know, Cam. But if we can get a DNA sample, we can rule him out or arrest him," Titus said. He thought Cam was representative of the rest of the county. They wanted assurances, they wanted the man with the star to tell them the monster was defeated. They wanted magical answers from him, when he had to deal with real-world circumstances.

He went into the office and sat down behind his desk. He could feel that weight Pip had mentioned like a yoke on his neck. He went over a few other emails, reviewed the gas expense reports, checked the arrest log from last night, updated the sheriff's office's social media page with a request for information about Elias's murder. It felt strange to attend to the mundane and the profane at the same time, but that was a defining aspect of the job.

The day crawled by at a snail's pace. Trey was keeping an eye on Denver, but so far all he'd done was walk to the Tall King convenience store, buy a case of beer, and drink himself into a stupor. Dayane Carter was still unaccounted for and no one seemed to have any idea where she might be. Steve called in a report about two kids spray-painting graffiti on a headstone at the First Corinthian's cemetery celebrating the "Weeping Willow Man."

Thanks, Davy, Titus had thought when he got the call.

Titus called his three peers in Queen, Red Hill, and Gloucester Counties, respectively, and asked for any assistance they could give for the Fall Fest in two days. Queen County rebuffed him almost as a matter of course, but Red Hill and Gloucester promised to send three deputies each.

Not enough. Not nearly enough, Titus thought, but it was all he was going to get, so he tried not to dwell on it. As the dark began to rise, Titus stood from his desk and popped his back as he looked at his bulletin board.

"Everything you need to solve a crime is already within your grasp. It's like you are putting together a jigsaw puzzle of a snowstorm. You have to take a step back and see how everything fits together," Special Agent Tolliver used to say, before Red DeCrain's wife and kids blew him into a million little pieces.

Titus stared at the board.

It *was* there. He just hadn't stepped back far enough yet.

His cell phone vibrated in his pocket.

"Hello?"

"Hey, Virginia. You doing okay?" Kellie said.

"I'm fine. Sorry about the other night. Everyone was on edge," Titus said.

"It's okay. I was just . . . well, I'm glad you're okay. I was calling because I wanted to let you know we finished editing your portion of the episode. You wanna hear it?" Kellie asked.

"I guess I should, so I can make sure you don't make me look bad," Titus said.

Kellie laughed. "There's a lot of things I can do, but making you look bad isn't among them. I can send you the file, or you can stop by here and listen to it."

Titus didn't say anything.

He could just take the file. Have her paste it into a text message and be done with it.

He could do that.

He could also go over to her cottage and hang out with her and Hector. Maybe talk about old times. Maybe just breathe for a moment. Sure, Kellie would ask about the case, but they could also talk about the time she got locked out of the apartment in her underwear. It wasn't like he was going over there to hook up. Even if Hector wasn't a part of the equation, he was in love with Darlene. That was a vow he wouldn't break for anyone.

This was just two old friends talking. This was just Titus taking off the star for an hour or so and allowing himself a brief respite from his atonement and, really, was that a bad thing?

"I got a couple more hours here, so that'll make it around ten, is that too late?" Titus asked.

"No, that's perfect. Want me to grab some lamb chops for dinner?" Kellie said.

"Kellie . . ."

"Okay, okay, too soon. See ya later, Virginia."

TWENTY-SIX

Todd's Inn sat, like so many old homes and former plantations, at the end of a long circuitous driveway covered in crushed oyster shells and lined by lush dogwood trees. Titus thought Charon was a county made of rivers and long driveways. The driveway was also lined by soft amber landscape lights every twenty feet or so. They created an ethereal glow that seemed to spill over the road like St. Elmo's fire. Eventually he came to the actual Todd's Inn, a two-story structure overlooking Spill's Creek. The driveway split into a fork in front of the inn. The left fork stretched out toward the cottages that sat in the clutch of Todd's Wood. The fork to the right took you down to the cottages that overlooked the creek. He'd texted Kellie and she'd said they were in cottage number fourteen. A sign nailed jauntily to a tree told him that cottages one through fifteen were to the left. Titus turned his steering wheel accordingly and drove past cottages one through thirteen. All of them were dark as the Pit. Lucy Todd hadn't even turned on the porch lights for the unoccupied dwellings.

Titus's headlights bounced off the back of Kellie's van, then spilled across the cottage itself.

That was when he saw the open door.

Titus moved fast. He put the SUV in park, hopped out, and drew his gun all in one motion. An open door didn't necessarily portend doom, but one open this late at night when the temperature had dipped into the forties wasn't a detail to be taken lightly.

He held his gun in a tactical grip. The door wasn't just open, it had been kicked in with such force the doorframe had split. In the dark the gentle bleating and whistles of nightingales and white-tails with heavy bellies and all the other forest creatures that only stirred at night were momentarily drowned out by the relentless pounding of his heart. It felt like it was slamming against his rib cage.

"Kellie?" Titus yelled, alternately feeling foolish and hopeful. If she was here, she was probably hurt and she couldn't answer him. If she wasn't here, his words were useless and she was in danger.

Titus moved into the cottage proper.

Hector was slumped against a wall with his hands on his throat. Blood was seeping through his fingers and gurgling from his mouth. Titus moved to help him, when he heard a scream.

He heard Kellie scream.

He ran through the living room and into the kitchen.

"FREEZE!" Titus screamed so loudly his chest hurt.

There was a man standing in front of what appeared to be a closet or pantry in the kitchen. He was dressed in all black. Black jeans, black sweatshirt, black gloves taped to the shirt at the wrists.

The man was holding a red-stained bowie knife.

He was wearing a leather wolf's-head mask.

He had stabbed the knife into the door of the closet. Titus could see the hole it had made. Now he was rigid, with the knife held above his head. Kellie was screaming from inside the closet.

"GET ON THE FUCKING GROUND!" Titus yelled.

The man in the wolf's mask didn't move.

"I will kill you if you don't drop that knife. I promise you that," Titus said. The man still didn't move. They stood there locked in a silent battle of wills where neither one seemed willing to give a quarter.

Suddenly Hector fell against Titus, then brushed past him before falling face-first on the floor of the kitchen. Blood flew up as his body hit the tiles. Titus was pushed to his right. The man in the wolf's mask spun on the balls of his feet and threw the knife at Titus's head. Titus simultaneously ducked and fired at the man in the wolf's mask. His shot went wide and cracked the glass of the patio door in the rear of the kitchen.

The man in the wolf's-head mask ran full-speed at the patio door and crashed through the glass even as the door was still spiderwebbing from Titus's shot. Titus ran to the door and started to fire, but there was no light in the backyard. The man in the mask had disappeared like a ghost into the yawing maw of the night.

Kellie was still screaming in the closet.

Titus went to Hector first. That last burst of adrenaline had allowed the man in the wolf's mask to escape. That ill-fated attempt to rescue Kellie would be the last thing Hector ever did on this side of the veil. His skin was already cooling to the touch.

Titus went to the closet and opened the door.

Kellie fell into his arms still screaming, still pleading for him to save her, to help her, to keep her safe. He realized he had failed one of those requests, the most important one of the three.

Titus sat in his SUV with the door open as Carla and Davy stretched yellow crime scene tape around the cottage. Trey came to the SUV and stood near the open door.

"Kellie says they were here with your episode booted up when the door got kicked in. She said she ran for the closet as Hector confronted the guy. She didn't hear a car, so I guess we can assume he parked down the road a piece and came up through the woods."

"Didn't want them to hear the engine," Titus said. His voice was flat as a pancake.

"Yeah. So he was really wearing a wolf mask?"

"Yes. Dressed in all black with his sleeves taped inside his gloves. About five-foot-ten, maybe one-ninety to two hundred pounds. He was strong. I shot that window, but he blew through it like it was crepe paper," Titus said.

"Why you think he came out here?" Trey asked.

Titus held his hat by the brim and let it move back and forth.

"He was trying to hurt me. Kellie and I are friends." He paused. "We used to date. I'm surprised you don't know that. Everyone else does. The killer knows. That's why he came here," Titus said.

"Nah, I knew that, but why go after your ex? Why not go after Darlene, not that I want him to go after Darlene," Trey said.

"People were talking about Kellie. She was the new gossip," Titus said.

"Well, Carla is taking Kellie over to the Hampton Inn and spending the night with her. She wants to leave first thing in the morning. Are we letting her go?" Trey asked.

Titus stepped out of the SUV and stood to his full height. "Yeah. If we need her, we can always get her back. We got Hector's info. I'll notify his people."

"Hey, why don't you let me do that? You don't really want to have to explain to them what happened here, do you? They don't need the gory details," Trey said.

"No, I'll do it. I have to do it," Titus said.

"You said he wanted to hurt you. Why just you?" Trey said.

"He's focused on me. He blames me for breaking up his little triumvirate. I challenged him on the phone. Challenged him through Dayane. He called again today and I pushed him about his birth mother. Called him by his true name. The name Elias gave him." Titus put on his hat.

"He called again today? When were you gonna tell us that?" Trey asked.

"Tomorrow at the daily meeting," Titus said. He turned to look at the cottage. At the splintered door.

"He said my flock wasn't safe."

Titus put on his hat.

"I guess he was right."

By the time he got home, his father and Marquis were asleep. He climbed the steps and peeled himself out of his uniform. He put his gun in the nightstand. He'd have Trey write up the report of the discharge of a weapon during an attempted arrest. If the rule didn't apply to him as well as his team, then what use was the rule?

He lay back in his bed and stared at the ceiling.

The killer was a friend of Cole Marshall's. He was sure of that, but it was looking like he was a secret friend. A friend he wasn't seen with out in public. Dayane knew, but she was gone. Either scared off or face-up in a hole in the ground. He had never been so close to catching this bastard and never so far away at the same time. If he had gone after him instead of comforting Kellie, he might have caught him. Might have pulled off his mask and seen his face. The face of a monster who walked on two feet. But could he have looked at himself in the mirror if he hadn't pulled her out of that closet?

Titus pulled the blanket up around him. He didn't know how the man in the glass would have looked at him if he hadn't.

He heard his cell phone vibrate on the nightstand. He grabbed it and checked the time. It was a little after 1:00 A.M.

It was Darlene.

"Hello?" Titus said.

"Hey," Darlene said.

"Hey, you all right?"

"I should ask you that. Heard somebody got killed over at your friend's cottage," Darlene said.

Titus grimaced. There was an ache in her words. "Yeah. Somebody tried to break in."

"Can you come over?" Darlene asked.

"I . . . I mean, you sure? I don't want to put you in danger, Darlene. This guy seems to have it bad for me," Titus said.

"I need you to come over. Can you do that for me?"

Titus pulled up next to Darlene's car. Her little sedan was on his left, and on his right was a row of boxwoods that her dad had used as a property line since they'd moved in back in 1998. Darlene had told him that getting the Parker boy down the street to trim them for him now that his arthritis would no longer allow him to do it was one of the saddest days of her dad's life.

Titus got out of his Jeep and walked up to the front step. Darlene came out and met him before he could knock on the door.

"Y'all okay over here? Is somebody bothering you?" Titus asked.

Darlene shook her head. He saw that her eyes were red. "No. Daddy was sleeping with his shotgun right up until they left."

"Left? What do you mean, left? Where'd they go?"

"Patterson's Walk over in Williamsburg. It's a senior living place. We closed down the flower shop on Tuesday. Just haven't told anyone yet."

"Why didn't you tell me? I would've helped them move. I could have—"

Darlene cut him off. "What, Titus? What could you have done? You're working on this Spearman thing. And you should be working on it. People are scared to death. This is what you have to do. It's who you are. I know that. So I didn't bother you."

"You wouldn't have been bothering me, Darlene."

Darlene bit her bottom lip, then wiped at her eyes with the back of her damaged hand. "Titus, I'm leaving too."

Titus leaned against the railing on the step. "What do you mean, you're leaving? Where you going? What about us? What are we gonna do?"

Darlene smiled a wistful smile. "When we started seeing each other, I knew that you carried a lot on you. I could almost see it weighing down those broad shoulders. I told myself I could help you through it. And I tried. God knows I tried, Titus. 'Cause you, more than anybody I know, deserve to be happy. But you don't wanna be.

For some reason, you think you gotta suffer. And I'm not the woman you want to help you out of that hole you made for yourself."

"Didi, don't say that. I . . . I love you. Whatever's going on, we can work it out," Titus said.

"You don't love me, Titus. You want to. And I want you to so bad, but it ain't there. I've been trying to hold on to you, and that's like trying to grab smoke. When my parents told me they was moving, I think I realized I've been . . . spinning wheels here for too long. I'm thirty-seven years old and I've never been on a plane. I've never been out the Mid-Atlantic. I would tell myself I was staying for my parents. Then we met and I'd tell myself I was staying for you. But my parents done moved on, and we . . . I don't know what we are anymore."

Titus took her hands in his. Felt the warmth there. "We're in love, that's what we are."

Darlene pulled her hands away. "You keep saying that, because you're a good man and you think you have to. But . . . I mean, I'm glad you was there to save your friend, but why was you there at ten o'clock at night?"

Titus felt his mouth go dry.

"I . . . I was just gonna listen to the podcast interview. That is all, Darlene, I swear. We was not gonna do nothing. You know me."

Darlene leaned forward and kissed him on his cheek. She placed her hand on his chest over his heart. "I do know you. And I know you weren't going over there to cheat. I'm saying, if you loved me, you wouldn't have gone over there at all. If you loved me, you would have sent someone to check on me after it happened. But it didn't even occur to you, did it?" Darlene said. Tears shone bright like diamonds against her cheeks.

Titus didn't have an answer for her. Because she was right. He dropped his head and closed his eyes.

"Darlene, I—"

But she cut him off.

"I'm leaving in the morning for Atlanta. My cousin has a bridal shop down there. Take care of yourself, Titus."

She kissed him on the lips.

"Find somebody that makes you smile," she said. She turned and went back in the house. He stood there as he heard her lock the door, and then he watched as a hall light came on, then was extinguished like a candle.

The darkness won't be denied.

Everyone feels it now. It slips unbidden into their hearts like a cold winter wind. It infects the days like an eclipse and the nights like a blanket made of dread.

Preston Jefferies has gone to the doctor over in Red Hill to get something, anything, to help him stop dreaming. He hasn't awoken from a night's slumber without screaming since finding that crazy white preacher in his field. He wonders if he'll ever find peace beyond the wall of sleep again.

Paul Garnett has learned to be careful with the trash. There are bottles that clink together like castanets when he takes the garbage to the dump. Five, sometimes six bottles of Old Crow. He's taken to sipping from a flask during lunch. He tells himself it's the stress of the job. Times are stressful at the plant; sales are down from last year. The new president can't get his act together long enough to put in an order for American flags for all the federal buildings and military bases around the country. Paul didn't vote for the guy, but he never thought he'd be this bad. He tells himself that's why he's going to the liquor store three times a week. But it's Cole Marshall's skinned face that comes to him when he gets too close to sober.

Sundays bring little respite from the shadows swirling over Charon. From Methodist to Catholic to Baptist to Lutheran to Jehovah's Witness, ministers and pastors and elders and reverends find their words of consolation and spiritual strength falling on largely deaf ears. What God would allow such a curse to befall his people? No one will say it aloud, but many, many congregants are having a crisis of the soul. Many are putting their faith in shotgun shells and .357s, not the carpenter from Galilee.

The killer has become the Weeping Willow Man for the kids and teenagers of the county. Arcane rituals to summon him have become common practice at bonfires and house parties. For the younger children he is the latest incarnation of the bogeyman, except they can see his work on the local news. Lavon Macdonald has secretly started carrying a paring knife in his pocket just in case the Weeping Willow Man comes knocking at his door. He misses his brother, who could impersonate any cartoon character Lavon requested. He misses him so much he feels like he might be going crazy, if he only knew what going crazy actually felt like. His father can't seem to stop crying. Lavon wonders if that's what it really looks like when you lose your mind.

Darlene drives past the statue of Ol' Rebel Joe as she turns onto Route 18. She tells herself she is doing the right thing, even if she had to subtly threaten her parents to move into Patterson Walk by telling them she was leaving no matter what. She doesn't regret what she said to Titus but, she wonders, if the Weeping Willow Man hadn't tried to kill his ex-girlfriend, would she have broken up with him? Her girl Sandra called her brave for lighting out for Atlanta. She didn't have the heart to tell her it wasn't bravery or independence that was driving her. It was pure uncut terror. From the moment she heard about the attack, all she could think was, RUN.

Run from this town, from Titus breaking her heart inch by agonizing inch, from this killer who had targeted him and the people close to him. It wasn't that she didn't think he could protect her. It was the idea he might have to choose between her and his ex, or his father, or his brother. She couldn't see a scenario where she was the one that he chose. It was this realization that drove her down Interstate 95.

The members of the Fall Fest Committee kept planning the event with the grim determination of the musicians playing on the deck of the Titanic. *Death, darkness, terror: nothing would stop them from setting up the pie-eating booth and the crab-pot-pulling platform. Elizabeth Morehood, the chairperson, gave a rousing "Spartans at the Gates of Thermopylae" speech during the last planning meeting about how important the Fall Fest* was to the county. How they couldn't let a monster in their midst take this from them. How they couldn't let him win.

She didn't say how she had embezzled thousands of dollars from the committee treasury in the form of booth permits and the funds from the annual raffle. She didn't mention how she was planning on moving money from the parking fees and the carnival rides to cover the shortfall. She didn't say how she had no intention of letting that Black bastard slap handcuffs on her like he had bloody Alan Cunningham.

Ricky Sours found himself trying to talk down some of his most ardent followers who wanted to carry weapons on the day of the parade at Fall Fest. Talking to them now was like trying to pet a starving bear. There was a lust in their eyes that frightened him. They wanted a confrontation. They wanted to split skulls and rend sinew. They couldn't do it to the person killing their neighbors, so perhaps anyone who dared to stand in opposition to them on the day of the parade would do.

He felt like that old Mickey Mouse cartoon with the dancing brooms. His creation was no longer under his control.

Mare-Beth Hillington tried to cry for her husband, but she found herself too overcome by the knowledge that an unwashed glass in the sink wouldn't come with a backhand.

Dayane Carter welcomed the darkness. In its embrace she found peace. It was there she was safe. There she couldn't see what he'd done to her flesh.

TWENTY-SEVEN

Fall Fest was in full swing.

Titus stood at the corner of Main Street and Courthouse Lane in front of the old pharmacy. Courthouse Lane had been blocked off for the festival. It stretched from the corner of Main Street to the Brickhouse Road, which ran parallel to Main Street. In between the two was the courthouse, the old colonial jail, the county treasurer's office, and the courthouse green, a wide expanse of fescue with benches and water fountains. Courthouse Lane also ran past Ol' Rebel Joe's statue.

Most of the festival took place on the green. There were several carnival rides set up there, arts and crafts booths, the three-legged race, the pie-eating contest, food booths, cotton candy machines, and a bevy of accoutrements that saw the light of day only during a small-town community celebration.

The crab-pot-pull platform stretched thirty feet into the sky at the far end of the green, away from the crowds. Contestants would stand on the platform and see who could pull up the crab pots the fastest. Titus wondered if someone would finally beat his father's time. Albert Crown had held the record for the fastest pull for nearly thirty years. Jaime Chambers, a big ol' hoss of a boy who worked on the *Busted Bottle* fishing boat, had come close last year.

Titus watched as the crowd moved over the green and the closed street like some amorphous organism, flexing and relaxing, expanding and contracting as it enveloped the festival. There were way more people attending than Titus had expected. With everything going on, he would have bet the crowds would have been thin as hair on a balding man. It was rare for him to be wrong, but this was one of those occasions.

Titus heard kids shrieking, parents laughing, young people shouting. There was a breathtaking sense of jubilation that filled the air, like the scent of daffodils in the spring. Titus thought it felt forced. It was like the good people of Charon had all agreed they were going to have a good time or die trying.

Titus walked a little ways down Courthouse Lane and watched a few kids go down the carnival slide. He saw a group of high school kids taking their turn in the pie-eating contest. He saw faces he knew from the halcyon days of his youth, others he knew from the past two years since he'd returned home. Other faces were strangers to him, but they seemed to be reveling in the joy of attending a small festival in a small county deep in the Virginia lowlands.

It should always be like this, Titus thought.

He checked his watch.

It was 2:00 P.M. Ricky Sours and his boys were set to start walking up Courthouse Lane in fifteen minutes. Titus grabbed his radio.

"Heads up. Fifteen minutes to the march. Let's get the perimeter in place," Titus said.

"Roger that," Carla said.

"Roger. I mean roger, I got it, not Roger," Davy sputtered.

"Get in place, Davy," Titus said.

"Roger on that, we're coming up from the east past the green now," Danforth Sampson said. He was the deputy sheriff from Red Hill.

Titus took a deep breath and smelled fresh-popped popcorn and the sweet saccharine scent of funnel cakes. He hoped he was wrong about this march. He hoped Jamal had just been talking out his ass. He hoped Ricky Sours could keep his good ol' boys in check. He hoped he wouldn't need the extra help, but he'd rather have it and not need it than need it and not have it.

"Hoping is trying to swim across a river, preparedness is bringing a map to find a good place to cross," Special Agent Tolliver used to say.

They hadn't been prepared that day at the DeCrain compound. Titus didn't want to make that mistake again.

He heard a murmur break out under the laughter as Danforth and the four deputies he brought joined with Carla, Davy, Steve, and Pip on the left side of Courthouse Lane. On the right was Deputy Caldwell Thomas and six deputies from Maryville, the next county up from Red Hill. He'd met Caldwell at a state-mandated training session earlier this year. He'd been impressed by the wide-shouldered, garrulous man with the severe buzz cut. He was as close to a friend as Titus had made since becoming sheriff.

Titus touched his badge, ran his fingers over the edges of the star.

"They'll love you. They'll hate you. But you have to make them respect you. And you do that by calling it down the middle," one of his instructors had said. He'd been talking about being an agent, but Titus thought it applied to being a sheriff too.

"TENNNNNNN-SHUN!" Ricky Sours yelled.

Titus squinted.

"What the fuck?" he whispered.

Ricky and his crew numbered about thirty. They were all dressed in historically accurate Confederate uniforms. Jasper was playing flag bearer. He was carrying a flagpole that was about six feet long with a huge Confederate flag attached to it. Titus could hear a fife and a drum report, which he was sure was historically inaccurate, as the Sons of the Confederacy made their way down Courthouse Lane.

"Look alive, here they come," Titus said.

Titus felt his skin begin to crawl. He knew intellectually that it was 2017, that the Fourteenth Amendment had been passed more than a hundred years ago, that racism was alive and well, but he was a sheriff who could and would arrest anyone, white or Black, who got out of pocket.

And yet.

He felt an atavistic revulsion roll through his body. The sight of these men, men who thought their lack of complete success in their every endeavor was proof of the falsity of their privilege, in their dress grays, made him sick. Not afraid, not disquieted, but physically nauseated. Seeing them strut down the street was like biting into a steak and tasting maggots.

"Let's keep the crowd on the green back at least six feet," Titus said into his radio. He didn't really think that was going to be a problem. The majority of folks weren't paying any attention to Ricky and his boys. They were too busy playing ring toss and eating slices of whiskey watermelon. There was a smattering of people clapping and waving at the marchers, but even they didn't appear that engaged. It was more about politeness, not polemics.

"They're approaching the statue now," Carla said. She was a little farther down the road.

"Gotcha," Titus said. Ricky and his crew were allowed to walk to the end of the street past the statue, then turn around and head home to rail against immigrants, Blacks, and anyone not straight, white, and male in the privacy of their garages over a case of cheap beer and wounded pride.

Titus heard the sound of a chorus rise up behind him. He heard the words of the song before he turned around to face the choir.

"WE SHALL OVERCOOOOOOME."

A large group of people were turning the corner at Main Street and walking down Courthouse Lane. They were a cornucopia of the citizenry of Charon County walking side by side. Black, white, Latinx, gay, straight, old, young. It was everyone men like Ricky Sours feared.

"Ten-eighteen, ten-eighteen! I need backup at the corner of Main. I repeat, backup at the corner of Main," Titus yelled into his radio. He stepped off the sidewalk and stood in the path of the counterprotesters, who numbered at least sixty. In response, the counterprotesters linked arms.

Jamal Addison was in the middle of the front row. His eyes and Titus's found each other's for a brief moment. Titus didn't like what he saw there. Jamal had the eyes of a man who was resigned to his fate. A man who was willing, who expected, to have to withstand unimaginable agony.

He had the eyes of a martyr.

Titus had seen those eyes before.

"Stop! Stop right now! You don't have a permit! The Sons of the Confederacy have been allotted this time to march—"

"Fuck a permit!" someone yelled.

"We won't be replaced! We won't be forgotten!"

The refrain rose up behind Titus like a battle cry. He didn't have to turn his head to see it was coming from the Confederate apologists behind him.

"Stop now, y'all!" Davy said. He and Steve had joined Titus in the middle of the road. Titus saw Caldwell and his men get in front of Ricky and his boys. They were trying to keep some of the men in gray from breaking formation and rushing the counterprotesters.

"Caldwell, try and turn them toward the green!" Titus yelled into his radio.

"Will do," Caldwell said.

"Jamal, stop this!" Titus yelled.

Jamal looked at him, but he only sang louder.

"Fucking niggers!" someone from the Confederate group screamed. Titus felt the scream as much as he heard it. It was full of a wild idiot rage, the howl of an animal caught in a trap of its own making.

A brown beer bottle sailed through the air.

It shattered near Jamal's feet, shards exploding upward and outward like razor-sharp butterflies.

Goddamn it, Titus thought.

About twenty people from the counterprotesters broke free and rushed past him, Davy, and Steve. Caldwell's deputies met them, and for a moment they were able to hold them back, but that moment passed into the river of time and then some of Ricky's boys were pushing forward and now the fists were flying and now the rage and anger and fear had burst like an aneurysm and Titus was yelling into his radio for everyone to concentrate on the altercation and he was telling Steve and Davy to push the remaining counter-protesters back. Folks on the green were running and Titus could hear children crying, long mournful wails that cut through the air like needles into flesh.

It was then he heard the truck.

Its snarl superseded all the howls and the screams and the sad pathetic battle cries. Its engine was a dragon announcing his arrival, presaging the cataclysm he was about to bring forth.

Titus saw the counterprotesters begin to scatter. They ran up on the sidewalks or headed for the courthouse green. A few of the older ones, like Reverend Wilkes, weren't moving quite fast enough to escape the truck bearing down on them.

Titus watched as the reverend's body flew up in the air, his arms waving to and fro. Another body joined him, twisting and turning like a piece of paper caught in the wind. As the crowd scattered, Titus could see the truck fully now. It was a red and white box truck. The Cunningham Flag Factory logo was painted on the hood.

Titus looked to his left and his right.

Steve and Davy were gone.

He could see movement out of the corner of his eye. He realized they had joined the crowd running for the hills. Caldwell and his men had succeeded in turning most of the Confederates, but a few people were still in the street from both sides of the conflict.

Titus's mind was working at millions of miles per hour. His synapses were firing like firecrackers. He saw the driver of the truck staring at him through the windshield, his teeth bared.

Titus drew his gun.

He was standing in the middle of the street like some Old West gunslinger having a showdown with five thousand pounds of steel and fire.

Suddenly Carla was there by his side, with her gun drawn.

Titus aimed at the windshield.

"Get the tires!" Titus yelled.

Carla dropped to one knee.

The driver of the truck pressed on the gas and the truck went from a snarl to a monstrous roar. Behind him Titus heard voices calling out to God, to Jesus, to whatever deities may be lending an ear.

Titus pulled the trigger five times in quick succession. He heard Carla let loose with a barrage of shots aimed at the truck's front left tire.

The bullets pierced the windshield and slammed into Denver Carlyle like a hammer from the heavens. Titus watched as the truck broke hard to the left, then rolled up on the sidewalk and slammed into the front of Wild Iris Collectibles, coming to a stop with a vicious crunch. Titus moved toward the truck and braced his back against the trailer while reaching out with his right hand to open the door. Carla was behind him, the barrel of her gun still smoking.

Denver Carlyle's body flopped out of the cab and sprawled across the cool asphalt. Four of Titus's shots had caught him in the face. Denver wouldn't be having an open-casket funeral.

Davy and Steve came running over. Pip came up to Titus and stood between him and the body.

"You okay? Goddamn, that's the damnedest thing I've ever seen in my whole life. Y'all stared down a fucking truck," Pip said.

Titus holstered his gun and ran toward Reverend Wilkes. He passed the rear of the delivery truck, the exhaust spitting oil.

"Titus, you okay?" Pip yelled.

Reverend Wilkes was lying on his side. His right leg was bent behind him at an impossible angle. Both his arms were going the wrong way. Titus dropped to his knees beside him. His beard was soaked in blood. His mouth was coated in it. His eyes were open, but what they saw now was beyond the understanding of men like Titus. Reverend Wilkes belonged to the ages now.

Titus wished he could close the man's eyes, but he knew that only worked in movies.

He ran over to the other body lying near the courthouse green. It was a woman, twisted and torn like Reverend Wilkes, but she was moaning in pain. Titus dropped to his haunches. He recognized her as Sandra James, one of Darlene's friends.

He stood and faced his team. He faced Caldwell and his men. Danforth and his folks.

"She's alive! Call fire and rescue! Let's secure the scene. And get a sheet for Denver," Titus said.

No one moved at first.

"Go! Go! Let's do the job!" he yelled.

"You heard him, let's move!" Carla said.

As they began to attend to their duties Titus touched the badge again. Sometimes that star felt like a shield over your heart, sometimes it felt like an anchor dragging you down, and other times, well, other times it felt like a cheap-ass piece of tin.

The ambulance came and took away Sandra. The undertakers came and took away Denver and Reverend Wilkes. Titus had five of the Confederates and three of the counterprotesters arrested based on information from Caldwell and his men.

Titus found Jamal sitting alone on a bench near the statue.

"Are you okay? You need the EMTs to look at you?" Titus asked.

Jamal shook his head. He looked up at Titus with haunted eyes. "Reverend Wilkes was a good man. I told him he didn't have to come. He said it was his duty as a man of God." He covered his face with his hands.

"They're never going to change, are they, Titus? People like Ricky, like Denver, all the marching and singing in the world ain't gonna make a damn bit of difference. It's never gonna touch their hearts. And now Reverend Wilkes is dead," he said, his voice cracking.

Titus sat next to him on the bench.

"I don't know. All I do know is violence begets more violence and all violence is a confession of pain. Hurt people tend to hurt people. Ricky had his folks all worked up, including Denver. Then we arrested Denver for a DUI yesterday. That was his third in five years. That meant he was going to lose his CDL. Lose his job. This was about the statue, but it was also about him. His life was spiraling out of control. He felt like he was losing everything. His job, his life. For a lot of these folks that statue is just a symbol of everything they fear they've lost. And people like you, like me, like Reverend Wilkes, we make easy scapegoats," Titus said.

"You know what Ervin told me the other day? Said he was at the Watering Hole and he heard Denver tell a joke. About, what do you call seven dead Black kids in the woods? A good start. Those are the kind of people we're dealing with, Titus. I don't know. Maybe it's time to give up. Let them keep their fucking statue. Maybe Reverend Wilkes would be alive if I hadn't—"

"You didn't kill him. Denver Carlyle did. Don't give up, Jamal. One day that fucking statue is coming down. And boys like Ricky are gonna have to watch it fall," Titus said.

He left Jamal and went to Elizabeth Morehood.

He told her they had to cancel the rest of the festival. She refused at first.

"Elizabeth, two people are dead. The festival is done. It's over. Go home."

"Titus, I understand that, but we need this. Now, I propose we shut things down for an hour, then reopen for the street dance tonight."

Titus stared at her, dumbfounded. "Elizabeth, people just died on this road. Are folks supposed to get their boogie on in Reverend Wilkes's blood?"

"Of course we will clean up the street during the intermission."

"Elizabeth, go home, or I'll have you arrested for obstruction of a police investigation. Fall Fest is over," Titus said. He saw her face change then, and suddenly there was a bitterness there that aged her ten years. She turned and walked away with her face drawn up tight at sharp angles.

Titus got back to the station and went to his office. Pip came in the office and closed the door.

"You had no choice, Titus," he said.

"The hospital said Sandra might be paralyzed. Reverend Wilkes is dead. We got a crazy man running around chopping people up and killing kids. A teacher and the son of a friend of mine were helping him kill those kids. The Fall Fest Committee wanted to keep the festival going, did I tell you that? What the fuck is wrong with people, Pip? What the fuck is wrong with Charon?"

Pip sat down in one of the chairs in front of Titus's desk. He took off his hat and wiped at his forehead with the back of his hand. A shock of iron-gray and black hair fell into his face.

"My grandma used to tell me how the early members of the Mennonite church was against slavery because they thought owning another person couldn't be part of God's plan. They felt like being slave owners was an unforgivable sin that would curse them to hell. Stain their sons and daughters for generations." Pip took a breath.

"Charon's been the home of so many terrible sins. Maybe there's a curse here. One that's stained us all," he said.

"You been around the world, Pip. You can't believe that the Mark of Cain or Original Sin have made us suffer like this," Titus said.

Pip shook his head.

"You asked me what was wrong with Charon. That's the best I got."

Albert was sitting in the living room with Marquis when he got home. His father jumped up and came to him with his arms outstretched. He grabbed Titus in a tight embrace.

"Boy, you gotta stop scaring me like this," Albert said. Titus wondered how his father dealt with his fear for him when he was with the Bureau. He wondered how Albert would react if he knew how close he'd come to death. How he'd played judge, jury, and executioner for Red DeCrain.

Titus hugged his father back.

"I'm okay, Pop."

Albert released him and stepped back. Marquis popped him on the shoulder with a left-handed slap.

"You gonna have to make some room on the wall," Marquis said.

"What?" Titus asked.

Marquis pointed to the deer head above the mantel. The twelve-pointer Titus had shot when he was thirteen.

"You got another head to mount," Marquis said with a laugh.

Titus didn't join him.

"Sorry, trying to hide the fact that I was scared for you," Marquis said.

"Key say they talking about you on them internets," Albert said.

"Don't you worry about that, Pop. That's all it is, talk," Titus said.

"Yeah, but talk get them boys riled up. Jasper especially been running his mouth," Marquis said.

There was a coldness to his voice that disquieted Titus.

"Like I said, it's just talk. Don't worry about it, okay?" Titus said.

"Hmm," Marquis said.

"I mean it, Key. Leave it alone."

Marquis shrugged. "We out of 'shine, but I bought some Jameson."

"Nah, I'm okay, I think I'm just going to bed," Titus said.

Marquis shook his head. "Stop that."

"Stop what?"

"Stop trying to carry everything by yourself. Come on, have a drink with me and Pop. Let's send a toast up to Mom," Marquis said.

Titus looked at Marquis, saw how hard it was for him to even mention their mother.

Titus felt the weight on his shoulders lighten infinitesimally.

"All right," he said.

Albert tapped out after two shots. Titus and Marquis finished the bottle an hour later. Now Titus was sitting at the kitchen table listening to Marquis snore in the living room. He picked up the empty green bottle and carried it to the trash can. He felt loose and wild, like a mean dog suddenly let off its leash.

He hated feeling like that because a part of him, a part he had shared with few people besides Kellie, liked it too much.

He got a glass of water from the sink. He peered out the window into the night. Red DeCrain no longer waited for him in the land of dreams alone.

Titus finished his water and rinsed the glass and set it in the dish strainer. He splashed some water on his face.

He was tired. More tired than he could ever remember being before. Tired in his bones in a way that one night of sleep wouldn't cure. He needed to go into a coma for a month. Become a somnambulist so he could keep working.

His radio crackled.

He would have sighed, but he was too exhausted.

"Go for Titus."

"Hey, Titus, just got a 911 call from Calvin Macdonald. Lavon didn't come home from school today. They thought he went to the festival, then when they heard about the . . . thing with Denver, they came down to the station looking for him. Titus, it's nine P.M. Ain't nobody seen that little boy since his mama sent him to school this morning," Kathy said.

The weight crashed back down onto his shoulders hard enough to crush his spine. A hole opened in the pit of his stomach.

I saw your brother walking all alone today.

TWENTY-EIGHT

Titus's eyes were as dry as sandpaper.

He'd been up nearly twenty hours. Popping little concentrated energy drinks and guzzling coffee to fuel his body when his body was so far past the point of exhaustion, he was damn near hallucinating.

He'd pulled the whole department in to find Lavon. He'd notified the state police. He'd sent out announcements on every social media platform. He'd sent out an Amber Alert. He had personally driven up and down every back road in Charon County, even gone out to Piney Island.

Nothing.

He'd gone to see Calvin and Dorothy last night. They'd looked like phantom versions of their former selves. Their faces were ghostly, drawn tight across their skulls. Titus noticed they didn't sit together on the couch. Calvin sat in the recliner; Dorothy sat at the far end of the sofa. As if they couldn't stand being too close to each other. Tragedy can bring some folks together. It can also tear asunder old wounds and make them weep anew.

"Find him, Titus. Please, find our boy," Calvin had said, his voice heavy with grief. Titus's old friend was a study in fragility. He could see Calvin was close to breaking, on the verge of a dissolution that might be unrepairable. Dorothy seemed to be in another world. A world where her oldest son wasn't dead and her youngest wasn't missing.

Titus had left them without making any promises. He'd made

a promise to another child's mother, and so far that promise had borne no fruit. He wouldn't add hope to the heartbreak Calvin and Dorothy were experiencing. If they found Lavon unharmed that would be wonderful, nearly miraculous. But if they didn't find him, or if they did find what was left of him, that promise of hope would become a cruelty that Calvin and Dorothy didn't deserve.

"Calling Titus," Carla's voice came over the radio.

"Go ahead for Titus," he said.

"The state boys are here with the divers. You want us to wait for you or go ahead and get started?" she asked.

Titus closed his eyes. He thought he could feel his lids click. "No, don't wait for me. Go ahead and get started."

"Gotcha," Carla said.

He'd brought in the state police to drag the river and search the gravel pit pond. But he didn't really think they'd find anything. It was called due diligence, but in this case he was sure it was a waste of time. Lavon wasn't in a pond or a river or a ditch. If he was still alive, he was with the Last Wolf. The Angel of Death. And it was Titus's fault.

The killer, the Last Wolf, the Weeping Willow Man had outwitted him at every turn. Whether through good fortune or good planning, he was continuously one step ahead of them. He'd seen him, had him in his sights like that deer on the wall. He was just a man. A crazy, evil man, but right now Titus felt like he was becoming a myth. A rural legend that would join the long list of folktales and tragedies that haunted his hometown.

He'd brought them their season of pain, but now it felt like that season would never, ever end.

Titus's cell phone began to vibrate in his pocket. "Hello."

"Sheriff, it's Dr. Kim."

"Hello, Doctor."

"I wanted to let you know we have completed the autopsy on Denver Carlyle. Also, we are getting the toxicology back on the seven bodies today."

Titus didn't speak.

"Sheriff?" Dr. Kim said.

"Yeah, I'm here. Um, I appreciate you calling. Just so you know, I've brought in the state police. They are going to investigate the Carlyle shoot. And . . ."

Titus paused.

"And I'm going to let them take over the Spearman case. We will continue to provide backup and assistance, but I'm going to get them to take the lead on this. I think your contact will probably be Trooper Geary," Titus said.

The word *failure* seemed to glow like a neon sign in front of his eyes, but he knew that was just his pride talking. A good leader knew when he was in over his head or when he'd exhausted himself and his team. And Titus had exhausted them, pushed them to their limits. They were good people, every last one of them, but this case was just beyond their capabilities, and his. That was a hard pill to swallow, but he would bite down on it, crush it, and swallow it down. He didn't want to give up on the case, but what he wanted wasn't important. Finding Lavon, finding the killer, those were the important things.

His grandfather used to say doing the right thing was rarely easy, but it was always worth it. This wasn't easy, but he had to believe it would be worth it.

Dr. Kim didn't speak for nearly a minute.

"Although I have my concerns, I understand your decision, Sheriff," Dr. Kim said.

"Wait, what are your concerns?" Titus asked.

Dr. Kim was silent for a beat. "Titus, they are seven Black boys and girls."

She didn't elaborate, and Titus didn't require it.

"I'm not abandoning them. I'm not going anywhere. But the state police have more resources than we do here. My deputies have been pushed to the limit," Titus said. and immediately hated himself for doing so.

"I'm not accusing you of abandoning them, Sheriff. I know you

would never do that. I just . . . I don't know if the BCI will be as
dedicated to solving this as you are," Dr. Kim said.

Titus heard her not just with his ears but with his heart. He
listened to her not only as a sheriff but as a fellow person of color
in a position that typically conveyed power and respect but was
constantly under attack from those who sought to undermine and
delegitimize them.

"I'm not going to let them give up on these kids," Titus said.

Dr. Kim sighed. "I believe you. Maybe they can help us finally
identify this metal T thing. We've been able to quantify and catalog
all the other items we found in or on the bodies."

"The T thing," Titus repeated.

"Yes, you remember, it's like a T with a cylindrical leg and thin
crossbar," Dr. Kim said.

Titus felt like his skin was on fire. His stomach felt as hollow as
an open grave. He sat straight up in his chair.

"Dr. Kim, can you text me a picture of the T thing?" Titus asked.

"I thought you were passing this case off," Dr. Kim said.

"Not yet. Send me that picture."

This was the piece. This was the string he had to pull to unravel
it all. He was sure he was right, but he wanted to see the picture to
confirm.

"Sent."

A few seconds later, Titus's phone vibrated.

He stared at the picture. Saw past its rusted, corroded appearance. Saw it for what it was, but also what it would be for him, for
the county.

A key to finally let in the light and chase away the darkness that
had enveloped them like a mourning shroud ever since he'd first seen
those poor broken bodies among the roots of the weeping willow tree.

Titus parked in front of the public entrance to the CFF, or the
Cunningham Flag Factory, and hopped out of the SUV. He checked

his watch. It was 9:00 A.M. The first shift was just about due for their first break. That was fine. He didn't need anyone from the floor. He needed the plant manager. And everyone in Charon knew Caleb Cunningham didn't come out onto the floor unless it was to walk to his Hummer at the end of the day.

Titus walked in the front office and stood in front of the counter. There was a stout older white woman sitting at a desk, and beyond her was a glass-enclosed office, and beyond that Titus could see the shadowy labyrinthine inner workings of CFF. Black iron and steel sewing and embroidering machines that stretched on for what seemed like miles. Industrial irons and conveyer belts that hissed and growled like beasts hungry for fingers and hands. American flags, flags for the state of Virginia, and flags for the various branches of the military were sewn, embroidered, pressed, and then folded for delivery all across the country.

And up and down the East Coast.

The receptionist was looking down at her phone. She hadn't noticed Titus.

"Excuse me, I need to speak with Caleb," Titus said.

The woman raised her head and squinted at him. "Do you have an appointment?"

Titus tapped his badge. "This is my appointment. I need to talk with him. Now."

The woman opened her mouth, then abruptly shut it. She picked up a desk phone, pushed a few buttons. A few seconds later Titus watched through the glass window as Caleb picked up the phone in his office. He looked up, saw Titus, spoke in the phone, and hung up.

"He said come on in," the receptionist said.

Titus went to the hinged section of the countertop, flipped it up, and headed to the office. He went through a heavy wooden door into the glass cubicle. Caleb didn't stand or offer his hand. Titus could feel the thrum of the machines inside the plant in the soles of his feet.

"Titus, what can I do for you?" Caleb said in a voice that said he absolutely didn't want to do anything for him.

"Caleb, I need the truck logs for Denver Carlyle and the truck he was driving for the past few years."

"What? Why do you need our truck logs?"

"Police business," Titus said.

Caleb furrowed his brow. "Those logs are confidential; they are the property of CFF. I don't know about just up and showing them to you without a court order or something like that. Besides, we are still talking to our attorney about who is going to reimburse us for that truck that Denver crashed. We may have to sue the county. In light of that, I don't think I should even be talking to you."

Titus was too tired to roll his eyes at the idea of Caleb suing the county, because his driver had run down a crowd of peaceful protestors.

"You know about the kids found out by the weeping willow tree on Tank's property?" Titus asked.

"Well, yes, but I don't—"

Titus cut him off. "One of those kids had a truck lock shoved down their throat. See, the killer took one of those locks you use to make sure nobody hijacks your shipments and made a fifteen-year-old boy swallow it. I didn't recognize it at first, but then yesterday I saw it on the truck Denver was driving when he tried to kill Jamal Addison and his people. So I don't have time for a fucking court order. I need Denver's logs and I need them right now."

"I . . . I, uh."

"Caleb, did I fucking stutter? A boy's life might be at stake. Get me the goddamn logs," Titus said. His voice rose up over the sound of the machines in the plant. Whatever resistance Caleb had thought about offering was washed away by the gale force of Titus's command.

Caleb grabbed the phone on his desk.

"Gloria, pull Denver Carlyle's delivery logs for the, for—"

"The past five years," Titus said.

"The past five years. Yes, you can just send it as a document," Caleb said. "Last year we had all the previous logs scanned and we went to an electronic system."

Titus stared at him.

An alert went off on the laptop on Caleb's desk. He moved his fingers over the keyboard. Then he spun the laptop around. "Here it is."

Titus sat down in a plastic molded chair in front of Caleb's desk and started going over the logs. It appeared that Denver drove the same truck for the majority of his time at CFF, truck number 873. Titus pored over the logs, clicking the cursor and advancing page after page. A bitter taste built up in his mouth. The dates weren't lining up. He didn't need his notepad; he'd memorized the dates and the locations. He kept clicking, kept looking, kept hoping.

"Don't see what you need?" Caleb asked.

Titus didn't speak. He kept clicking the cursor.

"Wait, wait, these dates in the summer. These aren't Denver's initials," Titus said softly.

"What's that?" Caleb asked.

Titus moved the cursor. He went to the search bar. He typed in "August 1, 2015."

"Whose initials are RGL?" Titus asked.

"Hmm, let me see it," Caleb said.

Titus spun the laptop back around.

"Oh yeah, when we are really busy, which usually happens during the summer, we take on additional drivers for deliveries. We run some rental trucks in addition to our regular fleet. Denver volunteered to drive one of the rental trucks because the AC was better, so one of the temporary guys drove his usual truck. We used to really be rocking and rolling during the summer," Caleb said.

"The initials, Caleb."

"Oh right. Well, we like to get guys that already have a CDL. This is Royce Lazare, you know, the school bus driver? Already got a CDL. Dependable as hell," Caleb said.

Titus's mouth went dry.

Titus studied the sharp angular writing on the screen. The three letters had wicked edges like the serrated edge of the razor blade they used to use to prick your finger when he was a kid.

Royce Lazare.

Lazare. Move the letters around and they spelled a different word.

Azrael.

The Angel Of Death.

"Putting out a BOLO for Royce Lazare. He is armed and dangerous and I have reason to believe he has Lavon Macdonald with him. Repeat, Royce Lazare is to be arrested on sight. Take extreme caution when approaching him," Titus said into his radio.

"You think it's him?" Carla's voice came through the speaker.

"No, I know it's him," Titus said. "Cam, call the school garage and see if he's supposed to work and find out if he called out. I'm heading to his house. I'm only five minutes away. Someone see if his bus is still on the road if he did go to work today."

"I'm on the other side of the county. I'll be there in fifteen," Carla said.

"I'm on Piney, I'll be there too, about twenty minutes," Steve said.

"No, don't everybody come down. If he's not there, we don't need him slipping out of the county," Titus said. He was ripping down Route 18. He turned onto Zephyr Road, then slammed the pedal to the floor. He'd pulled up Royce's address from the DMV database on the SUV's computer. Royce lived at the end of Tall Chief Lane. Titus crushed the brake under his right foot and kept the gas down with his right and took a hard left onto Tall Chief Lane. Smoke from his back tires engulfed the SUV as he drifted to make the turn.

Royce lived at 2274 Tall Chief Lane. Titus scanned the mailboxes as he drove.

"Twenty-two-sixty-eight, sixty-nine, seventy," he said to himself. He slammed on the brakes.

There was a red truck idling at the head of the lane near the mailbox for 2274 Tall Chief Lane. Titus jumped out of the SUV.

"What are you doing? You gotta get outta here," Titus yelled.

Tom Sadler got out of his truck.

"I heard you on the scanner. I was up the road. I came to help," Tom said.

"You don't work for me anymore," Titus said.

Tom slammed the door of his truck shut. "You can't go down there alone. If it's him, you gonna need help. You can deputize me as a citizen. I got my own sidearm. I'm ready to go."

"I don't have time for this. Carla is on the way. Now move," Titus said.

"I'm here now! I can help. Titus, please, I need to do this. Please let me do this," Tom begged.

Titus looked down the long driveway that led to Royce's house. It bisected a field of dead brown grass as it wound down to a white two-story farmhouse.

"You got your vest?" Titus said.

Tom pulled up his shirt showing the black Kevlar vest.

"If he's here, he might have Lavon Macdonald with him. We are trying to take him alive, but don't hesitate to take him down if he doesn't look like he's going quietly," Titus said.

"Roger that," Tom said.

"Time to end the season of pain," Titus said under his breath.

"What?"

"Nothing. Let's go," Titus said.

itus and Tom parked next to each other at the end of Royce's driveway. Titus was on the left and Tom was on the right. Next to Tom's truck was an older Econoline van. Titus wasn't sure what Royce drove, but he thought a plain white old-school van was right in line with his MO. Hide in plain sight. Be so nondescript you're unremarkable. Blend in like just another brick in the wall.

Titus drew his gun. Tom followed suit.

The farmhouse was in good condition. There was a fresh coat of paint on the screened-in porch. A decorative weather vane stood off to the left in the field next to the house. The aluminum siding was immaculate like Royce had just pressure-washed it.

Was he getting rid of evidence or just sprucing up his house? Titus wondered.

He opened the screen door and stepped up onto the porch. There was some patio furniture on the porch and a clay chimney in the corner. Titus went to the front door of the house and banged on it. It was a six-light door with white grids in between the glass. When no one answered, he peered through the window. The house looked empty.

Titus banged again.

Nothing.

"What do we do now?" Tom said.

"We have probable cause to believe someone is in distress in here," Titus said, hating the taste of the lie on his tongue. If Royce wasn't here, if Lavon wasn't here, anything they found would be in-admissible in court. A first-year law student would see right through his story.

But his gut told him that this was the place. This was the abattoir. And Royce was the butcher.

Titus grabbed the doorknob.

The door was unlocked.

"All right. Come on," Titus said.

The house had a cloyingly sweet aroma. It was as if someone had lit too many fragrant candles. They moved through a sparse living room. There was a sofa, a love seat, and a small flat-screen TV hung on the wall over what appeared to be an unused fireplace. Titus noted there were no pictures on the walls. No family or friends, no moments in time captured for posterity's sake. They worked their way through a small parlor. Straight ahead was the huge kitchen. To the left was a closed door.

Titus pointed to the door with two fingers, but he didn't speak. Tom nodded. Titus approached the door. He flattened himself against the wall and reached out with his left hand and grasped the doorknob. Tom moved to the right of the door and copied Titus's stance. Titus counted to three with his fingers, then turned the knob and pushed the door open.

He went in, crouching low while sweeping his gun from side to side. It was a small bedroom, a single bed in the center. It was just as spartan as the living room.

Tied to the bed by her hands and her feet was Dayane Carter. She was naked and not moving. Titus went to her and put his fingers to her neck. She had a pulse, albeit a weak one.

"Jesus Lord," Tom whispered.

Most of Dayane's naked body was covered with cuts and slashes. These cuts and slashes formed words and phrases that had the tone of biblical scripture but weren't in any Bible he'd ever read. Royce had cut her and then apparently cauterized her wounds.

"He wanted to keep her alive for as long as possible," Titus mumbled. If that had been Royce's plan, it was only half working. Many of her wounds were infected. Titus realized now why Royce was using so much air freshener.

"Should we split up? I go upstairs, you check down here?" Tom whispered.

"No, you see those double doors in the kitchen? They probably lead to a root cellar. Call 911 for her. I'm gonna go check it out," Titus said.

"I can call and follow you at the same time," Tom said.

"Okay, fine. Let's move," Titus said.

Titus headed for the kitchen. He heard Tom on the phone giving the address and requesting an ambulance and telling Cam to send the whole crew. The kitchen was twice the size of the one at his father's house. Where the rest of the house was a study in austerity, the kitchen was laid out with lavish equipment. There was an espresso machine and a retro stainless-steel refrigerator, a huge stainless-steel blender, and a fire-engine-red mixer. There was also a large six-slice toaster and a garish ceramic cookie jar in the shape of a teddy bear. The floor of the kitchen was set in a black-and-white-checkered pattern made with marble tile. A large, somewhat oval-shaped candy-apple-red steel table sat in the middle of the kitchen. The double door was at the far end of the oval. To the left there was a screen door that led to the backyard. To the right was a tall pantry with a cloth curtain next to a large gas oven.

Titus paused.

"Let's check that pantry first," Titus said, keeping his voice low.

"It don't look deep enough for nobody to hide in," Tom said in a whisper.

"Let's check it anyway," Titus said.

Tom turned his head to say something to Titus.

The next thing Titus knew, Tom was shoving him to the right, hard.

An explosion thundered through the kitchen and Titus saw most of Tom Sadler's head disintegrate. Titus fell against the table chest-first. The table skittered across the floor, throwing him off-balance. Instinctively he held out both his hands to break his fall.

Royce Lazare came bounding through the ruined screen door, shirtless and without his usual baseball cap or his thick brown hair. He was holding a double-barreled shotgun. Titus spun around and ended up on his backside. As he began to raise his gun, Royce swung the shotgun like a croquet mallet and cracked the stock against the knuckles of his left hand, knocking the gun free.

Titus's ears were ringing so loud he didn't hear the gun clatter across the floor. He hopped up and launched himself at Royce, tackling him around the midsection and driving him back against his counter. Royce dropped the shotgun and started raining down blows on Titus's back. Each one felt like a cinder block slamming into his spine. Titus locked his hands around the man's waist and hoisted him off his feet.

He was about to twist his body and slam Royce to the floor when he felt a punch to his right side that hurt more than any punch he'd ever received. Suddenly he couldn't catch his breath. Titus dropped Royce and used both hands to push off Royce's chest to create space between them. He tumbled backward, slipping on Tom's blood and falling to his backside again. His right side felt warm and wet.

Royce came at him holding a bowie knife.

He must have a collection, Titus thought randomly as he felt something hard and unyielding under his ass.

Royce was almost on top of him when Titus pulled his gun from under his right thigh. Royce reflexively put his hand out as Titus fired.

The bullet went right through Royce's hand and grazed his cheek, tearing off a chunk of his left ear. Royce howled and dove for the back door. Titus rolled over on his side and tried to fire again, but that shot went wide and hit the espresso machine on the counter.

Royce scrambled out the door.

Titus lay on his left side trying to hold on to his gun, but it was so heavy. His shirt was soaked in a mixture of his and Tom's blood. A ray of sunlight came through what was left of the screen door and caressed his face. The sunlight was warm. It was a contrast to the marble tile floor, which felt so cold.

The floor isn't cold. You're going into shock, he thought. The idea frightened him, but he tried his best to fight the feeling. If he could just close his eyes for a moment, just one minute, he'd regroup, get himself together, and put a bullet in Royce Lazare's head.

But what about the shock? The blood loss?

"It's okay. It's okay. I just gotta rest for a second," Titus mumbled. He closed his eyes.

The darkness wasn't that bad. In a way it was comforting. It was a place he'd run from for so long, a thing inside him that he wanted so badly to excise that he'd never considered the possibility that this was where he was supposed to be, what he was destined to become. One with the shadows, part of an endless night.

"You better shut up with that noise."

Titus heard the voice, but he refused to believe it was real. Better to keep his eyes shut and drift off than open them and have his heart broken again when he realized she wasn't there and it was all in his head.

"Boy, you hear me talking to you. You gotta get up, Titus. You gotta get up. He's got Lavon and he's gonna do terrible things to him. You gotta get up, son. He's not gone far. They're close by, but you gotta get up."

"I'm so tired, Mama," Titus said.

"I know, baby, but you gotta get up. GET UP!"

Titus's eyelids shot open.

The ray of sunlight was still lovingly touching his face. There was no one in the kitchen except him and Tom. Titus rolled over onto his stomach. He reached out and grabbed the handle of the refrigerator. Grunting, he pulled himself up from the floor and leaned against the fridge. He touched his side. He was losing a lot of blood. He took off his shirt. Moving slowly, he tied it as tight as he could around his own midsection. He tried to take a deep breath, but it hurt so much he stopped halfway.

He looked down and saw his gun on the floor. He was afraid if he leaned over he'd pass out again, so he gingerly went down as far as he could on his haunches and snatched it off the floor. He stepped away from the fridge. He had painted the stainless-steel surface in his own bloody palm prints.

He stumbled toward the back door. He forced himself to take a deep breath, cried out, and kept going.

There was blood on the grass, and it wasn't his. He followed the blood trail like he had that long-ago day when he'd bagged his twelve-pointer. The trail stopped in front of a row of six azalea bushes. Titus looked to his left and then to his right.

To the left was a brown field, recently bush hogged. To the right was a lush meadow, thick with honeysuckle. He looked down at his feet. The blood trail stopped here. The grass where the blood trail stopped was not as vibrant as the rest of the lawn. For that matter, neither was the azalea bush where he was standing.

I did some work for a boy. Helped him put in this building.

Titus reached out and touched the bush in front of him. Ran his fingers on the leaves. Touched the branches.

It was plastic.

Titus grabbed the branches and pulled.

The trapdoor the bush was attached to opened on a hinge similar to one in the counter at CFF. Titus let the bush go and peered down into a hole lit by fluorescent lights. A metal ladder was attached to the wall.

Standing in the middle of the bunker Cole Marshall had helped him build was Royce Lazare. He was holding Lavon in front of him with a knife to his throat with his good hand.

"I was wondering if you'd find it. Toss the gun and come down and join us. Come to Tartarus," Royce said. He grinned at Titus from the depths of his dungeon, blood streaking across his chest, his face, his shaved head, a manic glint in his eyes, and for a moment Titus thought he did look like an angel. One who had fallen far from grace.

THIRTY

Titus tossed the gun to the ground with a trembling hand. He knew he was running on adrenaline and endorphins, and that was expensive fuel. He had to get down there and save Lavon. No matter what happened to him, he had to save Lavon. He had failed Latrell. He wouldn't fail his brother.

Titus descended into the bunker rung by rung.

The structure was larger than he had expected. He guessed it was a good twenty-by-forty-foot room. In contrast to the minimalist décor of the farmhouse, the bunker was an exercise in garish excess. There was red and blue LED rope lighting running along the perimeter of the ceiling. A half dozen beanbag chairs were tossed around the room. Lava lamps sat on TV trays next to the bags. A Saint Andrew's cross leaned against one wall. In the middle of the room an antique embalming table held court.

Then there were the angels. Angels everywhere. Framed paintings on the wall in the style of Caravaggio and Rembrandt and Bacon. Cheap mass-produced prints with manga and comic book angels. A gray granite statue of an angel that Titus thought was probably stolen from a graveyard sat at the foot of the embalming table.

Seraphim and archangels had all borne witness to the most perverse manifestation of free will Titus could imagine.

"You like that table? I usually keep it covered when I have a guest. Guests who are going to leave, I mean," Royce said. His massive forearm was doing more of the work holding Lavon in place than the bowie knife, but the blade was still too close to the boy's neck.

"Lavon, it's going to be okay. I promise," Titus said.

Royce clucked his tongue. "You shouldn't make promises unless you can keep them, Sheriff."

Titus ignored the statement.

"You wear a wig because you don't like growing your hair out, do you, Gabriel? It kinks up on you. Did the Hillingtons make you hate that part of yourself?" Titus said.

Royce frowned. "The Hillingtons made me realize that we serve a God who is a sociopath. He set us free and lets us do things to each other, terrible things, and he and his angels just watch and laugh like Romans in the fucking Colosseum. And who gets it worse than anyone? Niggers. They are the shit on the shoe of the human race. They live in a world where everything is put in place to fuck them up and fuck them over. I did those kids a favor. What kind of life would they have in America? In a land built on murder and death in the name of 'Sky Daddy.' A deadbeat daddy who's abandoned us all. No angel ever appeared from the ether to stop us. Not one. And I prayed for them to show up. I wanted to see the holy fire just ONCE!" Royce screamed.

"That's why you killed seven little Black boys and girls, Gabriel? Because you were angry God didn't rescue you from Henry Hillington?" Titus said. He glanced at Royce's hand holding the knife. Lavon had slipped farther to the right, closer to the crook of Royce's elbow.

He was going to have to make his move soon or he was going to pass out.

Royce grinned. "You think there's only seven?"

Titus kept talking.

"I think you killed Black kids because you were trying to kill that part of yourself. I think that's why you joined the Sons of the Confederacy, wore trucker hats, and listen to Hank Williams Jr. But you can never kill that part of yourself, Gabriel."

Royce tightened his grip on Lavon.

"Don't call me that. That's not my fucking name," Royce said.

Titus held his hands up palms out and lowered his voice. "I know what they did to you. Elias, Henry, the Hillingtons. That church. And I know you were afraid. And angry. And you felt hopeless. I know what that's like. I know how it feels to pray to God for something that you want so bad and feel like he doesn't care. When I was a little boy, I prayed to God to save my mother, prayed all night sometimes, the same way you prayed for him to save you."

"And you see how that turned out? He could have done it, but he didn't. Do you know what hell is? It's not lakes of fire. It's being ignored by God. I was in hell, and he never once reached his hand down into perdition to pull me up. I WAS A CHILD! I was a child," Royce said. His eyes were wide and brilliant like emeralds.

"Maybe this is that moment. Maybe he's giving you his hand now. Let me help you . . . Royce. Let Lavon go and let me help you," Titus said. He held out his hand.

Royce closed his eyes for half a second.

When he opened them, Titus saw the devil that lived in him.

"I tell you what. Why don't you pray that I don't cut this little boy's throat, and then let's see if Michael strikes me down with his sword."

Royce gripped the handle of the bowie knife.

Titus braced himself.

He noticed Lavon's little brown hand moving. He watched as he pulled something small and silver from his front pocket.

Titus flicked his eyes up at Royce.

Royce grinned at him as he began to move the knife across Lavon's neck.

Titus leaped forward just as Lavon jammed the paring knife into Royce's forearm up to the hilt. Royce screamed, a high-pitched sound incongruous with his huge frame. Lavon dropped to his knees and scrambled out of the way as Titus slammed into Royce.

Titus grabbed the blade with his right hand while he rammed his left hand into the soft flesh of Royce's nose and cheek. Royce brought his right arm over in a clubbing motion and smashed his forearm against the side of Titus's head. It felt like someone was hitting him with a bag full of cement.

Royce pulled the knife from Titus's grip, flaying open his hand in the process. He brought the blade up in a slashing motion and Titus felt the skin of his cheek part like the Red Sea. He jumped back as Royce tried to stab him in the gut. He grabbed the blade again with his right hand, but this time he twisted it and felt it come free.

It clattered to the floor as Titus struck Royce with his right hand. Royce roared, not like a man but like some evolutionary throwback, and gripped Titus around the throat with his left hand. Still howling, he pushed Titus back against a wall, shattering two framed angel paintings that fell to the floor.

Titus felt himself fading. Royce's hand around his throat was like a bear trap. He shoved his left thumb into Royce's eye, but Royce just tightened his grip. Small black dots began to dance in front of Titus's eyes. Royce bared his teeth at him like a wolf.

Titus pawed at his belt buckle.

He felt it click and unlatch.

He touched a lever on the back.

Four inches of razor-sharp metal shot out of the rectangular brass buckle.

Titus shoved all four inches into Royce's neck under his chin. Then he pulled the blade hard to the left. Blood exploded from the wound. Royce let go of Titus and staggered back, grabbing at his throat. He fell against the embalming table, then slid to the floor, blood still pouring out of the wound in his neck like a river made of claret.

Titus glided down the wall until he felt the carpeted floor of the bunker under him. He laid his head back and tried to take a deep breath, but he couldn't seem to fill his lungs.

Lavon approached him slowly.

"Is he dead?" Lavon asked.

"Yeah," Titus said.

"Good. He wouldn't let me off the school bus. I was going home cuz I didn't want to go to the festival. He said real bad things about my brother."

"Don't . . . don't listen to him. Your brother loved you," Titus said. He felt like he was floating.

"Hey, I need you to . . . go in my pocket. Get my phone. Call 911. Tell them where we are. They're not gonna know, and I need help," Titus said.

Lavon came to him and pulled out his cell phone. He dialed 911. "Yeah, we are . . ." Lavon stopped.

"At 2274 Tall Chief Lane. In the backyard, in a bunker," Titus said.

Lavon repeated the message.

"They say they almost here," Lavon said.

Titus closed his eyes.

"That's good."

Lavon sat on the floor next to him.

"You gonna be all right," Lavon said.

Titus couldn't tell if it was a question or a statement.

"I miss my brother. Mama says he was sick. But I still miss him," Lavon said.

"I bet he misses you too," Titus said.

Then there was only the endless night.

Titus felt like he'd been chewing raw cotton. He opened his eyes and saw Albert and Marquis sitting on either side of his hospital bed. Albert noticed he was awake and hopped out of his chair with surprising agility. He grabbed Titus's left hand and squeezed it so tight Titus felt it through whatever pain meds they had pumped into him.

"My boy, my boy. You came back to me. I knew you'd come back," Albert said. Tears rolled down his weathered face and caught in his gray beard.

"How long . . . I been out?" Titus said.

"Two days," Marquis said. He stood on the right side of the bed, his huge hands gripping the railing.

Albert rubbed Titus's forehead. "I love you," Albert said.

"Love you too, Pop," Titus croaked.

"Let me get you some water. The doctor said you could have water if . . . when you woke up," Albert said.

"Yeah, I'm thirsty as hell," Titus rasped.

"I'll be right back," Albert said. He shuffled out the room, his previous agility having abandoned him.

"What's wrong with my voice?" Titus asked Marquis once he was sure Albert was out of earshot.

"That motherfucker did something to your larynx. He also got you in the liver pretty good and nicked your gallbladder, but they said you don't really need that," Marquis said. "It was touch-and-go for a minute, but me and Pop told them you're too fucking stubborn to die. Who would keep us from stealing grapes in the supermarket then?" Marquis said. He gently took Titus's right hand in his own.

Titus turned his head. The window to his left showed a serenity garden in the courtyard of the hospital. Large quartz rocks in concentric circles interspersed with liriope and pampa grass. A little wooden bench sat in the center.

"You know, when he stabbed me, I passed out for a few seconds. I was lying there on the floor, lying in my blood, in Tom's blood, thinking I was going into shock, and . . ." Titus swallowed hard. It felt like barbed wire was sliding down his throat.

"And what?" Marquis asked.

Titus licked his lips.

"I thought I heard her," Titus said.

"Heard who?"

"Her. Mama. I know it was my fight-or-flight reflex kicking my adrenaline into overdrive, making my brain fire off like a bad electrical circuit, but it felt so real, Key. I knew it wasn't. Knew if I opened my eyes she wouldn't be there. But it got me up off that floor. I guess my mind just pulled up my strongest emotion and used it to kick me into gear," Titus said.

"Your strongest emotion is grief?" Marquis asked.

"No. It's guilt."

"Ty, come on, now. Ain't nothing you got to feel guilty about when it comes to Mama. I done told you, ain't nothing you could have done, ain't nothing me or Pop could have done. That was above us," Marquis said.

"I know, but I still feel like . . ."

"You know, I don't know nothing about adrenaline and fight-or-flight or all that, but . . . okay, you say it was your brain pushing you to get up and gut that motherfucker, and that's probably true, but . . . what if we just say it was her? Say she came back to help her boy. I know you don't believe in that, but wasn't it nice to hear her voice? Cuz I'd give anything to hear her one more time," Marquis said.

Titus felt his breath come in ragged bursts.

And then he was crying, crying from deep in his belly, crying in long loud sobs that reverberated through his body, and there was Marquis with his arms around him, pulling him close and holding him tight.

"I miss her so much, Key. I couldn't save her. I couldn't save her. I miss her so much," Titus cried.

"You saved Lavon. You saved Kellie. You saved Charon. Now it's time for you to save yourself, big brother," Marquis said.

They rocked back and forth like that for a long time.

THIRTY-ONE

The twilight sky looked like a magenta dream over Charon County.

The cold December wind howled around the corners of the Crown house. Albert took the dinner plates off the kitchen table and sat them in the sink. Marquis finished his beer and tossed the bottle in the trash.

Titus came downstairs. He was wearing a black leather jacket, black T-shirt, and blue jeans. He had a brown duffel bag on his shoulder. He sat the bag down and went to the kitchen.

"Y'all gonna walk me out?" Titus said. His voice still wasn't back to normal after a month and half. The doctors said he might need surgery, but he declined. He was done with people cutting on him. He'd called Kellie to check on her once he was out of the hospital. She'd heard his voice and burst into tears.

"Oh, Virginia, what did he do to you?" she'd said, choking back a sob.

They had promised to stay in touch, but Titus had his doubts. Seeing him, hearing him would just be a reminder of the most traumatic night of her life. The last thing he wanted to do was cause her more pain.

"I don't know why you can't wait until tomorrow morning to leave," Albert said.

"Pop, I got a fifteen-hour drive ahead of me. This way I get into

Baton Rouge at nine A.M. and I can go right to the college and get settled in," Titus said.

"I still can't believe you gonna be a teacher," Marquis said.

"Professor," Titus corrected him.

Marquis waved his hand. "Whatever, I just can't see you sitting behind a desk grading papers and handing out stickers."

"I'm teaching criminology, so it's not like I'm completely giving up on law enforcement," Titus said.

"I don't know, I think you gonna be bored," Marquis said.

Albert turned around and dried his hands on a dish towel.

"If the Watering Hole hadn't burned down, I'd say we should go by there and have a goodbye drink," Albert said.

"Ain't like I ain't never coming back, Pop. And the Watering Hole was a shitty place anyway. Somebody just decided to put it out of our misery," Titus said. He caught Marquis's eye. His brother didn't wink at him, but he might as well have.

"Watering Hole burn down, the flag factory closing. Cunninghams selling the fish house and leaving town, and now you done resigned. It's like Charon is falling apart," Albert said.

Titus thought of Carla's face when he'd handed her his badge.

"Can you . . . can you do this?" she had asked.

"I've already done it. I told the Board of Supervisors I'd made you deputy sheriff when I gave them my resignation. Now you're just gonna serve out my term and you'll probably have to run against Roger when that's up. That's if you want to run," Titus had said.

Carla had stared at the badge in her hand.

"I wish you weren't leaving," she had said.

"Remember when you asked me how I dealt with the thoughts in my head that came from chasing people like Royce?" he'd said.

"Yeah."

"I want to be able to dream again without being afraid of what I'll see. Now, if you want my two cents, I think you should run, and I think you can win. You get with Jamal Addison and he will get the vote out for you. You'll be a good sheriff, Carla. Better than me," he'd said.

She'd hugged him then.

"Sometimes you gotta burn off last year's crop to let the soil get renewed, Pop," Titus said now.

"All right, Farmers' Almanac," Marquis said.

Titus shook his head. "Come on, y'all, walk me out."

The three of them walked out into the chilly autumn evening, the sun just barely still visible over the horizon. They stopped and studied the sky for a long moment.

"All right, I'm getting on the road," Titus said.

Albert gave him a bear hug. "Call us when you get there. And when you stop for a break. Just . . . call us." He released Titus and stepped back.

"You know I'm coming to visit so we can drive down to New Orleans, right?" Marquis said as he wrapped his arms around Titus.

"I'd be disappointed in you if you didn't," Titus said in his ear.

They clapped each other on the back before breaking their embrace.

Titus got in his Jeep and started the engine.

He lowered the window.

"Y'all behave yourselves. I'll call when I get into town," Titus said.

"Go on, before we all start crying. Again," Marquis said.

Titus laughed. "Love y'all."

"Back atcha," Marquis said.

"Love ya, boy," Albert said.

Titus drove down Route 18 past the Safeway and the pharmacy. The roads of Charon were empty except for a stray possum trundling across the center line. Titus turned left on Courthouse Lane. He was going to take it up to Zephyr and then up to Route 19, which would take him out of the county. He'd have to go through Red Hill and Maryville until he hit the interstate just outside of Newport News.

He passed the courthouse and the Confederate statue of Ol' Rebel Joe.

Titus slammed on the brakes.

He put the Jeep in reverse until he was in front of the courthouse. He backed up into one of the diagonal parking slots in front of the building.

He got out and looked to his right and his left. There wasn't a soul in sight. The sky had gone from magenta to full dark with no stars.

Titus opened the back of his Jeep. He pushed his suitcases to the side. He pulled back the spare tire cover. He moved the jack and the tire iron. He moved the flares and the reflective hazard triangle his father had given him last year for roadside emergencies.

He grabbed the yellow tow strap his pops had given him along with the flares.

He walked over to Ol' Rebel Joe. He read the inscription on the base of the statue in the red light of his taillights: TO OUR FATHERS AND SONS AND BROTHERS WHO EXHIBITED UNFAILING BRAVERY AND DEVOTION AS THEY FOUGHT TO PRESERVE OUR WAY OF LIFE. 1915 CHARON COUNTY.

"Fuck that noise," Titus whispered.

He lopped the tow strap around the waist of the statue. He hooked the other end to the ball hitch on his Jeep.

Titus got in and dropped the Jeep into low gear.

At first he thought it wasn't going to move. His tires were smoking as they spun against the asphalt. The engine squealed with a metallic ferocity, but eventually he felt the monument give up like the Confederacy did at Appomattox.

When it fell, Joe's arm flew off and bounced down the road, sending sparks up like a swarm of fireflies.

Titus hopped out, unhooked the tow strap from the ball hitch, then jumped back in his Jeep and tore off down the road.

He laughed all the way to the county line.

ACKNOWLEDGMENTS

Writing a novel never gets easier, but when you have wonderful people in your corner it never gets harder either. I need to take a moment and show those people my gratitude.

Josh Getzler, my agent, the first person to believe in me and the first person who helped me believe in myself. Thank you for all you do, sir.

Christine Kopprasch, my editor, thank you for pushing me to challenge myself as a writer and an artist. Your steady hand guides my words and the worlds we create.

To Nikki Dolson, Chad Williamson, Bobby Mathews, Jordan Harper, Rob Hart, Rob Smith, Jonathan Janz, Eryk Pruitt, James Queally, and Mark Bergin. Thank you for reading the early version of this book. Thank you for your honesty, your support, and most importantly, your friendship. There is darkness in the world, but you all are the light.

And finally:

Thank you to Kim. She knows why. She's always known.

ABOUT THE AUTHOR

S. A. Cosby is an Anthony Award–winning writer from southeastern Virginia. He is the author of the *New York Times* bestseller *Razorblade Tears,* which was named on more than twenty best-of-the-year lists, won the ITW Thriller Award for Best Hardcover Novel, and was recommended by Barack Obama. He is also the bestselling author of *My Darkest Prayer* and *Blacktop Wasteland,* which was a *New York Times* Notable Book and named a best book of the year by NPR, the *Sun Sentinel,* and *The Guardian,* among others.

S. A. COSBY
ON AUDIO

Read by award-winning narrator

Adam Lazarre-White

"Narrator Adam Lazarre-White's voice exudes confidence
and depth; his performance is an example of how
the best audiobooks deliver pure storytelling."
—AudioFile on *Blacktop Wasteland*
(Earphones Award winner)

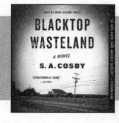  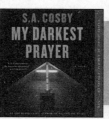 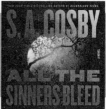

"Adam Lazarre-White's narration is multifaceted. His deep,
resonating voice creates an enveloping soundscape, and
he fully embodies the unique main characters."
—AudioFile on *Razorblade Tears*
(Winner of the ITW Thriller Award for Best Audiobook)

"Lazarre-White's performance is . . . a master class
in narrating a book from a single viewpoint."
—AudioFile on *My Darkest Prayer*
(Earphones Award winner)